FIVE DAYS TILL DAWN

Terry Cumberworth

DEDICATION

To the person who stood beside me through all the struggles and joy of writing this novel. The love of my life, Bobbie.

AUTHOR'S NOTE

This is a work of fiction. Mojave County and most of the other areas mentioned are solely from my imagination. The characters are also fictional and came from that same source — my imagination.

TABLE OF CONTENTS

ACKNOWLEDGEMENT

I am grateful for the help and encouragement I received in the research and writing of this book. They are Sam Siddiqui, Sophia Adams, Bobbie Cumberworth, Brett Kesler, Mike Hawkins, Jodi Kirsch, and Jene Beal. Also, many thanks to Officer Nick Barry and Lt. Tye Meeks of the California Highway Patrol and Sgt. Tim Miller (retired) of the San Bernardino, California, Sheriff's Department.

Chapter 1

The Weight of Quiet

Day One – 5:02 a.m.

Mojave County – Maria's Street → Desert Flats

The house held its breath.

Maria stood in the shadow of the hallway, one hand on the frame of her bedroom door, listening. Her father's snore rose and fell from the back room—steady, familiar, a metronome she'd grown up with. The swamp cooler ticked in the window, blades barely turning. Somewhere, the refrigerator kicked on and hummed; the sound seemed too loud. She waited anyway, counting to thirty, then another thirty, until the hum felt like part of the night again.

She had parked the car two houses down the evening before, under the broken streetlight where nobody looked twice. Her father never liked the sedan idling near the porch—said he could smell the exhaust in his sleep. She'd told him she was closing late at the café; he'd nodded without turning from the ballgame. She'd come home at eleven, left the car, and walked back in soft-soled shoes, practicing the route in silence.

Now she slid bare feet into those same shoes. The laces whispered against canvas. She lifted her backpack from the floor—the one with the loose zipper—and pinched the tab to keep it quiet. In the kitchen, she avoided the loose tile that clicked under her weight, stepping wide to the edge of the linoleum. When she tested the back screen door, the hinge complained with a delicate chirp. She paused, pulse tight, then pressed two fingers against the frame where the metal met wood and eased the latch free. The door gave with a sigh.

Outside, the desert fall air carried a sharp bite, cooler than summer nights ever allowed. The neighborhood was a hush of stucco boxes and gravel yards, ocotillo stripped bare of leaves, ribs of stalk cutting into the paling sky. A dog's collar jangled two streets over. She flinched and waited again, but no porch light snapped on, no voice called her name.

Gravel crunched softly under her steps as she moved down the block. The car crouched in shadow where she'd left it, windshield filmed with dew. She brushed it clear with her sleeve and peered back toward the house. No movement. The swamp cooler ticked. Good.

Inside the car, the seat was cold through her jeans. She closed the door carefully—pull, catch, then a slow press to settle the latch without the full click. The key turned; the engine caught on the second try. She winced at the sound, then waited until the idle smoothed. When she eased away from the curb, she kept the headlights off for the first half-block and used the moonlit asphalt lines like rails. At the corner, she flicked the lights on, low beams only, and turned toward the highway.

Her phone buzzed in the cupholder. A single line on the lock screen: We can't be seen together. People talk. Just meet me outside of town. Ten minutes, that's all. The message from last night again, pinned above a newer one: Almost there. Don't be late.

She put the phone face down. Her knuckles had gone pale on the wheel.

She told herself, again, to turn around. Go home. Wake her father. Confess everything. She pictured him in the doorway, gray hair mussed, the shape of his disappointment bigger than his body. She pictured Luis, too—hands raw from the warehouse, the earnest, stubborn way he loved. She remembered him waiting at the café once, long after his shift, holding a paper bag with a secondhand sweater inside. He'd noticed her shiver walking home at night and found it for her. He'd grinned as she pulled it on, proud as if he'd bought her the world.

She had told him they were over. She hadn't told him why. She had thought that was a kindness. Now, driving into darkness, she wasn't sure.

The highway shouldered her into emptiness where the desert met the road with nothing between. The world was two stripes of faded paint and her headlights sliding forward. To the east, a thin seam of orange unstitched the horizon, sharper in the crisp fall air. She lowered a window an inch. Cold air knifed in, carrying dust and the faintest trace of diesel from a truck miles ahead. The desert has a smell if you know it: creosote, old rain, metal warmed and cooling. She breathed it, steadying herself.

"I just want to do right by you," he'd said last night. "We'll figure this out. But no one can know yet."

He'd used the word we, and it had felt like someone opening a door when you're standing outside in the wind. But then he'd said: Turn your phone off before you leave. Airplane mode still pings sometimes. The kind of detail a person knew if he had reasons to avoid being seen.

Her fingers found the small rise of her belly beneath the hoodie. Not a bump, not yet, just a map of a thing that would be. Eighteen. A server at Della's Delights with tips in her pocket and a class she kept missing at the community college. A father who'd given her everything left in him. A boyfriend she had left because the truth had outgrown him. And the other man—the one in pressed shirts and a voice like a late-night radio host—moving through town as if the floor rose to meet his feet wherever he stepped.

Maria checked the mirror. The town had shrunk to a thumbprint of light. Ahead was the desert, endless and empty, as if it had been scrubbed clean for this one meeting. He had chosen well.

She left the highway at a service road patched with tar and potholes. The tires ticked over the repairs with a rhythm that reminded her of a second hand. To her right, a dry arroyo ran parallel—ragged brush, a sun-bleached tire half-swallowed by sand, the glint of a broken beer bottle catching the first low light. A raven lifted from a creosote, flared black wings, and circled once as if to mark her.

The pullout appeared as a half-moon scoop of hardpan, wheel ruts bit deep and fossilized. She coaxed the car to a stop with the nose facing the highway, a habit she didn't know she had until she noticed it. The engine ticked as it cooled. When she shut off the lights, the world slid one shade darker, and the horizon brightened in compensation.

For a moment, she just sat and listened. The desert is not silent; it breathes. She heard the grain-on-grain murmur of a small gust, the distant pop of a truck downshifting on the highway, the faint ping of heat leaving metal. Her own breath sounded too loud.

Her phone buzzed. Almost there.

Her thumb hovered over the power button. She hesitated, then held it until the screen went black. She placed the phone in the glove box, closed it, and ran her finger along the seam to be sure.

A pale dust plume grew on the road's horizon, narrow, controlled, like someone drawing a line with a pencil. A white SUV crested the low rise and rolled in slow, angling to stop with the driver's side in shadow. The windows were tinted darker than legal. The engine idled a few beats and cut. The dust drifted around them in a thin veil.

He got out in a neat button-down, sleeves rolled, a cap pulled low, sunglasses on though the sun was just a thought. Even here, in all this no one, he arranged himself like a person under observation. He didn't wave. He didn't hurry.

"Maria," he said, calm as if they were meeting inside an office where coffee was offered. "Thanks for coming."

She opened her door but stayed beside the car. "You said ten minutes."

"That's all we need." He glanced toward the empty highway, then back. "Phone off?"

"It's on airplane mode," she said. She wanted it to be enough.

"Turn it off." Gentle, but not a suggestion. "Airplane still pings sometimes."

She walked around to the passenger side, opened the glove box, showed him the black screen, pressed the power again for emphasis, though it was already dead. He nodded, pleased that she understood him, pleased that she obeyed.

"Walk with me a second." He pointed toward the arroyo. "Out of the wind."

There was barely wind, just the slow crawl of air that comes before sunrise, but she followed anyway. The ground sloped to the wash, crusted in places and loose in others. A bent soda can lay half-buried. A jackrabbit froze, then sprang, feet whispering on sand. The smell of creosote was sharp, antiseptic.

"I didn't sleep," she said. "I kept thinking—"

"I know." His tone went lower, confidential. "It's a lot. But I told you last night: I care about what happens to you."

"And the baby," she said, meeting his eyes. The sunglasses made them blank.

He looked past her at the horizon, a beat too long. Dawn opened another finger's width. "Right," he said. "That's why I asked you here."

"How?" she asked. "How will you do right by me?"

He smiled the practiced smile. "There's one answer. Quiet, simple. You end it."

She blinked. Even expecting something, she hadn't expected that so plain. "You want me to have an abortion?"

"You're eighteen." His voice warmed, persuasive. "You've got your whole life ahead. No one has to know. We can take care of it, clean and fast. No shame. No burden."

A cold narrowness passed through her chest like a blade. "No." The word surprised her with its shape in the air. She shook her head. "I won't."

The smile left him. His jaw moved once, settling. "Think carefully. If this gets out—"

"I don't care." Her voice trembled, then steadied. "I won't kill my baby."

Something colder than the morning slid into his face. "Who else knows?" he asked.

"No one. Not even my dad." She swallowed. "I told Luis we were over. But not why. He doesn't know."

He studied her as if she were a document to be initialed. Then his voice fell back into that measured, reasonable register. "That's good. It needs to stay that way. Truth without timing is a weapon in someone else's hand. If people find out now, they'll twist it. Ruin you. Ruin me. Is that what you want?"

"I want honesty," she said. "I want to stop hiding."

"Careful isn't hiding," he said smoothly. "It's survival."

Maria felt the desert around them as a fact: the open, the distance, the way sound carried. She realized her car was far enough to make running a plan that required too many steps. The SUV sat angled to the road, a better start.

"I won't do what you're asking," she said.

Silence held for three counts. Slowly, deliberately, he gave a small nod as if concluding a meeting.

The SUV's passenger door opened. A second man stepped out, broader in the shoulders, plain ball cap, no sunglasses, no expression. He didn't speak. He didn't need to. You could tell what he was by how he moved—efficient, as if his body knew which muscles mattered and which didn't.

The first man didn't look at him. He kept his eyes on Maria, as if this were still a conversation between civilized people. The sun lifted a degree and put a white line along the ridge of the arroyo. Somewhere, far off, a truck honked twice like a bird in a different world.

Maria's pulse climbed into her throat. She backed one step, heel slipping on loose sand. Her mind ran inventory: the distance to the car, the way her keys felt in her pocket, the fact that she could scream and the desert would lay her voice down and carry it nowhere. She pictured her father in his bed, the TV now an empty blue; pictured Luis on the loading dock rubbing his hands together to keep warm; pictured a baby no one knew, the single living secret holding her upright.

"I came because you asked," she said. "I'm leaving now."

The first man tilted his head, a sympathetic angle that didn't reach his mouth. "I'm trying to protect you, Maria. Don't make this harder than it has to be."

"Then let me go," she said.

The second man shifted his weight, a small scuff of grit. The sound was louder than it should have been. It was the sound of a decision being made elsewhere, by someone who did not care what she wanted.

Her fingers tightened around the zipper tab on her backpack. She didn't pray—she had prayed in the car—but she found herself thinking the single word she'd thought then too: Please.

He watched her a moment longer, then lifted one hand, palm down, two inches. A signal as quiet as a thought.

Maria turned. The sand gave under her shoes.

She had come for promises.

All she had was fear.

Chapter 2
The Desert Carries Silence

Day One – 7:21 a.m.

Mojave County – Desert Flats

The California high desert still held the night's cold, the kind that settled hardest in fall, but the sun was climbing fast. Mojave County Sheriff KC Talbird ducked beneath the yellow tape, boots crunching on gravel. Thirty-five, six-foot-three, broad-shouldered and lean, his hair cut regulation-short though his badge said elected, not appointed. Gray eyes swept the churned half-moon of sand where the body had been.

Too late.

A deputy straightened at the tape. Deputy Toni Salazar, early twenties, clutched a notebook in both hands. Her uniform was crisp, almost too new, the creases still stiff. Dark hair tucked under her cap, eyes steady, though her posture betrayed nerves. "Sheriff," she said. "I was first on scene."

KC's gaze stayed on the disturbed sand. The emptiness where Maria had been felt like an accusation. "Where's the victim?"

"Captain Parsons had her transported," Toni said. A beat. "Before you arrived. I thought you'd want her left in place."

"I did." KC's voice was flat. He turned toward her fully. "Report."

Toni flipped open her notebook, voice gaining strength as she read. "Witness was a teenage male on a dirt bike. Out here at dawn, likely skipping school. He spotted the body from the wash and called it in."

"Name?" KC asked.

"Captain Parsons spoke with him," she said carefully. "Didn't get one."

KC let the silence hang. The desert carried it like a blade. "Go on."

"No purse. No cell phone. No signs of a struggle around the body. The position suggested a single blow. Sand's too clean for a fight."

KC studied her. Green, but sharp. She saw what mattered.

Bootsteps crunched behind them. Captain Eddie Parsons strode up, sunglasses flashing. In his early fifties, stocky through the waist and chest, thick graying hair a shade too long for regulations, but still acceptable. He carried himself with the authority of a man who'd spent decades in the department and expected deference by default.

"Sheriff," Parsons said. "We've got this covered."

"Covered?" KC turned on him. "The body was moved before I arrived. The finder's name isn't recorded. How is that covered?"

Parsons' jaw twitched, but before he answered, his phone buzzed. He turned slightly, answering. "Parsons." A pause. "Good. Bring him in." He ended the call, sliding the phone back into his pocket with satisfaction.

"That was Akers," Parsons said. "Picked up the boyfriend—Luis Alvarez. He'll be booked at the jail by 7:30."

KC felt the words land heavy. "On what basis?"

"Cause and effect," Parsons said. "They were together. He's undocumented. He ran his mouth yesterday at the market. Plenty of probable cause."

KC's stare was cold. "Probable cause isn't a feeling."

Parsons shrugged. "It's action, which we took. I also called the DA to keep him in the loop. He appreciates being informed."

KC glanced at Toni. She kept her eyes on her notes, but the tightness in her jaw gave her away. She was paying attention. That mattered.

He pulled his small black notebook from his pocket, the one with block letters neat and disciplined, and wrote:

Witness (teen dirt bike) — find & interview personally.

No phone. No purse. No struggle.

Akers arrested boyfriend. Basis? Verify.

The scratch of a pen against paper sounded loud in the desert hush.

A county sedan eased to the shoulder. Theodore Dodd, Mojave County District Attorney, stepped out, adjusting his tie as though arriving at a press conference. In his sixth term, thin at about five-ten, white hair combed neat, dark eyes sharp above an immaculately cut suit. His shoes, polished to a mirror, scuffed instantly against gravel dust where the morning cold still clung in the shadows.

"Sheriff Talbird," Dodd said warmly, though the warmth stopped at his teeth. "Tragic morning. The community's going to need steady reassurance." His gaze sharpened. "I understand the boy's already in your jail."

"A suspect is in custody," KC said evenly. "The investigation is ongoing."

"Of course." Dodd's smile smoothed over the air. "But people sleep easier when they hear 'solved.'" He tilted his head. "We should be aligned on that."

KC slid his notebook back into his pocket. "We'll be aligned on the facts."

Parsons stood a half-step behind Dodd, arms crossed, silent but satisfied.

KC turned to Toni. "Diagram the scene exactly as you found it. I want your notes scanned and on my desk in an hour. Then find me every deputy who rolled through here and log their times."

"Yes, Sheriff." She was already moving, shoulders set with resolve.

Dodd's smile thinned. "I'll look for your update this afternoon."

"You'll have it when there's something worth saying," KC replied.

The wind tugged at the yellow tape, the only sound. KC looked again at the sand where Maria had lain. Too clean. Too fast. Too political.

He pressed his hand to the notebook in his pocket. Justice wasn't quick. It was careful. And already, this case was being stolen from him piece by piece

Chapter 3
Sherman's Market

Day One – 9:06 a.m.

Mojave County – Sherman's Market

The bell above the door at Sherman's Market gave a crisp jingle when Mojave County Sheriff KC Talbird stepped inside. Fall light slanted through the plate glass and laid bright bars across polished floors. A fine mist hissed over the greens, apples were stacked in neat pyramids, and a coffee urn burbled at a self-serve station beside a bakery case. This wasn't a chain, but it wore its Sunday best: aisles wide enough for two carts to pass, endcaps dressed with local peaches and school fundraiser flyers stamped with the store's logo.

Over the entrance, the painted sign he'd passed under read: Sherman's Market — Family Owned Since 1968. Herb's father had opened the place with one aisle and a butcher counter; Herb had turned it into a neighborhood anchor. The kind of store county politicians liked to be seen in.

Herb stood behind the glass of the butcher case, apron tied tight across a barrel chest, white stubble rough on his jaw. He was the size of a man who'd lifted crates half his life and only lately begun to soften. When the bell stilled, he looked up. KC saw grief fixed hard into the man's face, like plaster that hadn't set right.

"Sheriff," Herb said.

"Morning." KC took off his hat. A woman at the register counted bills with the checker; a teenage stocker rearranged soup cans with the intent focus of someone trying to listen. KC nodded toward the back. "Got a minute?"

Herb held his stare a beat, daring KC to do this in front of the tomatoes and coffee. Then he wiped his hands on his apron and jerked his chin. "Two," he said.

The office behind the meat counter had none of the shine of the sales floor. Old paneling bowed at the seams, a corkboard drooped under invoices and vendor cards, and a Polaroid of Maria at sixteen, grinning over a horseshoe-shaped cake, had faded to the permanent dusk of old film. A desk lamp leaned, throwing a low pool of yellow. The air smelled of paper dust and butcher soap.

Herb closed the door and planted himself, arms crossed like a barricade.

KC set his hat on the file cabinet. "There's no easy way to—"

"I already heard." Herb's voice had a rasp in it. "Beatrice Garrison called me. You know—Queen B." He made the nickname sound like a charge. "Said someone's in custody. Said you've got the one who did it."

So Queen B had reached him first. KC felt the familiar heat under his ribs and banked it. "We have a person in custody," he said carefully. "The investigation is ongoing."

"Luis," Herb said, like he was slamming a door. "She said it was Luis Alvarez. Girl dumps him, he runs his mouth over at Della's, and now my daughter's dead. What else is there to figure out?"

KC kept his gray eyes steady. "Being in a room with me isn't guilt. It's the start of questions."

Herb shoved away from the wall. The room was too small for his pacing; his shoulder brushed the corkboard, and a corner of a bill curled like a dry leaf. "Questions," he muttered. "Where were your questions at sunup?"

"On scene at seven twenty-one," KC said. "The body had been moved."

Herb flinched. His jaw worked. "Did she suffer?"

KC thought of the bare half-moon scrape in the sand, the way the desert had held its breath. One blow was a phrase he could not yet use. "I don't know yet," he said. "I'll bring you the truth when I have it."

Herb's gaze drifted to the Polaroid. He reached to straighten it though it hadn't been crooked. "She worked," he said, voice lower, words dragged up from somewhere deep. "School, here, and nights at your aunt's place. Girl never stopped moving." He swallowed. "She deserved better."

KC saw her as he had a dozen mornings at his Aunt Ruth's café—Della's Delights—threading through the window table with plates too big for her arms and a smile that made the old-timers sit up straighter. Ruth had said once, Maria's got her father's eyes. Looking at Herb now, KC believed it—same open shape, except his were red-rimmed and raw.

"She made people feel seen," KC said. "Ruth said the place felt warmer with her in it."

Herb's mouth twitched, not quite a smile. Then his face hardened again. "What happens to Luis?"

"I talk to him myself," KC said. "I verify his movements and calls. I make sure evidence is handled right. And I ask you to hold your fire in public until we've done it right."

"You think I'm running to the press?" Herb barked a humorless sound.

"I think Queen B already is," KC said. "She called you first to point out your anger. If you stand on these steps at nine a.m. and say we've nailed a killer, and the evidence says otherwise later, it breaks things that don't glue easy."

Herb studied him, anger cooling into something sharper. "So you think he didn't do it."

"I think I don't know yet," KC said. "And I won't turn your daughter's murder into a campaign line for anybody."

Silence settled. The desk lamp hummed.

"Some man came by last week," Herb said finally. "Asking about Maria. Well-dressed. Said he was from county mental health—'outreach.' Too smooth for that job. Said he'd seen her intake notes."

KC's chest tightened. Outreach with access to intake files wasn't outreach. It was a leak with a tie on it. "You get a name?"

"No." He grimaced. "He left a card. I tossed it."

KC took out his small black notebook, neat block letters ready, and wrote: Male, suit. Claimed mental health outreach. Saw intake notes. Last week. Follow up now. He drew a small square in the margin—his mark for urgent. "If he shows again, you call me. Or call Ruth. It'll get to me."

Herb nodded, eyes still on the Polaroid. "I'll do that."

KC slid the notebook back into his pocket. "One more thing. Who called you, besides Garrison?"

"Dodd. Left a message around seven." Herb plucked a Post-it from the corkboard and held it up: Dodd — 7:08. "Said he was checking on me." His mouth twisted. "First time that man's checked on anything in here that didn't vote for him."

KC made a second note: Dodd call to Herb 0708—verify logs. Then he set his hat back on his head. "I'll be back, Herb."

"You better," Herb said. He reached for the door, hand on the knob, then paused. "You bring me the truth, Sheriff. Not a headline."

KC met his eye. "That's the only thing I bring."

They stepped out to the polished front of the store. The teenage stocker was pretending to face the soup again; a little boy in a school sweatshirt tugged his mother toward the bakery case where cinnamon rolls glazed in neat rows. Everything in sight said the county was fine. KC knew better.

On the sidewalk, the fall air had already warmed a degree, but the shade from the awning held some of the night. A county sedan drifted down the block. KC recognized white hair and dark eyes behind the windshield before the driver turned his face to the road again: Theodore Dodd, making the rounds. Practicing concern.

KC leaned against the hood of his truck, opened his notebook, and wrote on a clean page:

Queen B—preemptive call to Herb

Dodd "check-in" 0708—verify with carrier

Luis—interview personally (this a.m.)

Outreach impostor—tie to Garrison funding streams? (Jodi K.)

He tapped the pen once against the margin, closed the book, and slid it inside his shirt. Across the street, two men leaned on a tailgate, watching him the way men watch a storm that might or might not drift their way. A school bell rang faint and far, the sound barely crossing the bright air.

KC started the engine of his truck. The clock on the dash rolled to 9:14. He glanced once in the mirror at the front windows of Sherman's Market, where Herb had already returned to the counter, jaw set like a man carrying two worlds: the polished one he showed the town, and the one waiting behind a shut office door with a faded Polaroid and a lamp that hummed.

The truth did not hurry, but it didn't wander either. KC meant to keep it that way.

Chapter 4
The Captain's Terminal

Day One – 11:02 a.m.

Mojave County – Sheriff's Office (KC's Office)

The Sheriff's Office smelled of floor polish and old coffee, the kind that lingered even when the pot was empty. Phones rang in the admin bay, printers chattered, and the buzz of fluorescent lights gave everything a false sense of motion.

Carlie Frye, KC's assistant and personnel clerk, looked up from her desk as he walked in. She was in her late twenties, five-four, with chestnut hair pulled into a clean bun and sharp brown eyes that missed little. Her blouse sleeves were rolled neatly to the elbow, a stack of files squared flush at her elbow, everything about her ordered and efficient.

"Sheriff," she said quietly, standing with a pink slip in hand. "Theodore Dodd called about an hour ago. Said he was checking in and would like to know if you'll be available later today."

KC hung his hat on the rack by the door. "Note that I won't. If he has questions, he can put them in writing."

Carlie's mouth tilted faintly. "I'll soften that before it goes back to him."

"That's fine," KC said.

She set another sheet on his desk. "This went out through the system at 10:38. 'Press availability, 2 p.m.—Sheriff to address homicide.' No signature line. It came from a captain's terminal."

KC read it once. The clipped phrasing carried Parsons' fingerprints, though he hadn't signed it. He slid the page back across the desk. "Take it down. If anyone asks, direct them to me. The official is at four. You set it up."

"Logged," Carlie said. She folded the paper once and tucked it into a red file marked pending.

KC moved into his office. The desk bore rings from other men's coffee, the corkboard behind it crowded with neat lines giving way to slanted tacks. He sat, opened his black notebook, and waited for Carlie to close the door.

"I need a file," he said. "Deputy Toni Salazar. Last eval, academy notes, training comments."

Carlie handed him a manila folder. "Pulled it when I saw her name on the first-on-scene log this morning."

KC opened it. Toni L. Salazar, 28. Academy: strong in reports, competent with firearms. Field training notes: Detail-oriented. Doesn't rush. Accepts correction. Keeps clear of lunchroom politics. An older remark: Quiet, steady. Detective potential.

"How is she in the building?" KC asked.

"Professional," Carlie said. "She eats off-site most days. Turns in clean files. She's not part of Parsons' circle."

"Careful good, or careful slippery?"

"Good," Carlie said. "That's my read."

KC closed the folder, hand resting on it. He remembered her steady voice that morning in the desert: I thought you'd want her left in place. She'd seen what mattered.

"Schedule her," he said. "Tomorrow. Eight a.m. Side door. Plain clothes. Put it in as personnel, not a meeting."

"Done," Carlie said, noting it down.

She hesitated, then added, "There's chatter in the squad room. ICE called twice asking about Alvarez. Deputies are passing it along like it means something."

KC's jaw tightened. Six months in this job, and already ICE was circling, Parsons whispering, and half the department still looking over its shoulder at Akers. "If ICE calls again, log it and direct them to me."

"Logged," Carlie said.

"Who booked Alvarez?"

"Deputy Núñez. Straight shooter. Parsons flagged the file for 'expedite interview' and handwrote 'ICE notified. '"

KC tapped his pen once on the notebook margin. "Set me up with Interview Two at noon. Alvarez in the chair, water on the table. No circus."

Carlie glanced at the phone. "Want me to place the call, or you?"

"Me." KC dialed the jail direct. Two rings, then a deputy's voice.

"This is Sheriff Talbird. Interview Two, twelve sharp. Alvarez prepped. Quiet escort, no observers. Understood?"

"Yes, Sheriff."

KC hung up and noted: 1200—Luis. Deputies may drag feet—watch the hall.

He stood, sliding Toni's file into his drawer, notebook into his shirt pocket.

Carlie waited at the door. "Anything else?"

"One more," KC said. "Call Dr. Jodi Kirk at County Mental Health. I'd like see her later. And pull any new outreach programs—ninety days. Names, vendors, grants. If they tie back to Beatrice Garrison, I want them."

"I've heard of a contractor through one of her defund-the-police projects," Carlie said carefully. "Community stabilization work. I don't have the name yet."

"Find it," KC said.

She nodded. "You'll get pushback on the two o'clock."

KC shrugged. "What's new?"

Carlie gave a faint smile. "Toni. Eight a.m. tomorrow. Side door. Plain clothes."

"Good," KC said.

When she left, the office seemed too quiet. On the corkboard, he wrote names on slips of paper. They formed a rough constellation: Maria. Herb. Alvarez. Parsons. Dodd. Garrison. Jodi. Outreach? Pins in a county where the lines ran longer than the eye could see.

KC took his hat, glanced once out the lobby window. Two deputies crossed the lot at an unhurried pace, men who thought the clock bent to them. Six months wasn't long enough to change a department.

At noon he'd face Alvarez. At four, the press. Between those times: no leaks, no shortcuts, no favors dressed as help.

KC set his shoulders and stepped into the hall. The building breathed around him, steady as always. The truth wasn't fast, but it was exact. He intended to match it.

Chapter 5

Do You Understand Why You're Here?

Day One – 12:03 p.m.

Mojave County – Jail (Interview Hall → Interview Room Two)

The jail corridor smelled of disinfectant and concrete dust. Fluorescents hummed overhead, washing the cinderblock walls in a flat gray light. KC checked the wall clock—12:03. He'd called for noon sharp.

Bootsteps came at last, unhurried. Two deputies turned the corner with Luis Alvarez between them. Luis wore county browns, the fresh-issued set hanging loose on his frame. His wrists were cuffed at the waist, a short chain clinking every other step. His dark hair was damp from the intake shower, face pale as unbaked clay.

The lead deputy was Núñez, steady-eyed, shoulders squared. The other, Davis, wore his smirk like a badge.

"You're late," KC said.

"Intake backed up," Davis offered, voice too quick.

Núñez gave the clock a brief glance and said nothing.

"Keys," KC said.

Davis hesitated, smirk lingering. "Cuffs stay. He's a flight risk."

"They come off," KC said, quiet but final.

Davis started to answer, but Núñez handed over the keys. KC unlocked the restraints himself. The steel clattered against the table, then coiled in a neat heap. Luis rubbed his wrists, then folded his hands tight on his lap as though afraid to move them.

KC slid a paper cup of water toward him. "Sit."

Luis sat. He didn't touch the water until KC gave a small nod. Then he lifted it with both hands, drank like he hadn't in hours.

Davis leaned in the doorway. "Captain Parsons wants to observe."

KC didn't look up. "Captain Parsons will get my notes. Wait outside."

Davis opened his mouth, but Núñez set a hand on the door and eased him back. The latch clicked shut, leaving just KC and Luis in the pale-lit room.

KC set his black notebook on the table, pen still capped. "Luis, I'm Sheriff Talbird. Do you understand why you're here?"

Luis's voice came low and raw. "They say... they say Maria is dead." The word broke on him. His eyes stayed down.

KC gave him a moment. "She is."

Luis drew a breath that sounded like it cut his ribs on the way in.

"I'm going to ask you questions," KC said. "You can stop at any time. If you want a lawyer, you tell me, and we stop."

"I don't have money for a lawyer," Luis whispered.

"If you want one, you'll have one," KC said. "Do you understand your rights?"

Luis nodded. "Yes. I signed the paper."

KC opened his notebook but didn't write yet. "I understand you had a fight with Maria recently?"

Luis blinked. "The night... two days ago?"

"Yes."

He swallowed. "We met at a fast-food place in town. She wanted to talk. No—she wanted to end it." His hands tightened. "I asked why. She wouldn't say. I got angry. Not... not hitting. Just words." His eyes flicked up, pleading. "She left crying. I stayed. I couldn't move. My food—it was still on the table."

"Anyone else see this?" KC asked.

"I think the manager. He came to see what was the noise. He saw her leave, saw me stay."

KC uncapped his pen and wrote: Fast food manager—witness.

"Is that the last time you saw her?" KC asked.

Luis licked his lips. "She was at Della's. Working. I tried to talk again. She shook her head. Said no. Walked away. I didn't touch her. I swear."

KC studied him. "Did she ever tell you why she ended it?"

"No," Luis said, voice breaking on the word. "She wouldn't tell me."

KC let silence sit before he asked, "Where were you last night and early this morning?"

"Humboldt Ranch," Luis said. "My shift ended late. I went home. My mother and brother were there. We live in the bunkhouse. I didn't go out."

"Names."

"My mother—Rosa. My brother—Mateo."

KC wrote both down. Alibi—verify.

He looked back at Luis. "Did Maria ever mention seeing anyone at County Mental Health?"

Luis frowned. "No. She just... sometimes looked tired. Like she was carrying something heavy no one else could see. That's all."

Before KC could press, a shadow filled the window in the door. The latch clicked, and Captain Parsons stepped in, sunglasses hooked on his shirt.

"We done dancing?" Parsons asked lightly. "ICE wants a word with our boy before lunch."

"Shut the door, Captain," KC said.

Parsons lingered, smile sharp. "You've got ten minutes, Sheriff. Then the gears turn."

KC stared until Núñez's shape appeared behind him. The door shut again, softer this time.

KC turned back. "Luis, some people want you to be the answer because it's quick. Quick isn't the same as true."

Luis's voice rose sharp for the first time. "I didn't hurt her. I loved her."

KC wrote one more line: Sincere.

He stood. "You'll go back to holding. No one talks to you unless I'm present. If they try, you tell them you want me. Or your lawyer."

Luis nodded fast. "I want you."

KC knocked twice on the door. Núñez opened it. KC pointed toward the cuffs on the table. Núñez re-fastened them without pinching. Davis trailed after, smirk gone.

KC sat alone for a beat after they left. The paper cup left a wet ring on the metal table. The fluorescent hum filled the silence, constant and tired. He didn't wipe the ring away.

Notebook open, he wrote:

- Fast food manager—witness. Maria ended it, left crying. Luis angry, but no contact.
- Della's—regulars at the window table. Verify if they heard words.
- Humboldt Ranch—alibi. Rosa and Mateo Alvarez.
- Deputies slow-walking. Davis—watch.
- Parsons interference. ICE pressing. No access without me.

He capped the pen, slipped the notebook back into his pocket, and left the cuffs where they lay.

In the hall, a trustee mopped a wet stripe down the tile. The buzz of the lights stayed constant, the same tired hum. KC pushed through the steel door to the admin wing, already shaping what he would—and wouldn't—say at four o'clock.

The truth wasn't fast. But it would stand, if he gave it room

Chapter 6
Courtesy Call

Day One – 1:15 p.m.

Mojave County – Sheriff's Office (KC's Office)

Carlie was already on her feet when KC pushed through the glass do. A wax paper–wrapped sandwich waited on his desk beside a sweating Cherry Coke, cap cracked but still cold.

"I figured you'd miss lunch," she said. "Italian sub. No onion."

KC set his hat on the file cabinet. "You read minds now?"

"Files," she said, with a small smile. "And schedules." Then she lifted a pink message slip. "Dodd called again twenty minutes ago— 'checking in, would like a word before the press conference.' I told him you weren't available and invited him to send questions in writing. I softened it."

"That'll do," KC said, dropping into his chair. The cushion breathed a tired sound. He took a pull from the Coke—the bite of cherry and carbonation waking a part of him that other drinks couldn't reach—and unwrapped the sandwich without looking away from Carlie. "All set at four o'clock?"

"Set and locked," she said. "Podium in the lobby. County PIO will stand to the side. I kept the invites tight. But others may show."

He nodded. "Good."

The desk phone rang with the clipped urgency of a line that only rang when it meant to. Carlie reached for it, glanced at the display, and handed the receiver over. "Line two. Says ASAC, federal."

KC slid the wrapped sandwich aside and picked up. "Talbird."

"Assistant Special Agent in Charge Stasovich, Homeland Security Investigations." The man's voice was crisp, practiced to travel across rooms and wires. "Sheriff, we're coordinating a custody transfer related to an immigration detainer. Five days from now, dawn, we'll be assuming control of Luis Alvarez at your facility. We'll also be taking family members at Humboldt Ranch into custody. I'm calling as a courtesy."

Carlie watched from her spot by the door. She didn't speak. She didn't need to.

"This is a homicide investigation," KC said. "Alvarez is a material witness and potential suspect. He doesn't leave this county without my say-so, and nobody touches his family without. They are tied to my case."

"The detainer is lawful, Sheriff," Stasovich said. "We're giving you five days' notice. Have Alvarez ready and stay out of our way with the family."

KC took a breath, measured it, let it out. "You planning to walk cameras onto my steps at dawn?"

"We don't carry cameras," Stasovich said dryly. "Reporters carry cameras. We can't control the press any more than you can."

"You can control timing," KC said.

"That's why I'm calling," Stasovich returned. "This isn't a negotiation. It's coordination. We'll move before first light, five days from today. If your charges change, if he's arraigned on anything that binds him there, send it over, and we'll reassess the sequence. Until then, Sheriff, plan accordingly."

KC looked past the Cherry Coke to the corkboard where names on slips seemed to be gathered in a protective constellation. He could feel the clock stilling the room—five days—a long time and no time at all. "You step inside my jail or roll onto Humboldt Ranch without telling me first, you'll find yourself explaining civil trespass to a judge."

"You've been on the federal side," Stasovich said, not quite a question.

"Yeah, I know how you work," KC said.

"Good," Stasovich said. "Then you know I'll be there at dawn. Five days." A faint rattle of paper. "Our liaison will follow with a memo."

The call clicked off.

Carlie exhaled the breath she'd been holding. "How... soon."

"Five days. Dawn." KC put the handset down, thumb resting on it for one extra beat. He leaned back. "There will be a memo coming in. Both Luis and his family."

Carlie nodded. "I'll log the call and print the memo when it hits," she said. "Do you want me to flag Humboldt Ranch contacts? Owner, foreman?"

"Not yet," KC said. "No rumors on the wind before I can look them in the eye."

Carlie jotted the time and "ASAC—five days—dawn" on her pad. "You need to finish that sandwich before the next fire hits."

KC took another drink, then the phone rang again—short-short-long, the line he'd asked his crime scene tech to use. He wiped his hand on the wax paper and grabbed it. "Talbird."

"Sheriff, Trisha Bell," a woman said—brisk, competent, a mind that moved in straight lines. "I'm giving you preliminaries from the desert pullout."

"I'm listening," KC said. He clicked his pen but didn't touch the notebook yet.

"Body position and imprint indicate a single downward blow to the head. Impact site consistent with a heavy blunt instrument—a pipe or large round rod of some sort. No obvious defensive wounds on the hands or arms. There's some post-contact drag artifact—short, maybe two feet—consistent with a reposition before removal."

"Which we know happened," KC said. Parsons' name crossed his mind like a shadow.

"We bagged trace from hair and clothing," Trisha continued. "Mostly desert grit and plant oils—creosote—what you'd expect. No purse, no phone. Shoes were still on. We have partial tread impressions in the half-moon pullout—AT pattern, wide spacing, likely an SUV. But the substrate is bad—crusted over old marks. I wouldn't stake a warrant on what's there."

"Time of death?" KC asked.

"ME will give you a tighter window," Trisha said. "But based on livor and ambient, I'm estimating pre-dawn—somewhere in the five to six a.m. range. You'll want Dr. Ram for the final."

KC opened the notebook and wrote, slow and exact: Single downward blow. No defensive. Drag artifact ≤ 2 ft. No purse/phone. Partial AT tread—SUV. TOD pre-dawn (Ram). "Anything that doesn't fit the scene?"

"How clean it is," Trisha said. "No scatter, no struggle signature. That pullout's used—old tire scrapes all over—but around the body, we've got almost nothing except what you'd expect from recovery. Whoever did this chose the spot or got lucky."

"Maria's car?" KC asked. "Anything?"

"Nothing," Trisha said. "It's also clean. Too clean."

"Prints," KC said.

Trisha huffed a humorless breath. "Whole car. Clean."

"Appreciate your report," KC said.

"You know I need help, Sheriff. I would've had my report to you sooner if I had."

"I know. I'm working on it." KC said.

"Appreciate that, Sheriff." The line clicked.

He set the phone down and drew a box around the words how clean, then underlined it. The room's hum felt louder for a moment, the old building reminding him it had outlived sheriffs before him and would outlast him, too.

Carlie's pen paused above her pad. "This... doesn't feel random?"

"No," KC said. He took a bite of the sandwich he barely tasted, and flipped back a page to his interview notes. "It's controlled."

"Do you want me to ping Toni and have her come in earlier?" she asked, staying with the practical because it was what held.

"Keep it as is," he said. "Eight a.m., side door. Plain clothes."

She checked her watch. "PIO called not long after the press time was set. Wants your talking points. Said Chairperson Garrison wants them well before four. I told him I'd pass that request along."

KC took another drink of Cherry Coke, the fizz fading now. "Talking points are simple. We're working. We won't feed you guesses." He paused. "Queen B moves fast." Needing control of the narrative.

"He'll call back." Carlie said.

"Take a message."

"Understood," she said, with a faint smile.

He took another bite, wiped his hands on the wax paper, and leaned back, eyes sliding to the corkboard. He picked up a fresh slip, wrote ICE—dawn (+5), and pinned it next to Alvarez. On another slip, he wrote Humboldt Ranch and pinned it low, a reminder to visit in person before anyone else did.

The phone buzzed again—internal line—and Carlie picked up, listened, then covered the mouthpiece. "ASAC liaison asking for an email to send the memo."

"Give them the generic admin inbox," KC said. "We'll print it." He didn't want the memo floating around the squadroom monitors like a weather warning.

Carlie relayed, hung up, and made the note on her pad: memo → print only.

KC finished the sandwich, or enough of it to call it done, and capped his pen. He could feel the day pulling apart—the four o'clock shaping itself like a storm wall, dawn five days from now standing beyond it like a darker ridge. Between those two, a narrow cut of time where work mattered.

"Anything else before I go put on a clean shirt and tie?" he asked.

"One thing," Carlie said. "Press have been sniffing specifically about Humboldt Ranch. Someone heard somebody say Luis lives out there."

"Keep that off the record," KC said. "If a reporter corners you, it's 'ongoing investigation' and 'direct questions to me'."

"Already in my script," she said.

He stood, the chair legs whispering against linoleum, and reached for his hat. The Cherry Coke had gone soft; he took one last swallow anyway. "When Trisha's photos hit, print two sets. One for me, one for tomorrow with Toni. And if Dr. Ram calls, break in."

"I will," she said. "Four o'clock is staged. I'll walk you there at 3:58."

He almost smiled. "You think I'll run?"

"I think you won't," she said. "But I like clocks."

KC tipped his hat, slid the notebook into his shirt, and took the still-cold half of the Coke with him. In the hallway, voices overlaid the AC hum, the day tightening down to the next hour. He stopped once at the window that looked over the parking lot. A news van idled by the curb. A deputy he didn't know well held the door for a cameraman as if he was somebody.

Five days, he thought. Till dawn.

KC turned from the glass and headed for the private locker room the previous sheriff had outfitted. He kept a shirt and a tie in his locker. His thoughts reeled, but the truth wasn't fast—it could keep pace with a clock when a man made room for it.

Chapter 7
Same Old KC

Day One – 3:30 p.m.

Mojave County – Sheriff's Office (KC's Office)

The wall clock ticked toward four. KC had his notebook open, scanning the lines he'd written at the jail and the crime scene, trimming them down in his head to the bare phrases he'd use at the press conference. Nothing extra. Nothing they could twist.

The knock came sharp on the door, but it opened before he could answer. Billie Akers strode in, brushing past Carlie Frye without so much as a glance. He crossed the office in three easy steps and planted himself on the front edge of KC's desk, close enough that his knees brushed the blotter.

"Kermit," Akers said with a smirk, rolling the name like it was a private joke. "Been a while."

KC kept his face still. On the inside, the name was a splinter. Kermit the Frog — the chant he'd heard in playgrounds until his fists or his silence ended it. Now it was Karole's burden too, bullies on the schoolyard turning the Talbird name against him. KC let the sting burn in quiet, refusing to give Akers the satisfaction of a reaction.

"What do you want, Billie?" KC asked evenly.

Akers leaned back on his hands, at home as if he'd never left this office. "I'm here on behalf of District Attorney Dodd. He's... disappointed you haven't kept him in the loop. Wants to be reassured you've got this under control."

KC didn't move, didn't blink. "I've got it under control."

Akers gave a small shrug, eyes glinting. "Then make it easy. I'm Dodd's investigator. Pass your reports to me. I'll see he gets what he needs without wasting your valuable time."

KC shut his notebook with a soft thud. "I don't report to you. I don't report to Dodd. The county elected me to do this job, and I'll do it. You want to know where we stand, Billie? Watch the press conference at four."

For a moment, Akers studied him, the smirk never leaving his face. He slid off the desk like he was indulging a stubborn child. "Same old Kermit. Always too proud to take a hand when it's offered."

KC stood just enough to make space, his voice level. "The name's KC. Don't forget it."

Akers chuckled low in his throat, brushed imaginary dust from his slacks, and strolled to the door. "See you around, Sheriff."

The door clicked shut behind him. Carlie, seated back at her desk, kept her eyes on her files, but KC saw her watch Akers turn down the hallway toward Parsons' office. She said nothing — for now.

KC reopened his notebook, but the words blurred for a moment before sharpening again. He checked the clock. Twenty-five minutes until he'd step in front of cameras. Enough time to settle his voice, not his temper.

Chapter 8
Rumor vs. Law

Day One – 4:00 p.m.

Mojave County – Sheriff's Office (Lobby Press Conference)

The lobby smelled faintly of wax and desert dust, the kind that never quite stayed outside. Folding chairs filled the tiled space, and cameras were already aimed at the podium when KC and Carlie stepped out of the admin hallway.

"Remember," Carlie murmured at his side, her voice low, meant only for him. "They'll try to bait you. Stick to facts. Don't let them drag you into their show."

KC adjusted his tie, giving her the faintest nod. "Facts are all they're getting."

The crowd was thicker than it should have been. County PIO had kept the invite list tight, but word spread fast in the high desert, and where news gathered, the vultures followed. Local reporters lined the front. A pair of network affiliates had wedged cameras behind them. In the second row, KC spotted the Latina blogger he'd heard about—sharp-eyed, notebook open, already writing before he spoke.

Along the side wall, Parsons stood with arms folded, his thick frame filling the space he hadn't been given. Akers was beside him, hands in his pockets, a smug smile carved across his face like he was the one in charge here. Near the back, Theodore Dodd had arrived with two assistant DAs, their dark suits and polished shoes marking them as men who expected to be noticed.

Carlie leaned in once more. "Clock says four sharp."

KC stepped to the podium. The mics bristled like iron weeds.

"Good afternoon. This morning, deputies responded to a report of a body found outside town. The victim has been identified as Maria Sherman, eighteen, a student and resident of Mojave County. This is a homicide investigation. At this time, one person is in custody, and the investigation is ongoing. Out of respect for the family, details will remain limited until we have verified facts."

Hands shot up before he finished.

"Sheriff, are you confirming the boyfriend is under arrest?"

KC held steady. "A suspect is in custody. No charges have been filed. The investigation continues."

Another voice cut in. "Sheriff, ICE sources tell us the suspect is undocumented. Shouldn't he be turned over to federal custody immediately?"

KC met the reporter's eyes. "He remains in county custody. As sheriff, my responsibility is to investigate the homicide. We follow the law. Not rumor."

Aker's voice carried across the lobby, pitched just loud enough. "Some might say holding back cooperation puts the public at risk, Sheriff."

The reporters turned, cameras swiveling. Parsons didn't move, but his smirk said enough.

KC gripped the sides of the podium. "Public safety comes from getting the truth right, not rushing it."

The Latina blogger rose to her feet without waiting for the mic. "Sheriff, isn't this the pattern? The undocumented are treated guilty before facts are gathered. How is that justice? How do you make sure prejudice isn't driving your department's case?"

The lobby hushed for a breath. KC looked at her, then at the sea of lenses waiting for his stumble.

"By treating evidence as evidence," he said evenly. "And by refusing to let anyone—federal, state, or local—decide guilt before the facts are in."

A ripple of murmurs moved through the press.

One of Dodd's assistants spoke up, voice polished, meant for microphones. "Sheriff, citizens are afraid. Don't they deserve protection more than delay?"

KC's jaw tightened. "Citizens deserve the truth. Soft is closing your eyes and calling it justice. I won't do that."

The words landed sharp, but Akers only smiled wider. Parsons shifted his stance like a man sure the ship was taking water. Dodd tilted his head, eyes narrowing, already calculating how the evening news would play.

Questions kept flying—about ICE, about the family, about how divided the department looked—but KC didn't give more. He repeated what mattered: Maria was dead, the case was active, and the truth would be found. Then he ended it.

"Thank you. That's all for now."

Carlie was waiting at his shoulder, already guiding him back toward the hall. As they stepped away from the flash of cameras, she leaned close again. "You held the line."

KC didn't answer. He'd felt the shift in the room—the optics already twisting against him. But Carlie was right about one thing. He had held the line. And for now, that had to be enough.

Chapter 9
The Name They Twisted

Day One – 6:42 p.m.

Mojave County – KC's Home (Above Della's Delights)

By the time KC climbed the narrow back stairwell to the apartment, the sun was low enough to paint the horizon in rose and rust. The smell of baked bread lingered in the air—yeast and flour that had risen before dawn and baked while the town still slept. Della's Delights was dark below, chairs stacked on tables, the ovens cooling, the hum of the walk-in freezer the only sound.

Inside, the apartment was warm and cozy. A table lamp glowed in the corner of the living room, casting long lines across the deck doors. Aunt Ruth sat in her wheelchair near the table, a knit shawl over her shoulders, her short dark hair streaked with the barest hint of gray. Blue eyes sharp, she was waiting.

"You made the news," she said as he set his hat on the rack. "Five o'clock spot. You didn't look rattled, but I know you. You're carrying more than you showed."

KC loosened his tie, gave her a faint smile. "It's part of the job."

"It's part of their job to twist it," Ruth said. "Don't let them make you doubt what you know is right."

The clink of a fork drew KC's eyes to the table. Karole sat there, tall for eight, with his father's gray eyes and his mother's softer features. He was pushing stew around in the bowl, not eating, his shoulders hunched like he wanted to disappear.

KC crossed the room, sat, and opened the waxy bag Ruth had left by his plate. Bread still warm, crisp crust, soft inside. He tore off a piece and chewed slowly. "Long day?"

Karole shrugged.

Ruth gave him a look that said more than words. "He's got something on his mind, Kermit. You should hear it."

KC stiffened just slightly at the name. Only Ruth used it without malice. He set the bread down and looked at his boy. "Go ahead."

Karole didn't speak at first. He kept his eyes on the stew. Finally, he muttered, "It's the older kids."

"What about them?" KC asked.

"They say my name's a girl's name. They laugh. They call me 'Carol' and worse." His voice cracked. "So I hit one. Then another."

KC leaned back, remembering Akers in his office that afternoon, drawling out "Kermit" like it was still playground season. He remembered being ten, fists balled, trying to swing away the sound of "Kermit the Frog."

He reached across the table, rested a hand on Karole's arm. "I know how that feels. They used to mock me, too. Same way. Called me a frog. Sang songs. Thought it made them big."

Karole's eyes lifted, uncertain. "What did you do?"

"Fought at first," KC admitted. "Didn't work. Made it worse. Until I learned something different." He leaned closer, his voice steady, quiet. "Do you know what a sheriff is called, Karole? A peace officer. That means my job—my whole purpose—is to keep peace, even when people push, even when they spit my name back at me. And that's not a weakness. That's strength."

Karole frowned. "So... I'm supposed to just take it?"

"No," KC said. "You stand tall. You tell them to stop. You walk away when you can. And if it doesn't stop, you come to me, or your teacher. But fists? That's their way, not yours. Being a peacemaker means you're stronger than the ones who throw punches first."

Ruth's voice was soft but sure. "Your father's right. Peace is harder than anger. But anger burns out. Peace stays."

Karole looked between them, chewing his lip. "What if they don't stop?"

"Then we'll face it together," KC said. "You're not alone in this. Not ever."

The boy's shoulders eased just slightly. He picked up his spoon and ate a mouthful of stew without prompting.

Ruth smiled, satisfied. She turned her chair toward the hallway. "That's enough for me tonight. I've got to be up before four to start the ovens."

"Thanks, Aunt Ruth," KC said quietly. Karole echoed, "Goodnight, Aunt Ruth."

Her wheels whispered across the floor as she rolled toward her room, shawl trailing just a little behind.

KC stayed at the table, watching his son—tall already, but still so young—finding his footing in a world that would always test him.

Later, when the dishes were cleared, KC stepped onto the deck. The desert air was cooling, the horizon dimming to indigo. He glanced down at the café below, dark and silent now, but solid—the foundation his family stood on. Karole padded out beside him, barefoot, leaning on the railing. Together they looked across Mojave County, a land wide and unforgiving.

"Dad?" Karole said.

"Yes?"

"I'll try. To be a peacemaker. Like you."

KC's throat tightened. He laid a hand on his boy's shoulder. "That's all I ask."

The lights of the county twinkled below, small against the vast dark. KC breathed deep, knowing storms were rising—both the ones outside, and the ones only a father could face.

Chapter 10

Not My Sheriff

Day One – 8:15 p.m.

**Mojave County Country Club – Private
Dining Room**

The country club kept its quiet like a secret. Beyond the tall windows, the golf course rolled into darkness, greens lit by low lamps like islands on a black sea. Inside, the private dining room was all polished wood and soft linen, the silver catching candlelight but never drawing attention to itself. A waiter in starched whites refilled a single water glass with the kind of care usually reserved for confessions.

Beatrice Garrison—Queen B—sat with her back to the window, the view behind her like a trophy she didn't need to look at. Dark hair, flawless skin that belonged to a woman twenty years younger, a dress that said old money even if Mojave County never quite had any. She didn't fidget. Power did not fidget.

Theodore Dodd arrived with the first course already down, his tie a neat line, white hair combed like a signature. He smiled as if he meant it and took the seat she indicated. The waiter ghosted a napkin across his lap and poured a measured inch of cabernet without being asked.

"You watched," Beatrice said. Not a question.

"I did," Dodd replied, settling his water, then the wine. "Your sheriff kept his voice even. That's something."

"He's not my sheriff," she said lightly. "He's the county's. And today he looked like a man trying not to drown."

"He chose caution," Dodd said. "Said what the law allows him to say."

Beatrice lifted her glass and studied the color. "Caution reads as weakness when the house is on fire, Theo." She tasted, set the glass down without a ring. "Right now, citizens want water, not philosophy."

The waiter slid away, returned with plates—rare steak for her, fish for Dodd—then vanished again. The door latched without a sound.

"ICE will move before dawn in five days," Dodd said, cutting once, precisely, then resting his knife on the edge of porcelain. "They called the sheriff. He's resisting coordination."

"Of course he is." Beatrice speared a bite, unhurried. "It's his nature to resist. He thinks that makes him noble."

"It makes him predictable." Dodd's smile thinned. "He's already set himself opposite my office. He won't give me updates, won't let my investigator streamline the flow."

"Akers went to see him," she said, eyes amused. "I heard."

Dodd took the amusement as it was offered and set it aside. "We both know Billie can be... forward."

"He's useful when directed," Beatrice said. "As is Captain Parsons." She tapped the stem of her glass once with a manicured nail, the faintest bell. "The department needs a center of gravity. KC hasn't provided it."

Dodd cut another small bite. "The press conference didn't help him. Too many questions he wouldn't answer."

"He couldn't answer." Beatrice's tone was soft, the blade wrapped in velvet. "But I can. And I will. If the sheriff won't speak to citizen safety, I will. 'We enforce the law.' It's not complicated."

"And if the boy is innocent?" Dodd asked mildly.

"Then the law clears him," she said. "But until then, we do not apologize for order." She dabbed at the corner of her mouth. "Order is what separates us from the desert."

Silence breathed between them long enough to be polite. The waiter refreshed Dodd's water; Beatrice ignored her wine until the quiet stretched, then took another measured sip.

Dodd set his fork down. "You seem particularly invested, Beatrice. Most weeks, you let me run my office without coaching."

Her smile did not quite reach her eyes. "I'm invested in stability, Theo. This county is a fence with too many broken slats. A girl is dead. The press smells blood. The sheriff hedges. That's how panic starts."

Dodd nodded, a small concession. But he had prosecuted men who smiled when they lied, and women who never raised their voice when they threatened. He knew the weight behind a tone that smooth. He stirred his fish with his fork, as if tasting for something that wasn't there. "Stability," he said. "Of course."

She let the single word sit. Outside, a grounds crew cart hummed past, a green dot of light moving over black grass.

"Julian was on my calendar this afternoon," Beatrice added, as if she'd remembered it. "Budget committee matters for the business community." She sipped again, casually. "He tells me the downtown initiative will finally break ground."

Dodd lifted his eyes. "Mr. Hahn is ambitious."

"Ambition keeps a town from dying," she said. Her tone made it an axiom, not a defense.

Dodd turned the stem of his glass a quarter inch. He did not ask why her nephew needed a slot on her calendar the same day a homicide turned the county inside out. He counted to three and exhaled through his nose, a habit that had saved him more than once. "Ambition needs rails."

"And I provide them," Beatrice said, the smile returning, warmer now. "As do you."

Dodd tried his wine, found it excellent, and set it down. "Then allow me a rail. Akers will report to me, not the sheriff. Parsons will keep an eye on internal temperature. We present a united message: the county will not be intimidated."

"Good." She cut, rested her knife, and finally looked past him, through the glass, toward the dark course. "In five days, federal agents will collect a man and perhaps his family. That will be loud. I want before then to be quiet—quiet enough that when dawn comes, no one is surprised by who stands where."

"And the sheriff?"

"If he insists on standing alone," she said, "we let him be alone." She reached for her glass. "Alone men fall."

Dodd's jaw moved once, a muscle ticking like a second hand. He thought of KC at the podium, saying soft is closing your eyes and calling it justice. He respected the line even as he prepared to bury the man who'd said it. "You're asking me to push him off the island."

"I'm asking you to hold the rope while he walks it," Beatrice said, the smile now bright enough to pass for kind. "If he crosses, good. If he doesn't—" She gave the smallest shrug. "Mojave County needs steadiness more than it needs pride."

"And your nephew?" Dodd asked, the question, placed with tweezers. He kept his tone neutral, pitched just above curiosity. "Ambition tends to place people near headlines. That can complicate stability."

Her eyes met his. Blue? Brown? In the low light, they were simply dark, and very clear. "Julian minds his business," she said. "And I mind the county's."

The waiter appeared with a tray of petit fours, sweetness offered like absolution. Dodd took none. Beatrice lifted a single square, turned it in her fingers, then set it back untouched.

"Five days," she said, raising her glass at last. "Dawn comes fast. Let's make sure it breaks on our terms."

Dodd touched his glass to hers. "On our terms," he echoed, and heard the hollowness of the words even as he spoke them.

When they rose, the waiter appeared with Beatrice's wrap as if he'd been waiting behind the door the entire time. She allowed him to drape it over her shoulders. Dodd thanked him and reached for his wallet. The waiter smiled and shook his head: "Already handled."

Outside the room, the club's carpet muffled everything. Beatrice moved with easy grace toward the lobby, a woman who had never found a door she couldn't open. Dodd lingered a half step behind, watching her profile in the glass as they passed.

He thought of rails and ropes, of sheriffs and dawn, and of a nephew whose name he would not say again tonight.

Then he followed her into the quiet, because that was how you lived to fight another day in Mojave County.

Chapter 11
The Ranch Table

Day One – 9:07 p.m.

Mojave County – Humboldt Ranch

The ranch road narrowed to hard-packed earth, the sheriff's Jeep Wrangler, his official vehicle, throwing a ribbon of light over fence posts and alfalfa stubble. Beyond the fields, low sheds hunched like sleeping animals; a windmill creaked once and stilled. When KC turned into the main yard, two heelers came barking out of the dark and then peeled off as a man on the porch whistled them down.

"Evening, Sheriff," Jack Humboldt called. His voice was weathered but even. He stepped into the porch light—a broad-shouldered man in his fifties with sun in the seams of his skin. "Dogs make more noise than sense this time of night."

KC killed the engine and climbed down. "Evening, Jack."

The porch boards gave a familiar complaint under KC's boots. He'd been out here before, in other years for other things—fence-line disputes, a strayed bull, a foreman's DUI that Jack had handled in-house with a severance and a prayer. The Humboldts were the kind of people who kept their own house in order and didn't ask for favors.

Eleanor Humboldt opened the screen door. She had a calm face and capable hands; the porch light caught the silver in her hair like river water. "Come in, Sheriff. Can I get you something to drink?"

"Water would be fine. Thank you."

Inside, the big house was tidy without being pretentious—saddles displayed with care, a faded photo of a 4-H ribbon on the wall, a dining table scarred from decades of meals and arguments. Eleanor set a glass of water in front of KC and sat across from him. Jack took the head of the table like he always did, not out of pride but out of habit.

"We were sorry to hear about Maria," Eleanor said. "Ruth at the café... she always spoke well of that girl. She worked hard."

KC nodded once. "She did."

Jack folded his hands. "We heard talk out here, Sheriff. You can't stop talking once it starts. They've got Luis in your jail."

"He's in county custody while we investigate," KC said. "That's all I'll say for now."

Jack held his gaze, then looked down at the table as if measuring a cut no one could see. "Luis has worked for us going on four years. Shows up early, stays late, doesn't steal time or tools. If he borrowed a wrench and couldn't find me to return it, I'd find it cleaned and oiled on my doorstep before sunup."

Eleanor nodded. "His mama, Rosa cleans the offices and helps in the kitchen during harvest. The boy, Mateo, does what he can—runs water, picks up trash along the fence. Good people. Quiet."

KC took a swallow of water that tasted of iron and ice. "I'm here because truth isn't something you hear secondhand. It's something you walk up to."

"What can we do to help?" Eleanor asked. No performance in it— only the question good neighbors ask when trouble comes to a door that isn't theirs.

"Two things," KC said. "One, be ready to speak plain if you're asked about Luis—his work, his character, his time. Two, don't let rumor drive this family off before the facts line up. People move because fear tells them to. Fear's not a foreman I answer to."

Jack breathed out through his nose, a thoughtful sound. "We won't push them. We've told folks to keep their mouths shut and their eyes open."

KC nodded. "Good to be prepared." He rose. "Would you introduce me to his mama?"

Eleanor stood. "I'll take you to Rosa. She'll open the door faster if I'm with you."

"I'd appreciate that."

They crossed the yard under a sky cut open with stars. The heelers followed at heel without a word, then settled under the steps of a small building tucked close to a tool shed. A single bulb burned over the door, moths drumming their wings against the glass.

Eleanor rapped once and called softly, "Rosa? It's Ellie."

The door opened on a woman in a clean house dress, hair braided and pinned. She was mid-forties with the kind of face that had forgotten how to rest. When she saw Eleanor, her shoulders eased a fraction. When she saw KC, they tightened again.

"Señora Alvarez," Eleanor said gently, "this is Sheriff Talbird. He wants to talk, and he wants to listen."

Rosa's eyes stayed on KC's for a long breath, weighing. Then she stepped back. "Come in."

The quarters were small and careful. A crucifix hung above the table. A pot of beans steamed on the back eye of a two-burner stove; the smell of onion and bay leaves clung low to the warm air. Mateo sat at the table with a workbook open and a pencil gripped in his hand like a nail. He was long-limbed for twelve, already working toward his brother's height, his chin set too hard for his age.

KC held his hat by the brim and did not put it back on. Rosa nodded to the chair. Eleanor took the second seat but stayed a little to the side, a bridge if one was needed, a shadow if not.

"I'm sorry for the intrusion this late," KC said. "I won't take more of your night than I need to."

Rosa folded her hands in her lap. The nails were short and clean. "You are the sheriff," she said. "If you knock, I'll open."

"I'm KC," he said. "Not just the badge." He looked once at Mateo. "And you must be Mateo."

The boy's eyes stayed wary. "Yes, sir."

"I'm here because I don't make cases out of rumor," KC went on. "I make them out of truth. I need to know where Luis was last night. I need to know who saw him and when."

Mateo spoke before Rosa could. "He was here," he said. "He came home late. I heard his boots on the steps. I got up to pee—I saw him. He was tired. He sat at the table and ate beans and fell asleep right here." He tapped the wood. "He snores a little."

Rosa made a soft sound of correction; the boy looked down, chastened but unyielding.

"What time did you hear him?" KC asked, voice mild.

"Late," Mateo said. "After I went to bed. After ten."

Rosa added, "He worked a long day. He is not a clock. But he came home. He slept here. This I know."

KC wrote that down. Home after \\ p.m. Slept at the table. Rosa/Mateo saw. He looked up. "Did Maria come by here in the last week?"

Rosa's mouth softened at the name. "María was like my own sometimes. She came when she could. She helped me when my back hurt. She laughed with Luis. She... ate with us." Her voice thinned. "He loved her."

Mateo nodded, the motion small and fierce. "She was nice. She would bring bread from Della's. She said Aunt Ruth gave her an extra sometimes."

KC thought of the apartment above the café, of Ruth's shawl and Karole's thin shoulders under his hand. He wrote Maria often here. Bread from Della's. He looked at Rosa again. "Did Luis ever raise a hand to her? Ever shout? Ever put a mark on her that you saw?"

"No," Rosa said, her chin coming up. "He is tired and sometimes he is quiet, but he is not cruel. He carries the weight of his father leaving. He does not throw it."

Eleanor spoke for the first time since they sat. "He's steady, Sheriff. We see it too."

Rosa's eyes misted and cleared. "Sheriff," she said, "does the truth matter here? Or only what people already believe?"

KC felt the question land where it always did—in that place in a man where duty and sorrow spar without witnesses. He thought of five days, of a dawn that would drag federal boots across this yard, through this door, into this small room that smelled of beans and clean oak. He thought of a boy who had just sworn that his brother snored.

"It matters," he said. He made himself hold her gaze. "To me, it matters. I won't move a thing I can't stand on. Not for a headline. Not for pressure. Not for anybody."

Rosa watched him a moment longer, measuring promises the way poor people have to. Then she reached for a dish towel, twisted it once, and set it down. "Gracias."

KC closed his notebook. "One more thing," he said. "When was the last time Maria was here?"

Rosa thought. "Maybe three mornings ago, after her work. She brought bread." A pause. "They broke up."

KC noted that she knew. "Did Maria say anything unusual when she brought bread? Did she seem frightened? Sick?"

Rosa nodded slowly. "Tired in her eyes. But she smiled at Mateo and kissed my cheek. I told her I would pray for her tests."

She saw KC's look. "At school—exams?" KC asked.

Rosa hesitated, unsure to say more.

Eleanor touched her hand. "You can trust KC."

Her eyes misted again. She wiped her tears with the dish cloth. "She was going to have a pregnancy test."

KC didn't want to cause more hurt, but he had to ask. "Was the baby Luis's?"

She shook her head. "I don't know."

"Thank you, Rosa." KC put his pen away. "I may need to speak with you again," he said. "If anyone comes here asking questions, you ask for their name and call me." He handed her his card. "You don't owe anyone this story but me unless a judge tells you so. Do you understand?"

"I understand," Rosa said. "But I am not afraid of truth."

"Good," KC said softly. "Neither am I."

They stood. Eleanor touched Rosa's shoulder in goodbye and left a folded slip of paper on the counter—a quiet promise of a ride, a meal, whatever might be needed when things turned. Rosa tucked it under the sugar canister without looking.

Outside, the air had gone crisp. The heelers thumped their tails once, recognizing that goodbyes smell different than greetings. KC and Eleanor walked back toward the big house, each watching their own stretch of ground.

"Thank you," KC said when they reached the porch. "For walking me in."

Eleanor nodded. "We look after our own out here. Even when they were born somewhere else."

Jack opened the door. He had a ledger in his hand and reading glasses perched low. "Everything all right?"

"As much as anything is," KC said.

Jack leaned the ledger against the doorframe. "If the feds come, we'll keep the peace best we can. But men with vests and letters on their backs make a lot of noise. If there's something we can do before it gets that far—"

"Keep the gates unlocked and the talk level," KC said. "No one needs to get brave at midnight. If I need statements, I'll call. If rumors get ugly, call me first."

Jack absorbed that, then held out his hand. KC took it. It was the grip of a man who knew how to hold a fence post steady while another man pounded the nail.

"Water for the road?" Eleanor asked.

KC shook his head. "I'm good. Thank you."

He crossed the yard alone, the white Jeep's dome light flaring when he opened the door. He took out his notebook and wrote by the glow:

- Humboldts vouch: steady, honest. Will support truth publicly.
- Rosa works ranch; Mateo helps. Home after 2200; slept at table.
- Maria often there; bread from Della's; tired eyes; promised cinnamon rolls. Possibly pregnant.
- Rosa's question: truth vs. belief. Hold the line.

KC stared at the line that said pregnant until the letters swam, then underlined it.

He could feel the weight in his chest—the knowledge he couldn't share—that in five days, before the sun cleared the ridge, strangers would knock not like neighbors but like storms.

When he looked up, Rosa and Mateo were framed in the doorway of the small house, silhouettes against the small light. Across the yard, the Humboldts' windows glowed warm. Two houses, one county, one future narrowing by the hour.

KC started the engine. Gravel cracked under the tires as he turned toward the road. He drove slow until the gate, then slower still once he was past it, as if easing the truck could soften what the next days would bring.

On the highway, the desert opened. He glanced once in the rearview and saw only stars. He kept his hands steady on the wheel and told himself, out loud so there was no mistaking it, "Truth first."

The words hung in the cab like a promise and a prayer, and the night took them the way it took everything—without reply, without hurry, and utterly sure of dawn.

Chapter 12
Tools, Not Shields

Day One – 11:02 p.m.

Mojave County – Queen B's Residence

The Garrison house sat on a rise above the country club greens, its windows glowing like a lighthouse against the dark sweep of desert. Inside, the air smelled faintly of lemon oil and polish—clean wealth, curated and controlled. A leather chair faced a wide desk, mahogany, imported. Paintings lined the walls: a desert landscape by a local artist, a modernist print from New York, a photograph of Beatrice at a campaign rally.

She sat beneath that photo now, a glass of sparkling water balanced in one hand. At sixty, she looked mid-forties in the right light—hair dark, skin firm, posture perfect. Every detail of her appearance was deliberate. On the mantel above the unlit fireplace stood a framed shot of her nephew Hahn in his college days, his smile careless, his future assured.

The grandfather clock ticked. A minute past the hour. Then two.

The door opened. Billie Akers stepped in, his shoes too heavy on the marble. He didn't wait to be called. He had the bearing of a man who once expected respect without earning it—five-ten, broad-shouldered, athletic, blue eyes, sharp but restless. He gave a tight smile.

"Evening, Beatrice. Roads were slow. Ridge was jammed."

She didn't answer. She let the silence grow until it filled the room, pressing against him. Akers shifted, his smirk fading.

"Two minutes late," she said finally, each word clipped. "Sheriff Talbird doesn't beat you with strength. He beats you with the clock. You can't even beat the clock."

Akers' jaw tightened. "I was with Parsons earlier. Making sure he stays in line, like you asked."

She set her glass down with a click. "That's not what I asked. Parsons is a tool, not a shield. What I want is leverage. Something on Talbird. Something the press can run with. Tomorrow. Noon."

"That's a narrow window." His voice had the faint edge of defiance.

"Then widen your effort." Her eyes stayed locked on his. "You grew up here. You worked in that department. You know the deputies, their wives, their drinking buddies. Someone's talking. Someone always talks. Find it. By noon."

Akers crossed his arms, testing her patience. "You think he's clean? Nobody's clean. He was Border Patrol. He's got dirt." His smirk returned, smaller this time. "And half that department still thinks I should've been sheriff. I can lean on them."

She gave a faint, cold smile. "Do that. But remember this—when people think you belong in the chair, that doesn't make you sheriff. Losing does."

He flinched, then masked it. "I'll bring you something. Press-worthy."

"See that you do."

Akers glanced at the photo of Hahn on the mantel. His brow lifted just slightly. "People still whisper about him, you know. About Maria. About—"

Her eyes cut to him like knives. "Family is not your concern."

"I didn't mean—"

"Family comes first," she said, each syllable measured. "Always. You keep Parsons busy. You dig on Talbird. But you don't touch family."

The silence stretched again. Akers looked away first.

She picked up her glass, took a sip, then continued. "And Billie—if there's blowback, it dies in your lap. Not mine."

He nodded, stiff. He hated being talked to like this—hated being the errand boy. Once, he'd run for sheriff. Once, he'd believed he had the office in his grasp. Now he was standing in Beatrice Garrison's home like a servant, waiting for orders. But he didn't show the anger, not here. Not to her.

"I understand," he said.

"Good."

She rose, smoothed a hand down her blazer, and walked to the mantel. With care, she straightened Hahn's frame until it sat level. Then she adjusted her campaign photo beside it. Symbols of power. Symbols of loyalty.

When she turned back, her smile matched the one in the picture—sharp, rehearsed, unstoppable. "Things are moving my way, Billie. Don't let me down."

Akers dipped his head. He told himself he'd bring her what she wanted. He also told himself that someday, the balance would shift.

For now, the clock ticked, and Queen B was winning

Chapter 13
Before Dawn, Four Days

Day Two – 7:32 a.m.

Mojave County – Sheriff's Office (KC's Office)

The desert held a fall chill that made the first light feel sharper. KC eased the white Jeep Wrangler into the gravel strip behind the Sheriff's Office, where staff parked out of sight of the lobby glass, and sat a moment with the engine ticking down. The eastern sky was a thin blade of pewter. Somewhere, a train horn laid a long line across the morning.

Inside, the building woke in low voices and paper sounds. The overnight crew signed off in murmurs; the day shift drifted in with the careful quiet people use when they aren't sure which way the wind will blow. From out front came a faint idle-thrum—reporter vans parked along the curb, cameras waiting like vultures for movement.

Carlie Frye was already at her desk, files squared to the edge, hair neat as a checkmark. She had a manila folder and a single sheet face down, waiting.

"Morning," she said.

"Morning," KC answered, hanging his hat on the rack. "What've we got?"

She slid the face-down sheet across. "The ICE memo came in late last night. It says five days from issuance at dawn. But that was yesterday—so we've got four days left." She tapped the upper corner where she'd stapled a routing slip with only her initials. "I printed it here and kept it off the squadroom printers."

KC read it once, let the language settle. Clinical words built to the sentence that mattered: HSI will assume custody of Luis Alvarez at 0500 five days from this notice and will execute related actions at the Humboldt Ranch contemporaneously. He folded the paper and slid it into his black notebook.

"Logged?" he asked.

"In a confidential file," she said. "Mine and yours only. Not in the general."

"Good." He nodded toward the front windows beyond the admin bay. "You see them?"

"One van parked. Another circling," she said. "They're trolling for scraps."

KC moved into his office. The corkboard filled one wall, a constellation of names on slips pinned with colored tacks. Overnight, he'd moved a few without thinking about it: ALVAREZ—ROSA/MATEO higher, almost level with MARIA; HUMBOLDT RANCH tucked under them like a foundation. AKERS, PARSONS, and GARRISON hung along the opposite edge like weather building.

Carlie followed and closed the door. "One more thing. At 3:51 yesterday afternoon, I saw Akers walk into Parsons' office. He didn't knock. Door closed behind him. They were in there for nine minutes—just before the press conference."

KC set the notebook on his desk. "Anyone else notice?"

"If they did, they didn't say it where I could hear."

"Thank you," he said. "Note it with the time in your confidential file."

"Already did."

He checked the wall clock. 7:33. "We're on for eight?"

Carlie's mouth made the small shape it did when she was pleased something had gone the way it was supposed to. "Deputy Salazar will arrive at the side door at 7:58 in plain clothes. I entered it as 'personnel review' in the log."

KC picked up a fresh slip, block-printed a new name—DIRT BIKE KID—and pinned it just below MARIA with an empty line between them, a space waiting to be filled. "When she gets here, bring her straight in."

Carlie nodded and left him to the quiet.

He stood a moment at the window that looked over the rear lot. Breath fogged faintly when a deputy stepped outside, hands shoved into jacket pockets—fall in the Mojave, long shadows and a sky that promised it would be mild by noon. Out front, a news van idled, camera angled like a hawk on a fence rail.

He flipped open the black notebook. Last night's lines looked steadier in morning light:

- Rosa works ranch; Mateo helps. Home after 2200; slept at the table.
- Maria—possible pregnancy (Rosa).
- ICE—4 days to dawn.

He underlined dawn once, then closed the book.

A soft knock. Carlie eased the door and stepped aside. Toni Salazar came in wearing jeans, a gray T-shirt, and a black windbreaker that could pass for nothing at all. No badge showing. No gun on her hip. Dark hair braided and looped low, eyes steady. She looked the way she had in the dust at the pullout—new to the job, not new to paying attention.

"Deputy," KC said, gesturing to the chair opposite his desk. "Have a seat."

She sat, hands flat on her thighs, a posture that said respect without fear.

"I asked you in plain clothes for a reason," he said. "The way we're going to work—if we work at all—is quiet. That means discretion beyond policy and a tolerance for me not explaining everything all at once."

"Yes, Sheriff," she said.

"In this room—" He tapped the wood twice. "—you can call me KC. Outside, you don't. Outside, you follow your captain's orders and the SOP. You don't change your gait, you don't change your lunch table, and you don't give anybody the itch that you're talking to me."

She held his gaze. "Understood."

"I'm going to give you a first assignment that tests whether you can move without adding noise." He slid a lined index card across. On it, in tight hand: Dirt bike kid—first on scene—no name recorded—find him, bring him in clean. "A teenage male on a dirt bike found Maria pre-dawn out past the wash. Parsons took the call and failed to log the name. I want the boy found and in an interview chair without Parsons knowing you lifted a finger."

Toni glanced at the card once, then back at him. "Any boundaries on how I find him?"

"Within the law," he said. "Within my office, not the rumor mill. Start with the obvious: who rides at dawn, who cuts class, who posts their dust trails like trophies. Check school lots by seven-thirty—look for fresh mud under a high schooler's rear fender when it hasn't rained. Talk to the crossing guard on the east side—helmet hair gives boys away."

A small smile touched the corner of her mouth. "Yes, sir."

"If you need traffic-cam stills and you can pull them without leaving a footprint in Parsons' inbox, do it. If you need a deputy as a shadow, you call me first."

"Yes, sir," she said, then corrected herself. "KC."

He nodded once. "When you have him, text Carlie. She'll route you and the kid through the side door as 'community outreach'. No cuffs unless he gives you a reason that would stand up in front of a judge."

Her eyes thinned a fraction. "If Parsons asks where I'm going?"

"You're on a personnel matter," KC said. "If he presses, you tell him to see me. He won't."

She tucked the index card into her windbreaker like it was something fragile. "I'll bring him."

"Good." He paused. "One more thing. If you think you're being followed, you don't test your luck—you test mine. Call me."

She didn't bristle at the caution. "Understood."

Carlie slipped back in with a blank personnel evaluation form and set it on KC's desk. "Paperwork ready," she said. "I'll file it as cover once Toni steps out."

Toni stood. "I'll start with the school lots," she said. "Then the east-side trailheads."

"Move," KC said, not unkindly.

She moved.

When the door clicked shut, Carlie waited one beat. "He'll feel it when she starts pulling threads."

"Parsons?" KC asked.

She nodded. "He's watching through blinds again."

"He can watch," KC said. "He doesn't get to touch."

Carlie's gaze flicked to the slip DIRT BIKE KID now hanging

under MARIA. "You want me to prep an interview room as 'community outreach'?"

"Two," KC said. "One for the boy. One for whoever shows up with him."

"Done." She hesitated. "Anything else before the morning spins up?"

"Two things," he said. "If Dr. Ram calls, break in—no matter who's in front of me. And call Dr. Jodi Kirk at County Mental Health. Tell her I'd like to stop by early afternoon on a personnel consult. Keep the words boring."

Carlie wrote personnel consult—J. Kirk (2:00 p.m.) in her neat hand. "You'll get pushback on confidentiality."

"I expect it," he said. "I also expect a human being to understand the difference between gossip and a dead girl."

A line formed in her cheek that might have been a smile and might have been a wince. "I'll make the call."

She left him with the hum of old ductwork and the early clatter of boots in the hall. KC opened his notebook, drew a line under the ICE memo, and wrote the day's first new entries:

- Toni—find dirt bike kid—no Parsons.

- Akers w/ Parsons—3:51 p.m.—9 min—pre-press.

- Jodi Kirk—2:00 p.m.—personnel pretext.

- ICE—4 days left.

He capped the pen and looked at the clock. 7:51.

Through the glass, the side corridor stayed empty until it didn't. He caught a flicker—Toni's windbreaker slipping past, her stride the same unhurried pace as any deputy on any morning. Then she was gone, swallowed by the building and whatever breadcrumb trail teenagers in a desert town left behind.

At 7:58, the desk phone gave a quiet chirp—Carlie's extension. He lifted it. "Talbird."

"Jodi can see you at two o'clock," Carlie said. "I framed it as personnel. Her voice was careful. Not cold."

"Take it," KC said.

He hung up and reached for his hat. The day outside was bright now, shadows long, breath still showing when doors opened and closed. Out front, the news van's camera had shifted toward the sidewalk, patient as a hawk.

His cell buzzed with a local number he knew. Dr. Ram.

KC answered as he walked. "Ram."

"Sheriff," the medical examiner said, voice low and precise. "I've got findings you'll want to hear. Are you free to come now?"

KC's pace didn't change. "Ten minutes."

He slid the phone into his pocket and kept moving. He passed Parsons' open doorway without looking, though he saw the man in his periphery—broad shoulders, thick hair, head tilted in that way that meant a smirk lived under it. KC didn't slow. He had a dead girl, a ticking clock, and a deputy he'd just sent hunting for a boy on a dirt bike in a town that liked to talk.

Truth wasn't fast. But it could keep pace with a morning if a man made room for it. KC pushed through the glass doors into the light.

Chapter 14
Struck Without Warning

Day Two – 8:47 a.m.

Mojave County – Medical Examiner's Office

The morgue was a squat concrete box on the edge of town, the color of sun-bleached bone. KC parked the white Jeep beside a county van and killed the engine. Morning sun threw long angles across the asphalt, but the air still had teeth—desert fall, the kind that pretends warmth until the wind shifts.

Inside, the corridor smelled of bleach and metal, the kind of clean that never feels clean enough. KC's boots sent small echoes down the tile until a door at the end swung open.

"Sheriff."

Dr. Arjun Ram was lean and precise, silver at his temples, lab coat crisp with the sleeves rolled once for work instead of comfort. His voice carried the finality of the morgue.

KC nodded. "Doctor."

Ram led him into the exam room. Cold air pressed the edges of every sound. A sheet lay squared on the steel table, corners folded exact.

"Cause of death is straightforward," Ram said, tone even. "One heavy downward blow to the occiput—the back of the skull. No hesitation. No follow-up."

KC's jaw flexed once. "Weapon?"

Ram tapped a photo clipped to the chart. "Blunt instrument, cylindrical, roughly one-and-a-half inches in diameter. The patterning is distinctive. A baton or nightstick is my strongest candidate—law enforcement issue fits."

"How certain?"

"Ninety percent if I had to testify."

KC glanced at the photo again. The image wanted to turn into a memory he didn't have—motion, momentum, the quiet before a strike. He kept his voice level. "Defensive wounds?"

"None." Ram slid another photo forward. "Positional evidence—abrasions, how the clothing sat—suggests she was facing someone. She didn't see the attack. The strike came from behind. There's a short drag artifact after impact—repositioned, then removed."

KC opened his black notebook. In square, clean letters, he wrote: Baton—occiput. No defense. Facing someone → struck from behind. He underlined behind twice. The room seemed to draw a breath and hold it. It wasn't only murder; it was betrayal. Someone she trusted had stood close enough for conversation and let her believe she was safe.

Ram shifted the chart again. "Preliminary tox is clean—no alcohol, no obvious drugs. We'll confirm when the full panel runs." He hesitated, then laid down a second sheet. "There is one more thing. Early pregnancy. Six, maybe seven weeks."

KC's pen paused. He wrote pregnant and circled it. The word blurred for a second. He made himself steady it, draw a second clean circle. In his mind, it wasn't a word; it was two futures folded shut—Maria's, and a child's that hadn't even had a name.

Ram watched him, unreadable. "This will complicate the case, Sheriff. The narrative. Motive. Anger. Shame."

"It adds truth," KC said.

Ram nodded once. "Truth has a way of widening rooms."

KC closed the notebook. "I need discretion here. I have to talk to her father before he hears this secondhand. Hold the file."

"I can't," Ram said, not unkindly. "Once I log preliminaries, the case packet becomes visible to the DA's office. They ping automatically. Your captain will see it the minute someone in his orbit asks. That's the system you and I both live in."

KC contained the flash of frustration with a breath that didn't show. "How long before you log?"

"I already entered the time of death and preliminary cause," Ram said. "Pregnancy marks as a note until the confirm hits—today's run tells me what I already know, but it won't be final-final for another day. The baton analysis is in my narrative; it's my opinion, but it's there."

KC looked at the sheeted table, then back to Ram. "Then I'm racing a clock." He opened the notebook and wrote: Herb—today. Before the leak.

Ram slid his hands into his coat pockets. "I'll speak precisely in my report and nowhere else."

"That helps," KC said. "One more ask—collect and compare DNA against Luis Alvarez. If he's not a match, I want that certainty as fast as the science allows."

"It's already drawn," Ram said. "We'll run paternity markers as soon as we can. I'll flag it as priority."

KC nodded. "Thank you."

Ram's gaze thinned, measuring him across the tired truce of two men who both answered to facts. "Sheriff—if the weapon points inward, it will not be a quiet storm."

KC met his eyes, gray and steady. "Storms have names. This one will too. A man's name, not just a rumor."

He stepped back into the hallway. The smell of bleach rose like a tide and fell again. Outside, the morgue's glass doors threw back a bent reflection of the Jeep, as if heat already wavered on a cool day.

On the hood, KC braced the notebook and added, under his last line: Struck from behind while facing someone—trust exploited. He drew a box around it. Then another note: Call Carlie → set with Herb now.

He climbed into the Jeep, hands at ten and two until the wheel felt like it belonged to him again. The drive back wasn't long, but the road kept narrowing—four days to dawn, and less than that until bad news found a father from a stranger's mouth.

He started the engine and told himself the same thing he told others when the ground gave way—truth first—even when it cut. Especially then.

Chapter 15

Hands on the Desk

Day Two – 9:32 a.m.

**Mojave County – Sherman's Market
(Owner's Office)**

KC pulled into the short row of angled slots along the side of Sherman's Market, the white Jeep nosing up to a curb painted red by some long-ago code tweak no one enforced. The bell over the glass door gave its same tired jingle as he stepped inside. Cold air rolled over him—refrigerated cases and citrus cleaner. The corkboard by the entrance looked exactly as it had the last time he'd walked in—the same yellowed Little League flyer, the hand-lettered ad for a used tractor, a church bake sale that had already come and gone.

At the register, an older, plump woman with dyed auburn hair and reading glasses counted change into a paper hand. She glanced up at KC, gave a small, respectful nod, and looked back to her till.

Herb was at the end of Aisle Three, tightening a cardboard sleeve around a bundle of paper towels. His hands were big and square, a butcher's hands. He looked up when he felt KC before he saw him, the way men do when bad news starts traveling ahead of itself.

"Sheriff." The word came flat.

"Herb," KC said, keeping his voice low. "Can we talk in the back?"

For a heartbeat, Herb didn't move. Then he dropped the sleeve on the shelf and jerked his chin toward the swinging door by the stockroom. "Two minutes," he called to the clerk. "Watch the front."

They passed sacks of flour stacked like sandbags, a corkboard peppered with vendor notes, the same faded Little League sign-up sheet tacked above a time clock. The office was a square room with a dented metal desk, a humming mini-fridge, and a calendar with a photo of the Colorado River. A picture of Maria was taped to the lower right corner—school portrait, blue, shy smile, hair pulled clean.

Herb shut the door with the heel of his hand. "You got some news for me?" he said. "Or a speech?"

KC took off his hat and set it brim-up on the filing cabinet. He sat. "I'm here because I have facts you need to hear from me."

Herb's mouth tightened like a fist. "Say them."

KC let the room settle so the words would have a place to land. "The medical examiner's preliminary shows a single blow to the back of Maria's head. She didn't see it coming."

Herb's shoulders hitched once. He looked at the calendar photo and then away. "Coward's work," he said, and it came out rough.

KC nodded. "No defensive wounds. Indications she was facing someone—talking, maybe—when she was struck from behind. One blow. Controlled."

Herb raked a hand over his jaw, eyes brightening and hardening at the same time. "And Luis is in your jail."

"He is," KC said. "He's in custody because that's the path others pursued yesterday. He has an alibi."

"Alibi," Herb snapped. "He would have one. His mama, huh?"

KC took that without flinching. "It's credible. I'm not naming witnesses to you, and I won't. But it exists."

Herb's hands braced on the desk. "That it?"

KC's voice stayed even. "Maria was pregnant. Early. Six or seven weeks."

For a second, Herb didn't hear it. The words ran past him and had to come back, slower. He put both hands on the desk and leaned into them like the surface might tilt. "No," he said, but he said it to the calendar, not to KC. "No, she... she would've told me."

"She might have meant to," KC said. "She might have been trying to figure out how."

Herb shook his head, mouth working as if he could grind the truth down into something else. "Then it was him," he said, grabbing the first shape in reach.

"Maybe," KC said. "We have his DNA, and the ME will determine whether he's the father."

Herb dropped back into his chair. "That's why he killed her."

KC stayed steady. "If the baby was his, Herb, why would he kill her?"

The room fell silent. Herb brushed his hand over the top of his head. His face went red, fists balling. "You saying someone else? You saying my daughter was—?"

"No," KC cut in quickly. "I'm saying we don't have all the facts. Nor motive."

"If it wasn't his—jealousy. That's your motive right there."

KC didn't dismiss it. "Jealousy is a motive we have to consider. Any decent investigator would. But what we saw out there wasn't a hot-blood scene. It wasn't rage. It was one precise blow from behind. No scatter. No struggle. If a man lost his temper, you usually see the storm he brings with him."

Herb stared at him, breathing hard, the line of his mouth a bruise. "So what are you telling me?" His fists uncurled.

"I'm telling you I won't hang this on anyone because it's easy," KC said. "I'm telling you, Dr. Ram is running a paternity test. When it comes back, we'll know whether Luis could be the father. If he isn't, your anger will have to find a new home. If he is... we'll handle that fact, too. But not by guessing."

Herb turned the desk calendar's page up with a thumbnail and let it slap back down. His eyes were rimmed red now, not from tears—

Herb didn't look like a man who cried where he could be seen—but from sleep that hadn't come. "Why didn't she tell me?" he asked, and that was the first real thing he'd said.

"I don't know," KC said, plain. "Sometimes girls hold a secret until they can put the words in a row that don't burn their throat. Sometimes they are scared."

"That's not how that works," Herb said, and his voice broke on it. He pressed the heel of a hand to his mouth and looked past KC to the far wall. "I could've... I would've..." He swallowed hard, found the edge of anger because it was easier to hold. "Whoever did this— whoever—" He swallowed again. "They took my girl from me. They took everything she was going to be."

KC let the silence stand there with them because a man needs to hear the shape of what he just said. Then he spoke softly, but there wasn't any softness in what he said. "They did," he agreed. "And I intend to put a name to the person who did it."

Herb's eyes cut to him. Something like respect flickered and went out. "You better."

"I will," KC said. He reached for his notebook but didn't open it. "Today and tomorrow, the talk's going to double. The pregnancy will likely get out before I can stop it. When it does, every man with a grudge and every woman with a story will tell you what you should've done. You don't have to listen to a single one of them."

Herb's jaw worked. "What do I do then?"

"You do two things," KC said. "You take care of your people— your employees, the ones who loved her, the ones who will say the wrong thing because they don't know what else to say. And you let me do my job. When someone comes in here with a rumor, you send them to me. When you want to hit something, you go out back and split wood." He let the next line hang because it mattered. "Don't turn on the ones who didn't do this just because they're close at hand."

Herb stared at him like he wanted to argue and couldn't find the place to start. "You think I don't know what you're telling me not to do?"

"I think you know exactly," KC said. "And I think you're the kind of man who can hold himself steady even when the ground moves."

Herb leaned back, eyes closed for a count of three, then opened them again. "You said paternity test."

"Yes."

"How long?"

"A day or two for the first pass," KC said. "Dr. Ram flagged it." He chose the next words carefully. "If Luis is excluded, it means certainty needs to shift. I need you willing to let it."

Herb's mouth twitched. "You telling me how to think?"

"I'm telling you how to fight," KC said. "You don't swing at shadows. You swing at the man who's in front of you when the light comes up."

A sound moved on the other side of the door—the thump of a dolly, the older clerk's laugh, small and human. Herb stared at the door as if he could make the noise stop with a look.

"Do I need to sit with you a minute," KC asked, "or do you want me gone so you can put your face back on for your people?"

Herb huffed a breath that wasn't a laugh. "You always talk this plain?"

"I try."

"It'll get you in trouble."

"It already has."

For the first time since KC had walked in, something like a smile touched Herb's face and died there. He reached for the corner of Maria's photo and straightened it a millimeter, a ritual too small to matter and big as anything a man could do. "You talk to Rosa?" he asked, eyes still on the picture.

"Last night," KC said. "She's solid. So's the boy."

Herb nodded once, slow. "Good woman," he muttered, as if it cost him something to say it and gave something back, too.

KC picked up his hat. "One more ask. When the paternity comes back—whatever it says—you don't tell a soul until I do. Not your friends at the club. Not the men who load your trucks. Not the council chair who calls you for checks. Let me say it first so it lands where it should."

Herb's jaw set. Then, after a long beat, he nodded. "All right."

KC set the hat on his head and reached for the knob. "If you need me before I call, you call. If someone comes in here with a camera or a microphone, you send them to my office. I'll stand between you and them as long as I need to."

Herb shook his head like he didn't believe anyone could do that, then surprised himself by saying, "Thank you."

KC paused with the door half open. He didn't say you're welcome. He said, "I'm sorry."

Herb's eyes flashed again and went wet at the edges. He blinked hard and looked away. "Bring me a name," he said, voice rough. "Don't bring me speeches."

KC stepped back into the hallway. The stockroom smell—cardboard, citrus, floor cleaner—hit him fresh. He waited for the dolly to wheel past before cutting across to the aisle. From the front door, he could see the strip of sky, hard blue now, the day brightening like it didn't have the sense to know better.

At the threshold, he took out the black notebook, braced it against the doorjamb, and wrote:

Told Herb: occiput; pregnant.

Jealousy motive (acknowledged) vs. scene = controlled; one blow.

Alibi exists—verify (no names).

Paternity test (Ram) flagged.

Herb—anger → grief. Beginning to bend toward truth.

He closed the book and slid it back into his shirt pocket. As the bell jingled over his head on the way out, KC told himself the same thing he'd told Herb inside: you don't swing at shadows.

Four days to dawn. The storm didn't have its name yet. But it would.

Chapter 16
Unity, They Call It

Day Two – 11:07 a.m.

Mojave County – Sheriff's Office (KC's Office)

KC stood before the corkboard, sleeves pushed to the forearms, pen cap against his teeth. The board had stopped being neat sometime earlier that morning; the lines he'd drawn between names had begun to look like a map of dry riverbeds—clear if you'd walked them, nonsense if you hadn't.

He pinned a new slip: PREGNANCY—underlined once, then again.

Beneath it: Paternity test (pending).

Off to the side: One blow—from behind.

And, lower, where he didn't want eyes to land unless they were his: Baton? LE knowledge.

He stepped back. The room hummed with old air and the memory of Lysol from the janitor's cart that had rolled through before eight. On the desk, his black notebook lay open to a half page that read simply: Trust exploited. He could still see Herb's knuckles whitening on the desk edge, the second when anger gave way to the heavier thing behind it.

A crisp knock came—once, then the handle turned before the second hit wood.

Parsons pushed in without waiting and dropped into the visitor's chair like it already knew him. He held his sunglasses by one arm and let them tap, tap, tap against his knee. His thick hair was combed back, too long for the regulations he ignored.

"Busy board you got there," Parsons said, chin lifting toward the slips. "Looks like you're doing a lot of thinking without your command staff."

KC didn't turn. "What do you need, Captain?"

"What I need," Parsons said, leaning forward, "is to know why the squad room thinks Toni Salazar's reporting straight to you."

KC glanced over, expression flat. "The squad room thinks a lot of things."

Parsons' mouth pulled thin. "She's not a rookie. She's one of my steadiest hands, and I'm short on patrol. If you've got her chasing your personal errands while we've got calls holding, that's a problem."

KC finally faced him. "Personnel assignments are my call."

"And I'm your operations," Parsons shot back. "It looks bad, Sheriff. It looks like favorites sneaking around protocols while the rest of us carry the weight. We don't make pets of deputies."

KC's voice stayed even. "If I need Deputy Salazar on something, I'll use her. If I need her on patrol, I'll put her there. Either way, you'll have the coverage you need."

Parsons spread his hands, mock-reasonable. "Then let's be reasonable. I've got a schedule to manage. If you're going to siphon her off, I need to backfill. You don't get to run side channels. Dodd's already asking why we aren't unified."

KC watched him for a beat. The unified landed like an accusation wrapped in a sermon. "You've had your say."

Parsons' eyes slid past him to the board again, lingering just long enough to be noticed. "You know what undermines unity? Whispering. Deputies seeing you pull people through the side door at odd hours. You want loyalty, you build it where everyone can see it."

KC didn't blink. "We done?"

Parsons's jaw worked. He tried a different angle. "You're new to this county's way of doing things, Sheriff. Folks don't love special paths. Paperwork goes through channels, captains get looped, and we don't make pets."

KC took one step closer, just enough to shorten the room. "If you've got concerns about my personnel, you bring them to me without a sermon. If you've got needs on patrol, you state them without guessing at my motives. You don't run your feelings through the squad room and call it unity."

Parsons leaned back, the chair creaking under his stocky frame. For a long second, the only sound was the faint tick of the wall clock. Then he smiled without warmth. "You've got four days till dawn, Sheriff. Might be a good time to stop picking fights inside your own walls."

KC held his gaze. "Might be a good time to stop making them."

A nerve twitched along Parsons' jaw. He stood, set the sunglasses on his face though the office was all fluorescent glare, and tugged the hem of his shirt like he was squaring a uniform that had stopped fitting right. "You want my advice—"

"I don't," KC said.

Parsons opened the door. "Dodd wants updates. Don't make him come looking."

"Close it on your way out."

He did, a little harder than necessary. The latch snapped home. Outside, KC heard Carlie's pen pause, then resume its neat run across a notepad.

KC looked at the door until the shape of Parsons' absence stopped vibrating in the air. He turned back to the board. After a moment, he wrote a new slip: Parsons → pressure and pinned it beside ICE: 4 days. On another line, smaller, he added: Fast arrest push. Interest in Toni. Watch.

He stared at Baton? LE knowledge until it felt like staring wouldn't change the letters. He thought of Trisha Bell's measured voice: How clean it is. He thought of Ram: Back of skull. No struggle. He thought of the way Parsons had stood at the press conference, a step behind, a half-smile that wasn't one.

KC picked up the notebook and wrote: Inside angle? Trained swing. Who gets within trust distance? Then, under that: Don't guess. Build it.

He closed the book and set it on the desk.

"Sheriff?" Carlie's voice through the jamb, a light knock that waited this time.

"Come in."

She slid in, a slim folder in hand. "You asked me to log ICE's liaison memo last night—done. And I've got your two o'clock confirmed." Her eyes flicked toward the door Parsons had just used. "He didn't wait, did he?"

"No."

"Do you need anything from me on that?"

KC shook his head. "Just keep your notes clean and your eyes open."

She nodded once, understood more than he'd said, and set the slim folder on his desk. "ME's office called. Dr. Ram will push your paternity run into the next queue." A breath. "You want anything else?"

"I want you to log all incoming and outgoing calls from Parsons. Confidential file."

She gave the smallest smile, the kind that didn't linger. "Understood."

When she left, KC returned to the board and, beneath Trust exploited, added one last line: Don't let them write your story for you.

He set his hat on his head and felt the weight of it settle. The clock said 11:14. Four days until dawn, and men with letters on their backs who didn't care what families they split—or what truth they buried. Between now and then, he had rooms to walk into while he still could.

KC left for an early lunch, notebook in his pocket, the board's questions still burning behind his eyes.

Chapter 17

The Storm I Named

Day Two – 11:46 a.m.

Mojave County – Queen B's Office

The oak-paneled office of County Chairwoman Beatrice "Queen B" Garrison carried its own weight. Heavy drapes softened the desert glare, throwing the room into a half-light that made the polished mahogany desk gleam like still water. A faint trace of sandalwood hung in the air, subtle but deliberate. Two framed canvases—one of the Colorado River at flood, another of a miner's camp at dusk—lent gravitas without warmth. The leather chair behind the desk was tall, severe, a throne in all but name.

Akers stepped in, file in hand, trying to mask his eagerness with composure. His thumb worried the folder's edge before he caught himself. Queen B did not rise. She watched him cross the rug with that level gaze that had flattened more than one political career.

"You're early," she said, her voice crisp, almost amused. "A dog that learns after one kick."

Akers gave a tight smile. "I don't like wasting your time."

"Good," she said, folding her hands on the desk. "Then let's not waste it. I asked for dirt on Sheriff Talbird. What do you have?"

He shifted and pushed the file across the desk. "He left Border Patrol after a conflict with his superior. Officially 'a difference of philosophy,' but if pressed, it can be spun as insubordination. I've got threads on his family, too. Nothing scandalous yet. And there's chatter about him running his deputies like pets. Salazar especially."

Queen B inclined her head slightly. "Not enough. Parsons needs to keep the pressure on from inside. I want you encouraging that fracture—feed his doubts, sharpen his anger. The worse the rift looks, the better for us."

"Yes, ma'am."

She leaned forward, eyes narrowing. "And don't forget the other levers. The union is restless, tired of frozen pay scales. Talk of a recall simmers—just enough heat to test the waters. Elections can be called sooner than he thinks. You use all of that. Quietly. No fingerprints."

Akers straightened a little. "And if something blows back?"

"Then it lands on you," she said evenly. "Not me. And certainly not Julian." Her gaze sharpened into a knife. "You will not put his name in a note, a whisper, or a breath. If anyone even suspects—"

"I understand." His tone faltered, then steadied. "Julian's shielded. Always."

"See that he is."

She let silence stretch before continuing, voice smooth again. "I'll handle the press. One reporter in particular owes me. I'll give her the angle—Talbird weak on crime, blind on immigration, already wobbling under ICE's deadline. You bring me bones, I'll dress them for slaughter."

"Yes, ma'am," Akers said. Greed flared behind his eyes for half a beat.

Queen B allowed herself the faintest smile. "And if this works—if Talbird is recalled, if the right winds blow—you could find yourself wearing that star. Sheriff Akers."

The promise gleamed brighter in the air than the threat, but both lived there.

Akers swallowed, nodded once, and backed away.

When the door closed, Queen B rose at last and walked to the tall window. She placed one hand on the cool glass, looking down at the courthouse square where people moved like pieces in her game.

"The storm I named," she murmured, "will land on his door."

Chapter 18
The Text That Stopped Her

Day Two – 1:42 p.m.

**Mojave County – County Mental Health
(Dr. Jodi Kirk's Office)**

The county mental health building sat two blocks from the courthouse, a squat beige square that looked more like an old insurance office than a place for healing. KC parked in front where the paint on the lines had gone pale. He killed the engine and sat for a beat, hat in his lap, watching the steady churn of traffic on Main Street. People going about their errands, all of them unaware that Maria Alvarez's name was pinned to a corkboard inside his office like a plea.

Inside, the receptionist gave him a practiced smile that faltered when she saw the pistol on his hip. "Sheriff Talbird. Dr. Kirk is expecting you." She buzzed him through.

The hallway smelled faintly of lavender air freshener. At the end, an office door stood wide open.

"Sheriff," a woman's voice called.

Dr. Jodi Kirk rose from behind her desk as he entered. She was tall, with long sandy hair drawn into a loose ponytail. Brown eyes watched him steadily, professional but kind. Appeared to be in her early 30s, maybe divorced, the ring finger bare. A navy blouse and charcoal skirt gave her the look of someone who wanted her clothes to be neat but not the subject of conversation.

"Thank you for seeing me on short notice," KC said.

She gestured toward the chair opposite hers. "Please. Sit."

The office was orderly without being cold. Stacks of case files neatly squared on a credenza. The Alcoholics Anonymous Serenity Prayer hung on the wall above the bookshelf, a small lamp glowing warm in the corner. On the desk sat a single manila file.

"Maria Alvarez," Jodi said, touching it lightly. "Did you already know she was a client?"

"I didn't. I asked to see you because a man visited with Maria's father, Herb Sherman, saying he was with mental health outreach."

Jodi hesitated, thoughtful. "We have case managers but no outreach positions. I don't know who that would be."

"I didn't think so." KC had to ask to confirm the information Carlie uncovered—the man was with one of Queen B's "projects." He'd follow up on that later with Queen B. He took out his black notebook, scribbled—follow-up, Queen B, outreach, MH.

"I need to know more about her coming here since you brought it up." KC leaned forward, forearms on his knees. "But I also know confidentiality is the wall you live behind."

"Yes," she said simply. "Confidentiality is sacred. Except in the case of imminent harm. And Maria... she didn't threaten herself or anyone else. She was private. Guarded."

KC let that settle. "I'm not asking you to violate ethics. I'm asking if there's anything you can tell me that helps me find the truth about who killed her. Anything at all."

Jodi folded her hands. Her eyes flicked once toward the prayer on the wall, then back to him. "She came here three times. The last session, she was nervous. Distracted. She kept glancing at her phone. She said she wanted to talk about pressure—family, expectations, something weighing her down—but when the phone buzzed, she stopped cold. One text, and she shut down."

KC straightened. "Did she say who it was from?"

"No. She excused herself, said she had to go, and walked out. She didn't reschedule. That was the last time I saw her."

"Did anyone encourage her to come here?"

"Yes." Jodi hesitated, then said, "Father Frank. St. Mary's. He thought she needed someone outside the family to confide in. He called me himself, asked if I'd personally take her as a client."

KC wrote the name in his notebook. "Did she ever mention Luis Alvarez? Problems between them?"

"She said they were very close, called him 'steady,' 'kind.' Said he cared for her, and she cared for him. But..." Jodi's eyes narrowed in thought. "She never spoke of him as the source of her stress. She seemed to separate him from it."

KC hesitated, then asked carefully, "Did she ever confide anything about... being pregnant?"

Jodi's face softened. "If that was what weighed on her, she never said it aloud. But she carried something alone. Whatever it was, she wasn't ready to share it."

KC's pen paused. "Cameras," he said suddenly.

"Excuse me?"

"Your building. Security system?"

"Yes. Standard exterior coverage. Entry and lot. Why?"

"If Maria left here after that session, those cameras might show who she left with. Or if someone was waiting."

Jodi's brows drew together. "I hadn't thought of that. The county IT vendor has the recordings. They keep them thirty days unless overridden."

KC made a note—check camera footage—then capped his pen. "We'll check into that."

Jodi studied him, then said carefully, "Sheriff, why does it matter if she was pregnant?"

KC's eyes lifted. For a moment, he considered not answering. Instead, he said, "Because whoever the father is may hold the key to motive. And because secrets don't stay buried when bodies do."

Jodi's face went still. "I don't think it was Luis."

KC nodded. He stood, slipping the notebook into his shirt pocket. "Thank you, Doctor. If anyone besides me should come asking questions, refer them to me."

She nodded once, resolute. "I want justice for her, Sheriff. She deserved that much."

At the door, KC paused. "So, I may be back, Jodi," he said, surprising himself. Then he turned to leave her quiet office and the serenity prayer that fit the moment.

"I'll be here, available, KC." She smiled.

In the hall, he wrote one more note: Jodi = guarded ally. Maria → Father Frank. Last session: abrupt exit after text. Cameras—pull.

He underlined "cameras" twice. Then he pushed out into the sunlight, hat low, four days shrinking fast.

Chapter 19
Not in Trouble

Day Two – 2:56 p.m.

Mojave County – Sheriff's Office (KC's Office → Interview Rooms)

Carlie was already standing when KC pushed through his door. Toni sat in the far chair, still looking neat near day's end, a neutral expression that was almost too careful.

"I brought her in the side door," Carlie said, low. "Captain's in the squad bay. Didn't look up."

"Good," KC said.

Toni rose. "Dirt bike kid's here, Sheriff. I put him in Interview One. His father's in Two."

"Names?"

"Boy is Evan Morales, fifteen. Dad is Daniel. Evan's the witness who called it in from the wash."

"Okay." KC set his hat on the file cabinet, crossed to the corkboard, and slid a fresh slip under Maria's name—Witness: Evan (15)—then turned back. "Toni, you sit in on the interview. Carlie, log the start and stop times. Put a hold on the tape once we're done."

Carlie tapped her notepad. "Already have the case file ready. Your eyes only."

KC nodded, then looked at Toni. "You good?"

"I am," she said. She didn't sound like it, which he preferred; people who said it with too much confidence usually weren't.

They walked the short hall. The building's tired hum was broken by a copier starting up and then choking itself quiet. KC eased the door to Interview Two open. Daniel Morales stood when he saw the badge, a broad-shouldered man in an oil-stained polo, jaw tight. Before he could speak, KC held out a hand.

"Mr. Morales, I'm Sheriff Talbird. This is Deputy Salazar. She's working with me." She extended her hand. KC continued. "Your son isn't in trouble for calling something in. I'm going to ask to speak with him. I'd like you present. If you say no to that, I won't talk to him right now."

Daniel's eyes went from KC to Toni and back. The tight line of his mouth loosened a notch. "I'm not happy he skipped school," he said. "But I want to hear everything. I'll be in there."

KC nodded. "All right. Then come with us." He glanced at Toni. "Ready."

She nodded, without conviction. KC remembered his first interview—the same hollow feeling, but without anyone steady beside him. That one hadn't gone well.

Inside, the room was the same as always: a metal table, four chairs, a camera eye in the corner that ignored everyone equally. Evan sat hunched, hands tucked under his thighs, helmet on the floor by his shoe. He looked smaller than fifteen until he lifted his chin, and there was stubborn there.

KC took the chair opposite. Toni slid into the one at his right, legal pad ready. Daniel sat beside his son with both palms flat on the table like he intended to hold it still.

"Evan," KC said, voice even. "I'm KC Talbird. This is Deputy Salazar. Your dad's here because I asked him to be. You're not in trouble for the phone call. You did the right thing. Do you understand?"

Evan nodded. His throat worked. "Yes, sir."

"We're recording," KC went on. "I need you to use your words. Don't shake your head. Don't say 'you know.' Start at the beginning and don't worry about making it sound good. Just make it true."

Silence held for a beat. Evan glanced at his father, then back. "I was riding in the wash," he said. "I left home after my dad had gone to work—he leaves before sunrise. I should've been at school, but I cut through the half-moon pullout. There's a rut there. I was gonna hop it." He swallowed. "I saw something in the sand. It... it didn't look right."

"What did you see?"

"A girl. Lying weird. Like she fell asleep, but not." His voice shook once and steadied. "I didn't touch her. I just stopped and looked. Then a car—no, not a car—uh..."

"Take your time," KC said quietly.

"An SUV," Evan said. "It came up on the highway, not in the wash. It was on the shoulder, then the pullout. I didn't see it at first, then I did. It took off fast. Kicked up dust. Like a wake behind a boat? Like that. It was white. I think." He grimaced. "It was bright out. But white."

"Make," KC asked. "Model?"

Evan shook his head, caught himself, and said, "No. Windows were dark. The back window, too. I could hear the tires. Mud tires, maybe? Aggressive tread. Loud on pavement."

Toni's pen moved, fast and neat. KC let the boy breathe a second.

"How long from when you saw her to when the SUV took off?" KC asked.

"Seconds? I don't know. I didn't see it pull in. I saw it leave." Evan looked at his hands. "I called 911 right away. Then I got scared and moved down the wash a little, so if they came back, they wouldn't see me."

"Did you see anyone on foot?" Toni asked, gently.

"No," Evan said. "Just the dust and the sound and then... it was gone."

"Anything on the SUV? Stickers? A rack? A dent?" KC kept his tone flat, not fishing, just trawling.

Evan's brow pinched. "A shade thing on the back window? Like a strip at the top. And the plate... I couldn't read it. Dust."

"You did good," Daniel said quietly to his son, surprising himself with the words.

Evan's shoulders raised a fraction.

KC nodded toward the helmet on the floor. "You always wear that?"

"Yes, sir."

"Good habit," KC said. "You said you left home early. Did you skip school?" He paused a beat. "That's between you and your dad later. In this room, you're a witness who did the right thing. I need you to remember that."

Evan blinked hard, swallowed. "Okay."

KC glanced at Toni. "Anything else that stands out?"

"Sound," she said to Evan, coaxing. "You said the tires were loud. Anything else? Rattles? A clunk?"

Evan searched the ceiling as if the memory might be written there. "It... hummed?" He made a low sound in his throat, embarrassed. "Like the road made it hum. And the brakes squealed a little when it hit the pavement and braked to turn."

KC let another small beat pass. "All right. We're going to write what you said. And you'll need to sign it." He looked at Daniel. The man nodded. "If we need you again, we'll call your dad. If someone at school gives you trouble for being out there, you tell them the sheriff said you did the right thing. Understood?"

"Yes, sir."

Daniel cleared his throat. "We're done here?"

"We are." KC stood. To Daniel: "Thank you for being present. I'll walk you out."

In the hall, KC shook the man's hand. Daniel's grip was strong and grateful in that tight way men have when they're trying not to show relief. "He was scared," Daniel said.

"Most of us are, when we see what he saw," KC said. "He called anyway. That matters."

Daniel nodded once. "Thank you."

KC watched them go—a father's palm briefly on the back of a boy's neck—and felt an ache that had nothing to do with casework. Karole's small hand in his, the too-large backpack, the way kids older than him could turn a name into a weapon. He pushed the thought aside before it took root here.

Back in his office, Toni slid into the chair opposite him.

"Good work bringing them in," KC said. "That was fast."

"Thanks." She tapped her legal pad and moved on. "You think his SUV detail is solid?"

"It matches what Trisha pulled from the treads." KC's pen moved over his notebook: Evan—saw white SUV, tinted, aggressive tread, brake squeal, wake of dust. He underlined white and drew a line to the earlier note: AT tread (partial).

Toni waited, a patient stillness that felt older than her twenty-eight years.

"Now for your next piece," KC said. "County Mental Health has exterior cameras. Dr. Kirk says County IT keeps thirty days. I want you to coordinate with Carlie to draft the request, then go in person and pull everything from the last week before Maria's death and the forty-eight hours after. Focus on the day of her last session with Dr. Kirk—that's three visits total—so back up the range accordingly. You'll need IT to hash it out, but don't let it drift to the vendor without eyes on it."

Toni nodded, already listing steps. "Time window?"

"Dr. Kirk didn't give exact times. Have Carlie call to get those for you. Pull all entries and exits for those spans. Vehicles: white SUVs get priority. I want stills printed and a copy on a drive that never leaves this building."

"Chain-of-custody logs?"

"From your hand to mine," KC said. "And Toni—" He held her eyes. "You use the side door going and coming. Don't broadcast this to the squad room. You see Parsons in the hall, you're going to Records to check a file, nothing more."

A corner of her mouth angled. "Understood."

"Last thing," KC said. "The boy's detail on 'dark windows'—check the county's list of assigned unmarked vehicles. See which ones are white with tinted rear glass. Check the city, too. Then... check our own." He didn't say Parsons' name. He didn't have to.

"I'll start with Fleet," she said, already rising. "Carlie can help me pull the assignment logs."

"She will," KC said.

Toni hesitated at the door. "Sheriff—"

"KC is fine when it's just us."

"KC," she corrected. "You think the kid's going to be okay?"

"He will if the adults around him do their jobs." He kept his voice even. "That includes me."

She nodded and slipped out.

Carlie stepped in a breath later with a manila folder. "Interview times are logged. Tape marked for hold. Anything else you need? Do you want me to set Fleet for Toni now?"

"Help Toni get dates from Jodi. She'll explain," KC said. "And print me a clean list of every county-issued SUV with tint. Start with Sheriff's. Then I want city PD, code enforcement, county admin motor pool if you can pry it loose."

Carlie nodded, smiled with a woman's intuition. "Jodi, huh? I'm on it."

KC ignored the jab, but her smile lingered after she closed the door.

He crossed to the corkboard. He wrote White SUV — eyewitness confirmed and pinned it flush beside Partial AT tread—Trisha. The lines between slips began to look less like guesses and more like a net.

The phone trilled once—internal ring—and went quiet. Somewhere, a deputy laughed too loud and then cut himself off, remembering the building he was in. KC left his hat on the cabinet and stood a moment with his palms on the desk, grounding himself the way his Aunt Ruth had taught him years ago: find center, release what you don't need.

Four days until dawn. He looked at the board and thought of white paint, dark glass, and a brake squeal on hot pavement. Some men believed precision made them invisible.

It only made the edges cleaner for the light.

If the weapon was a baton, and the SUV a county vehicle... then the killer wasn't just close. He was inside.

Chapter 20

Trap on the Steps

Day Two – 5:21 p.m.

Mojave County – Sheriff's Office (Front Steps

)

KC grabbed his windbreaker with SHERIFF written on the and took the rear corridor out of habit. The squad bay was thinning—graveyard drifting in, dayshift hunting keys and excuses. As he cut past the open doorway to Operations, Parsons leaned against the jamb like a man who'd been waiting all afternoon to be casual.

"Have a good evening, Sheriff," he said, smile soft as a bruise.

KC didn't slow. He touched the brim of his hat and kept walking. If there was a reply in him, it was the kind that didn't help anything.

The rear door breathed him into the evening. Heat had turned to cooling, but the metal door still held the heat from the day. He'd taken one step down when a camera swung out from behind the corner of the building and found his face. A lapel mic clipped to a woman's blazer gleamed like a pin.

"Sheriff Talbird—live with Channel Seven," she said, voice already warmed to the lens. The red light on the camera stared back, unblinking. "Dianna Cates. Do you have a moment?"

KC stopped because moving would mean running and running would look like guilt. A man with a sound bag flanked the camera. In the parking lot, a deputy about to get in his car pretended to study the keys he held in his hands.

"Quickly," KC said.

Cates' smile didn't reach her eyes. "Sheriff, viewers want to know: Did you leave the United States Border Patrol under a cloud? Sources say 'insubordination'—a conflict with your superior. And now, with an undocumented suspect in custody, are you soft on illegal immigration? Are you shielding Luis Alvarez from ICE?"

KC felt the hit land where she meant it to—two strikes, different doors, same room. Words leapt to the back of his tongue—angry ones—and then he swallowed them. He breathed once, quiet, the sort of breath a man aims upward. Lord, help me stand right.

"I left the Border Patrol to run for this office," he said, voice steady. "The sheriff's seat was vacant. I chose to serve my county."

Cates tilted her head like a hawk sighting thermals. "But isn't it true you had a 'difference of philosophy' with a supervisor? That phrase is in your file, is it not?"

"A difference of philosophy," KC said, "is a statement grownups make when they disagree about how to do a hard job. It's not a scandal. It's an honest line."

She didn't blink. "And on immigration—viewers are concerned. You're keeping a foreign national in your jail. ICE, we're told, intends to pick him up at dawn in four days. Why not turn him over now? Are you protecting him?"

KC let the silence stretch. The trick in a trap is to stop tugging the snare. He could feel the building behind him like a witness; through the metal door, a figure moved onto the back steps, shadowed and stilled. Parsons. Hands in his pockets, that same soft bruise of a smile.

"My job," KC said at last, "isn't to carry out ICE's schedule or to parrot what politicians want said. My job is to find the truth about a murdered young woman. That truth doesn't belong to any agency. It belongs to her and to this county."

Cates stepped half a pace closer, the camera tracking. "So you admit you're defying federal authorities?"

"I admit nothing of the kind." KC kept his hands still at his sides. "I'm conducting a homicide investigation. When the facts are ready, they'll move. Not before."

"Isn't it still true, though," she pressed, voice sharpening, "that you're weak on crime and soft on undocumented suspects? That you're creating an unsafe environment to make a point?"

KC looked past the camera for a heartbeat—the parking lot, the ridge gone purple with evening, the deputy still at the car fumbling his keys. He could feel the heat in his face cooling, the first flush gone. He thought of Maria's father gripping a desk, of Rosa's small kitchen, of a boy on a dirt bike trying not to cry. He thought of lies that travel faster because they've been given gas and a map.

"Let me be clear," he paused. "I ran for sheriff because I saw things in this county's justice system that weren't right. Think what you want. But if you're observant, you can already see what I mean."

Cates hesitated—just a breath—as the words landed. The camera didn't. It kept eating light.

"Sheriff, one more—did you order your deputies to hide evidence? We've heard—"

"No," KC said. "We preserve evidence. We follow the law. And we don't try cases on a sidewalk at dinnertime." He inclined his head to the lens. "You have my office number. If you want accuracy, call it."

He stepped past the camera, not fast, not slow. The sound man pivoted to follow; Cates moved with him, microphone glinting, but KC had already reached the bottom step. He didn't look back at the doorway, but he felt the shape there like weather.

At the curb, he stopped beside the white Jeep and let his hand rest on the metal where the paint ran thin on the edge. A breath in, a breath out. He lifted his eyes once more to the flag, to the line of ridge, to the place where the sky kept its own counsel.

Behind him, the reporter's voice stayed bright for the closing toss. "...live at the Mojave County Sheriff's Office, where questions remain tonight about Sheriff Talbird's record and whether his stance could put citizens at risk—"

KC opened the door and climbed in. He set his hat on the passenger seat and sat with the engine off long enough for the broadcast cadence to fade into regular air. Through the windshield, the building's glass held the last of the day like a verdict; in the reflection, a doorway figure turned and disappeared into the cool.

He started the engine. As he pulled away from the curb, he could hear the reporter, dramatic as an actor. Somewhere above the county, the storm Queen had named was drawing its lines. He put his hands at ten and two and said, not loud but not in his head either, "Truth first."

Then he eased into traffic and let the evening take him, cameras still hunting for angles he wasn't going to give them.

Chapter 21
Who's Watching You

Day Two – 6:42 p.m.

Mojave County – Apartment above Della's Delights

The smell of fresh bread still clung to the apartment, drifting up from the bakery ovens below. Ruth had set the table before KC came in, and now the three of them—Ruth in her wheelchair at the head, KC at the side, Karole across—were working through plates of roast chicken and rolls still warm enough to melt butter.

Karole poked at his plate more than he ate, tall for eight and already conscious of it. His shoulders hunched the way kids' do when the world feels heavier than they can say.

"Reporter was mean," he muttered at last. "Is she a bully?"

KC set down his fork, studying him. "Why do you say that?"

"She tried to make you look bad," Karole said, not looking up. "That's what bullies do. They pick and poke, try to make people small."

Ruth's eyes, sharp and blue, flicked from nephew to great-nephew. "Out of the mouths of babes," she said.

KC leaned in, voice quiet but steady. "Sometimes people ask questions because they want answers. Sometimes they ask because they want a fight. Either way, we don't let them decide who we are."

Karole finally looked up, frowning. "So... she's still a bully."

KC almost smiled. "Maybe she is. But the way to beat a bully isn't to shout louder. It's to stand straighter. Show them they don't get to tell your story."

Ruth's fork tapped her plate. "And stand straighter with more than your back, Kermit. Do it with your choices. Don't forget who's watching you."

Karole grinned at the name. KC didn't. He only nodded once.

After dinner, Ruth wheeled herself toward her room. "Up early tomorrow," she said over her shoulder. "Bread won't bake itself."

Karole trailed her, chattering about a school project, before slipping off to his room with a backpack that seemed to weigh more than he did.

KC cleared the table, stacked the dishes, and stepped onto the small deck off the living room. The night air carried the faint hum of Main Street and the cooling scent of flour and yeast.

When the rooms had quieted, he crossed to the small study at the back of the apartment. The desk lamp threw a circle of light on old case files and unpaid bills. Against the wall leaned the whiteboard he'd started keeping here—his private board, the one that stayed out of sight of every deputy and politician.

He uncapped a marker and wrote in block letters:

- White SUV → eyewitness (Evan)
- Partial AT tread – confirmed
- Maria pregnant – paternity test pending
- Baton? LE knowledge
- Parsons – pressure, fast arrest
- Father Frank – see tomorrow

He underlined SUV twice, then stepped back. The board looked cleaner than the cork one in his office, but the lines he carried in his head were no less tangled.

KC stood with the marker in hand until the quiet filled the apartment like a fourth presence. Then he set it down, drew a breath, and told himself the same thing he'd told Karole: stand straighter.

Four days until dawn.

Chapter 22

Hooks of Grief

Day Three – 6:42 a.m.

Mojave County – St. Mary's Catholic Church & Rectory

Mass had just ended, and St. Mary's breathed that soft hush a church keeps after words have been spoken and swallowed. The last hymn still hung in the rafters like a thread of smoke. A few parishioners lingered—an older man on the aisle with his fingers moving across a rosary, a young mother rocking a baby under the blue robe of the Blessed Virgin, a field hand in a sun-faded jacket kneeling with his hat pressed to his ribs. Incense and candle wax clung to the air. The morning light, thin and gold, spilled through the stained-glass saints and made colored pools on the tiles.

KC took it in from the last pew. He'd parked at the far edge of the gravel lot and called Carlie from the driver's seat before stepping inside: Going to see Father Frank. I'll be back after seven. Now he stood with his hat in his hands, brim up, a respectful stranger in a house where people came to talk to God.

The priest came out from the sacristy with the alb and stole folded over his arm, vestments set aside for a black shirt and collar. Father Frank was mid-fifties, maybe, hair gray at the temples, the kind of face that knew how to listen without snatching the words away. He saw KC, nodded once, and motioned him toward the side aisle.

"Sheriff," he said quietly, offering his hand. His voice had that warm weight that settles a room. "Thank you for waiting."

"Father," KC returned, keeping his voice low out of respect for the folks still knelt in the half-light.

"Walk with me?"

They passed a bulletin board pinned with pancake breakfast flyers and a photo of last spring's confirmation class, all awkward smiles and new suits. The stone underfoot was grooved where decades of shoes had made their own path. A votive stand flickered by the statue of St. Joseph; someone had left a tiny toy truck at its base, a child's prayer made of plastic.

Through a short corridor and a fire door they stepped into the morning again and crossed to the rectory. The house was adobe like the church, its front steps worn to a soft curve. Inside, the entry smelled of fresh coffee—not for KC, but for the steady trickle of early parish visitors—and something warm from the kitchen. Father Frank led him down a hall lined with framed photos: First Communions, wedding parties under the cottonwoods, a food pantry crew with hairnets and laughter. He opened a door into a small office with a window cracked to let the cool in.

"Have a seat," he said.

KC took the wooden chair opposite the desk. The room was orderly without being stiff. Bookshelves lined one wall: theology with cracked spines, grief counseling manuals, two dog-eared volumes on immigration law marked with Post-its. A crucifix hung above the desk. On the sill, a pot of basil, green and stubborn. A ceramic dish held a scatter of rosary beads and paper clips.

"I'm sorry to intrude so early," KC said.

"It's never an intrusion, Sheriff," Father Frank said, settling into his chair. "We do our best work early."

KC nodded. He rested the hat carefully on his knee and set his black notebook on the desk without opening it. "I won't waste your time. You knew Maria."

Father Frank's eyes softened. "I did." He drew a breath that touched something deeper than lungs. "And I know grief has hooks. It's caught her father hard."

"Herb's a man with his fists closed around the world right now," KC said. "He's trying to squeeze it into a shape he understands."

The priest gave a small, sad smile. "Some men split wood until their anger breathes itself out. Some men split people." He shook his head once. "I've prayed he chooses the first."

"Me too," KC said.

A quiet held between them, not empty. Then KC leaned forward, elbows on knees. "Father, I need to ask plainly. You referred Maria to Dr. Kirk at County Mental Health?"

"I did," Father Frank said. "She needed a place where she could speak on a different ground. She was careful. Guarded, but you could feel the pressure on her. I thought Dr. Kirk would be kind and competent."

"She was," KC said. "Did Maria confide in you before that?"

Father Frank rested his folded hands on a file that wasn't a file at all—just a yellow legal pad with the corners dog-eared and a pen tucked through the wire. "She did," he said. "But what she told me, she told me in confession."

KC met his eyes. "You know I have to ask."

"I do," the priest said gently. "And you know I cannot answer."

KC let the words run past and come back. "You know she was pregnant."

"I do."

"You know who the father is."

The priest looked out the cracked window at the cottonwood leaves shivering in the morning light. When he looked back, there was nothing evasive in his gaze—only sorrow and steel. "Sheriff, the seal is absolute. If I broke it for this, I would never be able to offer absolution to another soul and have it mean a thing. A confessional is either a refuge or it's theater. I can't make it theater."

KC held that. He'd asked men to do hard things for him. He'd done hard things himself. There were some lines you didn't cross without tearing up the ground behind you. "I understand," he said. "And I respect it."

"Thank you," Father Frank said. He exhaled. "I can tell you what is not bound, because it's known. I urged her to seek help. I told her the truth is lighter carried with another. She... nodded, but she was very young in her worry."

KC didn't move, but the edges of him tightened. "Father, I'm not here to make you betray your office. I'm here to catch a killer. If the name you hold could give me motive—"

"I know," the priest said softly. "And I have thought about that more times than there are candles in that church." He set his hands apart, palms flat on the desk. "I can give you this: it will not be a dead end if you look closely at what power asks to be kept secret in this town."

KC let that sit where it landed. He didn't write it down. Some things belonged off paper.

"Luis and his family," he said. "You know them."

Father Frank nodded with conviction. "Good parishioners. Rosa has a back that hurts and a laugh that still surprises her. The boy Mateo stares down the world like it needs reminding he's there. Luis... he is steady. He has the look of a son who chose to carry weight no one asked him to. They have given to the food pantry from what little they have. They volunteer without taking selfies. They pay taxes. They are neighbors."

"ASAC out of Phoenix will take him at dawn in three days," KC said, the words measuring themselves. "They say it's coordination. It feels like a clock set by someone who doesn't live here."

The priest's jaw tightened. "We used to call churches sanctuaries and mean it. We still do the work, Sheriff—feed, clothe, accompany—but there are men with letters on their jackets who will walk past a crucifix without seeing it at all."

"You thinking to shelter them?" KC asked, not as a challenge. As a reality check.

"I'm thinking to shelter them as far as the law allows and then two steps past that," the priest said, and the heat in it wasn't performance. "But I won't make martyrs out of Rosa and Mateo because I wanted to stand taller in my own eyes. If they need a bed for a night, they have it. If they need a ride in the morning to keep from being dragged out of their kitchen, they have that too. And if they need a man to stand in their yard and ask federal agents to show a warrant, they have that."

KC nodded once. "I can't promise you protection from that storm."

"I don't ask you to," Father Frank said. "I ask you to find the truth before the storm washes everything away that can't be nailed down."

"What I'm trying to do," KC said.

Silence again. A clock somewhere in the rectory ticked, the sound faint and regular. KC thought of Rosa's small quarters on the ranch, beans on the back burner, a boy with a pencil clutched like a nail. He thought of Herb in the square office with the humming mini-fridge, hands braced on a desk like he could hold the world steady by force. He thought of Maria—her future like an open road that had been folded shut by one precise blow.

"Herb," KC said. "You seen him?"

"Yesterday afternoon," Father Frank said. "He came and sat in the back pew like a man who wanted to fight God for five rounds. He didn't light a candle. He didn't kneel. He just sat there until the building had absorbed what it could. Then he left. I will go to him if he doesn't come to me."

"Tell him I said to split wood," KC said. "Not people."

The priest's mouth tugged in something like a smile. "I will."

KC reached for his notebook and opened it at last. He wrote in his tight, spare hand: Referred to Dr. Kirk (confirm). Knew of pregnancy. Seal—absolute. Luis & family: steady, pantry volunteers. Sanctuary if needed → careful. He capped the pen. "One more plain ask," he said. "Not to break confession. To guide me. Is there anything— anything—you can point me toward without crossing your line?"

Father Frank looked at the crucifix above his desk for a long breath. When he spoke again, his words were careful as a man placing glass. "How is Chairwoman Garrison's nephew doing?" he asked. "Have you spoken with him since the news broke?"

The room didn't feel colder, exactly. It felt narrower. KC kept his face steady. "Not yet."

"He is... a young man I pray for," the priest said, the pastoral phrasing doing its job. "Some boys think they can outrun what they owe. Some learn that debt collects at odd hours." He spread his hands as if to say that's all.

KC stood. "Thank you, Father. For what you could say. For what you couldn't."

Father Frank rose too. "I will not speak the name you seek," he said, and it rang as a vow. "But I will stand with you in everything else that is mine to stand in. When you find the truth, I will help this town look at it without blinking."

KC picked up his hat. "And if the Alvarez family needs it, they can call you."

"They already have my number," the priest said. "And if anyone asks, I'll say what I always say: we look after our own out here, even when they were born somewhere else."

At the door, he paused. "Sheriff," he said, softer. "I laid my hand on Maria's coffin yesterday in the mortuary chapel. Before I prayed, I told her we would do right by her. I do not break promises to the dead."

KC felt something in his chest give and settle. "Neither do I," he said.

They walked back through the hallway of wedding parties and charity drives. In the church again, two votives sputtered and steadied. The young mother had gone. The man with the rosary had put his hat back on and stepped into the day. KC dipped his head toward the altar, not Catholic but not careless either. Outside, the bell tower cut the bright sky.

On the rectory steps, Father Frank shook his hand. "Go with God," he said.

"Truth first," KC answered, and it wasn't a correction.

He crossed the gravel lot to the white Jeep. The door creaked the way it always did. He set the hat on the passenger seat and opened his notebook across his thigh, the paper catching the light. He wrote:

- Father Frank (St. Mary's): confirms referral to Dr. Kirk; knew of pregnancy; seal holds.
- Luis family: good parishioners; pantry volunteers; steady.
- Sanctuary: possible short-term; risk acknowledged.
- Hint: "How's Garrison's nephew?" → Julian Hahn.
- Note: Three days to dawn.

He underlined the last two lines once, then again. In his head the lines on his office corkboard realigned—the slip with WHITE SUV, the slip with PREGNANCY, the one pinned low that said TRUST EXPLOITED.

KC started the engine and let the radio stay off. Main Street was waking: hardware store lights popping on, a flatbed rattling past with hay bales strapped down and dust streaming in its wake. He pulled into traffic and turned toward the office, toward a board waiting for a new pin, toward a name he hadn't said out loud yet but could hear in the quiet that followed Mass.

Chapter 23
Bureaucratic DNA

Day Three – 8:15 a.m.

Mojave County – Sheriff's Office (KC's Office)

The morning light cut a clean rectangle across the far wall, dust drifting in it like slow rain. Somewhere beyond the door, a copier started, choked, then found its rhythm. Phones trilled and were snatched up; a stapler popped; a rolling chair barked across tile. The old building breathed out recycled air and the faint tang of floor wax from last night's mop. KC sat with his notebook open and a pen balanced across the wire, the calm before a day that had no intention of staying calm.

Carlie knocked twice and stepped in with two folders tucked to her chest. Her blouse sleeves were buttoned neat at the wrist, hair gathered into a no-nonsense bun, the kind that survived long days and worse news. She closed the door behind her with the quiet click of someone who understood that doors had ears.

"Morning, Sheriff."

"Morning," he said. "What do we have?"

She laid the top folder on his desk and kept her hand there a second longer than necessary, like she was making sure the contents didn't slide into the wrong day. "Parsons."

KC raised his eyes.

"He has a white SUV assigned to him through Fleet," she said, voice steady. "Two years running. Tinted rear glass. Aggressive tread tires. Service reports match AT pattern changes about six months ago." She slid a sheet out and turned it so it faced him—columns of dates and maintenance notes, the bureaucratic DNA of a vehicle's life. "Plates end in 5K3."

KC didn't look at the numbers long. They weren't the part that mattered. He saw Evan Morales' face instead—fifteen and trying not to shake—white SUV... windows dark... the tires were loud. He pictured partial treads in a crescent of sand, Trisha's voice on the phone: substrate is bad… wouldn't stake a warrant. He put a fingertip on the service line item that read REAR GLASS TINT—REPLACED/RESEALED and left it there.

"Anything else on it?" he asked.

"Fuel logs look clean. Parking logs are… light." She didn't have to explain that 'light' meant either lazy or careful. "It's assigned to him, but it rotates to pool when he claims off-desk training. Last rotation was two weeks ago for—" she glanced at a sticky flag "—an 'operations liaison' session."

"Who signed that?" KC asked.

She turned another page. "He did."

KC took a breath and let it out slowly. The air tasted like the inside of a filing cabinet that had swallowed too many lives. "All right."

She set the second folder beside the first. The tab read FINANCE COMMITTEE—Agenda. "Chairwoman Garrison wants you at ten-thirty. The clerk called twice. Dodd will be there. The agenda says 'review of criminal justice budgets.' I translated it for myself as 'we're sharpening knives.'"

"Accurate translation," KC said.

"I printed last year's line items for context and pulled the capital requests we inherited from the previous administration," Carlie went on. "If they bring up underspend on patrol overtime, remind them we were backfilling vacancies. If they bring up attrition, I've highlighted where we lost three deputies to the county across the river because their union negotiated a better package. I color-coded—green is us, blue is Dodd."

KC almost smiled. "You do good work."

"Thank you, Sheriff."

Beyond the door, a deputy yelled too loudly and then cut it off, remembering where he was. The copier coughed again and settled. A delivery hand truck rattled across the lobby tile. The banal sounds of a day trying to pretend it wasn't going to turn on anyone.

Carlie's eyes flicked to the corkboard on the wall. "Do you want me to add the Parsons assignment, or would you rather…"

"I'll do it," KC said. He stood, slid his notebook into his shirt pocket, and crossed to the board.

The board had stopped being tidy sometime yesterday: lines of twine sagging at odd angles, pins creeping outward like they were trying to leave the county. He took a clean slip, wrote in his blocky hand Parsons—white SUV (assigned) and pinned it flush under WHITE SUV—EYEWITNESS CONFIRMED and the older note AT TREAD (PARTIAL) – TRISHA. He didn't draw new string; he didn't need to. The lines were in his head.

For a long beat he just stood there, palms on his hips, feeling the tug that comes when a line you didn't want to believe in starts to hold.

Carlie spoke softly behind him. "You look like a man who found a rattler in his tool shed."

"I'm deciding if it's asleep," he said.

"Yeah," she said. The word was simple, not soothing. "And if it's alone."

He glanced back at her. "What are you seeing in the squad bay?"

"More eyes than mouths. That's better than the reverse, but it still means something's being passed hand to hand." She smoothed the edge of the finance agenda. "Yesterday's clip is bouncing around. The talking heads are saying you're soft on crime and immigration. There's a cut of you not saying anything for a good three seconds before you answered Cates, which they're using to say you were stunned."

"I was counting to three," he said.

"I know," she said. "They don't."

He gave the board one last look and came back to the desk. He sat, folded his hands for a second, then unfolded them. "What's Queen likely to swing at ten-thirty?"

"Overtime and fleet," Carlie said. "She'll say you're over-resourced and under-effective. Then she'll pivot to 'coordination with federal partners' and ask why you haven't turned Luis Alvarez over. When you say 'ongoing investigation,' she'll call that 'obstructionist posture.' Dodd will clear his throat and talk about community safety. He'll look neutral and lean her way."

"Talking points?" KC asked.

"I drafted facts, not slogans," she said, sliding a single page out—bullet lines, tight as fence wire. "You want them?"

"Yes," he said, and took the page. He read the first three lines: Body moved before sheriff arrived. No defensive wounds; single blow from behind. Evidence points to controlled act, not heat-of-the-moment rage. He tapped the paper once and set it down. "They aren't listening for facts."

"No," she said. "But they're afraid of plain sentences."

"I'll give them those."

Carlie hesitated at the edge of his desk, weighing something. "Sheriff," she said at last, "Parsons is he . . . is he involved."

"I don't know, yet," KC said.

"You know, he's also... tangled up with people who like to set fires and walk away before the smoke climbs." She looked toward the door like she could see through it. "If you move too soon, he'll play martyr. If you wait too long, he'll light the curtains."

"I know," KC said. He kept his voice even. "Today at two, I'll bring him in. Door shut. We'll talk. He can pick which line he wants to stand on."

She nodded. "Do you want me to put that on your calendar?"

"Yes. Two o'clock. And he doesn't set the time; we do."

"Logged." She flipped open a small steno pad and wrote it in neat, block letters. Below it, she drew a tiny box and filled it halfway, a habit KC had noticed when she marked priorities but never commented on.

He glanced at the clock. 8:22 a.m. The hour stretched ahead like a room with no chairs.

"Anything else?" Carlie asked.

KC considered. The morning at St. Mary's stayed with him—the colored light on tile, the quiet promise the priest had made not to the living but to the dead. He didn't say any of that. He said, "Yes. Keep Parsons' file current. Everything we see, everything we don't see. Calls in and out—not content, just times. Who he meets with officially. Who he meets with when he says he's at 'training.' Keep it confidenced."

"Understood." She slid the Parsons folder halfway back toward herself, then paused. "Sheriff... if this breaks the wrong way, it won't be just the board coming for you. It'll be some of our own."

"I know," he said again. "We'll give them fewer shadows to swing at."

The phone on her desk outside rang again. Voices crossed in the hall, one hushed, one too sharp. Carlie gathered the folders and stood square, ready to meet the day and whatever it threw. She made it to the door and stopped with her hand on the knob.

"Sheriff?"

He looked up.

"You're holding more than one job right now," she said. "Sheriff. Investigator. Wall." A quick breath. "Just—remember you've got people who will stand with you when the wind turns."

He let the words land. "Yes," he said. "And I see them."

She dipped her head, something like relief in the motion, and slipped out. The latch settled. The sounds of the office came back in: a printer spitting a long report, someone cursing softly at a jam, the flap of the interoffice mailbox as a hand pushed a thick envelope through.

KC stayed seated, palms flat on the desk, and looked at the two-page finance agenda. He could hear Queen B's voice in his head without trying—the polished amusement, the practiced outrage. He set the agenda aside and opened his notebook, turned to a clean page, and wrote:

- Fleet: White SUV → Parsons (assigned, 2 yrs, tint/AT tires).

- Press: Clip weaponized. Silence framed as stumble. (Let them have it—stand steady.)

- Committee @10:30: Cuts dressed as review. Overtime/fleet/"coordination" lines. Dodd = neutral, leaning her way.

- 2:00 p.m.: Parsons—closed door, choose a line.

He capped the pen and leaned back, eyes on the ceiling square where the paint had bubbled from a leak no one had fixed. The building had outlasted sheriffs before him. It would outlast him too.

He was a tenant in a structure that kept weather the way trees keep rings.

He stood and crossed to the corkboard again. He didn't move anything this time. He just read it like a map: MARIA at the top; PREGNANCY pinned beneath; LUIS—ALIBI (VERIFY) to the left; DR. KIRK—3 VISITS; LAST: TEXT/EXIT to the right; WHITE SUV centered like a nail; PARSONS—WHITE SUV (ASSIGNED) straight under it now. Off in the lower corner where only he looked, a slip that said Baton? LE knowledge with a question mark black enough to be a period.

He heard his own voice in the reporter's microphone from last night: I ran for sheriff because I saw things in this county's justice system that weren't right. He remembered the part he didn't say into a camera—And some of those things wear badges.

The door cracked an inch and Carlie leaned in just her head. "One more thing."

"Yes?"

"PIO emailed. Says Queen wants your 'talking points' by nine-fifteen 'to ensure a constructive dialogue.'"

KC stared at her a beat and then, very gently, said, "Tell them the sheriff's talking point is we tell the truth at ten-thirty. That's the whole point."

Her mouth twitched. "I'll soften it."

"Yes," he said, and in that small yes was a division of labor that worked better than any memo.

She vanished again. The clock ticked to 8:29. He picked up the finance sheet Carlie had color-coded—green bars for his office, blue bars for Dodd's. He glanced at the numbers—vehicles aging out, radios failing, vests past warranty—and knew how the conversation would go: You're asking for more money while doing less with what you have. There were sentences that only sounded like questions.

He closed the folder and reached for his hat, then stopped. He wasn't going anywhere yet. Instead he went to the small sink in the corner, ran the water until it didn't groan, cupped his hands, and threw a splash across his face. The cold took the last of the church and replaced it with the county building he'd chosen. He dried his hands on the paper towel, folded it once, dropped it in the bin, and stared at himself in the narrow mirror—thirty-five, gray eyes steady, hair that wouldn't pick a side and stay there. He looked like a man who had already gotten through worse mornings. He couldn't prove it with paper, but he knew it.

When he turned back to the desk, he snagged a fresh slip and pinned one more quiet note at the bottom of the board where only he'd read it: Pressure = weapon. Hold the line. The words weren't for evidence. They were a nail hammered into himself.

He checked his watch. 8:34. He had time to skim incident reports, to read the night shift logs, to pretend he wasn't waiting for a ten-thirty appointment with a woman who looked at the county like a chessboard. He sat, opened the inbox, and made himself read every line that mattered: a drunk and disorderly with no injuries; a welfare check that ended with a door opened and a cat found; a complaint about loud music that turned into a neighbor war. The work that was a sheriff's work even when the cameras were pointed somewhere else.

When he finished, he closed the email and laid his palms on the desk again. The building hummed around him, indifferent and faithful. He thought of Father Frank's office—the cracked window, the basil plant, the priest's promise laid like a hand on a coffin: We will do right by her. He thought of the words he'd written at the bottom of yesterday's page: Three days to dawn.

KC reached for his notebook and wrote it again at the top of today's: Three days to dawn. The letters looked like what they were—an hourglass turned by someone else's hand. He didn't intend to spend those grains arguing definitions with people who liked microphones.

He stood, squared the Finance folder on the desk, and straightened his tie. At ten-thirty, he'd walk into a room where they already knew what they wanted to say. He'd give them sentences that could not be bent without snapping. Between now and then, he'd keep his own house from burning down.

He picked up the phone and hit the extension for the front desk. "Carlie."

"Yes, Sheriff?"

"If Toni calls, patch her through. Otherwise, hold my calls until nine. I'm reading."

"Yes. Logged."

"Thank you."

He hung up, sat, and opened the notebook to the page with bullet lines running like fence posts, and began to work through them one at a time. Outside his window, a pair of pigeons fought for the warm strip of sun on the sill. In the hallway, someone wheeled a case of copy paper past at a wobble. In here, his world narrowed to names and lines and the next exact thing.

Three days to dawn. And right now, 8:41. Plenty of time for a man to choose how he would stand when the day began to lean.

Chapter 24

Typed in Tears

Day Three – 9:08 a.m.

Mojave County – Sheriff's Office (KC's Office)

The hum of the building carried through the thin walls—phones trilling, a printer grinding, Carlie's low voice at the desk outside. KC sat behind his own, notebook open, when the intercom clicked.

"Sheriff? Toni and Trisha on the line. They'd like speaker."

"Patch them through."

The button glowed red, and Toni's voice came first, brisk and measured. "Sheriff, we've got preliminary footage from County Mental Health."

Trisha's voice followed, cooler, precise. "We pulled the time frame from Maria's last session. Cameras don't give us everything, but they give us something."

KC leaned forward, elbows on the desk. "Go ahead."

Toni said, "She's seen leaving the front doors. She stops just outside—like she's hesitating. Then she pulls her phone, types fast. Less than ten seconds. Wipes tears from her eyes. Then walks off."

Trisha added, "A white hood—vehicle—edges into the frame. Only a sliver, but shape and height suggest SUV. It doesn't come fully into view. Doesn't block the building. It's parked off-angle. Then it's gone."

KC picked up his pen. On the page he wrote: Maria—last session → text. Tears. White SUV—hood visible. He underlined text twice, the ink pressing deeper into the paper.

"Any shot at clarifying what she typed?" KC asked.

Silence hummed for a second before Trisha answered. "Not from the video. Resolution's too low. But if the device is recovered, forensics might get fragments. Depends on encryption, depends on deletion. Without the phone—nothing."

"Maria's phone is still unaccounted for," KC said. His eyes flicked to the corkboard, the slip that read simply: Cell? Missing. "Could either of you see the recipient? Even just the name?"

Toni's voice was regretful. "Not yet. It's small on screen. We'll try digital enhancement, but it's iffy. I've asked IT to blow up the frames, but no promises."

KC tapped his pen once against the paper. "Do it anyway. Anything that clarifies that text matters. Work every angle. Who she was crying over may be who killed her."

"Yes, Sheriff," Toni said.

KC's tone softened. "Good work, both of you. Toni—check other cameras on that street. Traffic cams, county buildings nearby, even private security systems. If that SUV passed through, we'll find it."

"I'll start on it now," she said.

"Sheriff," Trisha said, "we did match the time stamps. The SUV's presence lines up with her walking out. The overlap is tight. Seconds."

"That's not coincidence," KC said flatly. "It's a shadow waiting at the door."

No one spoke. The silence stretched, the kind that hung between people who understood the weight of what had just been said.

KC let it hold, then said, "All right. Keep me posted. And thank you."

The line clicked dead.

KC sat a moment, pen still in hand. Then he rose, crossed to the corkboard, and wrote in block letters on a fresh slip: SUV?—seen at Mental Health. He pinned it beneath the earlier notes on the white SUV, the thread tightening another line in the net.

He picked up the black marker and went to the bottom corner of the board where his own questions lived. In heavy strokes, he added: TEXT MESSAGE—unresolved. He underlined it twice, harder this time, until the letters thickened into a warning.

The clock on the wall ticked to 9:12. Three days until dawn.

KC stood with his hands on his hips, staring at the board, and thought of a girl typing words no one had read, crying tears no one had wiped away, while a white SUV idled in the periphery like a ghost that refused to step into the light.

Chapter 25
Knives Behind the Dais

Day Three – 10:00 a.m.

Mojave County – County Board Finance Committee Hearing

The hearing room had the careful chill of places where public money was discussed: fluorescent lights, a screen that never quite calibrated right, the faint chemical bite of carpet cleaner. People filled the back rows—clerks with notepads, union reps with folded arms, a couple of reporters pretending their phones weren't already recording. At the long table below the dais sat two tented placards: DISTRICT ATTORNEY and SHERIFF'S OFFICE. KC took his seat at the latter, laid his black notebook beside the mic, and let the room settle around him like an old jacket that didn't quite fit.

Queen B presided dead center, gavel at hand, posture immaculate. The chair behind her was a touch taller than the others—no accident. To her right, Supervisor Borden chewed thoughtfully on a capped pen. To her left, Supervisor Mahoney scrolled his phone under the lip of the desk, the blue glow making his face look underwater.

"The Finance Committee will come to order," Queen said. Her voice carried the polished calm of someone who had practiced sounding reasonable. "We'll begin with the Sheriff's Office."

A staffer dimmed the lights. The projector stuttered, then threw up a slide of stacked bars—red for actual, gray for budget. The red crept over the line.

"Overtime," Queen said, almost gently. "Sheriff Talbird, your office exceeded budgeted overtime by thirty-two percent. Help us understand why taxpayers should be asked to fund this overage."

KC leaned to the mic. "Yes. The overage came from vacancies. Deputies covered shifts to prevent gaps in patrol. We didn't leave zones dark. We didn't miss calls. That cost overtime."

Queen smiled without warmth. "So you overspent to maintain basic service."

"I spent to keep people safe."

Pens scratched in the back. A reporter whispered, "Get that." Dodd, at the neighboring placard, adjusted his stack of papers until the corners lined up like soldiers. He looked exactly like a man who never had a hair out of place—white hair, dark eyes, suit pressed enough to cut.

"Fleet," Queen went on, clicking to another slide. "You've requested three replacements—two SUVs and one patrol sedan. You have vehicles assigned that, according to logs, sit idle."

KC kept his hands flat. "Those logs reflect court days and training rotations. Our vehicles are aging out; radios are failing; one ballistic vest is past warranty. The request isn't luxury—it's readiness."

"Mm." Queen turned slightly. "District Attorney Dodd, your office has also faced vacancies. Have you remained within budget?"

Dodd turned on the neutral. "Madam Chair, yes. We've managed within allocated funds while meeting our charging obligations."

"That's helpful context," Queen said, a quick glance sliding back to KC.

KC didn't look at Dodd. He was too busy counting to three inside his own head the way he'd taught Karole when frustration came hot: one, two, three—talk plain. He lifted his notebook a fraction, then set it down. Truth first.

"And now," Queen said, voice sharpening like a scalpel, "coordination with our federal partners. Immigration and Customs Enforcement has notified us of their intent to assume custody of Mr. Luis Alvarez at dawn in—" she consulted a paper she didn't need "—three days. Yet Mr. Alvarez remains in your jail. Why has he not been transferred?"

KC let the silence sit half a beat—no longer. "Because this is a homicide investigation. My office does not relinquish a suspect or material witness until the facts are complete. That's standard, not defiance."

Board Member Borden looked up from his pen cap. "Sheriff, we hear from citizens who are frightened. They want to know why a foreign national accused of killing a local girl isn't already in federal hands."

KC turned to face him, gray eyes steady. "Citizens should know we don't trade truth for speed. Mr. Alvarez is in secure custody. And being undocumented doesn't make you a murderer."

A murmur rolled, soft as a wave. Queen tapped the gavel once, not to quiet so much as to punctuate. "No one said undocumented equates to murderer," she replied, the word shaped like a gift she meant to take back. "But public safety requires decisiveness, Sheriff. Some would call your stance obstructionist."

"Some would," KC said. "It's not."

Dodd's mouth twitched—either a wince or a smile. He cleared his throat into the mic with the practiced cadence of a man planting a hedge. "Resources are finite," he said. "We all share responsibility for outcomes."

KC could have said: We don't share responsibility for shortcuts. He didn't. He thought instead of Rosa's clean kitchen, of Mateo tapping a table where his brother had snored, of Herb's fist tightening and then loosening when the word pregnant landed. He kept his voice flat. "Agreed. And outcomes are better when you don't cut corners."

Queen stacked her papers, alignment perfect. "We'll note your position. The committee reserves the right to revisit appropriations pending performance metrics and interagency cooperation." Her smile returned, polished to a shine. "That concludes this segment. Thank you, Sheriff."

The gavel cracked. Lights brightened. Phones rose. KC gathered his folder, spine the only straight thing he could control. He didn't look up at the dais. He didn't look back at the handful of cameras tucked by the wall. He stood and felt the room like heat on his back.

At the door, an elderly women in a windbreaker murmured, "Hang in, Sheriff." A man let his gaze slide away like he didn't know him. In the hall, KC exhaled, long and slow, and told himself not to look for a scoreboard in a room where the score was always written before you sat down.

Three days to dawn. And between now and then: fewer chairs, more knives.

He tucked the folder under his arm and walked toward the exit, already hearing the echo of Queen's voice in his head not as a question but as a strategy. You could fight a strategy. You just had to remember which hill you'd chosen.

Chapter 26
The Strong Hand

Day Three – 11:40 a.m.

Mojave County – Queen B's Office

The first thing Dodd always noticed was the quiet. Queen's office absorbed courthouse noise the way fine carpet drinks spills—no trace left. Heavy drapes cut the sun to silk. The air smelled faintly of sandalwood and polish. On the wall, the Colorado River roared in a painting that somehow made it seem tame. Power curated itself here.

She didn't stand when he entered. She didn't need to. She simply set down her pen and looked at him like a teacher waiting to see whether a student had done the reading.

"You didn't back me," she said, the words spare.

Dodd placed his file on the edge of her desk, parallel to the grain. "I spoke where it made sense."

"You hedged," she replied. "While I was making the case for fiscal discipline, you offered platitudes about finite resources. They cut my budget." She paused a beat, then added, "And yours."

Dodd smiled without showing teeth. "So we're both bleeding. Good to know you noticed the part past your reflection."

Her chin lifted a hair. "This isn't about me. It's about a sheriff who spends beyond his means and refuses to coordinate with federal partners."

"Coordinate?" Dodd let the word turn over in his mouth like a coin. "Or bend the knee in public, because it polls well?"

She didn't blink. "The public wants safety."

"They also want results that hold up in court," Dodd said. "I don't get convictions from rushed cases and television soundbites. You don't either, despite how far your voice travels."

A faint crack spidered in her composure—there and gone. "You could have pushed him. One hard question about Luis Alvarez and he would have flinched."

"He didn't flinch today," Dodd said, surprised to hear himself admit it. "He did what he always does—offered plain sentences and refused to perform. I can work with that. I can't work with a circus."

Silence pooled, the kind that made ordinary people talk to fill it. Queen let it stretch until it said something for her. When she finally spoke, her voice was smooth again. "You're protecting him."

"I'm protecting my office," Dodd said. "And my cases. We both know the math: you pick a fight that looks good on camera, I eat it in court when the optics don't line up with evidence." He glanced at the river on the wall. "You don't dam a river by yelling at it."

Her eyes didn't leave his. "What you're calling optics is leadership. The county wants a strong hand."

"Then give them one," he said quietly. "Just make sure it's steady, not theatrical."

He stood. The chair legs whispered on the carpet. He didn't gather his file right away; he let the moment breathe because he wanted to see which way she turned. She turned inward, calculating. He knew the look. He wore a version of it in mirrors.

"You attract more bees with honey than vinegar," he added, the line landing like a tack. "Today you poured vinegar. On both of us."

There it was—the crack widening a fraction. Not visible to a camera lens. Obvious to him. "You may not report to me, but your budget is under my control." She said. "And close the door on the way out."

The threat was clear and understood. In the corridor, sound returned: a clerk's laugh, a phone ringing somewhere, the scuff of shoes. Dodd exhaled and rolled his shoulders once as if to set them back onto a spine that remembered being separate from hers.

As he strode past Queen B's aide, he heard. "Get me Dianna Cates," she told her aide. Her voice was composed, already turned toward the next angle. "Tell her I have a story about our failing criminal justice system."

He had come up in this building knowing when to lean and when to stand. Today had been a stand. He didn't love KC Talbird, but he loved even less the feeling of being handed a script that ended with his office looking like an instrument, not a branch. If Queen wanted an instrument, she could find one. He was a survivor, not a servant.

By the time Dodd reached the stairwell, he had decided two things. First: he would not be caught on camera carrying her water again this week. Second: if a door opened that let him put a leash on her ambitions, he would take it. Honey or vinegar, he would choose what served him.

Whatever line Dodd had refused to carry, she would find another voice to say it.

Chapter 27

Cameras in the Blind Spot

Day Three – 12:06 p.m.

Mojave County – Sheriff's Office Rear Lot

KC eased the Jeep into his usual slot behind the building, nose toward the chain-link that rattled with every small wind. The meeting taste still sat in his mouth like old pennies—questions dressed as concern, budgets swung like bats. He killed the engine and reached for the door.

They came from the blind side where the air conditioner units sat: a camera first, then a woman with a mic, then two more with phones held high. The sound man moved like he'd trained for ambushes, cable already slung. The red tally light blinked on.

"Sheriff, Sheriff—quick comment—"

"Are you obstructing ICE—"

"Are you putting citizens at risk by sheltering an undocumented suspect—"

"Is it true your overtime is out of control—"

KC set one boot on the gravel, then the other. The breeze carried hot dust and the faint metallic scent of the rear door where paint had been rubbed to skin by years of hands. He didn't raise his voice. He didn't run. Running was guilt on camera. He kept his shoulders square and let the swarm press close enough for the mics to catch breath.

"Sheriff—why not turn Alvarez over now?" a woman pressed, eyebrow arched in performance.

KC thought of last night's red light and Dianna Cates' questions sharpened like awls. He thought of counting to three. He thought of not giving away seconds you couldn't get back. He opened his mouth—

His phone buzzed in his pocket. He pulled it free without looking at the screen, thumb sliding green by feel. "Yes."

Carlie. Calm as a level, all business under a soft edge. "Sheriff, your lunch appointment is now. Dr. Kirk is expecting you."

He glanced at the wall of lenses. "Right now."

"Right now." A beat. "And Della's has a bag at the counter with your name on it. You're providing lunch. Seems only polite."

KC let one corner of his mouth move. "Thank you."

"Drive safe," she said. He could hear paper moving under her voice, the sound of a day being kept on the rails by a person who liked clocks.

He slid the phone away and looked at the nearest camera, not unkindly. "Ladies and gentlemen, I have an appointment. My office will release a statement at the appropriate time. If you want accuracy, call it."

"Sheriff, are you soft on immigration—"

"Sheriff, is it true you left Border Patrol under—"

He stepped through them. Not fast. Not slow. Mics bumped his shoulder; a cord scuffed his boot. From the rear door's shadow, a uniformed deputy paused as if to watch a wreck that hadn't happened yet and then turned away, embarrassed by his own curiosity.

KC climbed into the Jeep and shut the door. Voices turned to muffled shapes. The red light stayed bright, insect-hard. He started the engine and let the idle thrum steady him. He could still taste the hearing. He could still feel Queen's clean cuts, how they bled optics instead of blood.

Della's was six blocks and a left. He took the alley to avoid the front steps where the flag would have meant stopping. The town moved around him like it always did at lunch—trucks nosing toward burrito stands, a delivery van crooked across two spaces, a woman in scrubs walking fast with her hair up and a paper bag clutched like the day depended on it.

At the curb in front of Della's, he left the engine running and jogged in. The bell over the door chirped, the pastry case fogged at the edges from heat meeting cold. Aunt Ruth's staff worked the line with the efficiency of a place that got through breakfast by muscle memory and kindness. A brown bag with DELLA'S DELIGHTS stamped crooked sat ready.

The cashier—Marta's niece, if KC remembered right—pushed it across with a smile. "Cherry Coke's in there," she said. "On the house. Aunt Ruth said so."

"Thank you," KC said. He meant the food and the lifeline.

Back in the Jeep, he set the bag on the passenger seat where his hat usually rode and hesitated a second before pulling away. The pleasant thought arrived uninvited: Jodi's office, quiet light, a table cleared of case files for forty minutes. Not romance. Not yet. Just a place where the chair across from him wouldn't be shaped like a throne and the questions wouldn't be designed to make him stumble.

As he turned onto Main, he caught his reflection in a storefront window—tall, gray eyes steady, hair that wouldn't pick a side. He looked like a man who had walked into a storm and decided not to drown in it. He signaled and merged, the bag rustling like a small promise.

He told himself he'd keep the conversation with Jodi on safe ground. He told himself he wouldn't lean on her. He told himself a lot of things men told themselves when the day had started its lean toward worse. He didn't have to decide any of them yet. He just had to drive.

At the red light next to the courthouse, a news van slid up in the adjacent lane. The cameraman glanced over, recognized him, and lifted a hand halfway before thinking better of it. KC lifted two fingers from the wheel in a gesture that meant nothing and enough.

The light turned. He moved forward. He didn't check the rearview to see if the van followed. He had a place to be that didn't require a microphone, and for twenty minutes, that was a kind of mercy.

Three days to dawn. A lunch before the next swing. He took the right toward County Mental Health and let the Jeep find the line between duty and the brief, simple grace of being seen without being put on display.

Chapter 28
Hope in a Paper Bag

Day Three – 12:32 p.m.

**Mojave County – County Mental Health
(Dr. Jodi Kirk's Office)**

The county mental health building didn't look like a refuge from the street, just a beige square with sun-faded paint and a drip line where the sprinklers overshot. But inside, the front desk clerk lifted a hand in quiet greeting, and the hum of the place was soft—printers whispering, doors closing without bang, a low conversation turning down at the end like a lullaby.

KC carried a brown paper bag stamped DELLA'S DELIGHTS, the bottom warm. The Cherry Coke inside rattled in its nest of napkins. He signed the visitor log—name, time, purpose—because he believed in paper, then took the short hall that ended in a door already open.

"Sheriff," Jodi said, rising.

Her office hadn't changed since the last time: orderly without being cold; the Serenity Prayer framed on one wall; a small lamp warming the corner; a neat stack of files squared on the credenza. Today a sprig of basil in a mason jar sat on the sill, leaves catching light. KC noticed a new photograph on the bookshelf—Jodi in trail shoes, standing on a ridge with a line of blue mountains folding into distance. She looked younger there, hair in a wind-tangled ponytail, smile unguarded.

"Thank you for fitting me in," he said.

"You're bringing lunch," she said, which was a yes and a you're welcome at the same time. "Come in."

He set the bag on the small round table, the kind meant for calm conversations and patient paperwork. Jodi fetched paper plates and real forks from a drawer—not a break room kind of drawer; a drawer in a space someone chose on purpose. He pulled out wrapped sandwiches, a tub of potato salad with Aunt Ruth's handwriting on the lid, and the Cherry Coke sweating already.

"Cherry Coke," Jodi said, amused as she reached for two cups. "You have a brand."

"I do," he said. "Aunt Ruth sent it. She sends hope in whatever form she can."

"That sounds like her," Jodi replied, and there was something in the way she said it that told him she'd already gathered pieces about his life he hadn't explicitly given. She poured water for herself, slid the Coke toward him, then took the chair opposite.

For a minute, they didn't talk. They unwrapped lunch the way people do who needed the ordinary. The sandwiches were simple—roasted turkey, provolone, lettuce with a bite to it, tomato that still remembered a vine. KC took a bite and felt his jaw unclench two notches he hadn't known were tight.

"How are you?" Jodi asked at last, not filing the question under intake or triage, just setting it on the table between them.

KC wiped his hands on a napkin. "Three days to dawn," he said. "And it feels like a lot of people want to make sure the sun rises on a story they like more than the truth."

Her mouth softened. "Rumors fly fast in this county. I heard Queen's hearing was rough?"

"She brought knives dressed like questions."

"And you brought sentences dressed like fence posts," Jodi said. "I watched the clip on the county channel during a break. You did fine."

"It didn't play that way in the room." He took a swallow of Cherry Coke—cold, sweet, the bite of carbonation exactly where he needed a reminder he was breathing. "Doesn't matter. You don't measure right by applause."

"No," she said. "You don't."

He glanced at the Serenity Prayer. "You keep that there on purpose."

"Every day," she said. "For my clients. For me." She nudged the tub of potato salad toward him. "For the sheriff who shows up with lunch and a world on his shoulder."

He took the tub, not because he wanted potato salad as much as because the act of accepting what was offered has its own kind of medicine. "This isn't therapy," he said. "I won't put you in a position."

"It isn't," she agreed. "And thank you for seeing the boundary. Two people can share a meal without me charting it." Her smile tilted. "If you start listing symptoms, I'll charge your insurance. Until then, I'm Jodi, and this is lunch."

He almost smiled back. "Understood."

They ate another minute in companionable quiet. Outside the window, a UPS truck eased into a space, the driver hopping down with a practiced step. Somewhere in the building a printer woke and, deciding it had been roused for nothing, went back to sleep.

"Have you seen Father Frank yet?"

"This morning."

"Want to share what he had to offer?" Jodi asked gently.

KC paused, time to trust a little more. "He confirmed he'd sent Maria here," KC said. "Confirmed she confided in him. He can't—and won't—share the name she gave him in confession."

"Good for him," she said softly. "And hard for you."

"I told him I understood," KC said, meaning it. "He gave me a different kind of hint on the way out."

She waited.

"Asked about Chairwoman Garrison's nephew," KC said. "If I'd spoken with him since the murder."

"Julian Hahn," Jodi said, not asking.

KC's eyes flicked to hers, impressed again by how she held the line—knew enough, didn't say more than she should. "I haven't spoken to him yet," he said. "I will."

"He's... around," she said. "Fundraisers. Ribbon cuttings. Outreach committees." She set her fork down. "Sheriff, I don't know what you can say and can't. But I can tell you this much: when Maria sat in that chair—" a small nod toward the space KC had used the other day "—she wasn't afraid of a boy who loved her. She was afraid of a weight she couldn't set down, and the fear wasn't small. She tried to carry it politely." Jodi's throat worked. "I hate that sentence."

"So do I," he said.

They let the silence stand a moment. KC broke it by reaching for the Cherry Coke again, the cold bottle giving his hand something to anchor. "The cameras," he said. "Your exterior system. We're pulling the last month."

She nodded. "Trisha Bell called me to make sure I didn't mind her moving fast. I told her to move faster."

"Good," KC said. "They think the lens caught the corner of a white hood near your entry."

Jodi's hands flattened on the table. "That makes my stomach hurt."

"It makes mine steady," he said. "I'd rather fight a thing I can see."

"Fair," she said. "Do you always do that?"

"What's that?"

"Translate fear into something with edges," she said. "So you can pick it up."

He thought of the corkboard—string starting to look like a net, not a mess. He thought of the small note he'd pinned where only he read it: Pressure = weapon. Hold the line. "I try," he said. "Aunt Ruth says when you're standing in a river you plant your feet where the rocks don't roll. Then you turn sideways."

Jodi laughed softly. "Your aunt would make a good therapist."

"She makes a good everything," he said. "She told me not to bring you anything from the pastry case because sugar isn't lunch."

"I like her even more now."

KC took another bite of sandwich, set it down carefully. "They're coming at dawn in three days. ICE. They want Luis and his family."

Jodi's gaze tightened. "Rosa and Mateo."

"Those names don't mean much on a clipboard," KC said. "They mean a kitchen that smells like beans and clean wood. They mean a boy with a pencil gripped like a nail."

Jodi looked down, and he had the sense she was praying without moving her lips. "Father Frank mentioned sanctuary?"

"He did," KC said. "I told him I can't tell a priest what to do with his church. But I can tell him not to trust cameras when men with letters on their jackets want a picture. He knows."

"Good," she said. "If it comes to that and you want me there, I will be."

"You don't owe me that," he said.

"I know," she said. "I'd still be there."

He let the words sit. They didn't feel like an obligation; they felt like a plank laid across a gap he hadn't admitted he'd been measuring. "Thank you," he said, and for a second the sheriff's cadence dropped out of his voice and left just the man.

"Can I say one thing you may not like?" Jodi asked.

"Probably," he said.

"You can't hold the whole county by yourself," she said. "You're already being the wall and the investigator and the face that gets hit. Find one more person you trust and hand them a piece. Not the heart of it. A piece."

He knew the answer before she finished. "Toni."

"She seems steady," Jodi said. "And you have Carlie. Trisha is there too. Let them hold parts of the weight. Not because you're weak. Because you intend to last."

He looked at his hands—broad, nicked, a scar along one knuckle from a fist fight with an undocumented that hadn't behaved. Ironic, he thought. Soft on them. "Parsons doesn't like that I use Toni."

"I've dealt with Captain Parsons with some of our homeless clients. He doesn't like not being the sun and the power that goes with it," Jodi said. "Parsons can file a complaint in triplicate and staple it to his own desk."

KC's laugh surprised him. It wasn't loud. It arrived like a small bird landing. "I have him at two o'clock today. We will come to terms. Or not."

"Good," she said.

He finished the Cherry Coke and set the bottle down, a ring of water left behind. "I don't usually talk this much," he said.

"You haven't," Jodi said. "You've said exactly what you needed to say and left the rest where it belongs."

He thought of Karole last night, working on his math, concentrating. A boy who had older children throwing rocks made of names. "You ever tell a kid not to say 'yeah'?" he asked, smiling at the corner.

"All the time," she said. "Out loud or in my head."

"I correct mine," he said. "Feels silly until it doesn't."

"It won't feel silly when he's twenty," Jodi said. "It'll be one of the rails he holds when the wind hits."

They cleaned the table together, an unspoken choreography—wrappers folded, forks rinsed at the tiny sink, the Coke bottle dropped into a recycling bin that clinked like a bell. Jodi dried her hands on a towel and turned back to him with something on her face that wasn't professional and wasn't not. Just human.

"You're a good man," she said, plain.

He didn't say thank you. He said, "I want to be."

"That counts," she replied. "And you're doing the work."

He checked the time: almost 1:30 p.m. The half hour between now and two felt less like a corridor and more like a field he could cross with his head up. He picked up the paper bag—lighter now, but not empty—and reached for his hat.

"I'll walk you out," she said.

They stood at the door a second longer than necessary. He wasn't a man who touched without reason; she wasn't a woman who offered touch as punctuation. She held out her hand anyway. He took it. It was a steady hand, warm, the kind you trust to hold a bandage or a secret.

"If Trisha gets anything off the footage," she said, "I'll be ready to help however I can. Phone, statement, whatever you need."

"I know you will," he said. "Jodi—thank you for lunch."

"Thank you for bringing it," she said. "And for the Coke brand loyalty. It's charming."

He tipped his hat, a small gesture that felt older than both of them and exactly what the moment could carry. In the hall, the air smelled faintly of lavender again. Behind him, her door closed with a soft click that wasn't goodbye so much as see you soon.

KC checked the time once more as he stepped into the daylight. The sun had slid past noon and found a better angle. The Jeep sat where he'd left it, the passenger seat smelling of warm bread and something he hadn't named yet because naming it would make it heavy.

He paused on the sidewalk and wrote a single line in his small black notebook, letters clean:

Jodi = steady ground.

Then he underlined it once—no flourish—and put the book away. Three days to dawn. A meeting with Parsons at two. A board that liked knives. Somewhere in a lab, a paternity test running toward a result that would move someone's anger from one target to another.

He slid behind the wheel and shut the door. The interior held a degree or two more heat than outside—the kind you could live with. He put the Jeep in gear and pulled away from the curb, the tires humming the way Evan had described—road noise, not menace.

For the first two blocks, he didn't think about Queen. He didn't think about ICE. He thought about a basil sprig in a jar and a photo of blue mountains and a woman who saw a man and not just a badge.

He let the thought sit beside him like a resting bird and didn't tell it to fly.

At the corner, he turned toward the office. He didn't look for cameras. If they were there, they could catch a sheriff with a lunch bag folded small on the seat and a face set to work.

Chapter 29
You Enjoy Trespassing?

Day Three – 2:00 p.m.

Mojave County – Sheriff's Office (KC's Office)

KC's boots struck the tile with a deliberate rhythm as he came down the hallway from the rear entrance. The building had that late-day smell—old coffee in the break room, Lysol from the morning still clinging at the edges, paper warmed by the copier. He wanted five quiet minutes to gather his thoughts after Jodi's office, but Carlie's expression stopped him cold.

She was standing at her desk, arms crossed, voice low. "Sheriff," she said, tilting her head toward his door. "He's in there."

KC paused, jaw tightening. "Parsons."

"Yes," she said. "I told him to wait, but he brushed right past me. I couldn't stop him."

KC's hand closed once into a fist, then opened again. "Did you see what he was doing?"

Carlie nodded reluctantly. "Taking pictures of your board."

KC held her gaze a moment, then gave the smallest nod. "All right. Hold Toni and Trisha in the outer office. No interruptions until I call for them."

"Got it."

KC pushed open his door.

Parsons stood at the corkboard, phone in his hand, shoulders square like a man caught but unwilling to flinch. The flash of the screen glinted across the twine and paper slips pinned like veins of a map. He didn't pocket the phone. He didn't even move.

"You enjoy trespassing in another man's office?" KC asked evenly, closing the door behind him.

Parsons turned, smile tight. "I figured if you were going to build your case with scraps and string, somebody ought to make sure it doesn't get lost. Transparency, Sheriff. Ever heard of it?"

KC walked past his desk and stopped halfway to the board. "Hand me the phone."

Parsons' grip tightened. "It's my property. My personal device."

"Not when it's pointed at investigative evidence." KC's voice stayed low, deliberate. "That makes it subject to seizure. Hand it over."

Parsons smirked. "Am I a suspect now?"

KC stepped closer, gray eyes locked on him. "Let's think it through. You've got a white SUV assigned to you. Witness says a white SUV fled the scene. Trisha's treads match your fleet tires. You pushed for Luis' arrest before evidence was even bagged. And now you're stealing pictures of my board." He let the silence ride, then added, "What would you call that?"

Parsons' face mottled red. "You don't know a damn thing. I've given this department twenty years. You think I'd risk that?"

"I think you've risked more already," KC said. "Now hand me the phone."

Parsons hesitated, jaw working.

"That's two strikes," KC said, voice steel. "The press stunt you pulled—that was one. This stunt here, two. And right now, you're at two and a half. Don't make it three."

Parsons shoved the phone into KC's hand hard enough the sheriff's knuckles stung. "Fine. Next time I'll have my rep sitting right here. You want to threaten my career, you'd better be ready to prove it."

KC powered down the phone without a word, then set it flat on his desk. "Next time, it won't be a conversation. It'll be a formal disciplinary action."

Parsons' breathing came hard. He looked like a man standing on a line and daring it to move. Then he spun, shoved the chair back with his knee so hard it hit the wall, and stormed out, the slam of the door rattling the frame.

KC stood still for a moment, palms resting on the edge of his desk, feeling the room settle again. Then he picked up the phone, pressed the intercom.

"Carlie."

"Yes, Sheriff?"

"Send in Toni and Trisha. And after I'm finished with them, I want you back in here with Parsons' personnel file."

"Okay."

A moment later, Toni and Trisha entered. They looked at each other, then back at KC, like they'd heard the storm but didn't want to name it.

KC motioned to the chairs. "Sit."

He slid the confiscated phone across to Trisha. "Catalog it. Full data extraction. Chain of custody form, logged and dated. I want everything on it, and I want it back in my hands by tomorrow."

"Yes, Sheriff," Trisha said, already reaching for the evidence bag she carried tucked in her satchel. She slid the phone inside, sealed it with a sharp press, and made her notes with neat block letters.

KC turned to Toni. "You and Trisha pulled the footage?"

Toni set a single printed still on the desk. The grainy enlargement showed Maria's phone angled just enough to betray the contact name: Julian Hahn. Clear as day.

KC studied it. His jaw flexed once, twice. "That gives me two ties to him now. Witness statements aren't the only thing pointing at Hahn." He tapped the photo, then looked at both women. "You comfortable taking this further?"

"Anything," Toni said, voice steady.

"Anything," Trisha echoed.

"Good." KC picked up a notepad, tore two slips. He handed the first to Toni. "Find the outreach worker at County Mental Health. Maria saw her—probably more than once. I want notes, schedules, anything that fills the hours we don't see."

"Will do."

He handed the second slip to Trisha. "You're already on the phone logs. Keep digging. Map Parsons' calls for the last two months—time, duration, destination. Don't worry just about content, patterns too. See who's in his orbit."

Trisha nodded, tucking the slip into her folder. "Understood."

"Report back when you've got traction," KC said. He tapped the board with two fingers. "This isn't string anymore—it's beginning to look like a net. I need you both to keep pulling."

They stood. Toni slid the photo back into its folder. Trisha cradled the sealed phone like it was a live grenade.

When the door closed behind them, KC let out a long breath. The office smelled faintly of Lysol and tension. He walked to the corkboard, unpinned the old slip that said WHITE SUV – Parsons (assigned) and replaced it with a new one: SUV – Hahn? Parsons? Then he drew a single line connecting Hahn's name to Maria's phone photo, the red twine catching on the pin like it didn't want to move.

"Two ties," he murmured. "And a shadow that doesn't stand still."

He stepped back, looked at the board. It was messy, but it was speaking. And it was time to decide who in this county still deserved the badge they wore.

KC pressed the intercom. "Carlie."

She entered with a manila folder in hand. The label was sharp in her block handwriting: Parsons, Evan J. She closed the door behind her, waiting for instruction.

KC stayed standing by the corkboard. "Add this to his personnel file: incident one—press ambush, insubordination in uniform. Incident two—entered my office without authorization, took unauthorized photos of investigative evidence. Both noted. Both acknowledged by me in conversation today."

Carlie flipped the file open, pen already poised. "Documented. Do you want me to log it as formal reprimand?"

"Not yet," KC said. "These are notes for the record. If he makes me go formal, I want the paper ready."

"Yes, Sheriff." She wrote quickly, steady script that looked like it belonged in a courtroom exhibit.

KC glanced back at the board. "Also note: he resisted turning over his personal phone. Only complied under direct order. That's two strikes. I told him the next would be formal complaint."

Carlie's eyes flicked up. "Understood."

She closed the file with a soft snap. "I'll keep it in the secure drawer."

"Do that," KC said.

She hesitated at the door, then added quietly, "Sheriff... you've already given him more grace than most would."

KC didn't answer right away. He looked at the twine crossing the board, Hahn's name pinned like a nail, Parsons' slip now underlined twice. Finally, he said, "Grace doesn't mean blindness. It means he's got one more chance to choose who he is."

Carlie gave a small nod and slipped out. The latch clicked.

KC turned back to the board, the office suddenly very still. Two ties to Hahn. Two strikes for Parsons. Three days to dawn.

Chapter 30

What Choice Do I Have?

Day Three – 3:23 p.m.

Mojave County – Queen B's Office

Parsons sat stiff in the waiting chair outside Queen's office, one leg bouncing so hard the secretary kept glancing up from her computer. He didn't care. His blood was still boiling from the scene in KC's office, and waiting only made it worse.

Finally, the intercom buzzed. "You can go in," the secretary said.

Parsons shoved the door open without knocking.

Queen didn't look startled. She rarely did. She sat behind her wide desk, legal pad in front of her, pen poised like she'd been expecting him. The heavy drapes muted the afternoon sun, and the faint smell of sandalwood hung in the air. She looked up at him with practiced calm.

"You look upset, Eddie," she said.

"Upset?" Parsons barked. "He practically accused me of being part of this murder. Said I'm tied to that white SUV, that I pushed Alvarez too fast, then called me out for taking pictures of his corkboard. He took my phone, Queen — my personal phone — and told me I've got two strikes. Two strikes! After twenty years in that department."

Queen folded her hands neatly on the blotter. "So Sheriff Talbird thinks he can cut you down to size."

Parsons leaned forward, voice rising. "He's trying to bury me. Acting like I'm dirty, while he runs around with Toni and Trisha whispering in his ear. He's locking me out of the investigation. Making me look bad to my deputies. On top of that I'm a suspect."

"And you're going to let him do that to you?" Queen asked smoothly.

Parsons bristled. "What choice do I have? He's the sheriff."

"You still have influence," Queen said, her tone measured but sharp. "Deputies trust you. The rank and file look at you as one of their own. They don't like being shut out, and they don't like watching their captain treated like a criminal. Remind them of that."

Parsons narrowed his eyes. "You want me to stir things up?"

"I want you to let things be known," Queen said. "That morale is cracking. That their sheriff doesn't trust his own men. That he hides behind outsiders while treating his veterans like suspects. If the deputies rally, the board will see the problem isn't resources. It's leadership."

Parsons' jaw worked. "Yeah, and the press is already painting him soft on immigration. Making him look like some bleeding heart who'd rather defend an illegal than protect this county."

Queen's lips curved in the faintest smile. "Leave the press to me. You handle your people. I'll handle the narrative."

Parsons straightened, fists tight at his sides. "Fine. If Talbird wants a fight, he's got one."

"Good," Queen said softly. "Make sure the deputies know exactly what kind of sheriff they're serving under. The louder the noise, the quicker the board will act."

Parsons turned on his heel, muttering, and slammed the door behind him.

Queen didn't flinch. She simply rose, smoothed the skirt of her suit, and walked to the window. Through a narrow slit in the drapes, she watched Parsons storm across the square, anger in every step. Perfect.

Only then did she press the intercom. "Get me Dianna Cates," she told her aide. "Let her know I have tonight's story. Unrest inside the Sheriff's Office. Deputies unhappy. Leadership in question."

She returned to her chair, sandalwood steady in the air, already arranging the next move.

Chapter 31
Three Darts, Three Prayers

Day Three – 5:58 p.m.

Mojave County – KC's House

The smell of roasted chicken and rosemary filled the kitchen, warm and grounding after a day that had run hot and jagged. KC hung his hat on the peg by the back door and let the tension of the office fall a notch. Ruth stood at the stove with her sleeves rolled, moving with the efficiency of someone who had been feeding family all her life. Karole sat at the table, chin propped on his hands, watching the food like it was a prize fight he already knew the winner of.

"Sit down, Sheriff," Ruth said, teasing just enough to soften the edge in her voice.

"Yes, ma'am," KC said, taking his chair.

The meal was hearty and familiar: chicken carved into thick slices, mashed potatoes piled high with butter melting down the sides, green beans with bacon, cornbread still warm from the oven. They ate with the quiet satisfaction of people who knew better than to waste food by rushing through it. Conversation came in pieces—Karole's math class, Ruth's story about a neighbor's runaway goat, KC's understated "long day."

When the plates were cleared, Ruth set the dartboard on the far wall of the den and handed out the darts like she was dealing cards.

Karole insisted on throwing first. His aim was improving—one dart in the outer ring, one low, one skittering off the floor. He groaned but grinned.

"Better," KC said, clapping his son's shoulder. "You'll get there."

"Yeah," Karole said automatically.

KC lifted a brow.

"Yes," Karole corrected, sheepish but smiling.

"That's better," KC said, voice gentle. "Respect shows in words."

Ruth's turn came next. Three darts in quick succession—thud, thud, thud—each one clean in the red rings. She rolled her wheelchair back, dusted her hands. "You boys should just pay me rent for the board. Seems I own it."

Karole doubled over laughing, and KC joined in, the sound catching him by surprise, like a muscle that hadn't been used in too long.

By the time the game ended Ruth was the clear victor. She accepted her win with only a small smile and a twinkle in her eye before declaring the den closed for the night. "I've proven my superiority," she said. "Now I'm going to bed."

Karole still had finished his homework before dinner. Now, darts done, it was time for bed. They strolled down the hallway together, chatting, chuckling. When they arrived at Karole's bedroom, KC suggested they kneel down and pray together. They knelt side by side at the bed, the boy's voice steady as they prayed together. Thanks for the food, thanks for family, strength for tomorrow, protection for those who needed it most. KC listened with pride to the growing cadence of his son's faith.

When Karole climbed under the covers, KC smoothed the blanket once, touched his shoulder, and whispered, "Good night, son."

"Good night, Dad."

KC lingered a moment, watching his boy's eyes close, then eased the door nearly shut. Ruth's room was already dark, the faint sound of a radio drifting through the crack in her door.

Back in his home office, the quiet wrapped around him. The whiteboard stood ready, marker waiting on the sill. He uncapped it and began updating the lines that were now starting to look less like guesses and more like a map:

- Julian Hahn – tied by Maria's text, tied by Father Frank's hint.

- Parsons – two strikes, trust eroded.

- Queen – fueling unrest, press engaged.

- Luis Alvarez – secure in custody. ICE countdown: two days to dawn.

KC drew arrows, underlined Hahn's name, circled "two strikes." Then he stepped back, arms crossed, studying the board as though it could answer him if he looked long enough.

He capped the marker, set it down, and whispered into the stillness, "Truth first. Steady hands."

The lamp cast a soft glow across the board as he switched it off, leaving only faint outlines in the dark. Upstairs, his family slept. Tomorrow would bring new battles. Tonight, at least, he had kept the walls standing.

Chapter 32
Public Outcry

Day Four – 7:59 a.m.

Mojave County – Sheriff's Office (Rear Entrance)

The noise hit even before KC cut the engine—chants echoing down the alley, the low roar of a crowd wrapped around the front of the building. The press had found their stage early. From the back lot, he could see camera lights flicker against the glass above the squad bay.

He parked in his usual slot near the chain-link fence. Voices carried faintly over the roof—sharp, angry, rehearsed. KC stepped out, straightened his jacket, and took the rear door into the hallway.

Inside, the hum was tighter than usual. Deputies clustered near the breakroom, half in uniform, half halfway through their first coffee. The talk cut off when KC entered, then picked back up in a lower key.

"Been like this since six," one deputy muttered to another.

"Queen stirred 'em up again."

"Cates went live ten minutes ago—Channel Seven."

KC stopped near the doorway. "Morning," he said, voice steady. "How's the shift?"

A younger deputy straightened. "Quiet enough inside, loud out front."

Another added, "Folks are saying you're catching heat, Sheriff."

"I am," KC said. "That comes as a surprise to anyone?"

A couple of nervous laughs. One deputy spoke more honestly. "Feels like we're walking on eggshells, sir."

KC nodded once. "That's fine. Just don't walk off them. Our job's the same today as it was yesterday—keep this county safe, tell the truth, and leave the noise to the ones who like it."

The men nodded. It wasn't applause, but something steadier— trust. KC gave a short nod in return and moved on down the hall.

Carlie was at her desk, sorting morning memos into neat stacks.

Her hair was pinned back, her expression already set to the day. "Morning, Sheriff," she said. "The deputies say it's been like this since six. You can hear the crowd clear down the hall."

"I heard it from the parking lot," KC said. "Any trouble?"

"Nothing serious. One guy tried to climb the rail but left when he saw cameras. They're loud, that's all."

"Queen's feeding them," KC said.

Carlie nodded. "And Parsons isn't helping. He's been walking the line in the squad bay, telling deputies morale's at rock bottom, that you've lost trust in your own people."

KC stopped mid-step. "He said that to you?"

"Not directly. But he's making sure I hear it."

KC's voice dropped. "Let him talk. Truth doesn't shout—it waits."

He continued into his office. The corkboard met him like a bare witness—stripped of evidence, pins and faint impressions where string had been. His desk was stacked with reports and last night's notes condensed onto a single sheet.

Carlie followed to the doorway. "The Board called again," she said. "Wants to know your next step with Alvarez."

"Same as yesterday," KC said. "Due process."

"They're saying you're defying cooperation orders."

He looked up. "I'm protecting evidence. That's the difference between a sheriff and a politician."

Carlie nodded. "I'll relay that—carefully."

"Do," he said. "And tell the deputies to hold steady. No confrontations with protesters. No comments to the media. Let the noise burn itself out."

When she left, KC stood at the small window that looked toward the back of the square. Even from here, he could see the tops of the protest signs bobbing above the parked cars, the red light of a news camera blinking like a signal flare.

He took his black notebook from the desk and wrote three clean lines:

Noise ≠ truth.

Queen fuels the fire.

Two days to dawn.

He underlined the last one twice.

The phone buzzed. Carlie's voice came through. "Sheriff, one of the news crews set up across the street. They're live right now."

"Expected," he said.

"They want a statement."

He watched the signs sway beyond the window, the heat already rising from the asphalt. "They'll get one when there's truth to tell."

He hung up and pinned a fresh note to the corkboard:

Hold steady. Truth first.

Then he turned the blinds just enough for the crowd to see him standing there—visible, unflinching, unmoved.

The chants went on, but he didn't blink.

This version preserves all your prior narrative and now includes a natural, believable exchange showing KC's rapport with his deputies—humanizing, steadying, and subtly reinforcing his leadership.

Chapter 33
Strings and Messengers

Day Four – 8:57 a.m.

Mojave County – Sheriff's Office (KC's Office)

The morning air inside the sheriff's office felt heavy but calm —
that kind of quiet just before the storm rolls back in. KC had been at
his desk since seven, reviewing the prior day's notes and sketching
arrows in his black notebook, when Carlie tapped lightly on the
doorframe.

"Sheriff," she said, stepping in, "Trisha's here. Would you like to
see her?"

"Yes."

He capped his pen and set it beside a half-empty bottle of water.
Trisha entered with her satchel and that quick, no-nonsense walk that
said she had something worth hearing. She looked tired but sharp, her
eyes bright with the kind of focus that came from hours at a monitor.

KC motioned toward the chair across from him. "You look like a
cat that caught a mouse."

"More like a rat," Trisha said, setting her bag on the floor. "And it's
trail."

KC leaned back slightly. "Go ahead."

She pulled a printout from a file folder and laid it flat on his desk
— clean columns of numbers, message snippets, and contact tags.

"It's Parsons' phone," she said. "I've gone through the primary
texts, some calls, and metadata logs. What I'm seeing doesn't make him
the ringleader. He's more like a messenger — a flunky feeding the right
people the wrong kind of information. A rat."

KC didn't move. "Meaning?"

"Meaning he's passing along internal chatter to Akers and taking
direction from Queen," she said. "There's a message from Akers the
morning Luis was arrested. It reads, 'Move on Luis Alvarez. He's the
killer. I'll handle Dodd. And I'll keep Queen B posted. Keep Kermit at

bay. Don't let me down.' Parsons replies, 'Understood.' No hesitation. And later. 'Feed me investigative reports. Thanks for the corkboard pic.' And there's more if you want it."

KC's jaw tightened. "Not necessary. What you've reported ties the arrest to politics, not procedure."

"Exactly. There's another chain between Parsons and Queen's office — her assistant's number — same pattern. Short messages, lots of voice calls that never last more than a minute. But the texts exist?" She flipped to another sheet. "Queen tells him, 'Keep stirring the pot. Alvarez is guilty.' Then later, 'Talbird can't ride out this storm forever. Keep the pressure on.'"

KC stared at the line. "She's still pulling strings."

"Every one of them," Trisha said. "And Parsons is just happy to be noticed."

"Anything about Hahn?" KC asked.

"Some cross-references. A few missed calls from Hahn's number, and one short text that reads, 'Don't let it come back to me.' Hard to know what that means without context, but given timing, it's after the day Maria's body was found."

KC exhaled slowly. "So Parsons feeds Akers. Akers feeds Queen, manipulates Dodd. And Hahn's afraid of something that might trace back to him."

"That's how it looks."

KC tapped his notebook once. "It fits what I saw yesterday. Parsons isn't working to find truth — he's working for the wrong team to subvert."

Trisha nodded. "Sheriff, I'm also still digging on Maria's phone. No new tower hits, no power-up, no SIM activity. I can try another proximity trace through the carriers, but I'm just one person. I could use another set of eyes or a stronger data pipe."

KC leaned forward. "I'll see what I can do."

"I appreciate that," Trisha said. "Oh — one last thing. The arrest timing? There's a text between Akers and Parsons, a few minutes before Luis was picked up. Akers says, 'Now or it slips away.' Parsons replies, 'On it.' That was sent twelve minutes before the arrest log timestamp."

"That'll do," KC said. "Send yourself home before you fall over. I'll get you help."

She gave a tired smile. "Thanks, Sheriff."

When she left, KC sat still for a long moment. He turned the bottle of water in his hand, condensation trailing along his fingers. He wasn't surprised — not really — but every new truth carried its own weight.

He reached for the phone, pulled his small, worn address book from the top drawer, and found a name he hadn't used in months: Elijah McKean. They'd worked the line together back when both wore Border Patrol green — KC out of El Centro Sector, Elijah out of Yuma. They'd spent more than one Christmas sharing old stories and blowing the wind along the fence. When KC left the Patrol to run for sheriff, Elijah moved to Homeland Security Investigations. The trust never left.

KC dialed.

"McKean."

"Elijah, it's KC."

There was a short pause, then a low laugh. "I'll be. Trouble chasing you again?"

KC smiled faintly. "Feels like it found me before I was awake this time."

"You always did have a way of attracting headlines," Elijah said. "How's life in Mojave?"

"Still dry, still loud," KC said. "You?"

"Different," Elijah said. "The job's changed. More politics than fieldwork. Harder to breathe some days. But I'm holding on."

"I know the feeling," KC said quietly.

"You didn't call to reminisce," Elijah said. "What do you need?"

"I've got a victim's phone — Maria Alvarez. It went dark right before she died. I need tower logs, pings, maybe a sector overlap if you can manage it. Nothing that crosses the line — just what's accessible through your channels. I want to see where that phone moved after it left signal range."

Elijah was silent a moment. KC could almost hear him thinking, weighing what he could and couldn't do.

"That's a narrow window," Elijah said finally. "And given ICE's posture around your county, anything connected to that name might get a double-take. You sure you want to poke that bear?"

"I don't poke," KC said. "I follow tracks. I'll take the heat if it comes."

Elijah gave a quiet chuckle. "You always did. Send me the identifiers — IMEI, last known cell, timestamps, and case number. I'll flag it as a cooperative review. It'll show up as a cross-agency assist, not a favor. Clean."

"Good," KC said. "If it gets you any flak, remember what I told you before you and I left Border Patrol — if I win this fight, there's a job here when you're ready to retire."

"You offering me desert dust over air conditioning?" Elijah said with a grin in his voice.

"I'm offering you peace and a good badge," KC said.

"Then that's worth more than most things these days," Elijah said. "I'll get what I can. But KC—be careful. ICE is sniffing around your county harder than usual. Rumor is they're coming back soon."

"I know," KC said. "And thanks."

"Always," Elijah said. "We stood in line together once. And I still do."

The call ended. KC set the receiver down, took a sip from his bottle, and reached for his notebook. He wrote Elijah's name beside Maria's:

HSI assist – tower records / Alvarez device – cooperative review.

He underlined it once, then drew a short line under the words Parsons feeding Akers, Queen pulling strings. The shape of things was starting to show itself, even without the corkboard.

A knock at the door. Carlie stepped in. "Everything all right?"

"Getting there," KC said.

She studied him for a moment. "Trisha, even though she looked exhausted, looked like she'd found the missing piece."

"She found a piece of the puzzle," KC said. "Now we just need to fit it."

Carlie nodded, her tone softer. "You want me to make the call sheet for tomorrow?"

"Yes. Put Parsons in for eight sharp. Closed door."

She wrote it down. "You think he'll come?"

KC looked toward the window, where the morning sun had just started to climb over the courthouse roof. "He'll come. People like Parsons always think they're immune."

"Anything else?" she asked.

"Make a note — Trisha's to get full credit in her file on the phone records. A Commendation. She's earned it."

"I'll see it's done," Carlie said, and left quietly.

KC picked up his pen and wrote one more line across the bottom of the page:

Two days to dawn. Truth first.

He sat back, the faint hum of the building filling the silence. Outside, the county kept moving—trucks, schools, lives that didn't know how close their peace sat to the edge of someone else's storm. KC took a long drink of water, capped the bottle, and rose.

It was time to prepare for the rest of the day.

Chapter 34
What the Evidence Says

Day Four – 9:30 a.m.

Mojave County – Sheriff's Office (KC's Office)

The argument carried through the hallway before KC opened his door. At first, just fragments—voices rising and cutting over one another, that edge of frustration that had been building since the protests began.

"...say what you want, but he's protecting the wrong people!"

"He's protecting the law, not your opinion."

That second voice—steady, controlled—KC recognized. Deputy Ron Latham. A solid man, quiet, one of the few who didn't bend with the wind.

"You call this law?" the first deputy shot back. "He's got the press all over him. Looks like he's coddling illegals. And we take the heat. He ain't on the streets to get the flak."

KC turned the knob and stepped out.

The conversation died like someone had flipped a switch. Four deputies stood clustered near the duty board. One avoided his eyes. Another suddenly found something to read on the bulletin. Latham, the one who'd defended him, straightened.

"Everything all right out here?" KC asked, voice even.

"Yes, sir," Latham said, meeting his gaze.

The others murmured agreement and scattered. KC nodded to Latham. "Appreciate the defense."

"Thank you, Sheriff."

KC didn't say more. He didn't need to. He took note. Loyalty mattered.

When he reentered his office, Carlie buzzed him. "Sheriff, Dr. Ram is on line one. Says he has news."

"Thank you."

He closed the door and crossed the room. He sat, picked up the phone, and said simply, "Talbird."

"Sheriff, this is Dr. Ram. Do you have a moment?"

KC uncapped his pen, poised it over the page of his black notebook. "Go ahead."

"I wanted to speak to you directly before the report moves through channels," the doctor said, his tone careful. "We finalized the paternity analysis in the Alvarez case early this morning. Two labs verified."

KC's pulse slowed, a habit he'd learned long ago—make space for what's coming. "And?"

"Luis Alvarez is excluded as the father," the ME said. "No partial match, no statistical ambiguity. The biological father is someone else."

KC wrote a single line—Luis excluded—Then who?

"You're certain," KC said quietly.

"Two independent confirmations," he replied. "We double-blind tested to eliminate cross-contamination. The confidence interval's better than ninety-nine point nine."

"Who else has that report?"

"Just me and my lead tech. We haven't uploaded to the DA's secure yet. I thought you'd want to know first."

KC's eyes went to the blinds. Outside, a dust devil twisted across the rear lot before breaking apart. "I do," he said. "And I need you to hold that information tight to your chest."

Dr. Ram hesitated. "Sheriff, I can hold it for a day. After that, chain-of-custody requires it to go to Dodd's office. Twenty-four hours, no more."

"That'll do," KC said. "Thank you for the courtesy."

"Of course," Dr. Ram said, voice softening. "I know what this means for the accused. For the father. For you too."

KC didn't respond right away. "You did good work, Doctor. Again, I appreciate you keeping it on the down low for a day."

The line clicked off.

KC sat for a moment, pen balanced against his thumb. The hum of the overhead light seemed louder now.

He wrote another line beneath the first: Maria – two months pregnant. Father unknown. Luis cleared.

He tapped the page once with his pen tip, thinking. The whole county had already decided Luis was guilty. Queen had made sure of that. The board had used him as their villain, the headline to buy fear. Now the one man who'd lost everything was innocent in the one way that mattered most.

He thought of Rosa's kitchen, of Herb Sherman wiping tears of grief from wearied eyes, of the boy Mateo still waiting for answers no child should need.

The truth had shifted, and truth always demanded payment.

KC leaned back, folded his hands, and stared at the ceiling for a long moment. He could call Dodd. It would be protocol, even polite. But Dodd's office had leaks—Queen's influence ran deep. She'd twist it into another weapon.

No. Not yet.

He reached for his bottle of water, took a slow drink, and set it aside. Then he opened his drawer, pulled out the printout from Trisha's report—Parsons' texts to Akers, Queen's orders, Hahn's short message: Don't let it come back to me.

"Hahn? Of course." He whispered.

KC rose, moved to the window. A small bird flew by, oblivious to the chants from the crowd. He sat back down, grabbed his notebook, and drew a clean line connecting Maria to Julian Hahn. Below Hahn's name, he wrote one word: Motive?

He leaned back, arms folded. Hahn has a political career. The motive—pregnancy—and now, maybe, the reason Maria had been silenced.

A soft knock. Carlie again. "Everything is set for the morning. Anything else?"

"Yes," KC said, without turning.

She hesitated. "Sounded serious."

"It was," he said. "Dr. Ram confirmed something I expected."

"You need me to start any paperwork?"

"Not yet." He turned then, eyes steady. "You've been with me long enough to know—sometimes the less we write, the better. For a day, keep everything quiet. Anyone asks about the Alvarez case, tell them it's still an ongoing investigation."

"You got it, Sheriff."

As she started to leave, he added, "Latham—Deputy Latham—pull his personnel file. I want to review it."

She nodded, understanding without needing explanation, and left.

KC went back to his desk and opened his notebook again. One new entry underlined twice:

Next: Confront Hahn.

He closed the book, slid it into his pocket, and looked once more toward the window where sunlight pressed through the blinds like bars of gold.

The truth had just changed shape. And he'd be the one to carry it where it needed to go.

Chapter 35
No Margin for Error

Day Four – 10:21 a.m.

Mojave County – Sherman's Market

The blacktopped lot in front of Sherman's Market shimmered in the late-morning autumn sun. KC eased his Jeep into a spot by the front entrance and sat for a moment with the engine off. The clang of dolly wheels from a bread truck carried across the lot. A soda delivery truck idled nearby, a man in ball cap unloading crates of bottled and canned drinks. The smell of dust and diesel mixed with the faint sweetness of fresh bread.

He adjusted his hat, squared his shoulders, and walked toward the front door.

Inside, the store pulsed with quiet motion. Aisles lined with bulk bins and stacked paper towels; a boy mopping near the front; an older man in a white apron filling grocery bags and chatting with customers about the weather. A woman compared prices on canned peaches, shaking her head. The place felt lived-in—solid, local, honest.

KC moved between the aisles, nodding to a few familiar faces. Near the back, Herb Sherman was stocking shelves, sliding jars of peanut butter into place. He looked up, saw KC, and gave a small nod toward the office tucked behind a beaded curtain. KC nodded back.

Herb followed him a moment later, wiping his hands on a towel. The little office smelled of cardboard and old coffee. Photos of Maria hung along the corkboard: her high school graduation, her behind the counter at the market, one with her parents at a town fair. The desk was stacked with invoices and a ledger open to a page half filled in pencil. Very similar to the last visit KC had made there.

"Morning, Sheriff," Herb said, settling behind the desk. "Didn't expect to see you today."

KC took the chair across from him. "Morning, Herb. I won't take much of your time."

"You're fine," Herb said, glancing through the doorway at the store. "Business is steady, but folks come and go. Hard to keep help lately." He sighed. "Guess that's everywhere."

KC nodded. "Everywhere."

They sat in a brief silence. Herb studied him, brow creased. "You look like a man carrying news."

KC leaned forward slightly. "I got a call this morning from Dr. Ram. It's about the paternity test."

Herb's hands stilled on the desk. "All right," he said carefully. "Go on."

KC took a slow breath. "The results came in early. They ran it twice, two separate labs. Luis Alvarez isn't the father."

Herb blinked once, twice. "What?" His voice cracked. "You sure about that?"

KC nodded. "Confirmed. No margin for error."

Herb leaned back, staring past KC at the wall. The clock ticked behind him. "Then who?" he asked finally.

"That's what I'm working to find out."

Herb's jaw flexed. "You're saying my daughter—she was with someone else?"

KC shook his head. "I'm saying there's more we don't know. I'm not judging her, Herb. I'm just following where the evidence points."

Herb pushed up from his chair, pacing a step. "You think I don't know my own daughter? She wasn't that kind of girl."

KC stayed calm, hands resting on his knees. "I know that. But whoever hurt her was close enough to betray her. That's the only reason I ask."

Herb stopped, eyes narrowing. "She worked hard. Spent long hours helping with that State Reps campaign—Julian Hahn. Believed in his message. She was in his office more than here toward the end."

KC kept his voice steady. "Did she ever mention any problems there? Anyone she didn't trust?"

Herb shook his head slowly. "No. But now that you mention it..." His eyes hardened. "You think that man could've—?"

"I'll be questioning him," KC said. "Soon."

Herb sank back into his chair, shoulders heavy. "They were so quick to put Luis in cuffs. The boy barely had time to breathe before they dragged him off."

KC nodded once. "That's been on my mind too."

Herb's voice thickened with anger. "Queen was out front, waving her hands, calling for justice. Justice, she said. I backed her campaigns, Sheriff. Twice. Thought she was one of the good ones."

KC's expression didn't change. "It's not the first time politics have stepped in front of truth."

Herb leaned forward, palms flat on the desk. "Then it's time somebody said so. I'll talk to the reporters—set the record straight. They need to hear from me. And now."

KC shook his head. "I wouldn't. Not yet. The story's still fragile. Let it settle, Herb. The truth will stand stronger when it's ready."

Herb gave a dry laugh. "You always this patient?"

KC almost smiled. "No. Just older."

The humor faded quickly. Herb opened a drawer and took out a small photograph—Maria at sixteen, wearing a red apron, a candy cane in her hand, smiling behind the register. It was much like the one he showed KC during an earlier meeting they had. The picture trembled slightly in his grip. "She wanted this place to matter," he said. "She thought she could change things, one person at a time. Now all I've got is this store and memories that hurt too much to look at."

KC's voice softened. "You raised a good daughter. What you built here—it still matters."

Herb's eyes glistened. "Then find who took her from me. Make it right."

KC nodded once. "That's the plan."

Herb rose and extended his hand. His grip was firm, calloused from decades of work. "You find him," he said, voice rough. "And when you do, tell me before the news does."

"You'll be the first to know," KC said.

They walked out together through the aisles. The same rhythm of carts and chatter filled the air. Life is going on, unaware of the fracture running through it.

At the counter, the old clerk nodded to KC. He nodded back, then stepped out into the sun.

He paused by his Jeep, flipped open his black notebook, and wrote:

Herb informed. Luis cleared. Hahn—next step.

Then beneath it:

Queen's storm grows. Truth tightens.

He closed the book, started the engine, and drove off, dust lifting behind him like a slow, rising ghost.

Chapter 36

A Question in Daylight

Day Four – 12:00 p.m.

Mojave County – The Club → County Highway Shoulder

The Club did not advertise itself. It didn't have to. The low, modern slab of glass and brushed steel sat back from the boulevard behind a desert-neutral privacy wall, its name etched in frosted letters on a single pane by the valet stand. Polished concrete glowed under the noon sun. A man in a dark vest stood sentry beside a row of agave planters and a rope line no one ever needed to touch. It was the kind of place whose silence did the talking—sleek, expensive, private.

KC parked across the side street where the shade from an under-watered palm tree threw a narrow band across his windshield. He unwrapped a Della's sandwich from wax paper, the bread still soft, and set a Cherry Coke in the console. Through the windshield, the Club's glass held his reflection for a moment and then gave it back to the sky. Behind the valet, a red Porsche waited nose-out, lacquer bright enough to turn heads without asking permission.

He ate without hurry. The habit had been knocked into him by men who learned the hard way that you don't sprint toward a door if patience will make the door open by itself. He wrote a note in his black book in his blocky printing—Hahn haunts The Club—then under it, in smaller letters: Watch the hands, not the smile.

The valet stepped forward, checked his phone, and stepped back. A pair of men emerged—suits that fit like they'd been told a secret, sunglasses that made the sun look expensive. They traded quick handshakes and peeled off to their cars. Then Hahn came through the glass.

Julian Hahn wore his clothes like he'd been coached: pale blue shirt open at the throat, jacket cut slim, vanity watch for anyone keeping score. He laughed at something the man behind him said, clapped the man's shoulder, then looked past him instinctively toward the street. His gaze found the white Jeep across the way. The laugh quelled. He nodded once to no one and moved for the Porsche.

KC set the sandwich wrapper aside and started the Jeep. He didn't pull out yet. He let Hahn reach the Porsche, let him fire it with a clean, hungry sound, let the nose swing wide to the street and the rear tires chirp a little like a dog eager for permission. When Hahn slid onto the boulevard with more throttle than goodwill, KC eased into the lane a car back and two over and rode the mirror.

Half a mile down—past the dealership that sold trucks no rancher could afford, new and a stuccoed office park that looked abandoned even when full—KC thumbed his light bar. The blues flared against the bright, a quiet insistence. The Porsche checked—hesitation, calculation—then indicated and drifted to the shoulder where the scrub gave way to caliche and a low fence wobbled into the distance.

KC parked a car length behind, angled, standard, and deliberate. He stepped out, hat on, wind teasing the edge of his jacket. The day smelled like hot road and creosote. He walked up the line of the Porsche and stopped just forward of the B-pillar, where a man can see your hands and you can see his.

The window slid down a measured four inches. Hahn looked up from behind sunglasses so dark they seemed painted on. The smile he tried on was the one he used for ribbon cuttings and Christmas toy drives.

"Was I speeding, Sheriff?" Hahn asked, pleasant the way a desert is pleasant before it remembers what it is.

"You were enthusiastic," KC said. "This isn't a racetrack."

Hahn set a hand on the wheel at ten o'clock and tapped a finger against the leather. "I'll keep my enthusiasm in check."

KC didn't write anything yet. He leaned his forearm on the edge of the window and let his voice go flat as level ground. "You've got a minute?"

"For?"

"Maria."

A tiny pulse jumped at the angle of Hahn's jaw. He didn't look away; he made a show of not looking away. "Tragic," he said. "Our whole campaign team's been shattered."

"You knew her," KC said.

"She volunteered," Hahn replied. "A good heart. Smart. Wanted to help the community. That's what we're building, Sheriff—community."

KC let that word hang in the cab for the second it deserved. "She was pregnant," he said.

Hahn didn't blink. His lips pressed together and then shaped sympathy. "That was the rumor. Ugly how people talk when a girl can't answer back."

"It isn't a rumor," KC said. "It's the medical examiner's finding. Two months along."

Silence then, real and clean. Hahn's throat moved once. The sunglasses made him look like a man hiding in his own face.

KC kept his voice gentle, because that's how you push without pushing. "Luis Alvarez has been excluded as the father."

"I don't know anything about that," Hahn said quickly, too quickly. "I barely knew the boy."

"I'm not asking you about the boy," KC said. "I'm asking about you."

A beat. Hahn smiled again, slower. "Me. Sheriff, I'm a public figure. My enemies stir lies every week. Comes with the territory." He lifted a shoulder. "If you're fishing, you picked the wrong lake."

KC took out his notebook and set it on the roofline, pen poised. "You spent time with Maria in your headquarters. People saw you together. You called her. She texted you. Ten minutes before she cut a session short at County Mental Health, a message came in, and she left. That message came from your number."

The smile cracked like a glaze crazing. "You reading my phone, Sheriff?"

"I read the world," KC bluffed. He didn't have access to Hahn's phone. Not yet. "And the world leaves marks."

Hahn looked past KC down the line of highway, where heat made the air seam and wobble. "This is harassment," he said, the friendliness draining from the next word. "You're trying to paint me because you don't want to admit you're soft on an illegal and wrong about a case."

KC didn't move. "I'm trying to find the father of a dead girl's baby," he said simply. "And the man who hit her from behind and left her in a wash. May be two separate men." Another bluff.

Hahn's fingers left the wheel and came back to it. He worked his jaw like he had grit in a tooth. "You think saying things quiet makes them less slanderous?"

"I'm not slandering," KC said. "I'm asking. Will you give me a buccal swab today—simple cheek swab—to eliminate you as the father? Five seconds. If you've got nothing to hide, it clears your name clean."

There it was, the part of a conversation where men who have rehearsed every answer find they forgot to practice the truth. Hahn's face went a color between desert red and paper white. He pushed the sunglasses up into his hair, blinked at the light, and tried a laugh that had no place to land.

"You're kidding," he said.

"No," KC said.

"On a roadside," Hahn said, pointing to the asphalt with an open palm. "Without a warrant. You think I'm that gullible?"

"I think you have an opportunity," KC said. "Men who are innocent usually take it."

"Innocent men also know their rights," Hahn shot back, heat rising now. "I refuse. This is a political ambush and I'm not feeding it."

KC wrote in his book: Offered voluntary swab—refused. Observed: agitation, defensive posture.

Hahn watched the pen move like it was a blade. "You're writing your fiction already."

"I'm writing what happened," KC said. He tore a copy from his citation book, filled the top line with the basic, ordinary truth of it, and slid the paper through the four inches of window. "This is a warning for erratic driving. You'll want to slow down."

Hahn took it and didn't look at it. "You're crossing a line, Sheriff."

KC set his pen down on the notebook and met his eyes. "I cross lines every day, Mr. Hahn. Most of them are chalk outlines. This one is a courtesy."

A muscle kicked in Hahn's cheek. "You think you can humiliate me in the middle of the day and get away with it?"

"I think you can choose to help or not," KC said. "And I think how men act when they're asked tells me what I need to know."

They sat there with the engine ticking hot between them and the desert pretending it wasn't listening. A semi rolled past in the far lane, wind rocking both vehicles and leaving a low hum like a warning under the noise.

Hahn slid the sunglasses back onto his face. When he spoke again, the voice had moved from wounded to cold. "You'll regret this," he said. "You don't know who you're making an enemy of."

KC didn't answer. He stepped back one pace, then another, the way you do when you've said everything that matters. He tapped the roof twice—a signal to no one—and walked to the Jeep.

Hahn lit the Porsche with a sharp rev and threw gravel when he pulled back onto the road, the red lacquer flashing once like a tongue of warning before the car melted into heat shimmer. KC watched until the tail lights were a mirage and then nothing. He opened the Cherry Coke, drank a long pull that steadied the hand he didn't realize had tightened, and set the bottle back in its ring.

He wrote quickly with the notebook braced against the wheel:

Hahn exit The Club → watched tail.

Stop @ MM 42. Window opened 4".

Discussion: Maria volunteer → pregnant (2 mo) → Luis excluded → text chain to MH → asked for voluntary buccal swab → refused.

Observations: defensive, practiced rhetoric ("my enemies stirring lies"), anger masked as certainty. Red Porsche, reckless start/stop.

Under that, he wrote one more line, smaller, the size of a thought he wasn't willing to say out loud yet: Motive + opportunity aligning.

A dust devil unwound itself across the flat, threw grit at the Jeep's door, and fell apart as if it remembered it had somewhere else to be. KC closed the notebook, slid it into his shirt pocket, and checked the side mirror. The shoulder was empty; the road was a ribbon pulling tight toward town.

He put the Jeep in gear and pulled out, the tires humming a low, steady note that fit the new shape of the day. Ahead lay the courthouse with its polished floors and cameras, the office with its board he'd stripped and rebuilt in his head, the names that now connected without string. Men liked to think money made them fast enough to outrun light. It didn't. It just made the edges cleaner when the light found them.

KC drove back toward the square, Cherry Coke cold between his knees, the red of a sports car fading in his mind to the color of a door he would open again—soon, with a warrant in his pocket or a confession waiting on the hinge.

Chapter 37
No Warrant, No Mercy

Day Four – 1:23 p.m.

Mojave County – Queen B's Office

Julian Hahn didn't remember parking, only the sound of gravel popping under the Porsche's tires as he swung it into a spot behind the County Administration building. His hands shook on the wheel. The air inside the car felt too tight, the sunlight too sharp. He sat there a full minute, forcing slow breaths, but they came ragged anyway.

KC Talbird's voice still echoed in his ears—"She was pregnant... two months along... Luis Alvarez excluded."

And the quiet after that, the kind of quiet that didn't forgive anything.

Hahn killed the engine and grabbed his jacket from the passenger seat. He didn't bother to button it. His legs felt unsteady as he crossed the square, the dry wind catching the edge of his shirt. Queen's office sat on the second floor of the administrative wing—a suite too polished for county business, too cool for comfort.

The receptionist, a young woman with dark hair and a gold pin on her lapel, looked up from her monitor. "Mr. Hahn—Chairwomen Garrison is preparing for a meeting."

"She'll see me," Hahn said. His voice came out rougher than he expected.

"I'm sorry, but—"

Queen's voice drifted through the partially open doorway. Calm, composed. "It's all right, Claire. Send him in."

The receptionist stepped aside. Hahn pushed through the door like a bull in a ring.

Queen sat behind her wide desk, a silver Mont Blanc pen poised above a notepad. The blinds were half-drawn, letting in slanted bands of desert light that fell across her desk and the neat row of framed photos on the wall—smiling officials, ribbon cuttings, charity galas.

The faint scent of sandalwood hung in the air.

Hahn stopped just inside the room, chest heaving.

Queen looked up. "Julian," she said smoothly. "You look like a man who's been running."

"I should be," he said, shutting the door behind him. "KC Talbird pulled me over."

She didn't flinch. "Did he now?"

"Accused me of being the father," Hahn said, voice rising. "Said Maria was pregnant. Two months. He's got the medical examiner saying Luis Alvarez isn't the father. He wanted a DNA sample. Right there, on the roadside."

Queen set her pen down with deliberate care. "Did you give it to him?"

"Of course not," Hahn snapped. "He had no warrant. He's out of line. I told him so."

"Good," Queen said, folding her hands. "Then you did the only intelligent thing you could have."

"He knows, Aunt Beatrice." The words came out low, almost a whisper. "He knows about Maria and me."

Her expression didn't change. "He suspects," she corrected. "That's different from knowing. Suspicion fades. Proof is permanent. You've given him none."

Hahn paced in front of her altar, running a hand through his hair. "You don't understand. He said he had texts. He's connecting me to her the day she died."

"Then he's fishing," Queen said, tone clipped but calm. "You're letting him see you sweat. That's his goal."

Hahn stopped pacing. "You're not hearing me. If he gets a warrant for my DNA—if that test comes back—"

Queen leaned back slightly in her chair, crossing one leg over the other. "If," she said softly. "You're building panic out of possibilities. That's not a strategy, Julian. That's a weakness."

He stared at her. "Weakness? I'm trying to keep this from exploding. You think the board, the voters, the donors will stay with me if they find out?"

Her voice hardened. "They'll stay if I tell them to."

That silenced him for a moment.

Queen rose from her chair and came around her altar. The heels of her shoes clicked softly on the dark oak wood flooring, the sound measured and precise. She stopped an arm's length away from him. "Let's be clear," she said, eyes level with his. "You won the State House seat because I made you viable. I shaped your campaign, built your image, gave you the seat you stand on. You owe every inch of that to me."

"I've done everything you asked," Hahn said, anger edging into his voice.

"Then stop unraveling," Queen said sharply. "This isn't the time to tremble. Talbird's desperate. He's cornered by the press, losing allies, clinging to scraps. If he can drag you through the mud, he buys himself a little more time."

"He's got more than scraps," Hahn muttered. "He's got my number in her phone records."

Queen's lips curved, not quite a smile. "How could he? He doesn't have the phone. He's bluffing."

Hahn wiped a bead off his forehead. "It's not that simple. He can find out."

"It is," she said coldly. "You avoid. You deny. You let me manage the rest."

Hahn turned away, pacing toward the window. "You don't get it, Aunt Beatrice. He's dangerous because he believes he's right. He's not bluffing. I saw it in his face."

"You saw your own guilt," Queen said. "That's what frightens you."

Hahn turned back, color rising to his cheeks. "You think this is minor, not serious?"

"I think you're being dramatic," she said, returning to her seat. "Sit down before someone outside hears you."

He didn't sit. "You can't fix this with spin."

"Spin," she said, picking up her pen again, "is what keeps this county from collapsing into hysteria every time someone like Talbird forgets which side he's on."

Hahn's voice cracked. "He's going to ruin me."

Queen's eyes lifted to meet his, cool and unblinking. "Only if you let him. Now stop acting like a scared child. Take control of your narrative. Smile for the cameras. Blame political harassment. Play the victim. You do that, and this storm will pass."

He shook his head slowly. "You don't care if I get blown away by the storm, do you?"

"I care about the county's image," she said. "And about stability. Chaos is bad for funding. Bad for elections. If you become chaos, Julian, I'll have to correct it."

He stared at her, the meaning sinking in. "You'd throw me to the wolves."

Queen tapped her pen on the pad, then set it aside, and gave him a look that was almost pitying. "I don't throw people, Julian. They simply fall when they stop standing where I tell them."

For a moment, neither spoke. The room felt smaller, the air tighter. Outside the window, a dust devil spun across the lawn and broke apart against the curb.

Hahn finally spoke, voice low. "You think I'll just let you hang me?"

"I think you'll do what's smart," Queen said. "Go home. Rest. Let me handle the optics." She turned to the intercom and pressed the button. "Claire, I'm free now. Send in my next appointment."

The door opened almost immediately. The receptionist's polite smile froze when she saw Hahn standing there, face tight with fury.

Queen didn't look up again. She was already writing something new on her pad.

Hahn stood there another second, then walked out, each step louder than the last.

The outer hallway was bright, the kind of brightness that exposes everything. He stopped halfway down, leaning against the wall, his reflection warping in a framed photo of Queen shaking hands with the governor. His pulse thudded in his ears.

She'd made him once. And now she'd kill his career just as easily.

He pushed off the wall, jaw set. If she wanted him to be her shield, she'd just made an enemy instead.

Chapter 38

The Rule of Evidence

Day Four – 1:45 p.m.

Mojave County – County Courthouse

The courthouse smelled of paper and polish, the kind of scent that outlasted the people who made decisions inside it. KC pushed through the glass doors, hat in hand, the echo of his boots trailing behind him as he moved down the marbled corridor. The ceiling whirled, and hummed above the low rhythm of whispered voices.

He had been here a hundred times before—for warrants, arraignments, hearings—but this time was different. This time, he was asking the system to turn on one of its own.

A bailiff sitting behind a metal detector nodded. "Afternoon, Sheriff."

"Afternoon, Ben."

The bailiff's eyes flicked toward the hallway leading to Judge Voss's chambers. "He's in. Been on the phone half the morning."

KC caught the tone—half caution, half warning—and gave a short nod. "Appreciate it."

He adjusted his hat under his arm and walked toward the frosted glass door that read Chief Judge Harold Voss.

Inside, the judge's secretary looked up from her desk. "He's expecting you, Sheriff. Go on in."

Voss's office was a long rectangle of order and restraint. Bookshelves lined with law volumes, a framed portrait of the State Supreme Court, a cactus near the window wilting from neglect. The judge himself sat behind an oak desk stacked with motions and rulings, a half-drunk cup of coffee cooling beside them.

"Sheriff Talbird," Voss said without looking up. "You're persistent. That can be a virtue or a nuisance. Let's see which it is today."

KC managed a faint smile and took the seat opposite him. "Hope for the first, settle for the second."

Voss finally looked up, his wire-rimmed glasses catching the light. "You said this was urgent."

KC laid a manila folder on the desk and opened it. "Medical examiner's report came in this morning. Maria Sherman—two months pregnant. Luis Alvarez's DNA excluded as the father."

Voss's brow furrowed. "That's unexpected."

"It is," KC said. "We don't have phone records yet, but Representative Julian Hahn—Maria did extensive campaign work for him—my instincts tell me| he's the father, and possibly connected to her death."

The judge's expression remained unreadable. "And you're requesting...?"

"A warrant for a buccal swab," KC said. "Hahn's DNA. Voluntary's been refused."

Voss leaned back, interlaced his fingers, and looked at the ceiling for a long moment before answering. "Sheriff, that's a steep climb. You're talking about compelling a sitting state representative to provide a DNA sample on the basis of circumstantial contact and what you call instinct."

"I call it evidence," KC said. "Not proof yet, but enough to justify testing."

The judge shook his head slowly. "Evidence requires connection. Motive and opportunity don't rise to probable cause unless you can link him directly to the crime scene or the victim's last known location."

"I'm working on that," KC said evenly. "I believe there are many texts on her phone that came from his number. She left County Mental Health right after receiving one. I think it was from Hahn."

"That phone isn't in evidence," Voss said. "As I understand, it's missing. Which means you can't produce the record in open court."

KC stiffened. "How do you know the phone's missing?"

The judge's eyes flicked down to the papers on his desk. "Word gets around."

"Word from who?" KC pressed.

Voss didn't answer right away. He adjusted his glasses and said, "You're not the only man with sources, Sheriff."

KC leaned forward slightly. "Or maybe someone's making sure you're briefed before I walk in the door."

Voss exhaled through his nose. "You think Chairwoman Garrison doesn't know every move made in this building? She called earlier this afternoon—concerned about the 'direction' of your investigation. She's already talking to the district attorney. I'd say your instincts about this case are getting ahead of the facts."

"That's what happens when the facts are hard to come by. When politics obscure the truth," KC said quietly.

Voss gave a weary smile. "You and I both know what happens when a small-county judge signs a warrant against a state representative less than two months before re-election. My phone would light up before the ink dries."

"So politics wins?" KC asked.

"Politics endures," Voss corrected. "Justice survives where it can."

KC sat back. "I've got a murdered woman who was with child, and someone who thinks their title makes others bulletproof. That's not politics, Judge. That's obstruction."

Voss's tone softened, but not by much. "You've always played it straight, Sheriff. That's why people trust you. But this—" he tapped the folder and pushed it toward KC— "isn't enough. Bring me something I can stand on, and I'll sign it. Until then, you'd better tread carefully."

KC closed the folder, the sound crisp in the quiet room. "I appreciate your time."

"I mean that, Sheriff," Voss said. "Tread carefully. There are lines that once crossed can't be uncrossed."

KC stood. "Sometimes lines are drawn to keep honest men out."

The judge said nothing more.

Outside, the hallway felt cooler. KC walked slowly, the echo of his boots following him to the exit. He passed a janitor pushing a mop bucket and a young lawyer whispering into a phone. Everyone in the building seemed to know something he didn't, and that wasn't by accident.

Out in the lot, the sunlight hit hard, though the season was autumn. KC climbed into his Jeep and sat for a long moment without starting it. The courthouse windows mirrored the sky, but in one, he could almost see the judge's shape—small, still, safe behind the glass.

He pulled his notebook from the dash and flipped to the page he'd marked earlier. He wrote:

Warrant denied – probable cause "insufficient."

Queen called Voss. Hahn protected.

Find alternative route.

He capped the pen and looked across the lot toward the

Administration Building. Somewhere in there, Queen was already spinning her next move.

He started the Jeep, the engine rumbling low. Through the windshield, he saw a flash of red—a Porsche cutting across the far intersection, moving too fast. Hahn again, running hot from somewhere he didn't belong.

KC muttered, "Running won't save you."

He shifted into gear and pulled onto the street, the courthouse shrinking in his rearview.

He knew the system wouldn't hand him justice.

He'd have to take the long way around to find it.

Chapter 39

The False Referral

Day Four – 2:30 p.m.

Mojave County – County Community Solutions (Outreach Office)

The "County Community Solutions" sign was vinyl white on dark glass, the kind of semi-permanent you use when a program is funded by year-to-year grants and politics. Inside, cubicles divided a long room into polite rectangles. A water cooler hummed. A corkboard held flyers for food drives and coat swaps, the corners curling where the pushpins had missed their mark.

Toni checked in with a receptionist who wore headphones half-off one ear. "Is there someone here assigned as a mental health outreach worker?" she asked.

The receptionist pointed her toward a back office with a pane of glass on a brown door. She volunteered the man's name.

Toni glanced around to get a better feel, then made her way to the office. "Ruben Marteen?" Toni said, rapping lightly.

A man in his early thirties stood as if he'd been caught mid-step. Neat beard, thrift-store blazer over a pressed shirt, eyes that went quickly to wary when she flashed her badge.

Toni stepped inside and closed the door until the latch surrendered. He motioned her to a chair. The office smelled faintly of dry-erase marker and coffee that had been made hours ago.

"I'm Deputy Toni Salazar. I'm here investigating the murder of Maria Sherman."

Ruben's head flinched just a beat. "Please, have a seat. I...I don't know anything about that." He pointed to a chair in front of his tan metal desk.

"Before we start," Toni said, setting a small digital recorder on the desk, "I'm going to record so I don't miss anything. This is voluntary, and you're not under arrest. You can stop at any time. Okay?"

Ruben glanced at the glass pane that looked out onto the cubicles, then back at her. "Okay. I… appreciate you saying that. I don't want any trouble."

"Neither do I," Toni said. She clicked the recorder on, set her notebook beside it, and placed her pen across the top. "Please state your name and job here for the record."

"Ruben José Marteen

," he said, hands folded, voice shaking as he talked. "Outreach Liaison for County Community Solutions. Contracted, not staff."

"How long have you been here?"

"Ten months. Since the program spun up."

"What does the program do, in your words?"

"We try to connect folks to services. Food pantry, shelter waitlists, a little job placement." He lifted a shoulder. "Sometimes just listening and pointing them toward people who can actually help."

"Are you a mental health counselor?"

He shook his head quickly. "No. We refer to County Mental Health. We're just supposed to… bridge."

Toni nodded once. "Let's talk about your visit to Sherman's Market the other day. You spoke with Mr. Herb Sherman?"

Ruben's mouth tightened. "Yes."

"Why did you go?"

He hesitated, then decided honesty was better than guessing what she already knew. "I got a call from Mr. Akers. Investigator Akers from the DA's office." He said the title carefully, respectful by habit.

"When?"

Ruben scrolled his phone, then turned it face-up on the desk without being asked. "A couple of days ago. Mid morning. He followed it with a text." He looked up. "Can I...?"

"Go ahead," Toni said.

He slid the phone toward her. The thread showed a missed call, then a message from Akers and Ruben's response:

Akers (10:19 a.m.): "Swing by Sherman's Market. Tell the owner, Herb Sherman, you're with mental health outreach. You're concerned about him. Find out if he knows anything about her situation, boyfriend, other relationships. Be discreet. Be friendly. Call me after. —A."

Ruben (10:20 a.m.): "I'm not with mental health. Can't do this."

Akers (10:22 a.m.): "Today you are. Or quit. Understood?"

Ruben (10:23 a.m.): 👍

Toni slid the phone back. "Do you always do what Akers says?"

"Uh," Ruben hesitated. "He and the...uh...Queen, that's what we call her, Ms. Garrison, are tight. So, yeah, if I want to keep my job I do."

"Did he say why he was asking you to do this?"

"After the text he called. Said our program had 'credibility' with the community." Ruben's mouth tugged sideways. "And that the Sheriff's Office was 'overloaded,' so a friendly face would help the father during this tragic time."

"Did you report to Mr. Akers before this?" Toni asked.

"Yeah, uh, you know. Check on people. Make sure they are registered to vote. If they need assistance, I could expedite. That kind of thing. But not like this. This was... specific."

"Akers is the DA's investigator. You followed his orders even though he's not in your chain of command?"

Ruben looked at her, confused by the question. "Like I said. He and Queen are tight. He's her right hand. Everyone knows that."

Toni wondered if the Sheriff was aware. "Did anyone else contact you about the visit? Chairwoman Garrison or her staff?"

Ruben's eyes flicked to the glass again, then back. "Her aide. The same morning. Just a short call. She said, 'Appreciate you supporting Rapid Response. Keep me posted if the owner says anything the public should know.' I didn't call her back."

"Rapid Response," Toni repeated.

"That's what they called it," he said. "I hadn't heard that label before."

"What did you do?"

"I went," he said simply. "I'm contract. I don't have a lot of latitude to say no when people up the chain ask." He stopped, trying to measure his words. "I figured I'd listen, if nothing else."

Toni pulled out her small notebook, wrote a line—Akers → Ruben → Herb (pretext: bridge). "Tell me about the conversation with Mr. Sherman."

Ruben exhaled. "I introduced myself to him per instructions as 'county mental health outreach'—that was the phrase Mr. Akers told me to use. I said I was checking on him, seeing if he needed anything. He took me to his office in the back. I told him I was sorry for his loss. He looked... wrecked."

Toni pictured Sherman's Market. "What did you ask?"

"I asked if Maria seemed under pressure lately. If she'd mentioned trouble at home or with her boyfriend." Ruben's face tightened. "He didn't like that. He said she was a good girl. I told him I wasn't implying otherwise."

"Did you ask about Representative Hahn?"

Ruben looked down at his folded hands. "Yeah. That was in the follow-up text from Mr. Akers. He wrote, 'Get sense of Hahn connection—was she often at HQ? Any signs of something more?'" He swallowed. "It felt wrong to say out loud."

"What did Mr. Sherman say?"

"He said Maria volunteered a lot. He said she believed in helping. He didn't say more. His jaw—" Ruben made a small fist— "got tight. I backed off."

"Did you tell Mr. Sherman you were working at the request of the DA's office?"

"No," Ruben said. "I kept it 'outreach.' He'd already let me in his office; I wasn't going to make him feel ambushed."

"What did you do after you left?"

"I sat in my car and called Mr. Akers. Told him Mr. Sherman didn't say much. I said it looked like grief, not... whatever they're trying to shape on TV. He told me to keep my visit quiet. I did."

"May I take a photo of these screens?" she asked.

"Yeah," he said, pushing the phone closer.

She raised her department-issued, camera-only phone and snapped each screen with time, date, and a quick frame of the entire thread list as context. Then she set both devices flat and wrote:

– Screenshot: Akers text, Ruben's responses.

– Screenshot: Queen B's aide, fishing for info.

"Did you keep any other record of these events?"

He looked at his hands again. "Yeah, I thought if someone came asking why I'd stuck my nose into a grieving father's office, I wanted proof it wasn't my idea. I don't want to be anybody's pawn."

"You felt you were being used," Toni said.

"I know I was being used."

They let the quiet sit between them for a breath.

"Do you have any more information about Maria herself—any prior contact with her?"

He shook his head. "I never met her. I only knew the name. We worked on a canned food drive last fall, and her dad sent over a pallet—he's generous. That's it."

Toni nodded. "Would you be willing to send those screenshots to me directly, and also forward your written account to mine? Chain-of-custody matters."

"Yeah," he said. He hesitated. "Will my name be in a report that gets out?"

"I can't promise your name won't appear in discovery," Toni said plainly. "But I can promise retaliation is unacceptable. If you feel any pressure, you call me. Immediately."

He gave a small, grateful nod, like someone had set down a weight he'd been pretending wasn't there.

"You mentioned the aide called this 'Rapid Response,'" Toni said. "Have you gotten other requests like this since?"

"Two," he said. "Small. One was, 'Is the Sheriff talking to anyone in the Hispanic community? Any pastors?' I didn't answer. I'm not going to burn the people we serve." He paused. "The other was asking if I had a good word with the Alvarez family. I wrote back that the family wasn't ours to reach under the circumstances. No one replied."

Toni wrote both requests down, underlined once, then underlined again without realizing it. "You did the right thing," she said.

Ruben exhaled, some of the tightness in his shoulders easing. "I don't know if there's a right thing anymore. Feels like every door opens into a room that isn't about people—just power."

"Sometimes the right thing is saying that out loud," Toni said. "On the record."

He gave a faint, humorless smile. "Put it on the record, then."

Toni gathered the recorder and clicked it off. "We're done for today. If anyone contacts you about this conversation—anyone—call me. If you get new instructions like the ones you've shown me, call me first."

"I will."

She stood. Ruben stood too. At the door, Toni paused. "One more question: do you know why Mr. Akers told you to use the phrase 'mental health outreach' when he sent you to Mr. Sherman?"

Ruben nodded. "Yeah. He said it would open the door."

Toni's jaw set. "Thank you for being clear."

He held the door for her. In the cubicle field, a woman laughed softly at something on a screen, and the water cooler still hummed like a steady engine.

In the hallway, Toni took out her phone and snapped one quick photo of the suite sign—County Community Solutions—framed with the suite number. She preferred paper to memory when it mattered.

Outside, the light made her blink. She stood in the strip of shade cast by the building's overhang and typed a short, neutral text to KC:

Met "outreach." Not MH. Pawned by Akers. Queen's aide involved too. Has written report and texts.

KC's reply came quick: Good work.

Toni slid the phone away and took one slow breath. The wind was strong; it carried the smell of hot asphalt and a faint thread of bakery from two doors down. On the sidewalk, a young girl in a work apron balanced a stack of to-go trays, careful and quick.

She walked to her cruiser, opened the trunk, and pulled a thin evidence envelope. She labeled it with today's date and wrote: "Digital Images — Marteen device (Akers thread / Queen aide cc / 'Sherman Notes'). Source: consent capture by Dep. Salazar." She sealed it, signed the flap, and tucked it in the locked case.

Before she got in, she jotted the last line in her pocket notebook:

They called it outreach to open a door. It was politics to keep it closed.

She slid behind the wheel and started the engine. 3:15 wasn't far. Neither was the next piece of a picture that was beginning to show its shape—not string now, not guesswork, but the kind of lines you could lay over a map and start to navigate.

Chapter 40

The Blind Spot

Day Four – 3:15 p.m.

Mojave County – Sheriff's Office (KC's Office)

The building had settled into that late-afternoon rhythm when the air conditioner hums louder than the talk. The deputies out front spoke in low tones, filing reports or pretending to. KC's office door was half shut, the light slanting through blinds that painted his desk in thin bars of gold and shadow. He stood by the window with his hat off, his notebook open beside a half-empty bottle of Cherry Coke.

Carlie tapped on the doorframe. "Sheriff, Deputy Salazar's back."

He turned from the window. "Send her in."

Toni came in, her boots quiet on the hard wood floor. She looked like she'd been out in the field all day—dust on her cuffs, hair pulled tight, eyes clear but heavy. She carried a slim folder and one of the small, labeled evidence envelopes KC had taught her to prepare herself.

He nodded toward the chair across from him. "Let's hear it."

She sat, laying out her folder with the same precision she used at a crime scene. "I just left County Community Solutions," she said. "Talked to Ruben Marteen, the outreach liaison. He cooperated fully. Nervous, but honest."

KC leaned forward, elbows on his knees. "Go ahead."

"Marteen confirmed that Investigator Akers called him two days ago. Told him to pose as a mental health outreach and visit Herb Sherman at the market. The cover story was to 'check in'—a welfare visit after his daughter's death—but the real reason was to see what Herb knew. Akers wanted to know about Maria's relationships— presumably whether she was involved with someone besides Luis."

KC's jaw tightened, his gaze fixed on the far corner of the desk. "And he went along with it?"

"He tried not to. Texted Akers that he couldn't do it. Akers replied, 'Today you are. Or quit.'"

KC let out a slow breath. "So the DA's investigator is using county outreach workers as political scouts."

"Exactly," Toni said. "And it doesn't stop there. Marteen got a call from Queen's aide the same morning, thanking him for supporting something called 'Rapid Response.' Told him to keep them posted if Herb said anything the public should know."

KC repeated the phrase under his breath. "Rapid Response." He shook his head. "That sounds like a crisis management team, not community help."

"That's what Marteen said too. He's had other small requests—checking on local pastors, even asking about the Alvarez family—but this one felt wrong. He kept everything. Screenshots, notes, timestamps. He's sending them to me tonight."

KC reached for his black notebook, his writing deliberate and square.

Marteen—used under pretense. Akers directs. Queen's aide aware. 'Rapid Response' label.

He underlined it twice, then drew a line connecting the names.

"Good work," he said. "What else?"

"I also went back to County Mental Health," she said. "I wanted to check the camera coverage again. There are interior feeds—hallways, reception. Outside, only one camera that gave a view of her leaving the building. No city cameras, no street footage. The maintenance director told me that other exterior cameras were never installed because of budget constraints. He got that news from Queen's office a day or two before Maria was murdered."

KC frowned. "No eyes where the truth walks out the door."

Toni nodded. "Exactly. If Maria met with someone outside, there's no video. It's a perfect blind spot."

"Perfect for who?"

She hesitated. "Whoever needed her to disappear quietly. Or whoever didn't want anyone to see who may have confronted her. Or followed her."

KC's pen tapped once against the notebook. "No coincidence, then."

"I don't think so."

He stood, walked to the whiteboard along the wall, and began adding names and arrows with a dry-erase marker:

Akers → Queen → Hahn

Then beneath it: Containment, not inquiry.

"They're not investigating," KC said. "They're managing fallout. Akers didn't send that outreach worker to gather evidence—he sent him to monitor Herb. To see if the man was talking. That's protection, not procedure."

Toni crossed one leg over the other, arms folded loosely. "Protecting who?"

KC capped the marker. "Who do you think?"

She didn't answer. She didn't have to.

KC turned back toward his desk. "I went to Judge Voss earlier this afternoon. Tried for a DNA warrant on Hahn. He turned it down— said I didn't have probable cause. Too risky politically. He didn't accept my reasoning. He was quick to remind me about 'election optics.'"

Toni's brow furrowed. "Queen called him, didn't she?"

"She did," KC said. "Before I ever walked in the door. Told him the investigation was getting 'reckless.'"

Toni let out a quiet scoff. "So we're back to rules for them and rules for us."

"Something like that."

She leaned forward. "So what's next? You're not just letting this drop."

KC smiled faintly. "No. We find another way. Hahn spends time at The Club?"

"I'm familiar with it," her thoughts calculating. "High-end, private. I can get in. I know one of the bartenders owes me a favor. Hahn won't think twice."

"Could you get close enough for a DNA sample?"

"Glass, napkin, something he handles. Yes."

KC watched her for a long moment, the quiet in the room holding its breath. "You're sure?"

"I can handle it," she said. "I won't push it, just play it natural. He's arrogant, not careful. That's a combination that usually pays off."

He nodded slowly. "All right. Do it tonight. And Toni—don't underestimate him. Hahn's scared. He can create problems. Or his protector can."

"I'll be fine," she said, with that small spark of confidence he'd come to rely on.

KC picked up the bottle of Cherry Coke, took a slow drink, and set it back down. "You've got instincts I trust. Use them."

That earned the faintest smile from her. "You sure you're not saying that because I agree with you more than Parsons ever did?"

KC's eyes softened. "Maybe. But you've earned more in days than he has since the election."

She looked down, fighting a grin. "You know, you're not much for compliments, Sheriff, so I'll take that as a big one."

"I save them for when they matter."

Toni closed her folder, slipped the envelope inside, and stood. "If I can get the sample, you'll have it by morning."

"Good," KC said. "If you can't, don't force it. He'll make another mistake. They always do."

At the door, she paused. "You ever get tired of the fight?"

"Every day," he said, a hint of grit buried under fatigue. "Doesn't stop me from trying again tomorrow."

She nodded once, gave a small salute with two fingers, and left.

The silence returned, heavier now but clear. KC sat for a while, listening to the steady tick of the clock and the hum of the building's old air ducts. He opened his notebook again and wrote in neat block letters:

Day Four – 3:45 p.m.

– Ruben Marteen confirms Akers/Queen coordination.

– No exterior cameras – blind spot confirmed.

– Hahn protected by politics.

– Toni assigned covert retrieval.

He looked at the word she'd underlined in her notes earlier—Rapid Response—and shook his head. "More like Rapid Cover."

Outside, the sheriff's building stood quiet while flags snapped hard in the wind, a dry rattle echoing across the square. The sun had tilted west, shadows stretching long through the glass.

KC rose, stretched once, and stared at his notebook—lines, names, arrows, all pulling toward one center. Hahn.

He picked up the pen, twirled it around his fingers and said softly, "All right, Julian. Let's see how fast you can run when the truth catches up."

He turned off the lamp, the last light on his desk falling across the words he'd just written—

Truth First—before the office settled back into stillness.

Chapter 41
The Hearing Goes Public

Day Four – 5:00 p.m.

**Mojave County – Sheriff's Office (Break Room →
KC's Office)**

Carlie's knock was quick and light, the kind you use when the news has already started without you.

"Sheriff," she said from the doorway, voice low, "I just heard from a friend at the County Building. Queen's holding a live press conference—on air now."

KC stood, left his notebook open on the desk, and stepped into the hall. The afternoon hush in the bullpen had thinned—more bodies than voices, the kind of waiting air that comes right before something breaks. He didn't say a word. Carlie fell in beside him as they moved toward the break room.

The TV had already drawn a crowd. Deputies lined the walls and clustered around the table—styrofoam cups, a forgotten box of donuts going stale, a microwave clock blinking the wrong time. KC took the back corner near the doorway and didn't announce himself. He wanted the room to be honest before it knew he was there.

On the screen, Chairperson Garrison stood behind a podium dressed with the county seal, the county building columns framing her like a set she owned. The 5 p.m. sun lit the edges of her hair. Two flags crisped in the breeze behind her. Akers and her aide were posted over her shoulder, placed for the angle, not the substance. Reporters' mics and tape flags jabbed up from the scrum.

"—deeply concerned," Queen was saying, calm and measured, "that the Sheriff's Office has used its authority for political retaliation."

A murmur rolled through the room. Someone muttered, "Here we go."

"Yesterday afternoon," Queen continued, "my nephew, State Representative Julian Hahn, was pulled over by Sheriff Talbird after leaving a private meeting with community leaders. The stop was not for a legitimate traffic violation. It was to intimidate and harass an elected official, who is part of my family, because I've opposed the Sheriff's budget requests."

"Liar," someone breathed near the fridge.

KC didn't react. He watched her mouth form each clean sentence the way a blade is honed.

"This is not how our county operates," Queen went on. "We do not use badges as weapons. We do not target our public servants because they stand up for fiscal responsibility. We do not endanger the civil liberties of anyone—citizen, resident, or representative—for the sake of salvaging a failing investigation and a failing department."

Deputy Ron Latham, near the coffee maker, shook his head once. "Hogwash. He doesn't work that way," he said, voice level.

Across from him, Deputy Hartman—newer, loud in the way new sometimes is—snorted. "You weren't there, Ron. None of us were. Maybe the chairwoman knows something."

"The Sheriff doesn't need a reason to warn a driver like Hahn. I've pulled him over myself," Latham said. "It's called doing the job."

"Or it's called harassment," Hartman shot back.

A reporter on the screen called out, "Chairwoman, are you alleging malfeasance and abuse of power by Sheriff Talbird?"

Queen lifted a hand like she orchestrated both question and hush. "I am calling for an independent inquiry into the Sheriff's conduct—specifically his treatment of Representative Hahn, and broadly his pattern of antagonizing federal partners. Our county deserves transparency. It deserves leadership that does not mistake stubbornness for integrity."

Someone in the back whispered, "She's good."

"She's poison," another answered.

Queen leaned into the microphones. "Let me be crystal clear: this is not about politics. This is about protecting our citizens from a Sheriff who thinks he alone decides which laws matter and which do not."

That one landed. KC didn't feel it in his gut so much as he felt the room re-tune itself around the line. Some shoulders squared in anger. Others sank, weary, like they'd just been given permission to doubt the man who signed their evals.

"Questions," Queen said, face ready for the press.

A cascade: "Do you support ICE action in three days?"—"Is Mr. Hahn cooperating with the homicide investigation?"—"Will you seek a recall vote?"

Queen smiled without warmth. "We will cooperate with all lawful processes, including ICE. Representative Hahn has nothing to hide and will work with any impartial inquiry. As for internal personnel issues, that is a matter for the board and for the people who put us here."

The feed cut to the anchor's clean summary. Volume dropped a notch as a few hands fumbled for remotes and then gave up. In the break room, the murmurs rose and hardened.

"That's trash," Latham said, not loud, not quiet.

"Yeah? Or she's finally saying what people are thinking," Hartman answered. "He's been picking fights with everybody. Now it's blowing back."

"Picking fights?" Latham turned. "He's been picking facts. That's different."

"Tell that to the budget," Hartman said. "Tell it to the press out front."

A chair leg scraped; a second voice chimed in—Deputy Cole, eyes fixed on the black screen like it still held answers. "Parsons wouldn't have let this happen," he said.

"Parsons helped make it happen," Latham said evenly.

Hartman stepped closer, heat rising. "Watch your mouth."

"You watch yours."

The shove was shoulder to shoulder, more insult than intent, but it tipped the balance—coffee splashed, chairs scraped, a sharp word cut through the air. Voices jumped, layered—don't—hey—knock it—

"That's enough."

KC didn't raise his voice. He didn't have to. The room stopped like a hand had closed around its throat. Heads turned. Eyes widened. They hadn't realized he was there. Now they did.

He stepped forward two paces, nothing theatrical. "We're not going to finish their work for them in our own break room. You want to argue? You do it after you've read the full case file and learned how to disagree without swinging. Until then, you stand down."

No one moved. He let the quiet hold.

"This uniform," he said, steady as a plumb bob, "doesn't swear loyalty to me or to Chairperson Garrison. It swears to the law. If that's not why you wear it, you come see me and hand it back. Otherwise, you act like it means what it says."

He turned and walked out. No flourish. The scrape of his boots on tile was the only sound for a breath. When he reached the hall, the noise behind him stayed low, chastened and sullen, like a scolded dog still thinking about its teeth.

Back in his office, he shut the door completely and let the latch click settle the room. The blinds cast thin bars across the far wall. He stood for a second, palms on the edge of the desk, then sat. He didn't reach for the TV remote—there wasn't one. He reached for his notebook instead.

A soft knock, then Carlie slipped in and closed the door again behind her. Her jaw was set, eyes worried.

"She's painting you into a corner, Sheriff," she said gently.

"Then we build from the inside out," he said. "She can shape a story in public. We'll make the truth fit in court."

Carlie hesitated. "Some of them are scared," she said. "Some are angry. A few... they just want to be told which way to lean."

"They'll figure out what they believe soon enough," he said. "That part's not my job. My job is the case."

She studied him a second, then nodded once. "Need anything?"

"No, thanks."

She started to go, then paused. "Latham's a good man," she said. "If you were measuring."

"I was," KC said.

The phone rang before the quiet had time to return. Carlie glanced at the display. "Dodd," she said, picked up and handed the receiver to him.

"Talbird," KC said.

"Sheriff." Dodd's voice always sounded like it came through pressed cloth—controlled, careful. Today it carried a scrape. "I assume you saw the show."

"I saw it."

"Pressure hit my office before the cameras cooled," Dodd said. "Queen wants an independent inquiry into your conduct. Formal request lands at 8 a.m. tomorrow at the Board. She's got the votes to open it."

"Of course she does."

A breath on the line, not quite a sigh. "You and I both know this is about the case, not about a traffic stop," Dodd said. "But she's going to make hay while she can. She thinks getting you on your heels keeps her nephew off his."

KC leaned back, the chair giving a small complaint. "She thinks my heels are the weak part."

"Are they?"

"No."

Silence again, the kind that tested where lines were.

Dodd dropped his voice. "I don't have appetite for theatrics. I do have appetite for cases that hold. If you have something real on Hahn, get it to me clean. If you don't, don't bring me a rumor with a badge."

"You'll get facts," KC said. "And you'll get them soon."

"Sheriff," Dodd added, tone flatter, "you're in the crosshairs now."

"I've been there since Maria died," KC said. "Now they're just aiming in public."

"I'll do what I can to keep this tidy," Dodd said. "But tidy is not today's weather."

The line clicked off.

KC set the receiver back in its cradle, the plastic sounding louder than it should have. He sat still, listening to the building—ducts humming, a copier cycling down, footsteps moving past and away. He pulled the notebook close and wrote in his block hand:

Day Four – 5:30 p.m.

— Queen goes public: accuses harassment/retaliation.

— Division inside: break-room fight stopped. Latham steady.

— Dodd pressured: independent inquiry pushed by board; 8 a.m.

— Truth unchanged. Stay the line.

He capped the pen and set it on the open page. For a long beat, he stared at the badge resting on the blotter—metal worn smooth at the edges where habit met duty. He wasn't a man who made speeches to objects. But he did sometimes mark the difference between what men said the job was and what it asked in the quiet.

"Truth first," he said, not loud, not a vow, just a line to step onto.

Outside the window, the last of the day slid west, stretching the shadows long. Somewhere in front of the building, a door opened and closed, voices moved, then thinned. Inside this room, the air steadied. He flipped the notebook shut and let his hands rest on the desk until his pulse slowed to match the quiet he'd have to carry into the next hour.

If she wanted a war in daylight, she would have it.

But daylight cut both ways. It lit the podium and the wash, the courthouse steps, and the quiet map he was building—name by name, choice by choice.

Chapter 42

Lessons at the Table

Day Four – 5:40 p.m.

Mojave County – Apartment Above Della's Delights

The evening light lay warm across the paved lot in front of Della's Delights, the bakery windows already dark—closed since two, as always. The hand-painted DELLA'S DELIGHTS script looked softer with the shades down, the front door latched and the bell quiet. KC parked at the curb, stepped out, and took a second to breathe the faint trace of sugar and yeast that still clung to the air like a remembered song.

He climbed the interior stairs two at a time. From the top landing he could hear Aunt Ruth humming under her breath—one of the old hymns she carried from a different decade—pots clinking gently, a drawer sliding shut. He opened the door and the room met him with warmth: butter and onions, a whisper of apples and cinnamon cooling on the sill.

"Wash your hands, Sheriff," Ruth called from the stove, teasing folded into the order.

"Yes, ma'am," KC said, already moving to the little sink. He hung his hat on the peg by the pantry and caught sight of Karole at the kitchen table, hunched over a lined notebook, pencil hovering mid-air like a bird deciding where to land.

"What are you working on?" KC asked, drying his hands.

Karole glanced up, grinning with a boy's mixture of pride and worry. "It's a story for class—about friendship. I thought it'd be easy, but my teacher says 'be specific, not just nice.'"

KC pulled out the chair beside him and sat. "Specific works."

Karole bit his lip, then read the first few lines. "Friendship is when someone sits with you at lunch and doesn't ditch you when a cooler kid shows up." He snuck a look at his dad, seeking approval.

"That's honest," KC said. "What else?"

Karole tapped the page, thinking. "I wrote: 'Friends listen to you, even when you're not saying much. They don't make fun of the quiet parts.' And 'A good friend helps you—homework, secrets... life stuff.'" He frowned. "I need one more."

"Try the hard one," KC said, voice gentle. "A real friend sticks up for people when it costs something. I don't mean money. They step in when it's easier to step back."

Karole tilted his head, pencils of light from the window making a ladder across his cheek. "Like... if someone's getting pushed around."

"Exactly," KC said. "And you can add: 'A real friend tells the truth—even when it's hard—and keeps his word.' That's how I pick mine, for what it's worth."

"So... honesty, keeping your word, listening, helping, sticking up," Karole said, ticking them off on his fingers. "That's five. My teacher will like that." He scribbled, tongue in the corner of his mouth, then looked up again. "Do you have a lot of friends, Dad?"

KC smiled at the page. "Fewer than I used to. Better than I used to."

From the stove, Aunt Ruth spun her chair, wooden spoon raised like a conductor's baton. "Save philosophy for after supper. Plate up, boys."

The small table took the weight of a full comfort spread: hamburger steaks with caramelized onions and brown gravy, mashed potatoes riding high, sautéed green beans snapping bright, and a loaf of homemade bread cut thick enough to honor butter. On the sill, a cooling apple pie threw off a soft perfume.

KC served Ruth first, then Karole, then himself. The simple rhythm smoothed something in him he hadn't known was bristling. They ate, talked small, and let the day ease off their shoulders. Karole told a sideways joke about his science teacher's pet tarantula; Ruth countered with a story about a county clerk who once stapled her sleeve to a file and pretended she meant to. KC gave the day only in safe slices—"busy," "lots of paper," "people not listening closely enough"—and nobody asked for more.

When the plates were cleared and pie vanished into clean forks and satisfied hums, Ruth wheeled to the side cabinet and set a well-worn deck of cards on the table. "Skyjo," she announced. "House rules: if I win, the two of you do dishes for the next two nights. If either of you wins, you still do dishes, but with less complaining."

Karole laughed.

"High stakes," KC said.

KC dealt the first spread, the colored numbers blinking up like traffic lights. The game moved quick—flips, swaps, that short sting when a card betrayed you. Ruth played with the same quiet ruthlessness she brought to everything worthwhile; Karole played bold; KC played as if he could steady the board through patience. The first round fell to Ruth—she drummed the table once, satisfied. The second, Karole dragged a perfect low row and crowed, "Pay up your rent," echoing her favorite line with a grin that showed all teeth.

"Rent's due on time this month," Ruth returned, eyes dancing.

They ran a short third round that ended in a tie nobody argued about, then Ruth pushed back from the table with a satisfied sigh. "I've proven my superiority. I'm off to rest this superior brain." She touched KC's shoulder as she rolled past. "You look better already."

"Yes," KC said softly. "I am."

Ruth's door clicked shut a minute later, the apartment settling into a cooler quiet. KC rinsed plates while Karole dried, and they fell into the easy rhythm of hand-off and towel. When the counter was clear and the last cup stowed, KC nodded toward the back. "Deck?"

They stepped out onto the upper back deck, where the town fell away and the desert opened clean. No road behind them, no traffic, only the low breath of evening wind over scrub and the mountain line inked blue in the distance. Overhead, the Milky Way arced without apology, a pale river of light that made the rest of the world feel honest again.

Karole leaned on the rail. "I think my story needs a scene," he said. "Not just a list."

"Good instinct," KC said. "What kind of scene?"

"Maybe... a kid sees someone getting shoved, and he sticks up for the other kid, even though he might get shoved too." Karole glanced sideways. "Does that sound too... maybe... like I'm trying to be a hero?"

"It sounds like you're trying to tell the truth about friendship," KC said. "Make it tighter: show the moment he decides. Why doesn't he walk away? And maybe add the quiet afterward—no applause, just a clean inside."

Karole nodded, eyes on the thin bright seam of stars. "My teacher says scenes have consequences."

"They do," KC said. "Good ones do, anyway. A friend who stands up learns something about himself. And sometimes the people around him learn something too."

Karole was quiet a beat. "Some kids at school... they push the same kid a lot."

"You talking about yourself or someone else?"

"Both," Karole said. "But sometimes the teacher catches it—most of the time she doesn't."

KC tilted his head, listening to the night. "You keep doing the right thing. Stand near the kid. Don't throw the first punch—ever. But you don't run from the hard part either. Use your words first, and remember walking away is smart if it keeps people safe." He looked down at his son. "And pray for them, even when it feels unfair. That helps more than you think."

Karole breathed out, a small cloud in the cooling air. "I'll write the scene tonight."

"Good," KC said. "Keep your pencil sharp."

They stood another minute, letting the sky finish something in them that words couldn't. Then KC squeezed Karole's shoulder. "Bed. Say your prayers."

"Yes," Karole said, and slipped back inside.

KC stayed on the deck until the last edge of night filled the mountains. When he went in, the apartment felt like a space held by kind hands. He moved to the small office nook—a narrow desk, a lamp with a warm shade, and the whiteboard he'd claimed for home, lines clean where the office corkboard had grown dangerous.

He uncapped a marker and updated what the day had sharpened:

QUEEN — press control / narrative warfare
AKERS — manipulation ("Rapid Response" conduit)
HAHN — fear + motive; refused voluntary swab
DODD — pressured; neutral posture (for now)

PROOF — DNA route (Toni glass), Maria's phone → HSI assist

He drew a tight triangle from Queen to Akers to Hahn and wrote under it: Containment, not inquiry. Then, beneath everything, he wrote the line that had started to push up through the day's noise: Friends tell the truth when it costs something. He glanced toward the kitchen, thinking of a boy with a pencil and a page to fill.

He wiped his hands absently on his jeans, then reached for his cell phone and scrolled to Dianna Cates.

She answered on the second ring, newsroom clatter faint behind her. "Cates."

"It's Talbird," KC said. "I need you at my office at seven sharp tomorrow. Off the record, for now."

A beat, then: "Seven it is, Sheriff. You bringing coffee?"

"I don't drink coffee," he said. "But there'll be truth."

"That'll do," she said, and hung up with a half-laugh that sounded more like relief than humor.

KC wrote CATES – 7:00 a.m. on the corner of the board, capped the marker, and let the room rest. He checked on Ruth—lights out, a soft rhythmic snore and peace. He checked on Karole—asleep, notebook open on the comforter, a half-sketched scene about a kid and a shove and a decision not to look away. KC slid the notebook onto the nearby table and pulled the blanket straight.

At the living room window, the street below sat quiet and empty, bakery sign bright, the lot a flat, clean slate. The desert wind threaded under the frame and lifted a corner of the curtain, then let it fall.

"Tomorrow we start clean," he said to the stillness—not a promise, not a wish. A plan.

He turned out the lamp. The apartment settled into a finer dark, the kind that made the Milky Way look close enough to touch. Somewhere far off, a single truck sighed over a seam in the highway and kept going. KC stood a moment longer, then went to his own bed with his shoulders set and his breath even, the day stripped down to the one line that always survived the rest:

Truth first.

Chapter 43

The Glass Between Them

Day Four – 9:00 p.m.

Mojave County – The Club

The Club sat on the corner of third and Palm, where the glass was always clean, the music low, and the crowd practiced at pretending they weren't watching one another. The valet stand gleamed under soft amber light. Toni pulled up in her silver RAV4, passed the key to a young man in a pressed vest, and gave the street one last sweep before stepping inside.

The cool from the evening clung to the stone walkway, but the air inside was warm, perfumed faintly with citrus and gin. Conversation drifted like smoke—lawyers, donors, local officials, the kind of people who knew which cameras to smile at. She'd dressed the part: simple black dress, low heels, hair loose, makeup light. Enough to blend in. Enough to be seen without being remembered.

The bar ran the length of one mirrored wall. Hahn was easy to spot—tie loosened, jacket hanging off the stool beside him, the proud fatigue of a man who'd been drinking confidence by the glass. She slid onto a stool one space away, ordered sparkling water with lime, and let the silence settle until it invited attention.

Hahn glanced to see if anyone was going to join her. Seeing no one, he turned slightly. "You here alone?"

Toni smiled, calm, effortless. "Just unwinding after a long day."

"I don't think I've seen you here before. I'm sure I'd remember." A practiced seductive look that didn't seduce.

"It's my first time here. A friend told me it's a good place to unwind."

"Let me be the first to welcome you." He slid to the empty stool between them. "I'm Julian. You are?"

She smiled inviting more but not flirtatious. "I'm Toni. Nice to meet you."

He extended his hand and held hers a beat too long.

"What do you do?" His words were smooth, but the edges of control had begun to fray.

"County government," she said. "And you look like someone who's had a week and a half in three days."

That opened him like a latch. He chuckled, waved for another round. "You could say that. You watch the press conference?"

"Only part of it," she said, keeping her tone curious but light.

He laughed into his drink. "My aunt knows how to handle a microphone. Talbird's finished, mark my words. He can't keep running a county Sheriff's department like it's still the frontier."

"Sounds like politics," she said, letting him talk.

"Politics?" Hahn's smile turned thin. "It's survival. My aunt knows how to keep the wolves at bay. That sheriff—he's not one of us. He doesn't play the game."

Toni let the pause stretch just enough. "Maybe that's why people like him."

He shrugged, looked at her more closely, then lost the thread of suspicion somewhere in the fog of his drink. "You've got opinions for someone in county government."

"I have a few," she said. "What about you? Always busy with politics, or just this kind of week?"

That was all the permission he needed. He started talking—about voters, about fundraising, about how unfair it was to work for good and still get smeared. And he made sure Toni knew how important he was in the state legislature. She nodded, smiled, asked small, harmless questions. He talked louder, laughed harder, and ordered another round. She took measured sips of her water and waited.

When he pushed back his stool, he drained his glass. "Back in a minute," he said, and wove a little toward the hallway at the rear.

Toni waited, counted to three, then lifted the glass, wrapped it neatly in a folded napkin, and slipped it into her purse. The movement was clean, invisible beneath the rhythm of the bar. Her pulse quickened. She kept her breathing steady.

The bartender came over with a fresh drink for Hahn. "Where's his glass?"

"He might've taken it with him," Toni said.

The bartender frowned. "That's strange."

"He's had a few," she said with a shrug.

He hesitated, then set the new drink down and turned away. She slid off her stool and walked out, heels clicking softly against the tile. She didn't look back.

Outside, the night felt cooler, she shivered, but not from the cool breeze. The valet stand was lit by a single overhead bulb that caught the soft shimmer of her dress. She waited, eyes flicking toward the door, every second stretched thin as wire. The valet jogged up in her RAV4, engine quiet, key in hand. She tipped him and slipped into the driver's seat, heart working faster than the car's ignition.

The engine turned once, caught. As she was shifting into gear, the door behind her burst open. Hahn stepped out, scanning the lot. "Hey—wait!"

The valet glanced at her, then back at Hahn. "Don't waste your time, man," he said, half amused. "She's a cop."

Hahn froze. Even at a distance, she could see the color drain from his face, pride and panic colliding behind his eyes.

Toni didn't wait. She pulled out fast, tires crunching over the curb edge as the car shot forward into the dark. The mirror caught one last flash of Hahn standing in the glow of the club's lights, stunned and still.

Two blocks later, she slowed enough to breathe again. The streetlamps blinked past, rhythmic and even. She reached into her purse, pulled the napkin-wrapped glass, and slid it into the pre-labeled evidence sleeve she'd packed in advance. Her handwriting was steady:

Subject: Rep. Julian Hahn

Source: Glass – The Club (20:12 hrs)

Chain of Custody: Dep. T. Salazar

She sealed it, pressed the tape firm, and tucked it into the small cooler on the passenger floor. Her phone buzzed once.

KC: Status?

She typed back: Sample secure.

A few seconds later: Good work. Home safe.

She glanced in the rearview mirror—only ordinary lights now, no pursuit, no danger chasing her down the quiet Mojave street.

"The truth's in the glass," she murmured, and drove on toward home, the night unfolding ahead like something that might finally give answers if she just kept following its line.

Chapter 44

The Queen's Nephew

Day Four – 11:52 p.m.

Mojave County – Chairwoman Garrison's Residence

The gated neighborhood slept in neat precision—lawns squared, porch lights on timers, the desert wind whispering through iron fences. Then the peace broke. Tires squealed against the curb outside Chairwoman Beatrice Garrison's stucco two-story, and a red Porsche fishtailed halfway up the driveway before stopping at an awkward angle.

Julian Hahn stumbled out, his jacket half off one shoulder, his breath sharp with whiskey and panic. He slammed the car door hard enough to wake the street. A motion light snapped on. Curtains in the houses across the cul-de-sac shifted like nervous eyes.

He went straight to the front door and pounded with both fists.

"Beatrice! Open the the door! Now!" He pounded both fists again on the door.

The bedroom lights of the neighbors on both sides came on.

Nothing at first—only the hum of the porch light and the clicking of a nearby flagpole rope in the wind. He hit the door again. "Beatrice! It's Julian! Open up!"

Somewhere behind him, a dog barked. Another porch light blinked on.

Inside, a light flared at the top of the stairs. Then footsteps—measured, deliberate. When the door opened, Queen stood framed in the foyer light, silk robe tied perfectly, expression carved from cold marble.

"Do you have any idea what time it is?" she said.

"Almost too late," Hahn slurred, shoving a hand through his hair. "They got me."

Her tone didn't change. "Who?"

"That cop—some woman. At the Club. She took my glass. My DNA, Aunt Beatrice! My DNA! She's a cop, and she's got it!" His voice cracked on the last word. "I'm finished. You have to fix this!"

Queen's eyes narrowed, but not from surprise. From irritation. "Stop shouting. You're making a spectacle."

"Don't you get it?" Hahn said, stepping closer. "She's going to take it straight to Talbird. They'll test it, and when they do—" He stopped himself, the next words clawing at his throat.

Queen crossed her arms. "When they do what, Julian?"

He stared at her, sweat shining at his temple. "You know exactly what I mean."

Her voice sharpened. "Lower your voice. My neighbors vote."

"Your neighbors are watching already!" he snapped, gesturing wildly toward the windows. "You think they won't figure out what's going on when the sheriff's cars show up at my door?"

"You're drunk," she said. "And you're sloppy."

"I'm desperate!" he shot back. "You're supposed to protect me!"

Queen's gaze went flat. "I protect order. You were supposed to manage yourself."

He blinked, uncomprehending. "You made me. You said we were in this together."

Her lips curved, almost a smile. "I made a candidate. Not a liability."

That landed like a slap. He stepped forward, voice breaking. "You think you can just throw me away? After everything I did for you? For your donors? For this county?"

"I can, and I will," she said, voice icy. "You can't be tied to me if you can't control yourself. You walk down those steps, you're on your own."

He stared, mouth open, the words lost somewhere between fear and rage. "You're not human."

"I'm pragmatic," she said. "Now leave. Before you give the press another story."

When he didn't move, she turned and started to close the door. "Don't come back."

He lunged forward, voice ragged. "You can't do this to me!" he shouted. "You owe me!"

The door closed with a heavy click. The porch light buzzed.

Hahn stood there a moment, chest heaving. Then the anger came in full, raw, and hopeless. He slammed both fists against the door. "You hear me? You don't get to walk away! You owe me!" His voice carried down the quiet street, harsh and broken.

Across the cul-de-sac, a curtain moved. A phone glowed in a window. Then another porch light clicked on, then another, until the whole block looked awake enough to witness the unraveling of a man who'd mistaken privilege for protection.

Hahn kept shouting, pounding the door until the sight of flickering lights curled around the corner. He turned toward the flashing red-and-blues—one Sheriff's cruiser rolling up slow, lights strobing over the manicured hedges. The deputies inside stepped out, their hands resting near their belts but not drawn.

"Sir," one deputy called evenly. "You need to step away from the door."

"She's my aunt!" Hahn barked, half laugh, half sob. "You tell her to open it!"

"Sir," the deputy repeated. "Step away. Now."

The front door stayed shut.

Hahn backed down one step, swaying. The blue lights washed over him—tie loose, shirt untucked, pride gone. "She said she'd fix it," he said softly, voice cracking. "She said she'd fix everything."

The deputy didn't answer. He just waited until Hahn sat down hard on the bottom step, head in his hands.

"Sir, you need to come with us."

Hahn stood, swaying. Each deputy took an arm and escorted him to the their cruiser. A small crowd of neighbors had formed, whispers that rang out loudly.

Behind the windows, the lights upstairs went out one by one until only the porch light remained, burning over the wreckage of Queen's perfect calm and her nephew's collapse.

The night held its breath again, as if trying to forget what it had just seen.

Chapter 45

The Quiet Before Morning

Day Five – 12:40 a.m.

Mojave County – Apartment Above Della's Delights

The phone rang once, then again. KC stirred, half awake, the room still thick with the kind of darkness that feels solid. He reached for the receiver on the nightstand, voice rough with sleep.

"Talbird."

"Sheriff, it's Latham," came the voice on the other end, low and weary. "Sorry to wake you, but we've got Representative Hahn in custody."

KC sat up, rubbed a hand over his face. "What for?"

"Public drunkenness. Disturbing the peace. Neighbors called it in. Happened around midnight."

KC swung his legs to the floor. "Where?"

Latham hesitated just long enough to make the answer matter. "On the porch of Chairwoman Garrison's place."

KC blinked once, the gears in his head turning faster than the clock on the wall. "That so."

"Yes, sir. Says he's her nephew. He was banging on her door, shouting. My unit responded—two of us. She wouldn't open up. Whole neighborhood came out to watch. We brought him in quiet."

KC reached for his notebook on the nightstand and flipped it open to the last page. "He's in holding now?"

"Yes, sir. Sleeping it off, or trying to."

"Anyone else seen him?"

"Just me and Deputy Miller. I ran a double today, short staff. Figured I'd keep an eye on him till morning."

KC nodded into the silence. "Good call."

Latham cleared his throat. "You want us to cut him loose in the morning? Or drive him home?"

"No," KC said. "Keep him right where he is. Don't release, don't book, don't process. Just keep him secure until I get there."

"Yes, sir."

"And Latham—nobody sees him. Not Parsons, not Akers, not anyone from Queen's office. You understand?"

"Yes, Sheriff."

"I'll be in by six-thirty. Stay posted till then."

There was a pause, then Latham said, "Copy that. I'll be here." His tone carried fatigue and something steadier beneath it—loyalty that didn't need applause.

KC hung up, the click echoing small in the dark. For a long moment, he sat still, listening to the hum of the refrigerator below the floor and the desert wind moving against the glass.

He exhaled slowly, a sound that wasn't quite a sigh.

He had the DNA.

He had Hahn in custody.

And, if he read it right, Queen had just locked her own door against the man she'd built.

KC stood, bare feet on the cool floorboards, and walked to the small desk by the kitchen. The lamp cast a thin circle of light across his whiteboard. He uncapped the marker and wrote, block by block:

Hahn — DNA / arrested / abandoned?

Then, beneath it:

Now truth begins to move.

He capped the marker, stepped back, and looked at the line until it settled in his chest.

Through the window, a shooting star floated across the vast sky. The night was dark, but for the first time in days, KC felt like the darkness might finally be on its way out.

Chapter 46
After the Arrest

Day Five – 6:45 a.m.

Mojave County – Sheriff's Office

The morning came pale and thin, the kind that forgets warmth for a while. KC parked out back in his usual spot and sat for a moment with the engine idling. The lot was full—first shift rolling in, third shift grinding to a close. He shut the engine, pocketed his keys, and stepped into the slow hush of the early hour.

Inside, the building felt busy, a quiet buzz filling the locker room and break room. KC caught fragments—the talk about Hahn's detention. The fluorescent lights hummed, seeming to give their own opinions on the matter. Somewhere near the front, a printer cycled through half a page before quitting. KC carried his notebook down the corridor, the soles of his boots whispering against the tile.

He stopped first at holding. Through the narrow window he saw Hahn asleep on the cot, one shoe off, one still on. The man's jacket was draped over the bench, his hair matted. Whatever polish he'd worn to The Club had long since worn off. KC took in the picture silently.

"Morning, Sheriff," said Latham from a chair near the door. His coffee cup steamed, and his face carried the gray fatigue of someone on his second sunrise without sleep.

"Morning," KC said. "How's our guest?"

"Out cold. Asked for water once, mumbled about his lawyer, then passed out again."

KC nodded. "Keep him that way if you can."

"Yes, sir." Latham rubbed the bridge of his nose. "You want me to hang till shift change?"

"Till Deputy Salazar gets in. You've done enough, but I'd rather have eyes I trust till then."

"Yes, sir," Latham said again. No complaint. Just the quiet loyalty that kept small counties standing.

KC clapped his shoulder lightly, then headed down the hall. The air had the familiar smell of floor cleaner and copier toner, that permanent perfume of public service. He unlocked his office, flicked the light on, and set his notebook on the desk. The corkboard behind it was still blank—the whiteboard at home had enough written truth for both.

He barely had time to settle before a sharp knock hit the door. Parsons.

The captain pushed in before permission, jaw tight, voice already in motion. "You holding Hahn here?"

KC didn't look up from his notes. "Morning to you, too, Captain."

"Don't do that," Parsons said. "Don't pretend this is business as usual. Queen's already calling the DA. She wants to know why you've got her nephew locked up like a drunk."

"Because he was," KC said flatly.

"That's not how this works," Parsons snapped. "You can't make this office a political circus."

KC looked up slowly. "Captain Parsons, the circus started when politics got in the way of the truth. I'm just cleaning up after it."

"This'll blow back hard," Parsons warned. "She'll make it about abuse of power, just like she did yesterday."

"I've seen the broadcast," KC said. "And if you're done rehearsing her talking points, you can get to work."

Parsons flushed. "You're playing with your badge, Sheriff."

KC stood, calm steel. "And you're walking on thin ice. Now get out of my office. And, Captain, do not stop at the holding cell. You hear me?"

Parsons hesitated long enough to show the hit had landed—KC was clearly in command—and it was best not to test the ice. He turned and left without another word. The door clicked shut behind him.

KC let the quiet breathe again. He checked his watch—6:59. Right on cue, another knock, lighter this time.

"Come in," he said.

Dianna Cates stepped through, all business and composure. She wore a gray blouse, slacks, and that deliberate neutrality reporters cultivate like armor. A notepad was tucked under her arm, her recorder small and silver in her hand.

"Sheriff," she said. "You said seven sharp."

He gestured to the chair. "Appreciate punctual people."

"I make a living off deadlines," she said, sitting. "You said this was off the record."

"It was," KC said, flipping open his notebook. "Still can be. Depends on what I decide in the next few minutes."

She lifted an eyebrow. "So this is a test?"

"Call it a conversation," KC said. "I'll talk. You listen. Then we decide what belongs on your recorder."

Cates gave a small nod and waited. KC outlined the investigation— broad, clean strokes, no names, no accusations. He described patterns instead: how evidence had been redirected, how resources were pulled to obstruct the investigation, how outside influence shaped procedure. He spoke like a man marking a map, not giving a speech.

Cates took notes quietly. "You're suggesting interference."

"I'm suggesting," KC said, "that justice doesn't move straight in this county."

She leaned forward, the recorder still in hand but off. "Why tell me now, Sheriff? It appears you've been sitting on this since the tragic incident."

KC looked straight at her, his eyes steady. "Because silence lets the wrong story win. I've been chasing facts. Now I have enough to start talking about them."

"That press conference yesterday," she said. "Garrison accused you of harassment, retaliation, and budget manipulation—"

"You've just made my point," KC interrupted. "Politics rules, not truth and justice. She's protecting something or someone."

"And you, Sheriff, are you protecting something or someone?"

"I'm protecting what's left of the truth."

Cates tilted her head. "You realize, off the record or not, I can't print half of this without attribution."

KC thought about that, then closed his notebook. He looked past her, out the window, where sunlight was beginning to show itself through the partially opened blinds. When he spoke again, his voice was measured, deliberate.

"Turn it on," he said.

Her brows rose. "You're sure?"

"Turn it on," KC repeated. "You want a statement. You're getting one—on the record. Just print it straight."

Cates clicked the recorder. The red light came on, and something in the air shifted. KC leaned forward, elbows on the desk, voice low but firm.

"This department doesn't work for politics," he said. "It doesn't bow to campaigns, or donors, or people who think their title makes them untouchable. We work for the law. That means following evidence wherever it leads. Some of that evidence got buried. Some of it's clawing its way back up. But it's coming."

She asked, "You have proof?"

"I've got enough to know I'm standing on solid ground," he said. "And when more comes in, you'll see it."

"Who's responsible?" she pressed.

KC shook his head. "Politicians and their minions. You'll get names when I start making arrests based on solid evidence. Not before."

She paused, studying him. "You know this will paint a target on your back."

"There's already a target there," he said. "Let's see who aims first."

The faintest smile flickered over her face. "You ever consider politics, Sheriff? There's a need for integrity."

"No," KC said. "And every day I'm grateful I don't live in that playground."

Cates nodded, then clicked off the recorder. "That's a quote."

He smiled faintly. "So's most of what I said."

She stood, tucking the recorder into her bag. "I'll run it straight. If you're playing me, you'll hear from me."

"I expect nothing less."

At the door, she paused. "You're betting a lot on people, the voters, still caring about the truth."

KC leaned back in his chair. "I'm betting the truth still cares about people."

She left without another word, her footsteps fading down the hall.

KC sat there for a long moment, the silence holding steady around him. The blinds had caught the sun rising higher, thin gold bars striping the wood floor. He picked up his pen, opened his notebook, and wrote in his square, deliberate hand:

Day Five – 7:40 a.m.

— Parsons confronts; pressure building.

— Cates briefed, on record.

— Hahn in holding, asleep.

— Queen's narrative being challenged.

— Truth ahead of politics.

He set the pen down, exhaled through his nose, his thoughts focusing on Hahn down the hall in holding. Somewhere behind those steel doors, the next piece of the story was waiting to wake up.

He stood, stretched once, and grabbed a Cherry Coke from the small refrigerator in the corner. He stepped in front of the window, letting the rising sun spill through the glass, warming him like something earned.

For the first time in days, KC didn't feel behind the clock.

He felt exactly on time.

Chapter 47

The Sheriff's Story

Day Five – 7:45 a.m.

Mojave County – Sheriff's Office

The door clicked behind Dianna Cates, and the air felt like it had shifted direction. KC stood for a long moment, staring out the window at the gathering crowd. His breath stayed even despite the commotion. The story had left his office. The truth, or at least enough of it to matter, would soon move out into the world.

Protesters were out early—voices carried in rhythm, the kind of sound that swelled with anger but didn't yet know its shape. KC moved back to his desk and sat. He'd seen it before: cardboard signs, a camera truck, frustration dressed as conviction.

A soft knock came at the door. "Come in."

Carlie stepped in, her headset crooked around her neck, hair pulled into a tight bun. "Morning's getting loud," she said. "Protesters out front—more by the minute. Local news is set up by the front steps. And I just saw Cates out there with a cameraman. Looks like she's going live any minute."

KC smiled faintly. "Good."

Carlie blinked. "Good? Sheriff, they're chanting for a recall. They've got signs calling you soft on illegals and others calling you enemy number one. It's chaos."

"Means people are paying attention," KC said. "That's the first step to daylight."

She hesitated, then nodded, a small grin tugging at her mouth. "You talked to Cates, didn't you?"

"I did," KC said. "She's got the story—on record this time."

Carlie let out a breath that was half relief, half disbelief. "So... that's why she's out there. She's going to tell it straight."

"That's the plan," KC said. "Now let's do ours. Bring in Toni when she gets here. And call Trisha. Have her meet me in my office as soon as she clocks in."

Carlie gave a sharp nod and slipped out, the sound of phones ringing and muffled conversation swelling behind her.

KC leaned back in his chair, picked up his notebook, and ran a finger down the last lines from earlier that morning.

— Parsons confronts; pressure building.

— Cates briefed, on record.

— Hahn in holding.

— Truth ahead of politics.

He closed it just as Toni knocked and stepped in.

"Deputy," he greeted.

"Morning, Sheriff." She looked alert, though there was a faint tiredness under her eyes from the night before. "The sample's been dropped at the ME's office. Labeled, sealed, and logged. I asked for preliminary results before day's end. Dr. Nash said he'd do his best, but no promises."

KC nodded, pleased. "Good work. You've progressed quickly."

"Thank you, sir," she said, her voice even but carrying quiet pride.

Before they could say more, another knock. Trisha pushed in, tablet under her arm with eagerness in her eyes. "Carlie said you wanted to see me, Sheriff?"

KC motioned to both women to take seats. He stayed standing, his hand resting on the armrests of his chair.

"Hahn's in custody," he began. "Picked up just before midnight for public drunkenness and disturbing the peace."

Trisha's eyebrows rose. "Didn't see that headline coming."

KC's voice stayed flat. "Neither did he. Apparently, he showed up on Queen's doorstep. She locked him out."

Toni leaned forward, frowning. "That's why he was shouting?"

"He must be awake by now," KC said. "Latham and Miller handled it quiet—no booking, no paperwork. Hahn's been sleeping it off in holding. Until now."

Trisha tapped her tablet. "You want me to process him?"

"Not yet," KC said. "First, relieve Latham—he's been running a double. Transfer Hahn to Interview Room One. Keep him dark. No greeting, no small talk, no explanation. Make sure he's cuffed. If he yells, ignore it."

Trisha nodded. "Copy that. What if Parsons tries to intercede?"

"Leave him to me. And Trisha—thank you for stepping up. We couldn't do this without you."

She gave a quick smile. "Somebody's gotta keep this place functioning."

KC nodded. "That's why I brought you in."

She stood to go, but paused. "Want the recorder running once he's in the room?"

"Absolutely," KC said. "This one's for the record."

When she left, KC turned to Toni. "We'll meet him once Trisha gives the all-clear. Stay calm and quiet. When it registers, he'll see you as the enemy—the person who set him up—and his fear will peak. That's what we want."

Toni nodded slowly. "You think he'll break?"

"Maybe," KC said. "That's my plan."

The door opened again—Carlie, back with updates. "Sheriff, Cates just went live. She's standing in front of the crowd now. Looks like she's going live."

KC tilted his head toward the window. "Good. Let her report."

Carlie frowned. "You trust her? And do you think she'll report the truth for you?"

"She won't do it for me," he said. "She'll do it for the story. And stories have a way of changing when truth walks in."

Carlie looked from him to Toni, reading something in the stillness between them that steadied her nerves. "You want anything before you face him?"

"Cherry Coke," KC said. "Cold."

She nodded. "Should I bring something in for Mr. Hahn?"

"No," KC said without hesitation. "Not yet."

Carlie slipped out again. Through the half-open blinds came the faint echo of the crowd—chants, the heat of public anger breaking against the front steps like surf. KC stood and looked out the window for a long moment, then turned back.

"I want you with me in the room," he told Toni. "Trisha too."

"Yes, sir."

"You'll see where I'm headed soon enough. Just stay calm but stoic—let me lead. He needs to feel the guilt, the weight of what he's facing."

Toni straightened her shoulders. "You're thinking plea?"

"I'm thinking confession," KC said. "He'll be looking for an exit, if I'm successful. Let's make sure it leads to the truth."

The intercom on his desk crackled softly. Trisha's voice came through, steady and composed: "Sheriff, it's ready. Subject's in Interview One. Latham's gone home."

KC pressed the button. "Good work, Trish. We're on our way."

He shut off the intercom and reached for his notebook, sliding it into his inside jacket pocket. "Let's go see how much man is left in the politician."

Toni followed him to the door, and together they stepped into the hallway. The noise from the protests swelled faintly as they passed the reception area, a reminder of the other battle being fought outside these walls. Deputies moved aside for them, quiet but tense, the ring of phones and the hum of dispatch blending into one steady undertone.

At the end of the hall, the narrow glass pane of Interview Room One glowed with fluorescent light. Trisha stood beside the door, tablet in hand, eyes alert. "Everything's live," she said. "Video and audio running."

"Good," KC said. He met her gaze, then Toni's. "Let's get to it."

Toni drew a slow breath. "Ready."

Trisha nodded, resolve firm in her face.

KC gave the faintest smile. "As I mentioned, Toni—stay quiet, calm, and stoic. You too, Trisha."

They nodded in unison.

He pushed open the door and stepped inside. Hahn sat slumped at the table, head in his hands, blinking against the light. KC paused a beat, letting silence do the work.

Outside, the first full chant of the day echoed faintly through the glass: Truth first. Truth first.

KC shut the door behind him and said quietly, "Morning, Representative. Let's talk."

The latch clicked, sealing them in.

And after nearly five days, KC Talbird felt the ground shift toward something that looked a lot like justice.

Chapter 48
Truth and Counsel

Day Five — 8:10 a.m.

Mojave County — Interview Room One

The room smelled of stale whiskey, bad breath, and sweat. Fluorescent light hummed overhead, impartial and bright, catching the thin film of perspiration on Julian Hahn's brow and bleaching the color from his cheeks. He sat slumped at the table, sleeves pushed up, a half-drunk paper cup in front of him. His suit was a rumpled concession to the evening before; the hundred-dollar tie hung loose like a question mark.

KC entered with Toni and Trisha, a half step behind him. The camera in the corner blinked a steady red; Trisha gave the tech a curt nod and the feed rolled. KC set his notebook on the table and chose the chair opposite Hahn with the casual care of a man who knows how to sit so the other man can't hide.

"Representative Hahn," KC said, voice even. "It's 8:11. For the record, is it okay if we start?" He watched the man's face for the small motions that tell a truth.

Hahn blinked. "Start what?"

"Talking," KC said. "About last night, about Maria Sherman, about why you were on Chairwoman Garrison's porch at midnight." He let the weight of the sentence sit there, not a hammer blow but a steady press.

Hahn let out a humorless sound. "You think you've got something?"

"We have a dead woman," KC said without flourish. "We have her body. A young woman whose name you've heard plenty before now." The name—Maria Sherman—fell cleanly into the air. Hahn's jaw clenched, a small, involuntary knot.

"You've got a body," Hahn parried. "That doesn't mean you have anything on me."

KC watched the man's fingers pick at the lip of his cup. "Two months pregnant," he said quietly. "That's a fact from the ME. And you were in contact with Ms. Sherman just days before she was murdered. Those are things that trigger an investigation." He watched the reactions rather than expecting them. "Right now, you're a man in a small room. By the end of the day, we'll have a DNA report and a cell-phone assist from federal partners. Those things make problems hard to walk away from."

Hahn's mouth flattened. "You don't scare me, Sheriff. You can't hold me on a whim."

"We can hold you for forty-eight hours. That's the law. Time began at midnight when you were arrested," KC said. "You can use it to stonewall. Or you can use it to start making sense of what you know. Either way, you've got time. Use it well."

Hahn spat the words out—brittle and sudden. "I want a lawyer."

KC didn't blink. "You will have one. You have that right." His tone stayed flat and factual. "Consider this—cooperation determines how people who make decisions view deal making. If your attorney steps in now and throws up obstacles, then my ability to negotiate and influence the outcome is severely limited. I can't promise anything I don't control. If you elect counsel immediately, the chance to make meaningful practical arrangements through me will evaporate."

Hahn's eyes narrowed. "So what?"

"So you'll lose my support," KC said plainly. "Not my silence. Nor my interference. But if you come clean, early, I can take what you tell me to our partners. That can change how things proceed. Once counsel arrives, the process goes where lawyers push it." KC sat very still. He would not bargain for immunity; Hahn did not deserve that. He could only outline the real mechanics of cooperation and what could result.

Hahn swallowed and looked away. For a moment, he seemed like a man weighing an internal ledger: pride on one side, preservation on the other.

KC let the silence settle. He noticed Toni watching with a careful face—she had seen an interview or two and read reports, but she hadn't seen the small dynamics that just occurred. The way truth slides out of a man when he believes the consequences are worse than silence. KC used stillness as a tool, a technique he wanted her to internalize. Here, she experienced the quiet education of apprenticeship: how he could take the room's temperature and use it like a thermometer.

Hahn shifted. He leaned forward, voice going small. "You have nothing. You've got a dead woman. You've got rumors. You've got a paternity test that's not even in yet. You can't hold me forever." The words were defensive, fast, and weak.

KC traced a finger across the notebook as if marking a line that had been crossed. "You're right about one thing—we can't hold you for murder. Not yet. But we do have a path." He met Hahn's eyes, clear and steady. "A path that will lead to life in prison if not death row."

Hahn's face went stony, then angry. "She—she was always a volunteer. I helped the campaign. People are twisting it."

KC folded his hands. He had no intention of piling accusation; he wanted confession or cooperation. "You said something last night that matters," he said. "You were loud enough to be heard. You said—on the porch—'You know what happened to the last woman who crossed me.'"

Time contracted. Hahn's mouth opened, closed. The laugh that came out was a poor imitation. "I was talking about someone else— when I was a kid. It has nothing to do with Maria."

KC let the possibility hang. "That sounds like a confession of harm to me," he said softly. "If you meant someone else, tell me who. If you meant—" He paused, choosing words like stones to build a bridge. "If you meant harm to Ms. Sherman, say it plainly. If you meant another story, say that plainly. Don't let a slip become the story that ends you."

Hahn's eyes bulged for an instant—the raw fear of a man who had seen how fast a life could be unstitched. "I said something stupid. I was drunk. I didn't mean—" His voice broke. "You don't have anything."

"Maybe," KC said. "Maybe you did. Or maybe not. That's why you're here." He gestured once. "You can use the rest of the clock to decide what you want your later self to remember you for. Talk. Or don't. The law will take its course regardless."

Hahn closed his eyes, a small, animal motion. When he spoke again, his voice was thin and urgent. "I need to be out of here. I want my phone call."

"You'll get your one call," KC said. "It will be recorded and logged. Make it count." He looked at Trisha. "Mark the call and record the number." Trisha nodded, fingers already moving through protocol.

As they stood to leave—routine, by the book—Hahn lunged with half a plea, half a demand. "And if I want counsel—if I call a lawyer, you can't—" He gestured wildly, words tumbling.

KC held up a hand. "Call counsel. That's your right. But understand this: cooperation without counsel allows me to do things for you I might not be able to do once an attorney intervenes. That's the practical truth. Not a threat. A fact."

Hahn's face crumpled in a way that had nothing to do with his hangover. "You don't understand what she can do," he whispered. "She's—" He broke off and hammered his fist on the table. "You don't know who you're tangling with."

KC's voice dropped to a near whisper. "I've got a fair idea. Tell me who she is, or tell me you won't talk. Those are your options."

Hahn's eyes flicked to the glass. "If I start pointing fingers, I want a deal. Not just promises. Real—" He gulped and swallowed back whatever arrangement he imagined. "And I want Dodd at the table."

KC did not smile. "I will talk to Dodd if you can start now by telling us what you know. I can't negotiate without knowledge."

Hahn sagged back into the chair like a man who had grown tired of pretending the world would save him. Or his aunt. KC watched as Hahn grabbed the styrofoam cup and stared into it. He downed it like a shot of whiskey.

KC waited. The silence felt heavy, thick. He watched as Hahn buried his head in his hands, sweat beads dripping from his forehead— the heavy burden of making a life-changing decision.

"I want a lawyer," Hahn said.

"Take him back to holding."

Hahn was cuffed, then escorted out by Toni and Trisha. He shouted as they took him—half threats, half pleas—something about being ruined, something about Queen. As they closed the door behind him, his last words trailed off like a belief that someone would answer.

When the room was empty, KC sat for a long moment. He did not write immediately. The hum of the camera seemed louder. The protest noises through the outer walls were distant but raw—like a reminder that the world outside was still watching.

Finally, he picked up his pen and wrote in careful block letters:

Hahn — DNA pending; arrested (public intox/disturbance); slip: "what happened to the last woman..." Possible confession. Wants a lawyer. Need Dodd.

He placed the pen aside and stood. The stale smells lingered—whiskey, sweat, fear. Outside the hall, someone's coffee carried through the vents, a faint roast that smelled like morning trying to start again.

Inside, the building seemed to hold its breath for what came next.

Chapter 49

The Chairwoman's Visit

Day Five – 11:15 a.m.

Mojave County – Sheriff's Office

The noise from outside rolled through the walls like a pulse — chants, drums, the occasional blast of a bullhorn. The crowd had doubled since dawn. Cardboard signs leaned against the barricades, deputies held the line, and every television in the building seemed to carry the same running headline: TALBIRD UNDER FIRE.

Inside, the hum was constant — phones ringing, printers spitting pages, the faint smell of coffee turning stale in the pot. Carlie's voice cut through it all, steady but strained, as she handled calls at the front desk.

KC sat at his desk, reviewing his notes from the Hahn interview. The lines were firm, the handwriting square: Possible confession—incriminating statement—needs counsel. Forty-eight hours started at midnight.

He'd been in this office long enough to know the rhythm of backlash. Every truth worth telling had an echo, and every echo drew a crowd.

The office door burst open so hard the blinds rattled.

"Sheriff Talbird," Beatrice Garrison barked.

KC didn't flinch.

Chairwoman Garrison — Queen to everyone who'd ever worked under her — swept into the room in a cloud of perfume and rage. Her sunglasses were still on, though she'd come from inside the building. Behind her trailed Leonard Pierce, County Counsel, trim and expressionless in a dark suit, and Valerie Hahn, pale, tired, clutching her purse with both hands.

Carlie was right behind them, flushed and trying to regain control. "Ma'am, you can't just walk into the Sheriff's office unannounced—"

Queen didn't slow down. "Watch me."

KC set down his pen, calm as stone. "Chairwoman. Counselor. Mrs. Hahn."

Queen pointed a finger at him. "You've overstepped your authority. You have my nephew locked in a cell like a criminal. I want him released — now."

KC leaned back slightly, voice even. "Representative Hahn was arrested for public drunkenness and disturbing the peace. He was yelling and pounding on doors in a residential neighborhood at midnight. In fact, your door, Madam Chairwoman. That gives me the right to hold him for forty-eight hours. That clock hasn't expired."

"You're making this political," she snapped. "You're trying to humiliate my family. And me."

"I'm trying to keep order," KC said.

County Counsel Pierce cleared his throat, stepping between them like a referee. "Sheriff, we're formally requesting Representative Hahn's release. There are no pending charges, and continuing to detain him without arraignment could expose the county to liability."

KC nodded once, slowly. "Noted." He looked at Queen. "He's also being held pending review of additional charges."

Queen's voice sharpened. "What additional charges?"

"Statements he made last night," KC said. "On your porch. Heard by neighbors. Those statements are incriminating."

Her chin lifted a fraction. "That's absurd. You have no evidence of his involvement with that girl."

"We'll see," KC said, tone unchanged. "He's on tape. And I did not mention anything about a girl. Are you referring to Maria Sherman?"

County Counsel, sensing her error, intervened before she could say more. "If those statements were recorded during questioning and he requested an attorney, they're inadmissible. You know that, Sheriff."

KC's gaze didn't move. "We'll see."

The silence stretched. Valerie Hahn's fingers tightened on her purse. The sound of chanting seeped through the window — muffled but rhythmic, relentless.

Queen stepped forward, voice rising. "You're bluffing, Sheriff. You have nothing."

KC regarded her calmly. "You sound nervous."

Her eyes flashed. "I am furious that an elected official would weaponize his badge to harass a state representative. You will regret this."

Pierce raised a hand, trying to cool the temperature. "Let's bring this back to process. Sheriff, we request a private meeting with Representative Hahn. I'll accompany his wife and Chairwoman Garrison. We'll need a confidential space."

KC studied the three of them — the lawyer's polish, the wife's trembling composure, the Chairwoman's cold fury — and nodded once. "Fine. I'll make arrangements."

He pressed the intercom. "Carlie, have holding transfer Representative Hahn to the private conference room. Two deputies stationed outside, eyes on the door at all times. No one else enters."

Carlie's voice came back through the speaker. "Yes, Sheriff."

Queen folded her arms. "You're walking on dangerous ground, Sheriff. You won't survive this politically or professionally."

KC rose slowly, letting the weight of his height fill the room. "Then it'll be a short walk."

Her mouth tightened. "Enjoy the view while it lasts." She turned sharply and strode out, the others trailing in her wake. The sound of her heels echoed hard down the hallway until the outer door closed.

Carlie lingered at the doorway, her headset still around her neck. "You want me to log this, Sheriff?"

"Yes," KC said. "Time, names, purpose of visit. Note that two deputies are posted."

She nodded, then added quietly, "Crowd's getting louder. Press vans are setting up across the street."

"Let them," KC said. "Noise doesn't change truth."

Carlie gave a small, uneasy nod and left to file the report.

KC sat back in his chair. The walls hummed faintly with the vibration of chanting outside, a sound like the sea against stone. He reached for his notebook, opened it to a fresh page, and wrote in his clean, square hand:

Queen — protecting or silencing Hahn?

Pierce + wife — damage control or setup?

He paused, looking toward the door she'd stormed through. Her perfume still lingered faintly in the air — something expensive trying to cover the scent of fear.

He stared at the closed door, then allowed himself a quiet breath. "Every queen," he muttered, "knows when her pieces start falling."

He closed the notebook, the sound quiet but final, and leaned back in his chair. Outside, the chants swelled again, as if the whole county were waiting for someone to blink first.

Chapter 50
The Family Meeting

Day Five – 11:30 a.m.

Mojave County – Sheriff's Office (Private Conference Room → Hallway)

The private conference room was all county utility—rectangular table, four chairs, a whiteboard that no one used, blinds drawn against the courtyard light. Two deputies stood outside the door, posted shoulder to jamb. When Leonard Pierce, County Counsel, stepped in with Chairwoman Beatrice Garrison and Valerie Hahn, the deputies uncuffed Julian long enough for the meeting, then closed the door and took their position again.

Hahn looked smaller without the shine of last night. The good suit had wilted, collar askew, eyes red-rimmed. He rubbed the fresh grooves at his wrists and tried to sit in a way that didn't betray the tremor in his hands.

Pierce set a slim legal pad on the table and motioned to the chairs. "Let's keep voices low," he said, the tone of a man who solved problems for a living and disliked theatrics. "This is a privileged consultation."

Queen didn't sit at first. She stood at the head of the table, hands resting lightly on the chair back, jaw set. Control, not comfort. When she finally lowered herself into the seat, it was with the air of a judge, not an aunt.

Valerie took the chair opposite Julian. She'd dressed in haste and dignity—plain blouse, no jewelry, hair pulled back so tightly it made resolve out of bone. She didn't look at him right away.

Pierce opened. "Julian, I need your account of last night and of any contact with Ms. Sherman. Facts only. Then we can discuss what happens next."

Hahn tried a smile that failed halfway. "What happens next is you get me out of here."

Queen's head tilted the smallest degree. "You put yourself here."

He flinched at the voice more than the words. "Aunt—"

"Don't," she said, the single syllable flat as a gavel. "Not in this room."

Pierce held up a hand. "One at a time." He turned to Hahn. "Start with midnight. The porch."

Hahn swallowed. "I drove over after... after The Club. I needed help." He risked a glance at Queen. "I told her that a cop—some woman—took my glass. I told her—"

"You shouted," Queen said. "You pounded on my door and woke an entire block."

"I was scared," he shot back, the veneer cracking. "They're coming after me. He pulled me over in the street like I'm nobody. Now his deputy has my DNA."

Valerie's eyes lifted. Quiet, sharp. "Then why were you talking to her in a bar, Julian?"

"I wasn't—" He broke off. "I was minding my business."

Queen leaned in, voice low and controlled. "Your 'business' has now made me look inept. That is intolerable." She enunciated the last word like a verdict.

Pierce interjected before Hahn could answer. "Let's leave optics aside. Julian, did you make any statements on that porch that could be interpreted as a threat?"

Hahn blinked, dragged a hand down his face. "I don't remember exactly what I said. I was upset."

Valerie let out a small, disbelieving breath that was not quite a laugh. "You mean you said something reckless."

Pierce tapped his pen once. "Neighbors heard you. The Sheriff will argue that those statements are incriminating. Whether they're admissible is another question, but the sound bites alone cause damage."

Queen's gaze never left Julian. "You didn't just damage your image. You damaged mine. You dragged my door into it. You dragged my neighborhood into it. You have blown years of work in a single week."

He stared at her, incredulous. "Your image? I could go to prison."

"Your future was my project," she replied, almost clinically. "I built the scaffold. You set it on fire."

Valerie's voice found its place, steady and clean. "He set our marriage on fire first."

All three turned to her.

She folded her hands so tightly her knuckles paled. "I'm done, Julian. With the lies. With the late nights. With the girls who 'believe in the campaign.' I've been humiliated enough."

Color rose up his neck. "You have no idea what pressure I'm under."

"I had an idea for years," she said, not raising her voice. "I just stopped pretending it made you decent."

Hahn's jaw worked. "You think I wanted any of this? I married you because—" He broke off, then plowed ahead, anger choosing the path. "Because Aunt—" he caught himself, swallowed, amended clumsily, "—because she told me it would stabilize donors. 'Family man,' remember? It was never about us."

Queen didn't blink. "I advised optics. You chose appetites."

Pierce's pen clicked once. "Enough." He looked at Julian. "Listen carefully. Right now you're being held on misdemeanors. The Sheriff is signaling something more serious may be coming tied to Ms.

Sherman. If there is a paternity confirmation, the calculus changes—legally and publicly. You need to decide whether to invoke counsel formally and say nothing further, or to cooperate with the Sheriff in hopes of negotiation."

"Negotiate what?" Valerie asked, still watching her husband like a patient watching a storm track. "What are you going to bargain with?"

Hahn's eyes flicked to each of them, then down to his hands. Sweat stood on his brow that had nothing to do with the stale air. "You told me you'd fix things," he said to Queen, voice small now, a boy's voice trapped in a man's mouth.

"I fix order," she said. "I protect stability. You are neither."

It landed slower this time—less a slap than a closing door.

Hahn stared at the table, the thin wood grain suddenly fascinating. "So that's it," he whispered. "You're done."

Pierce leaned forward, gentling his tone the way you do when the facts take one shape only. "Julian, I can request release on my authority, but the Sheriff is within his forty-eight hours. If a new charge is filed, that clock restarts. My advice—say nothing substantive without me present, and decide whether your best interest is to cooperate. But my advice only matters if you follow it."

Valerie stood. "My advice," she said, "do whatever you're going to do. You always follow your own advice, anyway. Good luck with that." She looked to Pierce. "I'll be calling my own attorney. Today."

"Valerie—" he began.

"No," she said, final as a bolt on a door. "I'm not staying for the next headline."

She pushed her chair back, the legs rasping against tile, and moved to the door. She paused with her hand on the knob, eyes never softening. "You wanted power more than a family, Julian. You got the power. Now live with it."

She left.

Silence took the room for a beat that felt longer than the second hand allowed. Out in the corridor, voices moved, a phone rang, the chant outside swelled and thinned. Inside, the air seemed to thicken.

Hahn looked at Queen one last time. "You'll regret this," he said, but the words carried no teeth.

"No," she replied, rising. "You will." She smoothed the sleeve of her jacket. "Sheriff Talbird has chosen a fight. You chose to hand him a weapon." She glanced at Pierce. "Counselor."

Pierce gathered his pad, stood. "I'll speak with the Sheriff about next steps."

Queen reached the door, paused, and without turning added, "You are finished in politics, Julian. Do not make the mistake of thinking you can trade your way back."

She opened the door and stepped out. Pierce followed. The deputies reappeared immediately, professional and impersonal. One of them—Ramirez—gestured. "Hands."

The cuffs clicked back around Hahn's wrists. He didn't protest; he didn't have anything left to protest with. Sweat had pooled at his collar. He drew one breath as if it might be his last easy one for a while, then nodded toward the hall. "Let's go."

They walked him out between them, a quiet march down a corridor that had seen worse and better in equal measure.

KC was at Carlie's desk when they came through—Queen first, then Pierce, both moving fast and not seeing anyone. The scent of Queen's perfume trailed behind her like a papered-over crack. They didn't look at KC, didn't speak. Their silence was louder than a threat.

A beat later, Hahn came down the hall between the deputies, cuffed, head down. His shirt clung damp to his back. The fight that had animated him for years—donor dinners, bright lights, easy applause—had drained out somewhere between the conference table and the door.

Carlie glanced up at KC. "Log their exit?"

"Already done," he said. "But, yes, log it in the record."

They watched the holding door swing open, swallow Hahn, and close with the hollow metal sound that feels colder than it needs to. The echo ran a few feet down the hall and faded.

KC opened his notebook on the counter, his square hand steady:

Queen—cut him loose. Fear visible. Confession close.

Pierce—process over rescue.

Valerie—done.

He tapped the nib once against the margin, then added one more line:

When protection fails, truth follows.

He folded the notebook shut and tucked it under his arm. Outside, the chanting pitched up again, waves against stone. Inside, the corridor felt suddenly cooler, the kind of quiet that comes when a wheel finally starts to turn the other way.

"It's turning," he said softly.

Carlie didn't ask what he meant. She heard it too—the hinge somewhere in the day, creaking toward something that sounded a lot like consequence.

Chapter 51
The Fifth Day Crowd

Day Five – 12:30 p.m.

Mojave County – Sheriff's Office, KC's Office

The noise outside hadn't stopped since dawn.

It came in waves—chants, drums, the distant crackle of a bullhorn turning words into static. Through the blinds, KC could see the edges of the crowd spilling across the courthouse lawn. Signs bobbed in rhythm with the noise, camera crews huddled by their vans, and a handful of deputies held the barricades steady.

Inside, the air carried a different rhythm—phones ringing, keyboards tapping, printers whining, the faint smell of burnt coffee hanging in the corners. Carlie's voice rose now and then from the front desk, even and firm, keeping order where order still held.

KC watched the muted television on the wall.

The headline scrolled in bright red:

QUEEN CALLS FOR INVESTIGATION INTO SHERIFF TALBIRD.

He didn't need the sound. The picture said enough. Beatrice Garrison stood at the top of the courthouse steps, the flag angled perfectly behind her. The posture was practiced, the expression deliberate. Parsons hovered at her shoulder, chin lifted, hands clasped—the loyal soldier following his general into whatever storm she created.

KC switched the screen off. The office fell quiet again, but the echo of her face lingered in the glass reflection.

The phone buzzed once. He picked up.

"Talbird."

"KC? It's Jodi."

Her voice was calm but tight, threaded with frustration.

He leaned back in his chair. "Hey."

"I just watched her," Jodi said. "Your favorite chairwoman is out there claiming you're abusing power, retaliating because she cut your budget, and that she's demanding a special counsel to investigate you."

KC exhaled through his nose. "She's playing her part."

"She's playing it well," Jodi countered. "Every network's running it. Even the local anchors look like they're buying it. Are you okay?"

"I'm fine."

"Fine," she repeated. "That your public statement or the truth?"

He smiled faintly. "Somewhere in between."

Jodi sighed, and he could hear her moving papers on the other end. "They've put it on the board agenda for tomorrow. Motion to appoint special counsel. They'll vote on it first thing in the morning."

KC's tone didn't waver. "Politics eats its own. They'll gnaw on me awhile, then find someone new to chew."

"You always act like none of this gets to you."

"I've just learned not to bleed in public."

That quieted her. When she spoke again, her voice was softer. "You don't have to do this alone, KC."

He looked toward the window. The sunlight fell through the blinds in narrow stripes across his desk, cutting through the faint dust hanging in the air. "I've been alone in worse rooms," he said quietly.

"That's not an answer."

He smiled again, though she couldn't see it. "No, it's not."

A pause settled—long enough to shift from tension to something closer to understanding.

Then Jodi said, "Come to dinner tonight. My place. Seven o'clock.

You need a night without a badge."

KC hesitated only for form. "You sure that's a good idea?"

"I wouldn't offer if it wasn't."

"I'd like that," he said—too quickly.

She caught it. He could hear the smile in her voice. "Seven, then. And bring that calm voice of yours—I think my nerves need it."

"I'll do my best."

"KC?"

"Yes?"

"Don't let her get to you. She's loud because she's scared."

He almost said so am I, but didn't. "See you at seven."

When the line went dead, the noise outside still pulsed, but the air in the room felt lighter. KC sat for a long moment, listening to the hum of the building. Then he flipped open his notebook and wrote, neat and square:

Queen – protecting self or Hahn?

Jodi – possible light.

He tapped the pen once, then set it down.

Outside, the chants rose again—less united now, more scattered, like anger losing its rhythm. KC stood, walked to the window, and watched as sunlight flashed off camera lenses and the movement of signs.

For the first time in days, the noise didn't feel like opposition. It felt like the ground shifting.

"Maybe," he said softly, "truth's starting to get noisy."

He let the blinds fall halfway, dimming the light, and turned back toward his desk. The chants faded to a low, steady hum—the sound of a county waking up to something bigger than politics.

KC sat, steady again, and reached for his notebook.

There was still work to do.

Chapter 52
Proof of Blood

Day Five – 2:09 p.m.

Mojave County – Sheriff's Office (KC's Office)

The air in the building had gone still, the kind of desert stillness that comes when afternoon settles in and nothing moves unless it has to. Outside, the protest rhythm carried steady across the square—chanting voices, the low drone of reporters filling the gaps.

KC sat at his desk, reviewing his notes from the Hahn interview when the phone rang. He checked the caller ID: Dr. Ram – County Medical Examiner.

He lifted the receiver. "Talbird."

"Sheriff, it's Ram," came the voice—measured, professional, but with a hint of tension beneath it. "You have a minute?"

KC leaned back. "Sure. Go ahead."

"The paternity results came back. It's conclusive—Representative Hahn is the father."

KC let that sit for a moment, absorbing it more as confirmation than surprise. "Understood."

"There's something else," Ram said. "Chairwoman Garrison called me not long ago. She wanted the results—said she was entitled as County Chair."

KC's tone hardened. "And you gave them to her."

"I had no choice," Ram said quietly. "Technically, my office reports to the county. She asked that the results not be released to your office until she'd reviewed them. I told her that wasn't how it works."

"Good," KC said. "You followed procedure."

"She wasn't pleased," Ram went on. "Implied I might want to think about job security. I told her I'm a doctor, not a campaign worker. There's always somewhere else to practice."

KC nodded to himself. "I appreciate you telling me. You did right."

"I thought you should hear it straight from me. She's rattled, Sheriff. Whatever's behind this—she's worried."

"Thanks, Ram," KC said. "I'll take it from here."

Ram's tone softened. "Be careful. This isn't just politics anymore."

The line went quiet, then clicked off.

KC set the receiver down slowly and stared at the phone for a long moment. He could almost hear the faint ring of pressure behind the silence, like a wire pulled tight.

He opened his notebook and wrote in his clean, square hand:

2:09 p.m. – Dr. Ram confirmed: Hahn = father.

Queen aware. Tried to suppress release.

He underlined once, then closed the book halfway, thumb marking the page.

A light knock at the door. Carlie leaned in, headset hanging loose around her neck. "Everything okay, Sheriff?"

He looked up. "For now."

"Press is still camped out front," she said. "Crowd's holding steady. Nothing new."

KC nodded once. "That's fine. Let them talk. We've got work to do."

She hesitated, reading his face. "You look like you've got a plan."

"I do," he said, reaching for his pen. "Next move's Hahn."

Carlie gave a short nod and stepped out, closing the door softly behind her.

KC sat a moment longer, letting the quiet of the office settle back around him. Then he opened the notebook again and wrote a single final line beneath the others:

Next move — Hahn confrontation.

He closed the cover, slipped it into his pocket, and looked toward the window where the dull afternoon light stretched across the square. The noise outside went on, but KC's focus had narrowed to one point—the interview room down the hall and the man waiting inside it.

"Time to finish this part," he said softly, and rose from his chair.

Chapter 53

Fifteen Hours

Day Five – 3:05 p.m.

Mojave County – Sheriff's Office (Interview Room One)

By midafternoon, the light through the narrow windows had turned amber—autumn sun stretched thin across the desert, more glare than warmth. The air inside the sheriff's office had gone flat, dry, a faint metallic tang clinging to the hallways.

KC walked the length of the corridor toward Interview Room One, his boots quiet on the tile. The hum of conversation and distant chanting from outside faded the closer he got. He paused once by the holding area, where Deputy Ramirez stood guard, alert but calm.

"Is he ready?" KC asked.

Ramirez nodded. "He's awake, Sheriff. Pacing like a caged cat."

"Let's move him."

Hahn was brought in, wrists cuffed in front this time, the marks from the earlier restraints faintly visible. He looked worse than that morning—paler, eyes bloodshot, jaw tight with the dull ache of a hangover and a night spent without sleep. His tie was gone, collar wilted, hair uncombed.

The deputies sat him down. KC waited until the door closed behind them, the latch clicking into the kind of silence that has its own pulse.

"Representative," KC said evenly, taking the chair across the table. "How's your day going?"

Hahn let out a bitter half laugh. "You're enjoying this."

"Not especially," KC said. "I'm enjoying progress."

Hahn rubbed his wrists. "You've had me locked in a room for almost fifteen hours. I know my rights. You can't—"

"I'm within forty-eight," KC interrupted, voice calm but firm. "You were arrested at midnight. You know how the law works."

Hahn glared. "So what is this, another fishing trip?"

"No," KC said, sliding a folder onto the table. "This is the part where truth starts to surface."

Hahn's eyes flicked to the folder that sat on the table in front of KC. "You don't have anything."

KC leaned forward slightly. "Dr. Ram called me about an hour ago. The paternity results came back. Maria Sherman was carrying your child."

Hahn went still, the color draining out of his face. "That's—" He tried for composure, failed halfway. "You can't prove that."

KC didn't blink. "It's conclusive. And the Chairwoman knows it too. The report was shared with her office as well."

That landed. Hahn's breath hitched, shoulders slumping as if the floor had shifted beneath him. "She—she knows?"

KC nodded. "And based on her visit earlier, I'd say she's not coming to your rescue."

Hahn's mouth worked, no sound at first. Then came a thin, furious whisper. "She told me to keep my head down. That she'd handle it."

"Maybe she changed her mind," KC said. "Maybe you're the piece she decided to sacrifice."

He waited, letting silence do its work. Outside, the faint pulse of chanting threaded through the walls like a reminder that the world was watching even if they couldn't see.

Hahn rubbed his temples. "She built everything. My campaign, the donors, the press... she said I'd be protected."

"Looks like protection is running out."

Hahn slammed a hand against the table, a burst of sound too quick for control. "You don't get it! She doesn't forgive. You think she'll let this ruin her?"

KC met his eyes. "I think she already decided who's taking the fall."

That quieted him. His jaw clenched; he swallowed hard. Fear had started to show itself, stripped of the arrogance that usually masked it.

KC opened the folder slowly. Inside, a copy of the lab summary, the photo of Maria, the chain-of-custody slip with Toni's handwriting. He set the photo on the table—Maria smiling, her badge from a community fundraiser still clipped to her shirt.

"You cared about her?" KC asked.

Hahn's gaze flicked to the image, then away. "She was... she wanted too much."

"She wanted honesty."

"She wanted a future with the baby," Hahn said bitterly. "I told her that wouldn't work. She didn't listen."

KC's eyes narrowed. "That sounds like a confession is coming, Representative."

Hahn shot back, voice breaking, "I didn't kill her!"

KC stayed still, quiet. "Then who did?"

Hahn's eyes darted toward the glass panel as though he could see through it. "You wouldn't believe me."

"Try me."

"She told me she was pregnant. I panicked. I told someone. They said they'd take care of it."

KC's tone hardened. "Who?"

Hahn looked away, sweat standing on his forehead now. "You don't understand how this works. You think this county runs on justice. It runs on loyalty."

"I understand loyalty," KC said. "I just don't confuse it with fear."

Hahn's laugh was sharp and desperate. "You think you're immune? You go after her, and you'll end up like—" He caught himself, shut his mouth, shook his head.

"Like who?" KC asked quietly.

Hahn's hands trembled. "You wouldn't believe me," he whispered again.

KC folded his hands on the table. "You're running out of chances, Julian. You've got two paths: lawyer up and let your aunt bury you, or tell me what you know and start saving yourself."

Hahn looked up, eyes glassy but calculating. "If I talk, I want a deal."

KC didn't move. "That's not mine to give. But if I take your statement to Dodd and you've given me truth, you'll have leverage. If you wait until your lawyer shows, that leverage disappears."

Hahn sat back, voice raw. "You promise me he'll listen?"

"I promise I'll call him," KC said. "And I'll tell him you're ready to talk. That's all I can do."

Hahn nodded slowly, a man measuring the edge of a cliff. "Fine. Call him."

KC stood. "I'll make the call. You sit tight. Don't say a word to anyone else."

As he reached the door, Hahn spoke again, low and hollow. "You don't know what she's capable of, Sheriff."

KC turned. "I'm starting to."

He stepped out into the hallway, closed the door behind him, and exhaled once. The noise from outside felt sharper now, the day heavier.

He walked back to his office, picked up the phone, and dialed Dodd's direct line.

The DA answered on the second ring. "Talbird."

KC's tone was clipped but steady. "Hahn wants to make a deal. I told him you'd want to hear it firsthand."

Dodd was quiet a beat, then said, "I'll be there at five. Let him sit with it a while."

"Understood."

KC hung up, opened his notebook, and wrote:

3:42 p.m. — Hahn confirmed fear, betrayal, named Queen without saying it. Wants deal. Dodd coming 5:00.

He drew a short line beneath it, then closed the book.

Outside the window, the square had gone almost golden, sunlight slanting against the courthouse dome and the cluster of news vans. The desert day was nearing its turn to evening, and inside the sheriff's office, the pressure of truth was building.

KC stood, slid the notebook into his pocket, and whispered, "Time's catching up to all of us."

Chapter 54

Loss of Command

Day Five – 4:12 p.m.

Mojave County – County Administrative Building (Chairwoman's Office)

By late afternoon the light had turned copper against the courthouse square, the same color as the dust that rose from the parking lot when the wind kicked. From the wide windows of the County Administrative Building, the protest banners below looked like scraps of fabric caught in slow motion.

Inside, the air-conditioning hummed quietly but couldn't quite push back the warmth that had settled through the walls. The Chairwoman's office—orderly, perfumed faintly with lavender polish—was a fortress of control. Every pen aligned, every paper squared to the edge of her desk.

Beatrice "Queen" Garrison sat behind it, still in her pale jacket from the morning's confrontation at the Sheriff's Office. Her expression was fixed, unreadable, but the rhythm of her fingers against the desktop betrayed her: an unconscious metronome of irritation and calculation.

On the edge of her desk lay a thin manila envelope, the one that had arrived from the Medical Examiner's office an hour earlier. She hadn't opened it immediately. She hadn't needed to. She already knew. When she finally slit it open with her letter knife, the words on the report were concise, clinical, and fatal:

Paternity: Positive – Representative Julian Hahn.

The confirmation sat like a stone in her stomach.

She leaned back in her chair, eyes fixed on the ceiling molding, her thoughts working the way they always had—fast, precise, without mercy. Damage assessment. Narrative control. The game she'd played for decades.

He had ruined everything. The fool. She had spent years cultivating power in a county that could barely hold itself together. And now, because of his weakness—his recklessness—everything she'd built was sliding toward exposure.

The phone rang—two sharp tones, the direct line, the one only a handful of people ever used.

She stared at it for a moment, then lifted the receiver. "Garrison."

A pause. Then a man's voice, low, even, distorted slightly by distance or intention. "It's done. He's talking. Sheriff called the DA."

Queen's fingers tightened around the receiver. "Are you sure?"

Another pause, deliberate. "Yeah, I am. Thought you'd want to know before the evening news does. He's making a deal."

For the first time all day, her composure wavered. The pulse in her throat quickened. "You're positive this is confirmed?"

"Yeah, I'm positive. I know how the DA and the Sheriff's office move when they smell blood." The voice was irritated, but unhurried. "Your nephew's about to trade family for freedom."

She pressed her thumb against the desk edge until it went white. "That's impossible."

"It's happening."

Silence expanded between them—the kind that carried too much meaning to fill with words.

When she spoke again, her tone was different—still measured, still cool, but the edges had softened in that dangerous way that meant her mind was already moving ahead. "Then you know what to do."

A beat of silence on the line. "You sure?"

"I said take care of it," she replied, each word clipped, almost clinical. "I don't want to hear details. I want results."

The voice gave a short nod of sound. "Understood."

The line went dead.

Queen held the receiver for a moment longer before setting it down, perfectly, back in its cradle. Her pulse had steadied again, but her mouth was dry.

For the first time in years, she realized she didn't know how far her control still reached—or how exactly this news would roll out. It felt strange.

She rose and crossed to the window. From up here, the square looked small, almost peaceful. Protesters still clustered near the Sheriff's Office steps. The TV crews were breaking down some of their gear, the early light fading to the gray-gold of desert evening. She could see the reflection of her own face in the glass—composed, painted, but tired around the eyes.

"You brought this on yourself," she murmured, but it wasn't clear if she meant Hahn or herself.

Her phone buzzed once—a text alert from the County Administrator's office.

Special Counsel Appointment – Board Agenda 10:00 a.m. Tomorrow.

She stared at it, lips pressed into a line. Tomorrow, the fight would be public. "At least I still control them," she muttered to herself.

She turned from the window, the lavender scent seeming suddenly sharp. On her desk, the medical examiner's report still lay open, its edges fluttering faintly in the draft from the vent. She reached for it, folded it once, and slipped it into the bottom drawer of her desk. Then she locked the drawer, the click loud in the otherwise silent room.

For a long time, she simply stood there, one hand resting on the desk edge, staring at the locked drawer as if it might open itself.

Outside, the desert light began to thin. A single helicopter moved across the horizon, its blades chopping faintly through the air like a distant heartbeat.

Queen exhaled once, quietly. The breath sounded like surrender—but only to someone who didn't know her.

To her, it was just calculation resetting itself.

She turned off the desk lamp and let the office fall half-dark.

Tomorrow would come, and she would be rea

Chapter 55
Suspension Order

Day Five – 4:50 p.m.

Mojave County – Sheriff's Office

The afternoon had thinned to its late light—amber sliding through the windows, shadows stretching long across the walls. The heat outside had lost its edge, and the air inside the sheriff's office had taken on that dry stillness that came before evening.

KC sat behind his desk, sleeves rolled once, reading through his notebook spread open in front of him. He examined every entry—times, statements, thoughts. Earlier that afternoon, he had assigned Toni to make sure the case journal was updated. No gaps, no loose edges. That was how you kept a case from slipping through the cracks once the lawyers got involved. He made a brief note, squared the pen, and let his eyes rest on the clock: 4:50 p.m.

The phone rang.

He checked the caller ID—E. McKean—and lifted the receiver.

"Elijah."

"Hey, Sheriff," came the voice, low and even, but with fatigue tucked beneath it. "Got a minute?"

"For you? Always," KC said. "Tell me."

"I pulled what strings I could on Maria Sherman's phone trace," Elijah said. "But it flagged internal systems. Somebody higher up noticed. They're calling it unauthorized database access. I'm suspended pending review."

KC didn't answer right away. "You were doing your job," he said finally.

"True," Elijah said, half a laugh without humor. "I told them that. Didn't change much. Guess truth still isn't a line item they fund."

KC leaned back. "What's next?"

"I think I'm done," Elijah said quietly. "Even if they clear me, I'm retiring. My wife's been saying it for a year. Might be time to listen."

KC's voice softened. "You ever think about staying in the game, just closer to the ground? We could use someone with your experience."

Elijah was silent a beat. "You mean Mojave County?"

"I mean somewhere where it still matters," KC said.

"I'll talk to my wife," Elijah replied. "That's a drastic change. But I'll think on it."

KC nodded, though the man couldn't see it. "You'd fit here. Keep me posted."

"I will," Elijah said. "And, KC—watch your back. This thing's kicking up dust in more than one place."

"Always do," KC replied, and the line went dead.

He sat there for a moment, phone still in hand, listening to the hum of the building. Then he set it down and wrote in his neat, square hand:

Elijah suspended — internal investigation. Tried to help. Possible recruit.

KC rose, stretched the stiffness from his shoulders, and walked down the hall. The air smelled faintly of printer toner and old paper—as usual. He found Trisha in the evidence room, cataloging sealed bags under the fluorescent lights.

"Elijah McKean's out. He had no luck with Maria's phone," he said. "They hit him for trying to trace it."

Trisha looked up from her clipboard, frowning. "He's the Homeland guy, right?"

"Was," KC said. "Seems doing the right thing gets you written up now."

She shook her head, exhaling through her nose. "That's backwards."

"Yes," KC said quietly. "Seems to be the trend."

Back in his office, KC picked up the phone again and dialed Toni. She answered on the second ring.

"Deputy Salazar."

"Toni, it's me," he said. "How's the case journal coming?"

"Up to date through this morning," she replied. "I added the Hahn interview transcript, ME notes, and timeline updates. I'll finish today's entries once we meet with Dodd."

"Good," KC said. "Keep it current. It's going to matter soon. I'll have Carlie give you the ME report. Hahn's the father."

"Yes, sir," she said. "I'm not surprised."

"Inevitable." He paused, shifting the weight in his voice. "I need you to pick up Rosa Alvarez and her son. Take them to St. Mary's. Father Frank knows they're coming. He'll make sure they have a place for the night."

"Sanctuary?" Toni asked softly.

"That's right," KC said. "It'll buy them some time before ICE gets here in the morning."

Toni was silent a moment, then said, "Understood. I'll take care of it."

"After that," KC continued, "come back here and pick up Luis. I'm releasing him for the night so he can be with his mom and brother."

Toni hesitated. "That's—kind, Sheriff. Not what most would do."

KC's tone stayed even. "He's earned a few hours of peace. So have they."

"Yes, sir," she said. "I'll handle it."

He ended the call, the quiet settling around him again. He opened his notebook and added a line:

Luis – release tonight. Rosa + son to St. Mary's. Family together before dawn.

The intercom buzzed. Carlie's voice came through. "Sheriff, DA Dodd just called. He's running late."

KC glanced at the clock—five minutes to five. "What's keeping him?"

"He said he got delayed at the Administrative Building," Carlie replied, though they both knew what that meant.

"Queen," KC said. "She's leaning on him."

Carlie hesitated. "You think he'll cave?"

KC's answer was simple. "Depends if he remembers who he works for."

"I'll let you know when he gets here," Carlie said.

"Thanks, Carlie," KC replied. "Get the interview room ready."

"Yes, Sheriff." The line clicked off.

KC leaned back, folded his hands behind his head, and looked out the window. The square was bathed in fading gold, the courthouse dome reflecting the last of the day. The protest crowd had thinned to scattered clusters of signs and small groups still chanting half-heartedly. The hum of news vans drifted faintly through the glass.

He reached for his notebook, flipped to the last page, and wrote:

4:50 p.m. – Dodd delayed. Queen's interference likely. Calm before storm.

He closed the book, the sound soft but final.

Outside, the desert light was slipping into amber twilight. The quiet inside the office felt like the pause before thunder—steady, waiting, inevitable.

KC glanced once more at the clock, then toward the hallway that led to Interview Room One.

"Everything's about to move," he said softly, and rose from his chair.

Outside, the first siren of evening wailed somewhere distant, thin and rising—a reminder that nothing stays still for long.

Chapter 56
Under Authority

Day Five – 5:21 p.m.

Mojave County – Sheriff's Office

The day was giving up its color.

By early evening, the last light over the square had gone amber-gray, casting long shadows across the windows of the Sheriff's Office. The protest crowd had thinned to small clusters along the barricades—voices low now, tired but still simmering. The courthouse dome glowed faintly in the distance, and across the square, the lights in the County Administrative Building had already come on.

Inside, the hum of the building had softened to an expectant quiet. Paperwork rustled. Phones clicked. And from the front reception desk, Carlie caught sight of District Attorney Dodd stepping through the glass doors, five minutes late and looking like he'd rather call it early.

"Evening, Carlie," Dodd said, giving her a practiced half-smile.

"Evening, Mr. Dodd," she said. Her tone was polite, but the edge of irritation was there. "Sheriff's been waiting."

"I'm sure he has." He adjusted his tie as if it could smooth out lateness. "You know how these political meetings go."

Carlie's eyes didn't move from him. "We've had our share of those around here." She gestured toward the door. "He's in his office."

Dodd gave a courteous nod and made his way to the office door. His shoes echoed against the tile—a sound too confident for someone already running behind.

KC was standing when Dodd entered. His notebook was open on the desk, the pages marked with square, neat lines of ink. The expression on his face didn't shift.

"You're late," KC said evenly.

Dodd closed the door behind him and gave that politician's shrug—half apology, half excuse. "Chairwoman Garrison wanted a word. You know how she is."

KC leaned against the edge of his desk, arms crossed. "Interference. That's what we used to call it."

"She's still the County Chair," Dodd replied, voice mild. "We answer to her for budgets and staffing. I'm sure you've noticed the trend."

"I noticed," KC said. "Doesn't make it right."

Dodd smiled thinly. "Right doesn't always keep the lights on."

KC didn't respond. He just let the silence stretch until it started to itch. Then he said, "Julian Hahn's ready to make a deal."

That caught Dodd's attention. He moved closer, the sharp interest flashing behind his eyes. "What kind of deal?"

"The kind that points fingers," KC said. "He's scared. Betrayed. And from what I know, he's ready to trade what he knows for protection and leniency."

Dodd rubbed his chin. "That could work for both of us."

KC's expression didn't change. "Explain that."

Dodd paced a slow step. "If Hahn gives me enough to put Garrison close to obstruction, I'll have leverage. Control. The county board listens when their queen's crown slips. She becomes manageable—and that's good for everyone. You get stability; I get cooperation."

KC's tone flattened. "You want control. I want accountability."

Dodd sighed. "KC, don't get self-righteous on me. You take her down publicly, the county loses confidence, and we both lose funding. Let's be smart. Better to work with who we know—especially if she's compromised."

KC shook his head slowly. "Justice doesn't get managed."

The line hung between them like an oath. For a second, neither man spoke.

Then KC straightened, closing his notebook. "Let's get to it. Hahn's waiting."

They walked together down the hall toward the conference room. The air smelled faintly of disinfectant and copier toner—the scent of offices that had seen too much tension for one day. Two deputies stood outside the door.

KC glanced around. "Where's Hahn?"

"Not here, sir," said one of the deputies. "Captain Parsons came by about twenty minutes ago. Said he was taking Representative Hahn over to the DA's Office for processing."

Dodd stopped cold. "Processing? Under whose authority?"

"Yours, sir," the deputy said, uncertain now. "He said you requested it."

Dodd's face darkened. "No, I didn't."

KC turned to him. "Your office is right across the square. He couldn't have gotten far."

Dodd pulled out his phone and dialed his secretary. "Mara, it's Dodd. Is Parsons there with Hahn?"

The voice on the other end came muffled but clear enough: "No, sir. Haven't seen either. Were they headed here instead of the Sheriff's Office?"

Dodd's frown deepened. "What about Akers?"

A pause. Then, "He left early, sir. Didn't say where he was going."

Dodd's voice went tight. "All right. Call me if either shows up." He hung up and slipped the phone into his pocket, his easy confidence gone.

KC's voice was steady, but there was weight under it. "They're not at your office."

"No," Dodd said. "And they're not supposed to be anywhere else."

KC folded his arms. "Captain Parsons couldn't pull this alone. His phone's impounded—he's been a person of interest since the start."

Dodd stared at him. "Then who?"

KC didn't hesitate. "Akers."

The name hit like a stone in a quiet pond.

Dodd blinked. "You're saying my investigator kidnapped a suspect?"

"I'm saying Maria Sherman was beaten to death with a blunt weapon," KC said. "Not Parsons' style. He probably hasn't laid hands on anyone in years. Akers, on the other hand—he's trained, built for enforcement when needed, and close enough to cover his tracks. He's got access, experience, and motive to tie up loose ends for Queen B."

Dodd's mouth tightened. "You think he's working for Garrison?"

KC's eyes narrowed. "I think he's working for himself first—and taking orders from someone who can make him sheriff."

They stood there in the hall, the hum of the fluorescent lights pressing in around them. Somewhere outside, the last chants from the square drifted low and steady, like a heartbeat the night hadn't claimed yet.

Dodd exhaled. "If you're right, this gets ugly fast."

KC's reply was soft but final. "It already is."

Dodd adjusted his tie, trying to recover something of his

composure. "I'll pull what records I can. Warrants, logs, comms data. A search is needed."

KC nodded once. "That starts now."

Dodd turned for the exit. "You'll hear from me," he said, and walked out.

KC stood for a moment, alone in the hall. The weight of what was coming settled on him—the thin, dangerous quiet before pursuit.

He called out, "Carlie!"

She appeared from behind her desk, headset half-cocked. "Yes, Sheriff?"

"Get Toni, Latham, and Miller," he said. "Tell them Hahn, Parsons, and Akers are missing. Last sighting—Parsons said he was taking Hahn to the DA's Office. That was twenty minutes ago. Parsons' phone's impounded. Akers' is likely off or destroyed. Start with vehicles, radio logs, and the back lot. Move."

Carlie's eyes widened, but she nodded. "On it."

She hurried off, and within seconds the bullpen came alive—radios snapping, chairs scraping, urgency finding its footing.

KC stayed where he was, looking down the hallway toward the holding area—empty now, humming with echoes of the day.

He opened his notebook, the pen steady in his hand, and wrote:

5:45 p.m. – Hahn missing. Parsons missing. Akers unaccounted. Dodd confirmed interference. Search initiated.

He underlined once, hard. Then he shut the notebook and tucked it under his arm.

Outside, the light was fading fast. Inside, engines were starting, radios crackled, and a county that had already seen too much was about to see more.

Chapter 57

When the Chain Snaps

Day Five – 5:48 p.m.

Mojave County – Sheriff's Office (KC's Office → Back Lot → Bullpen)

The square had cooled from gold to pewter. Out the window, the courthouse dome held a dull sheen, and the clusters left at the barricades had settled into tired chants that rose and fell like a tide that didn't know how to quit. Inside the Sheriff's Office, motion had a quieter sound—radios popping, the rattle of a printer, shoes on tile.

KC pulled his phone, stared at Jodi's name a beat, and hit call.

She answered on the first ring. "You're going to be late."

"Things are happening. I can't make dinner."

Silence, then the softness that comes when someone already knew. "What happened?"

"Hahn's missing. Parsons is badly beaten. Akers is in the wind."

She let out a breath. "That's terrible."

"Maybe," he said, tiredness coming through loud and clear.

"You always seem to minimize the seriousness of something before it gets worse."

"I'm giving you the short version," he said. "We're running a search now."

"Of course you are." The edge in her voice wasn't anger; it was knowing. "Call when you can, KC. Don't disappear."

"I won't."

"Good," she said, and the line clicked off with more care than the word.

He scrolled down and dialed home. Karole picked up, a boy's voice trying to sound steadier than he felt. "Hey, Dad."

"Hey, kiddo. Put Aunt Ruth on?"

"She's right here."

A rustle, then Ruth's voice, warm and already reading the weather in him. "Is this one of those nights when you forget to come home?"

"Maybe," KC said. "There's a lot going on right now. I don't have time to fill you in. We have an all-out search and rescue that will take time. Maybe all night."

"Be careful, child," she said, gentle but firm. "The truth doesn't protect you—doing right doesn't, either."

He smiled at the floor. "Sometimes they have to mean the same thing."

"Amen," she said, and he could hear the prayer begin as he lowered the phone.

He slid the phone into his pocket and stepped into the hall. The bullpen was already alive—Latham at a terminal pulling camera hits; Miller on the radio with Highway Patrol; Carlie at the front fielding three calls at once without losing the thread. The noise wasn't panic. It was work.

Trisha strode in from the side corridor, hair pulled back, an alert tightness in her face. "Sheriff—back lot. You need to see."

They crossed the rear corridor, pushed through the heavy door, and stepped into the purple edge of evening. Between two cruisers at the far row sat Parsons' white SUV, nose to the fence, no lights, no engine tick. The back lot lamps gave the car a flat sheen, like it had been painted onto the asphalt.

KC reached the driver's side, tried the handle. Unlocked. He opened it slowly.

Parsons slumped against the seatback, wrists zip-tied at his lap, face a ruin of swelling and blood. One eye purpled shut, the other trying to find light. Dark streaks climbed his collar where it had soaked and dried. His breathing came in short, sharp pulls that said pain lived in the ribs.

"Get EMS," KC said, already reaching for the pocket knife he carried, slipping the small blade under the tie and cutting clean. "Careful—jaw looks broken."

Parsons' good eye found him, swam, tried to center. The words came thick, slurred. "Akers... not... what you think..."

KC put a hand to the man's shoulder. "Not now," he said. "Let's get you to the hospital."

Parsons tried to nod and flinched instead. A little rectangle skittered from his lap to the pavement—his badge, knocked loose. KC bent, picked it up, and slipped it into his pocket without a word.

Paramedics jogged across the lot with a backboard and kit. In quick motions they collared him, lifted, and slid him into the rig. Doors thumped shut; the siren didn't sound—no need. The ambulance rolled slow out of the gate and turned toward County General without looking back.

KC watched the taillights a second longer than he needed to. Then he turned and walked fast for the door.

Inside, the bullpen held the same hum but harder. Toni stood at the big map, marking Xs along the western gas stops with a dry-erase pen. Latham leaned over a monitor, scanning a flood of license-plate hits. Miller had a phone wedged to his shoulder, tapping notes with the free hand.

"Report," KC said, and the room adjusted to face him.

Latham pointed to the screen. "Akers' county-issued SUV—last log shows fuel at 1532 hours at our motor pool. No gate cam on the back exit. Plate readers picked him up two blocks south at 1701.

Nothing after."

"Forty-five minute head start," Toni said, eyes on the map. "If he went east, he's in open desert by now. If north, foothills first—roads get thin. West leads to populated areas. South roads turn east toward Four Corners. Doubt he'd head that way."

KC nodded. "Akers would have a plan. I don't think this is spur of the moment."

Carlie stepped from behind her desk. "APB went to Highway Patrol and neighboring counties. Airport desk notified—nothing yet."

"Good," KC said. "Flag all rural fuel stops within a hundred-mile radius. Not just highways. The mom-and-pop with a single pump is where he'll most likely land when he thinks he's invisible."

"Copy," Miller said, already typing.

"And locate Hahn's red Porsche," KC added. "Akers may use that; he may be switching vehicles."

"On it," Latham said.

KC looked to Toni. "Any hits on Akers' known contacts?"

"Working it," she said, scanning the computer screen. "Pulled his recent court dockets, investigators he's cross-assigned with, and the last three phone numbers he called before he shut it off. Two county, one private. I'll chase the private."

"Do that," KC said. "And check to see if one of those calls was to Queen B."

He stepped back from the ring of motion and crossed to the windows. The square outside had dimmed to a sheet of dusk. The ambulance lights from a minute ago were gone. News vans idled like quiet whales at the curb, their masts lowered for once. On the glass, his reflection looked like someone older standing inside his own outline.

He opened his notebook and printed the day's pivot in square, sure letters:

5:48 p.m. — Parsons found, beaten but alive.

Akers + Hahn missing. ~45-min head start.

Why spare Parsons?

He stared at the question, then wrote underneath it:

Because dead men can't mislead.

He closed the book, the cover soft from the week's hard use, and tucked it under his arm.

"Sheriff," Toni said, coming up beside him, quiet under the noise. "Ambulance just pulled up to the hospital emergency room. You want me to ride over?"

"I'll go," he said. "Keep pushing the grid. Latham—pull every radio log from 1500 on and cross with gate swipes and motor pool keys. See if Akers checked out another vehicle. Miller—get me last-known on Hahn's wife's vehicle too. If Akers needed a clean car, he might've reached for that one as well."

"Copy," both said.

Carlie approached, headset askew, a pencil tucked behind her ear. "Media's asking if we've opened a manhunt."

"We've opened a search," KC said. "Tell them that. Tell them we're coordinating with other counties and Highway Patrol."

"Is that all?" she asked.

"For now—and be ready for a long night," KC said, and that ended that part of the conversation.

The bullpen didn't spike; it steadied. Radios spit; printers ran; the map gained more ink. The building had that feel it hadn't had for a long time—like a ship at sea, engines deep, everything aimed at one point on the horizon.

KC paused in the doorway and took a last look around—Carlie fielding calls faster than they came in; Toni scanning the computer, typing with breakneck speed; Latham and Miller pulling threads he'd handed them and spooling them into something useful. Work wasn't noise in a room like this. It was trust you could hear.

He slipped the notebook into his inner pocket and headed for the exit. The outside air was cooler now, the smell of dust clean again. Patrol lights flickered along the perimeter in red-blue whispers. Somewhere toward the east, the desert spread flat and unlit, the kind of distance men used when they wanted to be forgotten.

KC stopped at the top of the steps, eyes up at the dark line of the mountains. If Akers wanted everyone running at stone and scrub, he'd given them a story that fit. Parsons beaten but breathing. A head start that suggested a direction. Or misdirection.

He asked himself the question once more—Why spare Parsons?— and got the same answer.

Because dead men can't mislead.

He drew a breath that settled his shoulders. "We'll find out why," he said to no one in particular, and took the steps down into the evening that was about to become night.

Chapter 58

The Witness Who Lived

Day Five – 6:32 p.m.

**High Desert Community Hospital –
Parsons' Room**

High Desert Community Hospital sat at the far end of the square, its white walls catching what was left of the day's color and turning it the same dull gray as the sky. The parking lot was half-empty—shift change, twilight—when KC stepped out of the Jeep and made his way inside.

The air smelled of antiseptic and tired flowers. In the hallways, murmured voices carried like static—orderlies, nurses, the shuffling of carts. There was a buzz moving through the place, a current of rumor that outran facts. Names followed it: Parsons, Sheriff's Office, cover-up. None of it was flattering.

KC ignored the looks as he walked past the nurse's station. The clerk behind the counter glanced up, recognized him, and nodded toward the west wing. "Room 214," she said. "They're finishing up his scans."

Outside the door to 214, a young doctor in blue scrubs waited, arms folded, expression drawn from too many hours and too few breaks. "Sheriff," he said, extending a hand. "Doctor Hayashi."

KC shook it. "How is he?"

"Alive," Hayashi said, tired professionalism giving the words their weight. "He's got multiple contusions, several broken ribs, and a damaged eye socket. One knee's shattered—he'll need surgery if he wants to walk without a cane. A jaw contusion, no fracture."

KC's eyes narrowed slightly. "No fracture?"

"Bruised hard, but intact."

KC nodded once, slow. "So he can talk."

The doctor gave him a look—half curiosity, half warning—but said nothing. KC's tone had the edge of deduction, not surprise.

"Can I see him?"

"Don't be long. He needs rest."

KC stepped inside.

The room was dim except for the narrow beam from the wall lamp. Machines hummed softly, steady as breathing. Parsons lay propped up on pillows, oxygen tube looped beneath his nose, one arm in a sling, IV lines trailing to the stand. His face was swollen and raw with bruises—colors ranging from deep violet to yellow at the edges. The good eye tracked KC as he entered.

KC stopped at the bedside. "You're lucky, Captain."

Parsons' lips cracked into something like a smile. "Don't feel lucky."

"Doctor says you'll keep the knee," KC said. "After surgery."

Parsons gave a short, pained breath that might have been a laugh. "Guess that's one way to slow a man down."

KC pulled a chair closer and sat. "You want to tell me what happened?"

Parsons stared past him for a long beat, like replaying film in his head. When he spoke, his voice rasped—low, strained, but steady enough.

"Akers called the office," he said. "Said Dodd wanted Hahn transferred to the DA's Office for processing. Nothing unusual about it. I figured it was a courtesy transfer." He swallowed hard. "So I went to get him. Hahn didn't say much—looked scared, but calm enough. I got to my vehicle and that's when it happened."

KC didn't move. "Go on."

"Akers came out of nowhere. I turned—and he was already swinging. First hit landed on my knee. Dropped me. Next came to the ribs, the face. Didn't stop until I went down for good." He drew a shaky breath. "Hahn just stood there. Didn't do a thing. Looked like he was trying to figure out what side to stand on."

KC said nothing, just watched him.

"Akers told him to help," Parsons went on. "Made Hahn grab my arms, haul me into the car. Then he zip-cuffed my hands and threw my badge in my lap like a warning." His good eye flicked toward the window. "Said if I ever talked about his place up in the mountains—the cabin—I'd regret it. Said next time he'd finish what he started."

KC studied him for a moment, weighing every word. "So he knows you know about that place."

Parsons nodded weakly. "Built it himself. Hidden. Self-contained. Didn't say where exactly, but I've heard him talk about it after hours—his getaway spot. Power, water, satellite phone. He bragged about how no one could find it."

KC leaned back slightly, his thoughts aligning like gears catching. "He made sure you couldn't run," he said, almost to himself. "But he left your jaw intact so you could talk."

Parsons looked at him, confusion flickering behind the pain. "You think this was planned?"

"I think Akers wanted us chasing ghosts," KC said. "And you were the bait."

Parsons closed his eye, breathing slow. "I should've seen it coming."

KC shook his head. "He's been planning this longer than you realize."

A pause. Then Parsons said, softer, "What happens now? Do I still have a job?"

KC stood, hand resting lightly on the rail of the bed. "Let's get you through tonight first."

Parsons nodded faintly, and his breathing evened out into a rhythm that might've been sleep or surrender.

KC turned and stepped into the hall. Doctor Hayashi was there again, checking a chart. "He'll make it," the doctor said to confirm.

KC looked at him. "Yes, that's the point."

He walked down the corridor, the sound of his boots dull against the linoleum. The hospital doors whispered open, releasing him back into the desert air. Patrol lights from his Jeep painted the parking lot in alternating blue and red, fading against the dark horizon.

He opened his notebook under the glow of the Emergency Room's bright lights and wrote in clean, block letters:

6:58 p.m. – Parsons confirms Akers' ambush.

Knee broken to stop escape. Jaw spared to talk.

Misdirection confirmed. Time to pursue.

He closed the book, slipped it into his pocket, and looked toward the horizon—the long stretch of black desert that seemed to swallow light whole. Somewhere out there, Akers was moving, and the game had shifted again.

KC got in his Jeep, started the engine, flicked off the patrol lights, and let the headlights flare across the half-empty lot. Then he turned toward the road, the sound of pebbles crunching under the tires fading into the widening dark.

Chapter 59

A Light Kept Burning

Day Five – 7:10 p.m.

Mojave County – KC's Jeep → Sheriff's Office

The highway between the hospital and the square lay nearly empty, the kind of road that looked wider at night. KC drove with one hand on the wheel, headlights cutting a narrow tunnel through the desert dusk. The radio murmured quietly with dispatch chatter—updates on vehicle checks, false leads, routine noise that didn't amount to much.

He didn't have time to stop at St. Mary's, but he needed to know. He thumbed his phone, pressed the number he'd saved years ago.

"St. Mary's Rectory," came the familiar voice, soft and low.

"Evening, Father," KC said.

"Sheriff Talbird," Father Frank replied. "I thought you'd be halfway up a mountain by now."

"Not yet," KC said. "Wanted to check on the Alvarez family. How are they doing?"

There was a small pause, and KC could hear voices in the background—the boy laughing, the faint clatter of dishes, the rise and fall of Spanish conversation that sounded like home.

"They're all right," Father Frank said finally. "Rosa cooked dinner in the parish kitchen—rice, beans, carne, and tortillas. Her son ate like he hadn't in days. There's laughter here tonight. Feels good to hear it again."

KC nodded to himself, though Father Frank couldn't see it. "That's good to hear."

"I know why you're calling," the priest said. "You want to remind me what's coming."

"Yes. ICE will be at my office at dawn. I'll send them your way."

The silence that followed was long enough to carry meaning. "Sheriff," Father Frank said slowly, "what if I were to... redirect them?

Maybe send them out toward the Humboldt ranch. That could buy a few hours."

KC shook his head even though the priest couldn't see it. "That's obstruction, Father. It'll make things worse for everyone. Especially for Rosa."

Another pause, the sound of a sigh. "Then perhaps I could send them away tonight—Los Angeles, maybe. I've got friends there. They'd disappear."

"That's a bad idea," KC said, his tone steady but not cold. "ICE will respond more harshly. They'll hunt, not collect. The family needs to stay put. Do what's right, Father, even when it feels unfair."

Father Frank's voice softened. "You always were stubborn, Sheriff, even as a youth."

"My Aunt Ruth has said that many times. Sometimes that's all that's left when things look bad."

A small chuckle came through the line, tired but kind. "Then I'll do what's right. I'll keep them safe here tonight. I'm holding a special mass for them before dawn."

KC smiled faintly. "I appreciate that."

"You're welcome to come," Father said. "I'll delay it until four-thirty."

"I'd like to," KC said, "but I'm on a manhunt right now. If I can make it, I will."

"I'll keep a candle lit for you either way," Father Frank said.

"Thanks, Father."

"Goodnight, Sheriff."

"Goodnight."

KC ended the call and slid the phone onto the console. Ahead, the lights of the square came back into view—soft golds and whites against the deepening gray of desert night.

He parked behind the Sheriff's Office and sat a moment, engine idling, headlights washing the back wall of the building. He could see shadows moving inside—people still working, still chasing.

When he stepped through the side entrance, the sound hit him first. Radios popped, printers ran, chairs scraped. The bullpen was in full search-and-rescue mode—Toni at the computer, Latham cross-checking road grids, Miller on the phone with Highway Patrol. Carlie handling two calls at once, her headset crackling.

KC stood in the doorway, taking it in. The noise wasn't panic—it was a rhythm, the hum of people trying to keep up with something that didn't want to be caught.

"Stop what you're doing," KC said.

The words cut through the room. Conversations stopped, radios went quiet, heads turned.

He waited until the silence settled. "Everything we're doing right now is a waste of time. We've been running in the wrong direction."

A few uncertain glances traded across the room.

KC pointed toward his office. "Conference. Now."

They moved without question—Toni grabbing her notepad, Latham and Miller exchanging a look, Carlie setting her headset down. The bullpen filled with motion again, but it was quieter this time—focused, pulled inward.

KC held the door as the last of them entered, then closed it behind him with a quiet click.

"We've been chasing ghosts," he said. "Let's start over."

The hum of the office faded outside the closed door, and inside, the work of finding truth began again.

Chapter 60

The Fifth Night

Day Five – 7:30 p.m.

Mojave County – Sheriff's Office

The bullpen lights were low, only the thin hum of fluorescents over the hallway. The air smelled faintly of aftershave and light perfume. KC stood in his office doorway while the others filed in—Toni, Latham, Miller, and Carlie, each looking worn but alert.

Carlie and Miller rolled a whiteboard from the bullpen. KC nodded toward the corner. "Set it there. That's our new operations board. Forget the corkboard—that's old business."

They arranged themselves around the table, notebooks open, pens ready. KC closed the door and turned the lock. The sound was quiet, but final.

He leaned against the desk, hands on the edge. "We've been following a ghost."

The words hung for a moment before he went on. "I just came from the hospital. Parsons is alive, barely. Akers shattered his knee so he couldn't move. Left his jaw intact so he could talk. Told him if he ever mentioned the mountain cabin, he'd finish the job."

Latham frowned. "You think the cabin's a lie?"

"No," KC said. "I think it's bait."

He grabbed a black marker, turned to the whiteboard, and in square letters wrote TIMELINE across the top.

"Here's how it plays out," he said, drawing quick lines. "Akers calls Parsons, pretends he's acting on Dodd's orders. Parsons picks up Hahn, heads to his SUV. Akers ambushes him in the lot—first the knee, then the face. He makes Hahn help load Parsons into the car, zip-cuffs him, tosses his badge in his lap, and drives off."

He capped the marker, looked at the board. "He had ten minutes to subdue Parsons, five more to get control of Hahn, another ten to get out of sight. Call it thirty minutes of real movement before our lockdown started."

Toni leaned forward. "It's been closer to two hours now."

KC nodded. "Yes—but we had patrols and checkpoints up within fifteen minutes. He knows the system and knew the net would close fast."

He turned from the board. "So—where would you go if you were him?"

"L.A.," Miller said. "He could disappear before dawn."

"South," Toni offered. "Mexico's a straight shot."

Latham shrugged. "He could cut east, cross into Nevada."

KC listened, then shook his head slowly. "That's what he wants us to think."

He drew a rough outline of the county, circled the mountain range to the north. "Akers wants us chasing him toward the desert and the highways. That's the ploy. He planted Parsons to make sure we'd hear about the cabin, so we'd waste time on a wild trail. He's counting on that."

He studied the map for a long moment. "He'll lay low tonight, somewhere close enough to move fast but hard enough to reach in the dark. Then, at dawn, he'll go. That's his window."

He uncapped a red marker and wrote one word: DAWN, underlining it twice.

Toni looked up from her notes. "This began five days ago—when he killed Maria. Five Days Till Dawn isn't just about ICE. He planned everything—right down to that timing. Even the ICE raid's a distraction."

KC met her eyes. "You're right. He's been planning this from the start. Dawn's his finish line."

He faced the others. "So we stop following what he wants us to see. We find where he's really hiding."

He pointed the marker like a directive. "Toni, cross-check every county record for any property tied to Akers—his name, his family, any alias. Latham, wake whoever you have to in property and zoning. I don't care if they're home eating dinner. Get access to land deeds, tax maps, off-book parcels. Miller, coordinate with state GIS, look for anything new in the high-country grid. Carlie, keep the comms quiet. Nobody outside this office hears we've shifted direction."

Miller hesitated. "Some of those records are locked down for the night. We'll need county authorization."

KC set the marker on the desk. "Then I'll get it."

That ended it. The team moved out fast, voices low but purposeful. The bullpen came alive again—radios, typing, the scuff of boots. The rhythm was back, steady and sure.

KC stayed behind. The whiteboard glowed pale under the light, the word DAWN standing out in red. He looked at it a long moment, then reached into his pocket for his phone.

Scrolling through the contacts, he stopped at Queen Garrison. His thumb hovered for a breath, jaw set.

Then he pressed call.

The ring tone echoed in the quiet office, steady and hollow—like something beginning again.

Chapter 61

The Price of Cooperation

Day Five – 7:56 p.m.

Mojave County – Sheriff's Office (KC's Office → Bullpen)

The office was quieter than it had been all day. The storm of activity in the bullpen was now a steady hum—radios, low conversation, the scrape of chairs. Through the window, the square glowed under the sodium lamps, soft gold light on tired pavement.

KC stood by his desk, one hand resting on the open notebook, the other holding his phone. His thumb hovered over a name he didn't want to call but had to.

He hit Queen Garrison.

The line rang long enough to make him think she wouldn't answer. Then, finally, a click.

Her voice came cold, precise, and distant. "If this is about the reporters, Sheriff, I've had enough for one day."

KC stayed calm. "Reporters?"

"You don't know?" she said, tone hardening. "Dodd leaked the Hahn and Akers story to the press—called it a 'flight from justice.' They've been camped outside my building all evening."

KC's jaw tightened. "I didn't know about that."

"Oh, please." Her voice sharpened. "You expect me to believe you and Dodd aren't working together? He controls the headlines, and you control the narrative. Same game, different hands."

"I don't control Dodd, and I don't feed the press," KC said evenly. "I'm trying to bring two men in alive, that's all."

A pause stretched—long enough for her to decide whether to trust him.

"Then why are you calling me, Sheriff?"

KC took a slow breath. "Have you heard from your nephew?"

The question detonated. "How dare you ask me that? You think I'd hide a fugitive? My nephew's destroyed enough of what I built."

Her voice had dropped low and dangerous, every word meant to cut.

KC didn't rise to it. "Then you haven't heard from him."

"Of course not."

"Good," he said quietly. "Because I'm calling for another reason. We're trying to locate Akers. I believe he's gone to a mountain cabin he built. I need your authorization to open the county title and land records tonight."

"Why?" she asked, her tone shifting from anger to suspicion. "Why would I hand you access to everything?"

"So we can find them, bring them in," KC said. "That's why."

She let the silence run until he could almost hear the tick of her desk clock through the line. Then she said, "What do I get for it?"

KC's patience held. "You get to save your nephew's life."

"He's finished, Sheriff. You and your DA saw to that."

"He did that all by himself," KC replied. "Besides, he's your nephew, you're family."

Her tone was dismissive. "Family is an investment, and his account's overdrawn."

He waited. "Then what do you want?"

"I want credit," she said finally, voice cool and deliberate. "When this ends, the press will know I cooperated. That I helped."

KC closed his eyes for a moment, then said, "You want a headline, not justice."

"Justice is a story told by whoever gets to speak first," she replied. "You and Dodd made sure of that. Now I'll tell mine."

He let a beat pass, then nodded to himself. "Fine. You'll get your credit."

Her voice softened—almost pleased. "That's better."

KC reached for his pen. "Now, tell me where."

There was the faint scrape of paper on her end, a pause, then: "It's north of Kernville. Remote country near Shirley Meadows. You can't get to it by road. There's an old service trail—starts at a fire road about six miles out. He used to hike in with Julian. Called it his retreat."

KC's pen moved fast, square letters filling the page. "Service road— how close?"

"You'll know it by the gate marked Timber Wash 9. It hasn't been used in years. The cabin sits somewhere above that ridge."

He paused, reading back what he'd written. "He ditched his vehicle, probably has horses or bikes stashed up there."

"Likely," she said. "Akers always planned for contingencies."

"Thanks," KC said.

But before he could say more, the line went dead.

He stared at the phone for a second, then set it down carefully, as if it might still bite. He picked up his notebook and wrote:

7:56 p.m. – Queen confirmed: Cabin above Kernville, near Shirley Meadows. Trail access only. Provided info in exchange for publicity. Concerned with optics, not family.

He underlined the last line once, hard.

Outside the office, the bullpen was alive and buzzing with activity—voices, tapping of computer keys, phones ringing. He stepped out, the door swinging wide behind him.

They looked up—Toni, Latham, Miller, Carlie—expectant.

"I know where he is," KC said.

The room stilled.

"In my office," he added. "We've got a plan to make."

They followed him in without a word, the hum of the building fading behind the door as KC turned back toward the whiteboard where DAWN was still written in red.

It was closer now, and everyone knew it.

Chapter 62
Tell the Press I'm Away

Day Five – 8:12 p.m.

Mojave County – Sheriff's Office (KC's Office)

The sheriff's office had gone still again—an uneasy kind of quiet that meant everyone was waiting for direction. Radios whispered low. Keyboards clicked in a careful rhythm. Even the phones had gone silent, as if the building itself were holding its breath.

KC stood behind his desk, sleeves rolled once, eyes on the whiteboard glowing pale in the corner. The word DAWN stood out in red beneath the outline of the mountains. He turned toward the group gathered before him—Toni, Latham, Miller, Carlie—all waiting for what came next.

"All right," he said finally. "Here's what we know."

He stepped forward, tapping the whiteboard with his pen. "Akers' cabin is north of Kernville, near Shirley Meadows. No roads. Only an old service trail—six miles past the Timber Wash gate. Remote country. That's where he's headed."

No one spoke. The information sank in like a weight.

KC continued. "He's likely hunkered down there now, waiting for daylight to make his move. That gives us four hours to box him in."

Carlie crossed her arms. "So what's the play?"

KC turned toward her. "You stay here. Keep things calm. If the press calls, tell them I'm heading into the desert. Let that story roll—radio, scanner, whatever reaches his ears. That's our own misdirection."

Carlie nodded. "Make him think you're two counties away."

"Exactly."

KC looked to Latham and Miller. "We need the cabin surrounded quietly by midnight. No sirens, no chatter. Coordinate with the substation and pull every deputy you can get. Ask the Highway Patrol for help on the perimeter. You'll both take the helicopter out with us.

We'll drop you near the substation to coordinate. Latham, you're in charge." He turned to Miller, "you're second in command."

Latham scribbled quick notes. "Perimeter only."

"That's right," KC said. "No one goes in. Not until I say."

"Sheriff, what if command there balks?" Latham asked.

KC said, "Carlie, call the Kernville substation and let them know Latham and Miller will be there to coordinate. Make it clear that they are in command."

"Understood."

He turned to Toni. "You and I will hike in from the ridge. I don't want engines or rotors giving us away. Get some rest, grab a bite, and be back by eleven. Bring a pack, your sidearm, plenty of spare mags and something warm. It'll be cold up there."

Toni nodded once. "Got it."

"Good. Be ready to move."

She and Carlie exchanged a glance, then slipped out of the room—Toni already pulling her phone to check gear lists, Carlie heading for her desk.

KC hit the intercom. "Carlie."

"Yes, Sheriff?"

"Before you call Kernville, get ahold of the pilot. I want the helicopter prepped and in the back parking lot in thirty."

"Already on it," she said.

KC clicked off and looked back at Latham and Miller, both standing straight, waiting. "When you get there, keep your distance. Eyes open, radios low. I don't want anyone getting jumpy. If Akers moves, I want him boxed, not dead."

They nodded. "Roger that."

"Good. Get what you need and be ready when that chopper lands."

They left without another word, boots quiet against the tile. The office door swung shut behind them, leaving KC alone with the soft hum of the fluorescent lights.

He glanced once more at the whiteboard. The map of the mountains looked back at him—lines and names and coordinates drawn in careful black, the word DAWN underlined twice in red.

He closed his notebook and slid it in his pocket.

Time to eat. Gear up. Maybe an hour's rest.

Outside, the night had deepened—cool, still, a wind rising from the west. Somewhere far off, the faint thump of helicopter blades began to echo across the desert, steady and growing.

KC stepped into the dark, locked the door behind him, and started for home.

Chapter 63

No Sirens

Day Five – 11:00 p.m.

Mojave County – Sheriff's Office

The night held an eerie chill. Inside the Sheriff's Office, the fluorescent lights burned bright — they never dulled. The bullpen had settled into that particular hush of anticipation. A half dozen deputies from earlier shifts lingered near the Sheriff's office, eyes bright with the mix of boredom and eagerness that comes when something finally calls them off the bench. They looked like athletes who'd been warming up all day.

KC stepped through the rear door into the building. The sound of his boots rang loud in the empty hallway. When he entered the bullpen area, they straightened as if by muscle memory. He could read that wanting in them — the want to be useful — and it hardened his jaw toward a short nod. "Get back in uniform," he said. "We're going to need bodies up north. Move."

They were gone before he'd finished the sentence, boots thumping down the hall.

Inside his office, the team was already assembled. Toni, Latham, Miller, Carlie, and one more man — Sergeant Tyrone Rodman — who filled the doorway like a shadow that had learned to hold itself precisely. Rodman wore a flight jacket over dark clothes and had the easy, practiced stillness of someone who'd spent more nights in cramped metal than in beds. Rumor in county circles said he'd piloted classified missions long before Mojave, and KC had no interest in confirming gossip. The man's calm was all the confirmation he needed.

"Good to have you," KC said as Rodman ducked in without formality.

Rodman gave a small, polite nod. "If it's helpful, I've flown the line at night more than once. We'll keep low and tight."

KC walked to the whiteboard. The word DAWN, still there

written in thick red, looked like a promise and a threat at once. He took a marker and, with the quiet authority he'd used to shape other meetings, reviewed assignments.

"Carlie, you're here. So keep comms calm. Again, if the press calls, tell them the sheriff's team has headed into the desert tonight — make sure the wording makes it sound like we're driving south and east. That buys the one trick Akers wants: radio noise in the wrong place."

Carlie nodded and already had her phone half up, practiced with a public line. "Say we're doing a sweep of the highway south and east toward Trona," she offered. "And I've already given out that line a half a dozen times."

"Perfect," KC said with a small, wry smile. "Misdirection on the air."

Latham and Miller tightened their notepads. "You'll run perimeter from Kernville. Coordinate with the substation, Highway Patrol, and the deputies who have gathered in the bullpen. Remember, quietly — no sirens, no public chatter. Hold your positions. No one goes in until I give the go."

"You got it," Latham said. His voice carried the steady steadiness of a man who liked maps and rules.

Rodman spoke up then, practical and blunt. "Drop point logistics: I understand that I'll put these two deputies at the substation parking lot. For you, Sheriff, and Deputy Salazar, the plan is to drop you a mile out. In these conditions, you'll hear us coming several miles off. We can't hide that."

KC considered the map on the board. "What do you suggest?"

Rodman didn't hesitate, his experience talking. "Drop you at the substation as well. Go in on horses from there. Quiet and covert. Undetected."

Miller — who had worked the Kernville substation years back — nodded. "There are mountain horses kept at Kernville. Used for the rescue of hikers and such. They'll saddle faster than you think, but give them twenty to forty-five minutes to get mounted."

KC turned to Carlie. "Call them. Tell them to get the animals saddled and ready. Two riders — Toni and me. Their best horses."

"I'm on it," she said, already moving.

Toni stood with a pack slung over her shoulder and the look of someone who had slept little and thought a lot. She was younger than the rest of the room but had the composed face of someone who'd learned the weight of waiting. KC gave her a small nod. "Looks like you're ready?"

She swallowed and smiled without humor. "Been ready for two hours."

With that, they made their way out, except KC. He cast his eyes around the group and noticed the way the earlier-shift deputies lingered at the doorway. He wanted them on the perimeter, not on the front line — there were twelve of them.

"I appreciate you. Mount up. Two-by-two, go to Kernville now. Keep it quiet. Your task: secure the perimeter. Latham and Miller are in command. Follow their instructions. Clear?"

They moved like a single organism, practiced and obedient. Carlie, already at her desk, placed the call to Kernville, her voice steady as she explained who was in command and what they needed. Her tone was official but respectful — the kind that made people move. Fast.

KC went to his Jeep and opened the rear. He knew exactly what he wanted. He reached for a familiar, issued tool — the department's Remington 870 shotgun — and three extra magazines for his sidearm. He checked the weapon with a practiced hand, grabbed the mags, then slung the shotgun carefully over his shoulder. He also tucked a compact med kit and an extra thermal blanket into his pack; they'd need it, and he'd rather carry common sense than bravado.

Rodman was already outside, leaning into the chopper as the pilot and crew finished preflight checks. KC watched the rotors begin to stir, the low thrum that moved through the bones. Rodman caught his eye, and there was that quiet assurance in the man's face — no boasting, only focus. "ETA fifteen," he called once, voice steady above the burgeoning din of preparation.

Carlie's misdirection was already on the airwaves: a terse update to a local feed about a sweep near Trona. Small white noise in the scanner, a breadcrumb to make Akers think twice before listening too closely. KC appreciated the small theater of it; tactical deception required sleight of hand just as much as courage.

The helicopter blades had grown into a living thing by the time KC climbed the steps. Deputies were getting last-minute instructions from Latham, radios tuned to low channels. Miller handed him a roll of extra batteries and a pair of thermal gloves. Toni checked her pack twice, sealing zippers, testing straps.

KC paused, hands on the roof of the Jeep, and looked out over the dark line of mountains. The desert wind smelled of distant creosote and cold, the feel of an air that knew how to hold secrets. Dawn, he thought, was still hours away; a good plan could make those hours count. He thought of Maria, of the Alvarez family upstairs at St. Mary's rectory, of Aunt Ruth's voice telling him to be careful. He thought of Toni's steady, tense jaw. He thought of how easy it is to pretend the night is under control.

The copter's bow rose, the rotor wash starting to lift dust into small, spirited whirlwinds that flashed in the floodlights. Rodman, seated in the pilot's chair, nodded once. KC slid the shotgun into its sling, checked the balance, and climbed aboard.

As the chopper lifted, KC watched the Sheriff's Office fall away — the white rectangle of the bullpen window, Carlie's silhouette at the desk, the deputies moving like ants in the shallow wash of light. The blades ate the night, and for a moment, the only thing he heard was the throb of the machine and the steadying patter of his own breath.

Rodman's voice in his ear was close and practical. "We'll hold low, but fast. We'll be there ASAP."

KC settled his weight into the seat and looked once more at the dark sweep of land ahead. "Bring us in clean," he said.

Rodman's reply was as spare as the man. "We'll do more than that."

The copter slid into the black toward the mountains. Behind them, the Sheriff's Office became a square of gold, the whiteboard DAWN pulsing in his mind like a new map. Ahead, the night opened and waited.

Chapter 64
The Sheriff's Ground

Day Five – 11:54 p.m.

**Kernville Substation – Mountain Trail
toward Shirley Meadows**

The helicopter came in low over the dark ridge, lights off, only the pulsing red of the tail beacon cutting through the night. Below, the wide asphalt lot behind the Kernville Substation shimmered under floodlights. Every vehicle that usually crowded it had been cleared out earlier. Deputies on the ground, eyes wide, looked up as the rotors thundered overhead.

Rodman held the bird steady, easing it down slow and flat until the skids kissed pavement. The downdraft kicked dust and grit across the lot, scattering paper and dead leaves against a fence. When the blades slowed, KC pushed open the side door and stepped out first, coat flaring in the wind, followed by Toni. Latham and Miller jumped down after them, ducking instinctively under the spinning blades.

The air up here was thinner, sharper. The substation lights burned clean white against the mountain dark, and the line of trees beyond looked like a solid wall waiting to close in.

KC didn't waste time. He gave Latham and Miller a nod toward the outer lot, where deputies waited beside their vehicles. Then he motioned to Toni and walked toward the substation entrance. The heavy steel door clanged behind them as they entered.

Inside, the station buzzed in its own quiet way—radio chatter, printers, the hum of fluorescent lights overhead. The place was bigger than most outposts, not sprawling but substantial enough to matter. Maps lined the walls; coffee cups marked half-finished shifts.

Lieutenant George Harlan stood near the reception counter, arms folded, a square man with a square jaw to match. His expression said he'd been waiting for this moment and wasn't sure he liked it.

KC met his eyes. "Lieutenant," he said simply. "Appreciate the use of your space."

"Appreciate notice next time," Harlan replied, clipped. "I've been told I've got line deputies running my command."

KC didn't blink. "You've got deputies who know this case inside and out. Miller knows this terrain better than any of us. There isn't time to bring you up to speed. That's why I put them in command."

Harlan held his stare for a moment, then glanced at Toni, who stood ready but silent. The man's shoulders eased a fraction. He gave a sharp nod, but his jaw still worked, chewing on the loss of control. "All right, Sheriff," he said finally. "They're yours for now."

KC gave a short nod and noted the for now comment. He'd deal with that later. "Appreciate it."

He left the lieutenant to his radios and stepped back outside. The asphalt was already alive with movement—Latham and Miller moving among the deputies, checking assignments, radios, gear. A few SUVs idled low, headlights off, red tail lamps muted. Orders moved fast and quiet.

"Two by two," Latham called. "Secondary roads only. Keep it dark. Secure your sectors and hold."

KC crossed to him. "Perimeter by 0100," he said.

Latham nodded. "We're on track. Maybe sooner."

"Good," KC said and kept walking, Toni keeping pace.

Rodman stood near the helicopter, headset around his neck, hands in his pockets like a man unbothered by noise or cold. KC joined him.

"You stay here," KC said. "We'll call if we need extraction or eyes in the air. If you don't hear from us by dawn, take her up and begin a search west of the ridge."

Rodman's expression didn't shift. "Understood. Be careful up there. The trail gets narrow fast."

KC gave a half-smile. "Wouldn't be the first bad road I've taken."

"Fair enough," Rodman said, stepping back toward the chopper. The rotors were still now, the machine a dark shape crouched under a floodlight.

At the corral, two deputies waited beside a pair of mountain horses—broad-shouldered, trail-worn, steady under the halters. Their breath came in clouds in the cold air. One horse was a mottled gray, the other chestnut. Toni ran her hand down the gray's neck, checking the cinch and girth. KC tightened his stirrups, checked the straps on his pack.

He looked over at her. "We'll ride until the grade narrows. Then we walk the last mile in. Stay quiet, keep to the trees."

Toni nodded once. "Got it."

KC turned back toward the lot. The dozen deputies from HQ had arrived, joining the others gathered near their vehicles. They waited silently for his word. Though tired, they were alert and ready.

"Mount up," KC called. "Two by two, it's time to head out. Latham and Miller are in command. You secure the perimeter. Quiet, disciplined, no contact unless ordered. Understood?"

A chorus of affirmations came back. Then the group dispersed, engines turning over soft and low, red brake lights fading as they pulled into the dark.

KC glanced once more at Rodman, who stood by the chopper's frame, arms crossed, the faintest nod exchanged between them. No words needed—just the understanding between men who'd spent long nights counting on timing and trust.

KC swung into the saddle, the leather creaking under his weight. He looked toward the mountains. The ridge loomed black against the stars, a jagged silhouette cutting the sky. The air smelled of pine and stone and cold.

He nudged his horse forward. "Let's go."

Toni fell in behind him, her horse's hooves crunching over the gravel. They passed the substation fence and turned north onto the fire road. Behind them, the floodlights of the substation grew small, shrinking to a pale glow against the valley floor.

Ahead, the mountain rose—black, silent, and endless.

The night swallowed them whole—one step closer to dawn.

Chapter 65

Trail to the Cabin

Day Five – 11:58 p.m.

Sierra Range – Mountain Trail toward Shirley Meadows

The air was thin and cold enough to sting. Clouds drifted low across the ridge, breaking and reforming in slow, silent waves. The only sounds were hooves on rock and the faint creak of leather—two horses climbing the narrow trail beneath a sky the color of slate.

KC rode point, his flashlight capped in red to keep the beam low. The mountain loomed black above them, the trees closing in like sentinels. Behind him, Toni kept a steady rhythm, reins in one hand, the other resting near the holster on her thigh. Her breath came slow and even, though he could sense her nerves in the silence between steps.

They'd been climbing for over an hour. The substation lights were long gone, the valley below swallowed by fog. Only the occasional flicker of starlight through the treetops hinted at how far they'd come.

"Trail's narrowing," KC called softly over his shoulder.

"I see it," Toni replied. "Still clear?"

"For now."

He pulled his horse to a stop at a bend where the path narrowed to little more than a ledge. Beyond it, the mountain fell away into a deep ravine. Far below, a faint trickle of water caught the dim light.

KC dismounted, boots crunching against frost-crusted rocks. "We go on foot from here."

Toni swung down without hesitation. Together they tied off the horses under a copse of fir trees, brushed their muzzles once, and checked their packs.

KC scanned the path ahead, flashlight angled low, searching. "From here, stay close. Watch your step. No talking—whisper only if we need to."

"Understood," she said.

They started up the incline, moving through uneven terrain littered with pine needles and shale. The forest pressed tight around them, shadows layered upon shadows. The air smelled of sap and the cold iron they carried.

After twenty minutes of climbing, KC held up a hand.

Toni froze. KC crouched, sweeping the beam across the ground. The light caught a glint—fine wire stretched between two rocks, just above ankle height. He traced it to a crude trigger assembly half-hidden under leaves.

"Tripwire," he murmured. "Old-school."

Toni crouched beside him, squinting. "Looks fresh."

"Probably tied to a noise rig—maybe a flashbang if he's got them."

KC followed the line with his eyes, then eased his knife from its sheath and cut the wire cleanly. The faint metallic snap vanished into the wind.

"Won't be the last," he said.

They kept moving. Twice more, they found signs of traps—one a camouflaged pit lined with brush, another a small perimeter alarm, a motion sensor rigged to a battery pack. Akers had been busy.

When they reached a ridge clearing, KC dropped to one knee, motioning Toni beside him. Through the trees ahead, the faintest amber glow bled through the fog.

"There," he said quietly. "Cabin's down in that draw."

Toni adjusted her binoculars, glassing the slope. "Single lamp. Inside, maybe in a front room."

"Smoke?" KC asked.

She lowered the glasses. "None."

"Then they're conserving light," KC said. "Trying to stay hidden."

"Or waiting for us." Toni took one last look.

He didn't answer right away. The forest was still again—the kind of stillness that didn't feel natural. Every sound seemed to pause, even the wind. Somewhere far off, a night bird called once, then fell silent.

KC leaned close enough that she could hear him without raising his voice. "From here, we move slow. He's expecting company."

"Which means traps."

"Which means," KC said, "he's probably watching right now."

Toni gave a tight nod. "You think we're already in range?"

KC scanned the treeline. "We were in range ten minutes ago."

They moved forward, one careful step at a time, weaving between the pines. The glow from the cabin grew faintly brighter as they descended the ridge. The slope was slick, every loose stone ready to betray a sound. KC's shotgun was raised, steady, the matte barrel dark against the trees. Toni's hand hovered near her holster.

At fifty yards, they stopped again. The cabin was fully visible now—a small structure, no larger than a ranger's shack, half-sunken into the slope. The light inside flickered weakly through a curtained window. No movement.

Then—faintly—footsteps outside.

KC lifted a hand. They crouched.

A figure emerged from the cabin's shadow. Tall, hesitant, with a gun in one hand. Julian Hahn. His face pale even in the dim light, eyes darting toward the treeline.

Toni whispered, "He's armed."

KC nodded, studying his movements. "And alone."

"Where's Akers?"

"That's what I'd like to know."

They watched Hahn pace the clearing, scanning the woods like a man afraid of what he might see. He took a few steps toward the trees, then stopped. KC could see the fear in the stiffness of his shoulders. Hahn's hand trembled where it gripped the pistol.

KC leaned close to Toni. "Hold here. I'll circle right. Try to get eyes on the back side."

Toni nodded and shifted slightly, rifle ready.

KC eased along the contour of the slope, silent as the wind. Every instinct told him something was off. Hahn's movements were too staged, too deliberate. It was like watching an actor hit marks on a stage.

He reached a small outcropping of rock and knelt behind it, eyes narrowing. Hahn turned once toward the cabin, looked up the slope—and then his face changed, flicking to something unseen beyond the treeline.

KC's breath caught. He saw it too—a faint shimmer of light reflection, low, maybe thirty yards off. Metal. Optics.

His voice came out barely a whisper. "He's not alone."

He shifted back through the brush toward Toni. She caught his movement and started to rise, but he held up a hand.

Then he leaned close enough for his whisper to reach her through the dark.

"He's behind us."

Chapter 66
The Stillness Before

Day Five – After Midnight

Sierra Range – Below Shirley Meadows, near Akers's Cabin

The woods had gone still again, the kind of stillness that comes before something moves. KC's whisper hung in the air like smoke.

"He's behind us."

Toni froze. Her hand found the grip of her pistol, the slow, soundless draw of leather against steel. The fog hung low, brushing against their faces. A single breath seemed loud enough to give them away.

KC turned slightly, the red beam of his flashlight no more than a faint pulse against the ground. The trees behind them rose thick and black, the slope climbing into deeper dark. Nothing stirred—but that was the problem. The silence was too clean.

Below them, maybe fifty yards downslope, the faint glow of the cabin window bled through the mist. Hahn still paced the clearing, a gun loose in his hand. He looked small from here, nervous. A man trapped between sides.

KC motioned for Toni to shift right. She moved in a half-crouch, boots sliding carefully over damp leaves. The air was cold enough to sting through her gloves. They paused, eyes up, listening.

A twig snapped somewhere above them—sharp, deliberate, human.

KC mouthed, "Up slope, thirty yards." Toni gave a single nod.

Then came the softest sound—the unmistakable click of a rifle bolt sliding forward.

"Down!" KC hissed.

The first shot cracked the night open, the round tearing through bark inches above Toni's head. Splinters showered her shoulder. She dropped flat, rolling behind a fallen log, pistol drawn. KC hit the dirt, shotgun up.

Another shot followed, this one lower, punching into the ground where he'd been a heartbeat earlier. The echo ran through the trees and back again, bouncing off the ridge in quick, hollow bursts.

Akers had the high ground. And he was patient.

KC scanned the ridge. Through the fog, a faint glint flashed—metal catching stray moonlight. Scope. He tossed a rock into the brush ten feet to the left. Akers's next shot tracked toward the sound.

KC whispered, "He's pushing us downhill."

Toni's reply came quietly but certain. "Toward Hahn."

"Exactly."

The air smelled faintly of powder now. KC edged left, using the low brush for cover, motioning Toni to hold. She did—steady, calm, eyes fixed on the treeline above.

Down below, Hahn's voice broke the rhythm. "Akers? That you?" he called out, the sound raw, uncertain.

KC watched through the trees. Hahn turned toward the ridge, pistol half-raised, trying to see. The wind carried his voice thin through the fog.

No answer came.

Toni whispered, "He doesn't know where Akers is."

KC nodded once. "He's being used."

"What do you mean?"

"He's bait," KC murmured. "For us—and for himself. Akers is watching how he plays it."

The next gust of wind came colder, carrying the smell of wood smoke—or maybe gun oil. KC motioned for Toni to stay put and began to climb. The slope was steep and loose, every step deliberate. His boots found shallow holds in rock and root. Twice, he slipped, catching himself with a hand in the dirt. The ground here was colder, the fog thicker.

At the crest, he paused. Through the branches, he caught the faint outline of a man lying prone, rifle balanced on a bipod, scope angled downslope. The faint blue glow of a digital sight flickered against the shooter's face—Akers. Motionless. Focused.

KC steadied his shotgun, breathing shallow. The angle was bad—too much brush in the line of fire. The spread would scatter and lose power before it reached him.

Too much cover. Not clean.

He crouched low, tracing a new line around the edge of the ridge. Two short flashes of red from his light—Toni's signal. Ready.

KC angled for a better shot.

Then the night tore open again.

Hahn shouted from below, voice sharp with panic, "He's up there!"

And fired blindly into the trees.

The gunfire lit the fog in quick, white bursts. Akers pivoted his rifle toward the sound, reacting fast. The muzzle flare flashed once—then again.

KC seized the moment, breaking from cover and sliding downslope. Dirt and needles tore under his boots as he moved fast, using the chaos to get below Akers's line of fire.

Rounds ripped through the trees above him, the sound deafening at close range.

He hit the lower ridge beside Toni, breath harsh, heart pounding.

"Now we've got him looking both ways," he said, barely audible above the fading echo of gunfire.

Toni's reply was a whisper through clenched teeth. "Then let's make it count."

The forest went quiet again—but it was the kind of quiet that never lasted.

Somewhere above, Akers shifted position, and KC knew the next round was already in the chamber.

The mountain exploded into sound, and KC knew the night had just turned into war.

Chapter 67
The Fog Burns Red

After Midnight

Sierra Range – Near Shirley Meadows

The mountain exploded into sound.

Muzzle flashes stitched the fog like lightning trapped in trees. Splinters and pine needles peppered the air. KC slid downslope until his shoulder hit the fallen log where Toni had tucked in, breath coming hard in white bursts. Above them, higher on the ridge, a controlled volley clapped and rolled—short, precise, like a metronome set to violence.

"Flank right! Stay low!" KC shouted over the racket.

Toni rolled off the log, sliding on her hip through wet needles, crawling into a shallow crease that ran along the contour. KC rose to a knee, racked the pump, and sent a blast uphill—buckshot cracking a dead limb to powder. The fog gulped the sound and hurled the echo back at them. He dropped flat as answering fire stitched the brush just above his head.

The air smelled of cold sap and burnt propellant, of stone just starting to sweat under a thin skin of mist. A gust pushed the fog sideways; shadows leaped and settled. Up the slope, something metallic chimed once—quick, bright, like an ejected casing skipping off rock.

Then the voice came—calm, close enough to feel.

"You move quick for a desk badge, Kermit."

Akers. The syllables fell with an easy contempt, a man enjoying his own aim. The fire came again, a beat later, not panicked, not wasteful—two, three sharp reports from a steady platform, slightly left of where KC had expected him to be.

Toni's reply cut across the gap, measured bursts to keep that angle honest. Bark leapt off a trunk above Akers' last muzzle flash. The next second, he shifted, his position sliding laterally in the fog. He was herding them—pin from above, push them toward the little apron of open ground in front of the cabin.

Below, through the thinning mist, Hahn hovered at the edge of that apron, jittery, visible in staccato—the flash of his pistol, the white of his face. He fired uphill into the trees, again and again, the shots wild, too fast.

"Akers! Where are you?" he yelled, voice pitching thin.

KC ducked as one of Hahn's rounds cracked a branch ten yards off and zipped into the dark. "He's firing blind," KC said, low.

Toni slid to a new pocket of cover, pistol up. "He's shooting at shadows."

Another burst from above—one round hissed into the rock beside KC's cheek and skittered away in a spray of grit. He blinked stone dust out of his eyes and pushed higher, angling toward a wedge of basalt that jutted from the slope. The shotgun felt heavy and honest in his hands, the pump's rhythm settling his breath.

He found a notch, leaned out, and caught a flicker—metal and movement through fir boughs. He fired. The recoil thumped his shoulder; pellets chewed a black streak across the rock face where Akers had been a blink before. Nothing. Silence, then two taps from somewhere else entirely—deeper in the trees, east, down toward the ridge they'd climbed an hour ago.

"He's moving east," Toni murmured into the dark, voice barely a breath.

KC listened. The mountain spoke in small sounds if you let it—branches flexing, a heel scraping shale, the heavy hush of fog sliding through needles. He caught it: slow footwork, cautious, crossing slope with the patience of a man who'd done more of this than the night could hold. "Circling," KC said. "Trying to cut us apart."

The wind turned. Fog thickened, swallowing the cabin light until it was just a dirty amber smudge in the trees. The forest tightened in around them—the kind of tight that meant your skin knew you were being watched before your eyes did.

KC raised a hand where Toni could see the silhouette of it. Hold.

The slow steps came closer. Deliberate. The kind of walk you used when you wanted your next shot to be a certainty. Pine needles whispered.

The voice drifted out of that direction again, nearer now, amused. "You came fast, Kermit. Thought my little detour would keep you busy till dawn."

KC pivoted to face it, shotgun set. "Show yourself."

"Oh, I plan to," Akers said, closer than the sound should have allowed. There was the polite metallic click of a magazine locking home. "Brought a bullet for you?"

KC didn't answer. Fog billowed between trunks, ghost-white, then thin again. He could almost map the physics of it: their heat, the wind's eddies, the small differences that turned visibility into a coin toss.

Below, Hahn stumbled forward, away from the cabin, gun extended, two-handed like range training. He squinted into the trees, trying to reconcile sounds that refused to stay put. "We have to go, Akers!" Panic cracked the last word. "We have to—"

A shot snapped from upslope. Toni answered immediately, a clean, controlled pair. Silence slammed down hard after—so hard that Hahn's ragged breathing seemed to carry all the way up the incline.

KC edged toward Toni's last silhouette. "Status."

"I'm good," she whispered. "He's ghosting the contour. He's—"

A round tore a shower of needles six inches above her head. She flattened, rolled, and returned fire. KC leaned out of the notch and sent another blast a yard higher than her angle, forcing Akers to rotate.

"Push him," KC said, steady as if they were on a range and daylight.

They did, trading angles, giving the fog nothing to hang onto. For a fleeting second, KC caught glass—optics peeking through fir—and squeezed. The buckshot punished the limb; a dark shape melted sideways and was gone.

Akers laughed once—quick, breathless. "Not bad, Kermit. But not good enough."

A scuff sounded behind KC, so close his muscles fired before his brain did. He whirled, shotgun up. Toni's shape came into focus through the gray—she had moved, anticipating the flank. Their eyes met for a fraction. She pointed, two fingers, left and back.

KC nodded. The old rhythm returned—move on the exhale, count the feet, move again. He cut left, low, felt shale roll under his boot, and froze until the tiny cascade finished its glassy clatter downslope. The fog thinned just then, mischievous, and in that slot of clarity, he saw it—Akers, a darker dark behind a trunk, rifle high, cheek settled on the stock. The muzzle swung toward Toni's last position.

"On me," KC said, and stepped out, firing twice in quick succession.

The trunk jumped splinters. A round came back mean and fast; it hit the rock at KC's knee and slashed off into the void. He ducked in the same motion, rolled his shoulder against cold dirt, and came up with the shotgun tight in.

"Toni," he called, low and sharp.

"Here," she answered, a breath left of where he'd thought. Her voice was steady, but the breath behind it had that tightness that meant she'd felt that last close pass. "I'm good."

Hahn's pistol popped again—closer now, his footsteps noisy. He'd stepped out from the cabin's meager shelter and was edging toward the lip of scrub, eyes saucered. He fired at a shadow that wasn't either of them; the muzzle flash lit his face hollow and pale.

KC exhaled once. No fear left to spend on Hahn; the math was simple—Akers first.

Silence returned in a hush that made the trees feel like they were listening.

Then, ten feet behind and a hair above, the whisper of cloth on bark. A warmth in the fog where cold should have been.

Akers' voice, right there.

"Tell you what, Kermit. You put down the shotgun, I'll let your rookie detective keep her heartbeat."

KC didn't turn his head. "Bad deal."

A soft snort. "Figured you'd say that."

Out of the corner of his eye, through haze and timber, Toni shifted a fraction, bringing her muzzle to bear on the sound, using the trunk as a shield for everything but the barrel. KC's hands loosened on the stock, not to drop it, but to buy the next second.

"You planned tonight down to the hour," KC said, voice even. "Cabin stories. Parsons. The head start. Dawn."

"That's a compliment," Akers said pleasantly. "Or you trying to butter me up, Kermit? No matter. I got a bullet with your name on it."

KC drew a breath so shallow it barely moved his chest. "No, Akers. Not tonight. Your bullet will wait. I'll be taking you in for Maria."

For the first time, the voice cooled. "Not tonight, you won't."

A distant shape flickered below—Hahn pivoting, trying to find the source, his gun wavering. He was talking to himself, a low mantra of words the fog didn't carry. The cabin window went dark; someone inside—or something—had snuffed the weak lantern.

KC let the quiet stretch until it threatened to break on its own. He slid his left foot an inch, toes finding purchase.

"Toni," he said, the word so slight it rode the wind like another pine needle.

"I'm good," she answered, ready, keyed to his cadence now.

The fog edged closer around their ankles, thick and cold, and the forest held its breath.

The next move belonged to whoever trusted the sound more than the sight.

Chapter 68

Ends and Echoes

After Midnight

Sierra Range – Above Shirley Meadows

For a long second after the last volley, the mountain felt wrong—too quiet, the way air sounds after thunder. Smoke hung low, not fog but cordite and cold sap, a sour metal taste riding the back of the tongue. Dew slicked the rock; every breath turned into a small ghost.

"Move!" KC hissed, cutting left along the crease. A shot cracked from above and to the rear—tight, disciplined. He fired back, two fast pumps, not to hit so much as to break the rhythm. The hillside answered with small sounds—pebbles skittering, a pine bough flicking back into place, someone's sleeve brushing bark—each a point on the map.

"Toni—status."

"Here." Her voice came clean from six feet to his right.

Then a whip-crack from below—the apron in front of the cabin—and a sharp, wet intake of breath beside him.

Toni dropped flat, hand clamping her upper arm. Dark spread through the fabric in a heartbeat, the sleeve blooming. She gritted her teeth but couldn't swallow the sound.

KC slid on his side to her, dragging the med kit from his pack. "Talk to me."

"Through-and-through," she forced out, breath thin. "Upper arm. Burns."

KC took out his knife, slit her coat, then the sleeve. He found the entry and exit high on the bicep where muscle is thick and luck is thin. The bleeding was heavy but bright and steady; he pinched above the wound, packed quickly, tightly, and wrapped. Her fingers dug into the dirt until the knuckles went white. She kept her eyes on him and didn't blink.

Another shot from the apron. KC tracked the angle. Lower. Sloppier. The fog had lifted just enough to make the lantern smear on the cabin window. Hahn stood thirty yards downhill, wobbling in and out of the smear, both hands on the pistol like range class, muzzle rising after each trigger press.

"Hold pressure," KC said. "That came from Hahn."

Toni nodded once. "Wasn't Akers."

KC looked back upslope. The disciplined fire had gone quiet. Akers was moving again, using the noise below as cover. KC shifted, scooped the shotgun with his left, and pushed a strip of rock with his boot, slow and calculating. Somewhere to his ten o'clock, a twig cracked, soft, then nothing.

A whisper, close enough, the hair on his arms lifted. "She bleeds fast, Kermit. Put down the gun."

KC didn't turn. He set the shotgun on the ground in front of him—loud enough for the metal to kiss stone—and kept his right hand resting beside his boot, where he'd tucked his backup earlier: a snub in a kydex sleeve under a scrap of dead fern.

"You planned a clean dawn," KC said evenly. "Not this."

"You planned a sermon," Akers said, amused. "This isn't a church."

Below, the ATV engine coughed to life, then caught, low and mean. Hahn's silhouette jerked with the throttle. He looked back once toward the trees as if waiting for an instruction that didn't come. Then he gunned it. The machine lurched across the apron and tore into the scrub toward the east, cut, taillight smearing red in the mist.

"Hahn!" Akers barked, not loud, but with that command nuance men obey. The ATV didn't slow. The sound dropped out of sight and became the hollow buzz of a wasp nest far down the slope.

"Figures," Akers said, softer, almost to himself. "Shoots the woman, runs from the man."

KC drew two slow breaths and made his bet. "You protected him all week so he'd be grateful enough to save you tonight," he said, buying seconds, bleeding them into the dark. "But he won't. He'll save himself every time."

"You lecturing me on men?" Akers said gently. Closer now. "You know what I am, Kermit? I'm the man who finishes the job. Starting with—"

KC rolled.

His left hand swept the shotgun back; his right came up with the snub, already finding the silhouette. The world narrowed to a shape and a sightline. He fired twice in a snap pair at knee height—dirty shots close-in, where math beats aim.

Akers grunted and buckled as one round took his thigh just above the knee. He dropped to that side, caught himself on a trunk, and punched back with the rifle on reflex. The shot slammed into KC's flank where the vest stopped and flesh was unkind—raked across the edge and skittered off the rib. It burned hot and immediate, the kind of hurt that makes vision halo for a heartbeat.

KC felt the pain, cataloged it, shoved it away, and drove forward on instinct—the space between them suddenly a room instead of a hillside. Akers swung the muzzle again, too high now, fighting his own weight. KC shouldered the shotgun one-handed and fired into center mass.

The round hit hard. The vest held—but blunt force doesn't take orders. Air left Akers in a grunt that sounded like surrender dressed as surprise. He reeled back, thumped against the tree, slid a foot, and hung there, sucking at nothing.

KC kept the muzzle trained. "Drop it."

Akers stared up at him through the wash of pain and something like respect. Under the vest, something gurgled wrong. A wet rattle set into his chest.

"Should've brought... dawn," Akers got out, ragged. He looked past KC toward Toni, then down the slope after the ATV. "Kid... shot her... not me."

"We noticed," KC said.

Akers' mouth tugged into what might have been a smile. "You always were faster than your file."

He sagged, head listing, eyes blinking like someone trying to stay in a room he'd already left.

"I wanted you alive," KC said, low and true.

Akers' pupils tracked for a beat, then swam. His lips moved around a thought he didn't finish. The rattle deepened. His hands opened. The rifle slid away. The mountain took the rest.

KC held the sight picture a count longer than he needed to, then eased the shotgun down and crawled back to Toni.

"Talk to me."

She had her own belt above the bandage now, a makeshift tourniquet cinched tight. Her face had gone gray at the edges, but her voice was clear. "Still here."

He peeled his sleeve, looked at the blood slick under his vest where the round had grazed. "I'm nicked. You're worse. We need a bird."

He fished for his radio. Dead hiss. He thumbed Toni's. Same. The ridgeline and the weather had built a wall around them.

"Cabin," she said, reading his thought. "Maybe a shortwave inside."

"Can you move?"

She nodded once, jaw tight. "Help me up."

He slid her good arm over his shoulder, pulled her weight to him, and they moved in short, deliberate steps, downhill toward the dim square of the cabin window. The apron had taken enough rounds that the dirt looked chewed. KC kept one eye on the treeline, the other on her feet. At the sill, he eased her inside, then followed, closing the door with a careful hand, not a slam.

The interior was one room: a cot, a potbelly stove, a crate for a table, and a battered shortwave rig on a shelf over a propane lantern. The air smelled like cold ash and stale food. He sat Toni on the cot, rechecked the wrap, added gauze, and tied it off. She didn't ask him how he was. He didn't tell her.

KC found the power toggle on the radio and flipped it. Nothing. He traced wires with his fingers, found the battery box under the shelf, toggled the breaker there, and tried again. A small green eye winked to life. He lifted the mic.

"Rodman, Mojave One to Skyhawk, you on frequency?"

Static, then a voice, calm as always, cut through the grit. "Go for Skyhawk."

"Two officers, one critical, one stable with a graze. Suspect down. Secondary suspect fled east on ATV. We need pickup at the ridge above Shirley Meadows. Terrain tight."

"Copy, Mojave One. Hold your candle, I'm lifting. Give me three to find a hole, five to put metal on it."

KC looked to Toni. Her eyes had closed, but at his voice, they opened again. "Bird's coming," he said.

"Good," she breathed, the fight still in it.

He set the mic down and crossed to the door, cracked it, and listened to the dark. Far off, somewhere down in the country where scrub gives way to shale, the faint snarl of an engine dragged itself across rock and dropped away. Hahn, running on fear and luck.

KC eased the door shut and glanced to the stove, then to Toni's bandage. The lantern hissed softly. Outside, the mountain had gone quiet again, but not the safe kind.

He keyed the mic one more time. "Rodman—bring a line. We won't have room to sit down."

"Already packed," came the reply. "I can hear the rocks from here."

KC slid down the wall opposite the cot, shotgun across his knees, the shortwave's green eye winking steady between them. He checked his watch without meaning to. After midnight. Closer to dawn than not.

"Just hold," he said to the room, to her, to himself.

Outside, somewhere beyond the trees, rotors began to thrum against the dark.

Chapter 69
The Quiet That Waits

Near Dawn

Sierra Range – Above Shirley Meadows

The mountain had gone quiet again, but it wasn't peace.

It was the kind of silence that waits—dense, metallic, humming under the skin. Fog dragged across the trees like slow smoke, and the air smelled of burned powder and pine.

Then, faint at first, the deep thump of rotors rolled up the slope.

KC stepped outside the cabin, breath clouding in the thin air. A weak red flare hissed in the clearing, marking their position. The mist glowed around it like blood in water. The helicopter came through low, rotors biting the fog into ribbons. Dust, needles, and bits of paper shot into the air.

Rodman held her steady, steady as a stone in weather, and lowered the line. Two shapes dropped fast—a firefighter medic and a deputy— harnesses gleaming wet under the floodlight.

KC waved them in.

"Inside," he shouted. "Wounded officer, through-and-through, upper arm."

The medic didn't waste a word. He brushed past, bent over Toni, and went to work. She sat propped on the cot, gray-faced, her arm packed and bound. When KC crouched beside her, she managed a crooked smile.

"You said this would be quiet," she rasped.

"It was," he said. "Then it wasn't."

She let out a small laugh that died before it finished.

They lifted her into the sling. The flare hissed and spat beside them, its red glow trembling across her face as she rose toward the wash of light. KC watched until she vanished into the fog and the helicopter's belly swallowed her whole.

He turned back toward the pines. The deputy from the crew waited near Akers' body, camera light glinting off the badge that lay beside the rifle. Akers looked smaller now, slack-jawed, half turned toward the ridge like he'd tried to watch the dawn coming.

"Bag his gear," KC said. "Weapon, badge, vest, all of it. Chain of custody runs through me."

The deputy nodded. "Yes, sir."

KC crouched once beside the dead man. There was no anger left in him, just a low, settling weight. He reached out, pressed two fingers against Akers' throat out of habit more than hope, then stood.

The hoist line dropped again.

"Your turn, Sheriff," the deputy said.

KC slung his pack, clipped in, and rose through the rotor wash, boots spinning until they cleared the trees. The mountain tilted away beneath him—cabin, flare, the broken ground all folding into shadow.

When the chopper banked, the first true light of morning broke over the ridges, pale and bruised. The mist below turned to gold, and KC could see the shape of the land—the folds of the valley, the river's faint gleam, the scar of a narrow trail twisting down toward the east.

Inside, the cabin smelled of hydraulic oil and blood. The medic leaned over Toni, his hands steady, his voice soft but firm. She was conscious, eyes half-open, whispering something KC couldn't hear over the engines. He reached out, rested his palm on her boot, and she gave the faintest nod before her eyes closed again.

Rodman's voice came through the headset, even and calm.

"Sheriff, we've got chatter from the perimeter. One of Latham's units found tire marks leaving the ridge—looks like an ATV. The trail ends near a break in the slope."

KC leaned forward, eyes narrowing. "Show me."

Rodman banked east. The helicopter dropped lower, the fog tearing past the skids. Below, the faint ribbon of a trail cut along the ridge, ending in a violent gouge where brush had been ripped clean from the roots. Beyond that, nothing—just open air and a scatter of rock.

Rodman steadied the chopper. "That's where it stops."

KC stared down through the window.

At the edge of the cliff, the ground looked sheared and dark, as if something heavy had torn through and vanished. A thin line of smoke—or maybe dust—still drifted upward, catching the new light.

He keyed his mic. "Set us down near the ridge. If Hahn went off that drop, we'll know soon enough."

Rodman nodded once, adjusting the pitch. The helicopter swung in low, skimming the slope as the sun finally broke over the crest of the Sierras.

KC felt the weight of everything—the cold, the ache in his ribs, the sting of gunpowder in his throat—but the sight below pulled him forward. Somewhere down that cut, Hahn's escape had ended.

And the day that began five days ago was about to meet its dawn.

Chapter 70

The Brief Between Nights

Pre-Dawn

Sierra Range – East Ridge Above Shirley Meadows

The first light came in thin and bruised, a faint seam along the black lip of the ridge. It didn't warm anything. It just let the mountain show its bones.

Rodman kept the helicopter in a slow hover down-valley—rotors thumping the fog into tatters, searchlight hooded. On the ridge, KC dropped from the skid with a deputy from the Kernville substation—Quinn, lean and quiet, rope coil over his shoulder—boots biting into frost-slick shale.

"Hold station," KC said into the handheld.

"Copy," Rodman replied, voice calm in the small speaker. "I'll paint your edge and back off to low orbit."

The beam skimmed the slope, found the scar: brush ripped out at the root, dirt clawed raw, twin ruts knifed into the lip of rock. Past that—the nothing. Just air and cold.

Quinn crouched and touched the cut. "Fresh," he said. "Rubber still warm."

KC eased to the edge and lay flat on the granite, chest to stone, hat brim nearly kissing the void. He peered over.

The ravine dropped hard and mean—fifty yards of broken ledge, then a long, steep tumble to a rubble fan haloed by stunted juniper. Partway down, a shine: the ATV twisted into the crotch of two slabs, one wheel still spinning weakly, clicking against a bent fender. The sound carried up like a bad clock.

Ten yards farther below that—Julian Hahn on his back in the scree, half-turned, one arm flung overhead in a posture that had started as grasping and ended as surrender. The fall had wrung the life out of him. The color of his suit—whatever it had been—looked the same as the rock now.

KC blew out a breath that fogged and vanished. "I've got him," he said.

Quinn edged in. "Confirm?"

KC didn't blink. "Confirmed."

For a beat, there was only the soft grind of the ATV's wheel and the far-away chop of Rodman's rotors smoothing the air. The ridge smelled of iron dust and cold sage, the kind of morning that makes a man wish for coffee and silence. KC felt neither.

He keyed the radio again. "Mojave One to Skyhawk."

"Go," Rodman said.

"Subject located. Deceased. ATV wedged at the first bench. We'll mark and hold the top for recovery. No rope work until daylight and a proper team."

"Copy all," Rodman said. "Latham's units are staged west. I'll vector them to your position."

KC pushed back from the edge, stood, and the world felt wider again—sky opening east, the first gold pushing a line across the nearest peak. He looked out over the drainage, the black pines turning dark green in the newborn light.

"Never makes a sound you expect," Quinn said quietly, eyes still on the ravine.

"What's that?" KC asked.

"When a life ends," Quinn said. "Always thought it'd be louder."

KC didn't answer. He stepped to a scuffed patch of earth and crouched where the ATV's ruts bit deepest. A shoe print sliced across one rut—Hahn's—heels dug in, trying to stop a thing that had already decided. There was a moment drawn in that dirt: impulse, panic, gravity. Everything after had been the slope's story, not his.

He pulled his notebook—creased, blood-specked—and wrote the lines that mattered.

Ridge cut: fresh. ATV over. Hahn—deceased. No sign of a second rider.

He closed it and slid it away.

The radio cracked. Latham: "Sheriff, we're two minutes out from your ping."

"Bring tape, flags, and a long lens," KC said. "Leave the ropes in the truck until we've got the sun over the lip. No cowboying."

"Copy."

KC walked a slow circle around the cut, eyes taking pictures—broken manzanita, a tuft of denim on a thorn, a handprint where someone tried to pivot and didn't. He found the pistol—Hahn's—four feet from the edge in a pocket of crushed needles, the slide locked back on an empty mag. He knelt, photographed it with the small point-and-shoot in his chest pocket, then bagged it and marked the GPS on his phone.

Behind him, the helicopter's sound moved out toward the valley and back again—Rodman tracing ellipses, never still, a mechanical hawk holding sky. The light crept up the ridge face by inches, slow and relentless, painting frost into glitter and then into nothing.

"You want to say anything?" Quinn asked, a question that could have meant a dozen different things.

KC looked east. St. Mary's stood out there somewhere in the low country, a stone rectangle on a sleepy street. Four-thirty had come and gone—Father Frank with a small congregation hunched over pews, Rosa Alvarez's hands folded so tight her knuckles paled, Luis trying not to look at the door. Dawn would finish that chapter too—boots on a church step, papers read in measured tones, a family unstitched politely.

He swallowed the dust in his throat. "Just mark it clean," he said.

They set cones at the rim and ran blue tape in a neat rectangle around the scuffed ground. Latham and two deputies topped the rise a minute later, faces gray with the hour, eyes bright with the work. KC pointed, briefed, and handed off the scene with a few simple verbs—log, photograph, and hold. No speeches. The mountain didn't need them.

Latham peered over the edge and whistled low. "Long drop."

"Longer night," KC said.

He stepped back from the edge and keyed the radio one more time. "Skyhawk, you still with me?"

"Always," Rodman said.

"As soon as Latham's got this locked, take us straight to the hospital in China Lake."

"Copy. I'll be on the skids."

KC nodded to no one, looked once more down the ravine, and let the scene fix itself in his head—so he could put it away later without losing it.

He felt the ache in his side where the round had kissed him, a hot line under the vest. He felt the fatigue heavy behind his eyes. And he felt—unexpectedly—something like relief. Not triumph. Not joy. Just the absence of the next shoe waiting to drop.

"You good, Sheriff?" Quinn asked.

KC tipped his head toward the brightening east. "It's over," he said, and heard the truth in it.

The sun broke the ridge then, sudden and soft, turning the fog in the ravine to gold. For a heartbeat, even the torn brush looked tender.

He thought of Maria Sherman's smile in an old fundraiser photo, Toni's jaw set against pain in a dim cabin, Aunt Ruth's voice telling him to be careful, Father Frank's candlelight pooling warm around a borrowed table, the Alvarez family at prayer as the clock marched them toward the door. He thought of a note he'd written on a whiteboard in a quiet room: DAWN.

"Five days," he said under his breath. "Five days till dawn."

The rotor wash brushed his coat as the helicopter eased back over the ridge. KC stepped to the skid, grabbed the bar, and climbed. As the aircraft lifted, the ridge fell away—tape, cones, the raw earth scar tracing a single, final decision down the face of the mountain.

Rodman settled the bird into a shallow bank, the valley opening like a map below them. The light came up another notch. Shadows softened. The day began to take a breath.

"Hospital first," KC said into the mic. "Then St. Mary's."

"Copy," Rodman answered.

They turned south, the helicopter's shadow sliding over pines and granite, long and sure, as the sun reached for the county that had not slept.

Chapter 71

The Rose Light

Dawn

Flight, High Desert Community Hospital → St. Mary's Church (Ridgecrest, toward China Lake)

The helicopter cut southeast across the desert, the light ahead turning from ash gray to rose. The first edge of dawn brushed the ridgeline, and the world below began to take shape again—hard lines of rock, the pale streaks of dry riverbeds, the long reach of the highway toward Ridgecrest and China Lake.

Inside the cabin, Toni lay strapped to the stretcher, her face pale but steady under the medic's light. KC watched the bandages on her arm, saw the pulse in her wrist still strong. He pressed his palm against the side of his ribs, where the graze burned under his shirt.

He leaned toward the headset mic.

"Carlie, it's KC. Have my Jeep ready at High Desert. Engine running."

Carlie's voice came through faint but sure.

"Already done. And Sheriff—press are everywhere."

"Figures," he said, and killed the channel.

Rodman glanced back from the cockpit.

"You sure you're not the one who needs a gurney?"

"Not yet," KC said. "They're waiting at the church."

The helicopter descended over the flatlands, the town below edged in morning light.

High Desert Community Hospital was awake before the sun. Nurses and medics ran toward the pad as Rodman eased the chopper down. KC helped guide the stretcher out, one hand steady on the rail.

A doctor met them at the door.

"We'll take it from here."

KC nodded once.

"She's tough. Just make sure she stays that way."

The nurse looked at him—blood drying on his shirt, exhaustion drawn in the lines around his eyes.

"You need treatment too."

"Later," KC said.

He signed what needed signing, stepped out the side doors, and crossed the lot to where his Jeep idled. The keys were in it, just as he'd asked.

He drove east, the tires humming over asphalt, the first rays of sun stretching long shadows ahead of him. Ridgecrest was waking up slow—coffee shops opening, flags lifting in the wind. But near St. Mary's Church, the street was already jammed.

The scene looked like a standoff wrapped in a news story.

ICE vehicles and patrol cars filled the lot, lights muted but ready. News vans lined the curb, their satellite dishes craned like ears toward heaven. Reporters clustered near the church steps, microphones raised, camera lights throwing harsh splashes across faces still cold with morning.

Father Frank stood on the top step, robes stirring in the breeze, the Humboldts at his side—unmoving, defiant in their plain clothes. Parishioners clustered behind them, whispering the Rosary that rose and fell like surf.

When KC's Jeep turned in, the reporters moved as one.

"Sheriff Talbird! Are you going to resist ICE this morning?"

"Where's Akers—was he found?"

"What about Hahn—where is he?"

KC stepped out, the rising sun catching the stains on his sleeve. He didn't break stride, didn't answer. His boots hit the pavement with the calm finality of a man walking toward something he'd already decided.

Agent Brad Simpson spotted him first. He was standing beside an unmarked SUV, giving quiet orders to his team. When he turned, his face registered both surprise and understanding.

"Talbird," he said. "Didn't think you'd make it."

"Didn't think I'd be able to," KC replied.

Simpson's eyes swept over the torn shirt and dried blood. He gave a small nod.

"Hell of a morning."

"Not over yet," KC said.

He pointed toward the church doors.

"Let me go in. I'll bring them out quiet."

Simpson checked his watch, then looked back at KC.

"Five minutes, Sheriff. No more."

KC climbed the steps, brushing past the reporters and cameras, their questions following him like mosquitoes. He pushed through the heavy wooden doors and into the dim, quiet sanctuary.

Inside, the air was thick with candle smoke and the faint scent of incense.

Rosa Alvarez sat in the first pew, her hands folded tight, her youngest, Mateo, pressed against her side. Luis, acting strong, stood near the aisle, his jaw locked, eyes trying to be hard, but fear showed in them.

KC removed his hat as he walked toward them. His voice was low, steady.

"You don't need to be afraid. Nobody's here to hurt you."

Rosa looked up. Her eyes glistened.

"They'll send us back," she whispered. "To the same place where the gangs—"

KC knelt beside her pew, meeting her eyes.

"You've worked hard. Raised your boys right. I can't stop what happens today—but I can promise this: it won't end here. If you come peacefully, I'll help make sure you have a way back."

Luis straightened, his chin lifting a little. He didn't speak, but he listened.

Father Frank stepped forward from the back, rosary in hand.

"You have a plan, Sheriff?"

KC nodded once.

"Some kind of sponsorship—but it depends on the Humboldts."

He turned toward the doors.

"Brad—would you let the Humboldts in?"

After a moment, Simpson appeared in the doorway, the light behind him flaring like a second sunrise.

"Be quick, KC. I've got to move out."

The Humboldts entered—solid, steady, wearing work clothes still dusted from the ranch. KC faced them square.

"You know this family," he said. "You've seen them work your land. I need your help—to sponsor them when it's time to bring them back."

Mr. Humboldt looked at his wife, then back at KC.

"We already talked about it on the way here. We'll stand for them. They belong here."

KC's throat tightened just enough to make him pause before speaking.

"You'll be saving their lives."

Simpson stepped in again, checking his watch.

"Time's up."

Rosa rose slowly, clutching Mateo's hand. Luis turned once toward KC, his face solemn but resolute. He extended his hand. KC took it— firm, silent understanding passing between them.

Father Frank murmured a prayer as the family stepped past him toward the doors. Simpson and his men waited just outside, their posture measured, not harsh.

At the threshold, Rosa turned back once.

"Gracias, Sheriff."

KC nodded.

"De nada, señora. Mantén la fe."

The family crossed into the dawn, flanked by the Humboldts. Cameras flashed again. Reporters called with questions no one answered.

When the last ICE SUV pulled away, KC descended the church steps in quiet. The rising sun burned through the haze, bathing the stone and the stained glass in pale gold.

Father Frank looked at KC.

"You kept your word."

"But I missed your mass," KC said.

"You brought hope," the priest answered softly.

KC managed a tired smile.

He turned toward his Jeep, the sound of the engine breaking the still morning.

Behind him, the church bells began to ring—slow, steady, carrying across China Lake and the desert beyond.

The light grew stronger.

And for the first time in five days, KC felt the world begin to settle.

Chapter 72
The Notification

6:46 a.m.

Julian Hahn's Home

KC Talbird drove through the quiet subdivision as the first light pressed against the gray edges of morning. The streets were empty except for the occasional jogger and the mist curling up from neatly trimmed lawns. He'd made this kind of drive too many times — the kind where the destination sat like a stone in his gut.

Halfway there, he called HQ. The phone rang twice before Carlie picked up.

"Good morning," she said, her voice low and rough from being up all night. She'd been the contact during the search and rescue, running on caffeine and pure nerve.

"Morning," KC said. "I'm headed to Hahn's place now. I also need next-of-kin info for Akers."

There was the sound of papers rustling and a keyboard clicking in the background. "Akers is divorced," she said. "No kids. His ex-wife moved to Oregon. I've got her number."

"Send it."

"I'll text it to you now."

"Thanks, Carlie," KC said. "You should get some rest when you can."

A faint, tired laugh. "Not likely. Be careful out there."

"Always."

The text came through as he turned a corner. He called the number. It rang once before a woman answered — brisk, businesslike.

"This is Marlene."

"Ms. Akers, this is Sheriff KC Talbird, Mojave County, California. I'm sorry to tell you your ex-husband, Billie, was killed early this morning during a search and rescue."

There was silence on the other end. No gasp, no question.

"I see," she said finally. "I'll handle all arrangements. Send whatever you need me to sign."

"Yes, ma'am," KC said. "We'll be in touch."

The call ended. Short. Efficient. He drove on, the sun climbing higher, washing the windshield in pale light. Every death landed differently, and some — like this — didn't seem to land at all.

When he pulled up in front of the Hahn residence, the house was already awake. The smell of toast and bacon drifted through an open kitchen window. Somewhere inside, a child laughed.

He walked up the path and knocked. A moment later, the door opened.

Mrs. Hahn stood there in leggings and a loose sweatshirt, her hair twisted up, eyes sharp with the irritation of being interrupted mid-morning routine. She didn't look surprised to see him — only wary, like she'd already guessed why he was there.

"Mrs. Hahn," KC said, removing his hat. "May I come in?"

She hesitated, then stepped back. "Why not," she said flatly.

He stepped into the foyer. The house was spotless, everything in its place. Somewhere deeper in, a little girl's voice chattered to the television. KC stopped just inside. So did she.

He didn't waste words. "I'm sorry to have to tell you that your husband was killed early this morning. It happened during the search and rescue attempt."

Her expression barely shifted. No tears. Just calculation — or maybe confirmation. When she finally spoke, her voice was even. "Was he shot?"

"No," KC said quietly. "He tried to escape on an ATV, lost control, and went off the mountain."

She gave a single, sharp nod, eyes flicking toward the kitchen. "I told him at your office that I was finished with him," she said, a hardness in her voice. "Now it's final."

KC didn't respond. There was nothing useful to say.

"Is that all?" she asked.

"For now," he said. "We'll have someone contact you later about arrangements and benefits. If you need anything, call the number on this card." He set it on the entry table beside a small vase of fake flowers.

"Fine," she said. "If you'll excuse me, my daughter's eating breakfast."

KC nodded once. "Of course."

She turned and walked toward the kitchen without another word. He stood for a moment longer in the stillness of the foyer, listening to the faint hum of a cartoon. No grief lingered here — just life as usual.

He stepped outside, closed the door gently behind him, and drew in a slow breath. There were all kinds of widows in this job, and not all of them mourned.

He drove off toward the hospital.

Halfway there, his phone rang again — Elijah McKean.

"KC," Elijah said, voice crisp and direct. "What position do I have?"

"Captain over Operations," KC said. "You'll replace Zack Parsons."

Elijah was quiet for a second. "What are you going to do with Parsons?"

"Terminate him," KC said. "He's built himself a little network —

old guard, favors, politics. It's time to clean house."

Elijah let out a thoughtful hum. "You could do that. Or you could demote him. Keep the enemy close. Let him think he still matters, and while he's busy protecting his little circle, you map it and tear it apart from the inside."

KC didn't answer right away. He watched the road narrow ahead, the city hospital's tower just visible through the trees. "That's one way."

"It's the smarter way," Elijah said. "You don't burn a nest before you know how deep it goes."

KC exhaled through his nose. "I'll think on it. When can you be here?"

"A week. I'll be ready to start."

"Good," KC said. "See you then."

The call ended as he pulled into the hospital lot. He sat for a moment, watching nurses cross the pavement under the rising sun, their faces lined with the fatigue he felt himself.

He'd spent the morning with the dead.

Now it was time to deal with the living.

Chapter 73
Post-Op

7:25 a.m.

High Desert Community Hospital

The morning light cut hard through the blinds, slicing across the bed where KC sat with his sleeve rolled up. A nurse dabbed antiseptic along the graze on his arm and said something about lucky angles. He only nodded. He'd been lucky plenty of times; he just didn't always call it that.

The antiseptic burned. He watched the sting without flinching. Pain was familiar—part of the uniform. What he couldn't shake was the quiet. After days of noise, motion, and adrenaline, silence felt unnatural. The case was done, the dust settled. One battle over. The war, he knew, was still on.

Sleep, family, even that slow, uncertain thing with Jodi—he'd traded all of it for truth. He wasn't sorry. Justice had been served, fairness done its part. That was enough. For now.

When the nurse taped the last dressing, he thanked her and stood, the room tilting slightly before his balance returned. He flexed his arm, pulled the bandage tight, and moved down the corridor toward Recovery.

Toni's Room

Toni was sitting up when he entered, the window open to the desert light. She looked smaller in the hospital gown, but alert, alive. She smiled when she saw him.

"Hey, boss," she said, her voice soft but steady.

"Good morning." He stepped closer. "You look better than I expected."

"Feel better, too. The doc says I might even get out tomorrow."

KC nodded. "Good work out there."

She blinked, surprised. "I just followed your lead."

"You did more than that." He let a small smile edge across his face. "You asked the right questions, didn't freeze when it mattered. That's what makes a detective."

Her eyes widened. "Wait—are you—"

"Promoting you, yes." He took a breath. "Detective Toni Wells, effective when you get back on your feet."

Her mouth dropped open. Then she laughed, the sound thin but full of life. "Thank you, sir. I mean it. I learned more in the last five days with you than all the time in the academy and as a deputy."

"Don't thank me. You earned it."

A nurse entered, chart in hand, a smile breaking their moment. "Sorry, Sheriff," she said deliberately, "time for vitals—and for the patient to rest."

Toni sat up straighter as the nurse grabbed the blood pressure gear.

KC gave a half salute. "Rest up, detective." He turned for the door.

As he stepped into the hallway, he caught her reflection in the window—smiling, proud, ready. That would carry her a long way.

Parsonss Room

The smell of antiseptic and bandages hung in the air when KC entered. Parsons sat up in bed, face pale, arm strapped in a sling. His eyes narrowed as soon as KC appeared.

"You look worse than me," Parsons muttered.

"Not by much," KC said. "How's the shoulder and knee?"

"Hurts like it'll never stop." Parsons grimaced. "Guess you're here to tell me if I've still got a badge."

KC pulled a chair up beside the bed. "You do," he said. "But not the one you had."

Parsons blinked. "Meaning?"

"I've hired a new captain. You're staying on as sergeant."

The room went still. Parsons swallowed hard. "You're demoting me."

"I'm giving you a chance," KC said. "A fair one. You'll keep your job, your time, your dignity—if you earn them back."

Parsons looked down at his hands. The old defensiveness flickered but didn't light. "What do you want from me?"

"Loyalty," KC said. "Not to me. Not to Queen B. To the badge. To the truth."

Parsons's jaw worked. Then he nodded once. "I can do that."

"Good," KC said, standing. "Then we'll be fine."

He turned to leave but paused at the door, something in him not quite ready to move on. He waited a beat, listening.

Through the half-closed door, he heard Parsons's voice: low, urgent, into a phone.

"Chairperson Garrison? He didn't fire me. He demoted me."

KC stood still for a moment. Then he nodded to himself.

The fox was still in the chicken coop; Elijah had been right—wisdom didn't stop the rot, it just named it. Soon enough, the purge would come. He'd be ready.

The Parking Lot

Outside, the sun had fully broken the horizon, bright and sharp. The air was clear, the kind of crisp morning that smelled like a new start. KC's Jeep waited in the lot, dusted with desert grit. He leaned against the door for a moment, letting the warmth settle into his skin.

He called Carlie. She answered on the second ring.

"Hey," she said, voice hoarse with fatigue.

"Go home," he told her. "Get some rest. Tomorrow's a new day."

"You headed home too?"

"Yes." He looked out at the desert stretching wide and gold. "Soon."

They said their goodbyes, and he climbed into the Jeep. The engine turned over smooth.

He sat for a moment before shifting into gear, eyes on the horizon. The world looked clean again, but he knew better. Clean didn't mean pure. It just meant washed by light.

He pulled out of the lot, tires crunching over asphalt. The hospital shrank in the mirror. The desert opened ahead—bright, empty, endless.

One battle over. The war goes on.

He drove toward the office.

Chapter 74

The Drive Home

Late Afternoon

Home

The afternoon sun stretched long and low over the desert, the light sharp and clear, the air heavy with heat that hadn't yet given way to evening. KC turned off the city street, tires humming over the lined asphalt of Della's Delights. The Jeep settled into its usual parking space—as if it had memory.

He killed the engine and sat for a moment, hands on the wheel. The restaurant stood quiet beneath the green awnings, blinds in the residence above drawn against the glare. A faint wind stirred the dry sage and dust around the adjacent lot.

He thought about the day—hospital corridors, paperwork, the slow unraveling of adrenaline. The case was finished, officially sealed. He'd signed the last reports himself before leaving the office. Justice on paper, as close as it ever got.

One battle in a war that wouldn't end. But now he knew who was on which side. That counted for something.

KC stepped out, his boots crunching on the dirt. The air was cooler here, touched with the faint smell of mesquite smoke drifting from somewhere down the valley. He climbed the steps and opened the door.

Aunt Ruth

The familiar scent of stew, cornbread, and cooked vegetables hung in the air. Aunt Ruth sat at the kitchen table, her wheelchair angled toward the stove. A cooling pan rested beside her. She looked up as he entered, eyes narrowing with that mixture of relief and reproach he'd come to know too well.

KC hung his hat, gun, and keys in their familiar place. A burden lifted.

"You look like something the dog buried," she said.

KC managed a small grin. "You should see the other guy."

She poured him a glass of water and slid it across the table. "You win?"

"For today."

She studied him for a long beat, her expression softening. "Don't let it make you hard," she said quietly. "That's how the enemy wins."

He nodded, taking a long drink. "I know."

"I'm sure you do," she said. Then, after a pause, "Karole's been waiting to see you."

He set the glass down and gave a single nod. "Thanks, Ruth."

She turned her chair back toward the stove. "Dinner'll keep. Go on."

Karole

His son's door was half-open. KC knocked lightly.

Karole sat cross-legged on the bed, a tablet propped on his knees, earbuds hanging loose around his neck. He looked up when KC stepped in.

"Hey, Dad."

"Hey, kiddo." KC leaned against the doorframe. "Heard you've been waiting for me."

Karole shrugged. "Just wanted to know when you were coming home."

"Well," KC said, stepping inside, "that'd be now."

He sat on the edge of the bed. For a moment, neither spoke. Then Karole said quietly, "School's still bad. Not as bad as before, but... still."

KC nodded. "Kids can be cruel. But maybe it won't last forever."

Karole looked down, picking at the edge of the blanket. "Feels like it does."

KC's voice was gentle. "You don't fight every war alone, son. Remember that."

Karole looked up, eyes uncertain, then nodded. "Okay. But what about tomorrow?"

KC reached over, squeezed his shoulder once, firm and steady. "That's a good question. Maybe tonight, we can let tomorrow wait."

"Okay."

"That's my boy. Now let's go help Aunt Ruth in the kitchen. I'm hungry."

Karole jumped up. "Me too."

The Deck

Later, after Ruth had turned in and Karole was long asleep, KC stepped out onto the deck with a Cherry Coke in his hand. The bottle sweated against his palm, cold and sweet after a long day. The desert spread out in front of him, quiet except for the low hum of night insects and a coyote calling from somewhere beyond the ridge.

His phone buzzed. Jodi.

He answered. "Hey."

"You okay?" she asked.

"Yes. Finally."

"How do you feel?"

He looked out over the open land, the horizon just beginning to fade into blue shadow. "Like I can breathe again."

"That's good," she said. "You did good, KC."

He smiled faintly. "Thanks."

"Get some rest," she added.

"Planning on it."

"Night."

"Night, Jodi."

The line clicked off. He set the phone down beside him and leaned back, letting the chair creak under his weight.

Through the open door there was silence. A calm. A sense of peace. Five days behind him now, and the noise finally gone. He took another sip of the Cherry Coke and watched the stars glisten. They burned sharp above the ridges.

The air was still, the world quiet. He thought of Elijah's words, of truth, of the war that never ended. But tonight, it didn't feel like a burden. It felt like balance.

The desert breathed around him—vast, quiet, unbroken. And for once, he didn't feel alone in it.

ABOUT THE AUTHOR

Welcome!

Thank you for visiting my bio page. Let me share just a little bit about myself. I was born into a large family. I am the number 6 child of 14 total children. Yes, it was sometimes chaotic and always adventurous. There was never a dull moment with my six brothers and seven sisters. I grew up in the Midwest. I am an avid sports fan, especially football—I played in high school and college. I suppose you could say I followed in my parents footsteps by having seven children if my own with my lovely wife, Bobbie. We have twenty-six grandchildren.

I spent most of my professional life in behavioral healthcare as a therapist, supervisor and chief executive. I had the opportunity and honor of serving over 2000 clients during the many years I worked in that field. I cherish the many experiences I had with so many interesting and wonderful individuals and families.

Books were a large part of my upbringing. My mother was an avid reader of almost all fiction genres. She also read a variety of nonfiction. I developed a love for reading when she exposed me to Dante's Inferno when I was in high school. Writing became a desire of mine when I read Shogun by James Clavell. The more I read, the more my desire grew to write. But I kept that storytelling desire hidden for years until I watched an interview of a best-selling writer, Mary Higgins Clark. She has since passed, but her influence on me has steadily grown. Because of her, I gained the confidence to write fiction. And, a love for writing!

So there you have it. That's me in a nutshell.

9 798902 350279